MY
3RD MOTHER:
VIETNAM

and the Journey
Toward Redemption

JOHN ROZICH

DEFIANCE PRESS
& PUBLISHING

MY 3RD MOTHER: VIETNAM AND THE JOURNEY TOWARD REDEMPTION

ISBN-13: 978-1-963102-02-4 (Paperback)
ISBN-13: 978-1-963102-01-7 (eBook)
ISBN-13: 978-1-963102-03-1 (Hardcover)

Published by Defiance Press & Publishing, LLC

Bulk orders of this book may be obtained by contacting Defiance Press & Publishing, LLC. www.defiancepress.com.

Public Relations Dept. – Defiance Press & Publishing, LLC
281-581-9300
pr@defiancepress.com

Defiance Press & Publishing, LLC
281-581-9300
info@defiancepress.com

Dedicated to My Family:

Ex umbra in solem.

"From the shadow into the light."

To those who emerged from the shadows, join us in the light.

I love you all. But especially my boys, you were the first people who looked like me. This is our remembrance.

And a Condemnation:

To those whose hubris "knew" best and cost more than fifty thousand of our brothers and sisters.

Abundans cautela non nocet.

"One can never be too careful."

It is a journey filled with paradoxes. Of the love between a son and the mother he never knew. A son forcibly taken from her, now a man seeking forgiveness for actions taken within the obligations of honor and duty. It is the discovery of love for a woman who nearly destroyed him, and a final requital for the death of his mentor. It is a common journey for those of our children asked to shoulder their nation's legacy bound in difficult, if not appalling deeds. For them, as for this man, it is a struggle along a path often shadowed in mendacious absolution offered by their nation, now fatigued, if not bored, by the legacy once sought. It is accepting the need to cleanse one's soul before rebirth and a purposeful future can be achieved. What we ask of our children, and the redemption, the metanoia, we owe, is an unending cycle within our collective experience. Let us not forget.

BOOK I

Corpus Sine Pectore

"Body Without a Soul"

CHAPTER 1

THE BOY IS NOW A MAN

November 1970
Auribus Teneo Lupum

"Holding a Wolf by the Ears"
—Phormio (c. 161 BCE)

The mist hung thick and wet, covering everything and concealing even more. It was beautiful in its distortion of light, ethereal and soft, wrapping around each movement and muting each sound. Its moisture gave life to the jungle, dripping from broad green leaves, making tree bark glisten. The hidden figure was alert, however, to something else the mist could mask: death.

He was in his seventeenth year, big for his age with a wiry but muscular frame that concealed unforeseen strength within coiled quickness. His eyes missed nothing, set within a lean, almost gaunt face, eyes that conveyed both hunter and wonder.

His teachers had said he was endowed with a remarkable intellect. This, in combination with an authentic eidetic memory, had rendered physics, math, and languages almost painful in their simplicity. His instructors took note, particularly of his almost insatiable interest in history. Most were enthusiastically supportive—some even a bit jealous—as this man-child rapidly grasped their queries and mental exercises, often expanding his answers beyond any of their expectations. And so they were aghast when this teenage kid—whom some would say was gifted, but otherwise typical—disappeared from his suburban high school in January 1970. Eventually, rumors were confirmed that he had volunteered for the Marines and was destined to intersect with the Southeast Asian killing fields of Vietnam.

In letters from Patti, his classmate, she related that Mrs. Griffith had actually become a bit tearful at the news, ending American history class early the same afternoon upon being told of this former student's impending departure from San Francisco on a flight bound for Saigon. And here he was, not eight weeks later, nestled within this vibrant green jungle teeming with life, surrounded by birds calling to each other in reaction to the early morning sun in a forgotten corner of the world over 8,500 miles from home.

They had been asked by their president to partake in a collective national effort to benefit and protect this third-world agriculture-based society, and to do so by killing certain of its inhabitants. Indeed, America's obsession over the past decade with this ribbon of fecund green tropical land was as mystical as it was misguided, and the "strategic benefit" broadcast into countless Midwestern homes on the Cronkite-read nightly news had originally attempted to bolster the national necessity in taking these families' sons in the prime of their lives. Now, by 1970, not so much.

For Judah Connor Doolin personally, it was a practical apprenticeship where he was mentored by his elders, aging veterans from WWII and Korea, honing his skills to implant high-velocity projectiles into unsuspecting human beings who did not share his country's political viewpoints. But it was, in reality, something more—a need to answer darker worries held deep within him, as to his courage, abilities, and value as a man, or lack thereof. He would address each of these elements, but the answers were not always easy to derive nor pleasant to face.

Patti … he had been the ultimate inattentive fool in not recognizing her growing interest in him during the spring as he approached his sixteenth birthday. His perceptual failure with Patti had marked a mental promise he had made to himself, one that would save his life in the ensuing eighteen to nineteen months in Vietnam. Failure to absorb environmental contextual data in war can end one's life, and quickly. His failure with Patti was not to be repeated in the 'Nam. However, he did feel a bit tolerant of his initial poor performance with her. After all, she was the combination of everything "untouchable" for a guy like him: pretty, popular, and the proverbial focus of every upper classman's clownish superiority coupled with their varsity football player egos.

Her soft, almost straw-colored yellow hair, thick with half-completed circular curls, fell just below her shoulders. She routinely pushed it back behind her ears to prevent it from veiling her sharply cut cheekbones and obscuring her sight. Patti would look up suddenly from reading, half her face cloaked in golden whirls of ropey beauty, her silky blue eyes and aquiline nose partially hidden. Her long, slender neck was enough to almost make her face float above her body. A seldom-seen impish grin revealing white straight teeth was a reward always worth waiting for.

Out of his league, simply put. So, sitting next to her in class, Doolin had resigned himself to settle for her friendship. He helped her with math and shared the common banter regarding their teenage world views. But something odd had slowly transpired between them—they also began to divulge topics that ultimately progressed to a naked honesty. A sharing of their individual insecurities and inherent fears as people, as uncertain maturing beings.

Discussions for her centered on her father, a successful internal medicine physician who had walked out on her mother for a younger nurse and thus, of course, had also walked out on Patti. As for Doolin's story, he also had opened up a bit, sharing beyond his normal taciturn nature and, surprisingly, she had been careful with their conversations. It had been a month before finishing the first phase of Marine boot camp at Parris Island when the first letter arrived from Patti.

He couldn't say he had really *wanted* to read it at first, fearing that most of its contents—the letter was heavy, containing multiple pages—would be school gossip and might, in fact, open doors that Doolin had tried to permanently seal regarding choices he had made. It is odd that seminal moments in one's life can be filled with such emotional clarity only to subsequently find that reality sews discord and doubt into such previous conviction. He didn't care to revisit his choices, such as his sudden enlistment, or recategorize his personal doubts as to his earlier mentioned possession of—or deficiency in—fundamental courage and what that meant for his value as a man.

But the letter was a surprise: a careful analysis and sharing of her intimate pain and worry about her value as a reasonable steward to Christina, her younger sister. She wrote she was questioning the reflection she saw in the mirror each morning, judging it as often being too superficial and ill-informed. Patti, this seemingly happy young woman with her orthodontist-ensured perfect smile, was, in fact, hiding behind her soft cornflower-blue eyes the pain that each individual eventually learns to mask.

It was a meticulously written letter, and Doolin had spent more time than he might have imagined judiciously picking through her confessed inadequacies. Some were a bit dramatic, but then, indeed, don't most individuals have traces, if not more, of such self-directed hyperbole? But Patti was

slowly coming into her own as an adult, as a woman, regarding the disparities between having been told what was right and then seeing the deliverers
of such veracities, the adults in her life, fall miserably short in the practice
of each. She was rebalancing the scales between childhood ideals and the
often fetid real-world actuality. Adults never truly understand that children
easily see through the lies, unmask their faulty logic, and ultimately keep
score. Patti was examining the rules of the game and unveiling the tally that
should have been.

These memories took mere seconds to flash within Doolin's consciousness before he immediately pushed them into his mind's empty recesses—
movement had caught his peripheral vision. A small group of broad green
leaves in the jungle canopy moved incongruently. It was more a sense of
incorrect motion than certain confirmation, but the odd jiggle of leaves 290
yards and 20 degrees left of dead center suggested something or someone
had tugged, brushed, or pushed against the lower limbs. The more vertical
structures, once released from this force, then gave a slight but distinct rapid
two-cycle dance. While wind or a slight breeze rustled the emerald green
canopy of the jungle in countless directions, each minor movement occurred
in unison; singularity of motion or an atypical, arrhythmic choreography is
predatory until shown otherwise.

His position was almost completely hidden, the lens of Doolin's scope
veiled from any reflection of the sun. He was tucked into a fern-covered
stone crag only two and a half feet tall, nestled into a rising rock formation
jutting up from the earth, the likes of which were common in the highlands
of this beautiful land. The lush foliage hung limp and dripped over his clothing, providing narrow slits of visual access. His uniform was damp, and
actually soaked in areas where Doolin had tied the same foliage to his arms
and legs to obscure any traces of his human outline. His face was green; no
area of his neck remained uncovered, from either applied dirt or the waxy
stick of green paint used for camouflage, but even this applied "paint" was
then covered in erratic smears of damp jungle soil. The barrel of Doolin's
rifle was blackened and covered with moss and leaves, both hanging and
uneven. Judah Doolin was invisible.

However, Doolin refused to condescend to the groupthink—indeed, to
the arrogance of command, who repeatedly underestimated the skill and cunning of this indigenous enemy. This was their home, and they were remarkably alert to subtle, if not imperceptible, changes in this complex ecosystem.

Doolin absolutely needed to see them first and ensure they did not possess a newer upgrade in technology provided by the Soviets that had recently been deployed, as reported via US Army command, with their scouts: infrared or thermal-sensitive scopes.

Snipers had long possessed night scopes allowing uncanny visualization of movement within the nocturnal leaf-covered dome of the jungle, but if any of these rumors of new thermal hunters were true, whether in night or day imaging, looking for heat signatures tucked into trees or mountain out-croppings would expose an individual. He needed to see them and observe their rapid and quite competent scanning of each sector to ensure that they had no such technology.

The Vietnamese regulars—members of what was to be known as the People's Army of Vietnam, or PAVN—were remarkable soldiers. They were disciplined, committed, and often fearless, willing to endure unimaginable suffering to secure both their tactical and strategic goals. Examining each sector within zones of conflict and systematically combing through them for any indication of geographic structures likely to hide or mask threats, these hunter-killers would advance methodically, but often not predictably.

They would, for reasons simply unknown to the Americans, advance along a corridor or slice of a jungle zone only to veer off or double back and re-examine previous areas. They could also completely disappear, entering into their complex web of interconnected concealed tunnels, making it diffi-cult for Americans to ever gain comfort when attempting to track or provide close clandestine monitoring of their activities. Because this land was their home, they enjoyed an immense advantage. These soldiers were selected from among their best, trained to live off the land, to shadow, expose, and eliminate. Their similarity to trackers and scouts at various stages of the American Western expansion was an irony never lost on Doolin.

There! A shrouded but characteristic helmet outline momentarily ap-peared between low tree limbs. These were not Viet Cong, or Charlie, but regular ground troops from North Vietnam. And almost seven feet above him, again betrayed by the tugging and release of leaves, this time with water droplets misting toward the jungle floor, was an antenna—thus, a radio man. Doolin knew there must be others; communications specialists were not allowed to travel alone. It was a mistake to wear headgear without camouflage—a rather significant one.

Yet Doolin did not take comfort. Rather, he immediately sensed adrenaline being released in his body as he waited for evidence of a trap. He had marveled for some time now at their willingness to bait traps with comrades in an effort to expose US sniper positions. It often meant one clean shot, one dead comrade, and then one dead US Marine sniper as these hunter-killers expertly identified the US Marine loci. Doolin doubted they would deliberately sacrifice a radio man. Perhaps he was inexperienced, but more likely it meant that he was part of a larger patrol.

However, he could not detect any troop noise. If there were forward scouts with the radio man, but acting as part of a larger dispersed group, this meant they would be able to hunt more efficiently, covering a larger geographic area. This could spell trouble, and the hidden sniper felt his pulse quicken. Although he could not see them, they would likely be stopping every few yards, listening and looking. Identifying natural hiding places and targeting them. Sound is distorted in the jungle, muffled or baffled by moisture and plant growth, distorted but not absent. But Doolin had prepared for this as well.

Months before this US teenager had been deployed into the jungle, he had begun to systematically assess variables likely to get him killed. One area that had fascinated him was the use of new technology or enhanced existing technology that might counter these threatening elements and thus extend his shelf life. As a result, although Doolin's buddies thought him a bit weird, he had already prepared and practiced for hours with a self-constructed sound suppressor, or what was commonly called a "silencer" for his rifle. This was a very deliberate expression of his regard for personal "existential" concerns.

Yet, as noted, several of Doolin's rifleman colleagues in the US Marine sniper school scoffed at the use of a sound suppressor and, in fact, raised legitimate concerns that acoustic dampeners could negatively impact accuracy, consistency, and range. But Doolin saw the utility of such acoustic suppression as enhanced masking of his "nest" or location in the field. This, along with his own leaf-and-branch-covered customized ghillie suit—a forerunner to the camouflage suits issued by the Marines in subsequent conflicts—was his attempt to negate visual detection.

Incidentally, his eventual assigned operational parameters in Vietnam indeed demanded that every aspect of Doolin's activity be molded to allow for maximum stealth. Because he was able to shed most of the customary Marine regulations involved in sniper operations, his rather unconventional assignments relied on his ability to remain a "ghost." This meant no target indicators or remnant detritus—evidence of his having been present in an area—were allowed.

What Doolin could not have known is that as the years passed, modern sound suppressors actually did not harm accuracy in shooting. However, their use required the optics of the scope used by the shooter to be readjusted or retargeted, and this was the source of the altered, slightly diminished velocity of the exiting round. But such knowledge was not appreciated in the years of the Vietnam conflict. Command considered the use of sound suppressors for field operations unnecessary, if not hazardous. Still, Doolin methodically labored to understand the impact of such acoustic suppression. He heuristically examined length, size, and, most importantly, the actual composition or material used to ensure that employment of his acoustic dampener did not influence effectiveness. Not only did he continuously tinker with these mufflers, but even before Doolin had deployed to Southeast Asia, he had become adept in building several prototypes that resulted in effective tools that, in many ways, were precursors of what was to become the modern sound-modifying platform.

Doolin knew that his rifle emitted sound in at least three distinct ways. The triggered release of the firing pin followed by the initial explosion of the solid gunpowder in the jacketed round instantly transformed this solid material into a gas that expands dramatically at nearly three thousand pounds per square inch, plus or minus, dependent upon the model of the gun and the type of round used. This exploding gas seeks a release, or an outlet, and is then funneled down the barrel, forcing the projectile, the actual killing force of the gun, to exit the barrel at supersonic velocities. The explosive gas creates a huge sound that reaches upward of 160 decibels, which can ultimately permanently deafen the user of the rifle but, even more importantly, can also provide positional clues for an enemy. A sniper's temporary inability to hear and the enemy's ability to locate him are generally not advisable in the environment of war.

Thus, prior to his Asian deployment, Doolin had spent several months experimenting with aluminum or steel hollow tubes, one fitting within another, the inner tube having a Swiss-cheese appearance of holes that allowed for the expansion of the heated gas and the dampening of its aerosolized velocity. This in turn allowed for a differential effect on the velocity of the gas distinct from the exiting solid lead projectile. His high school physics teacher would have been proud of Doolin's near professional analysis of the mathematical–physical relationship between these materials and their final outcome, and his research would serve Doolin well as he traversed the unknown destiny awaiting him.

The ultimate result was a predetermined optimal size and spacing of the holes in the tube along with dampening material of the inner tube itself. He eventually chose a ceramic composite for this inner cylinder within the outer aluminum casing, one strong enough to withstand the vibrational impact of the superheated gas without harming the accuracy of his round. Ceramic was still a new material, and its innovative use in industrial and commercial applications was just beginning to dramatically expand among global competitors.

Doolin's exposure to this material came about through his interests in physics and his serendipitous introduction to a visiting materials science professor at the Marine sniper school in Quantico, Virginia. This academic rapidly formed a relationship with Doolin that went beyond the casual interest in a clever student. It was not an overstatement to infer that the university instructor was amazed by the intrinsic grasp of requisite knowledge linked to the younger man's subtle understanding of scientific principles. The professor was genuinely astonished by Doolin's intuitive breadth regarding the mathematics of the acoustic dampening, and working with this older educator and two of his graduate students provided Doolin with an expanding, not to mention unique, perspective in the area of materials science and their influence on ballistics.

For example, Doolin had systematically compiled limited tables of data, sharing these with the two graduate students and their professor, that demonstrated the influence of the holes within the utilized tubes. He took a special delight in demonstrating the impact of their spacing, size, and total number and showing how these variables dramatically affected the sound, distance, and precision of the round exiting his rifle. Afterwards, he enthusiastically discussed the variations and test results with this ad hoc team, who then were encouraged to "fully investigate" potential optimization of ballistic performance. Doolin didn't know if these two advanced degree candidates ever intended to use their materials science knowledge to refine the perfect "silencer," but the collective discussions were both fruitful and enjoyable to all involved. What little free time the teenager had had on the weekends at Quantico was spent combing through his experimental results.

The net effect was that this brief but intense period of experimentation resulted in consistent eight-hundred-yard bore accuracy for twenty-five rounds at a fast reload rate, and this could be maintained after adjustments for drift despite rain or temperature variability. Yet, Doolin didn't entirely trust it beyond 725 yards in a rapidly changing environment, such as heavy rain, or if his subsequent movement or redeployment to another secondary site for firing was required. He foresaw the need to minimize his exposure if he were to deliver a poor or ineffective first shot, thus giving any advantage to the opposing hunter-killers. To this effect, he focused on the need to ensure that his first shot had the characteristic response of killing the enemy target linked to a typical but variable time wherein they were pinned down, which Doolin felt this provided him with the time to reposition if necessary. Every individual action and response was considered; failure to embrace such options could mean not living through the experience.

But yet another development Doolin could not have foreseen was that within thirty-five to forty years, effective ranges for experienced military snipers would be routinely measured in miles, not yards. Indeed, a Canadian Special Forces operator purportedly eliminated a target 2.199 *miles* from him, but laser-based range finders and upgrades in ballistics, including fifty-caliber rounds, had yet to be employed in everyday use. The legendary sniper in Vietnam Carlos Hathcock registered a lethal effort at 2,500 yards using a fifty-caliber round. His shot was effective due to pretargeting, or a previously ranged object that coincided with the exact point where a Vietnamese combatant had paused during his use of his bicycle. Hathcock is credited not only for pushing the boundaries of useful technology, but also for expanding the psychology of "possibilities" for snipers as he continually pushed for more effective strategies.

So here Doolin was months later, wet and thousands of miles from Quantico, waiting to once again "test" his product. He remained motionless and watched: The helmet had rapidly appeared, then immediately disappeared, and additional movement was not detectable. Now it was raining again. There was a beauty in the pattern of water as each drop reached the ground, tickling different leaves on the way to the sodden debris that made a textured carpet for the jungle floor. But the rain created just enough background noise to insulate any slow-advancing noise of movement if one was careful, experienced, and patient, and these hunter-killers were all three.

Got it—tree limb movement side to side, 265 yards out, 35 degrees from dead center. That movement was not Mother Nature, but a dreaded signature: upright bipedal ambulatory motion.

Only seventeen seconds later, Doolin's scope picked up binoculars: Tento, Russian-made 20x60 regular visual spectrum optical binoculars, and not advanced thermal detection. The North Vietnamese soldier was looking to Doolin's left but slowly, meticulously moving his visual field to encompass his location. Doolin saw him through his sniper scope, the left border of his visual field registering the enemy's methodical scanning. The North Vietnamese helmet was adorned with leaves and sticks and now Doolin could confirm there were two, if not more.

The soldier was young, but older than the American—perhaps late twenties, small and almost petite. The body shapes of many Vietnamese were a blend of delicate muscle, slender yet strong. They were not to be underestimated in intimate physical combat; they were very quick. His cheekbones rode high on his face and his eyes, hidden from Doolin by the binoculars, carefully and systematically moved in a slow arc that would intersect with the American's position in about fifteen seconds. And from the right semi-circle border of Judah's scope, he saw the inconsistent bobbing motion of a thin black line: the antenna. The radio man was situated to the right of his binocular-laden comrade, perhaps two to three feet away and probably kneeling, as the antenna was at a sixty-degree angle from the ground. The twin round glass circles of his dark-brown-cased binoculars were nearly on Doolin.

Objectively, he doubted the man would be able to detect him and was almost certain he could not see him, but Doolin was unwilling to risk it. Thus, the American readied his most trusted companion—his rifle. Doolin's finger had been just off the trigger since he put his eye to the scope almost twenty minutes ago, but now he touched the metal hook with his index finger, almost caressing it. The metal was dry from the film of powder he had on his right hand; an element of mild tackiness persisted. His finger found the familiar resting position. Doolin silently inhaled, then exhaled. His head did not move, but the Marine's mind raced as he calculated the appropriate first shot for the radio man, then a second shot for the forward scout. He wanted to leave no time for emergency communication about their team taking sniper fire. Doolin's finger found the release point of the trigger and the gun kicked immediately, followed by the attenuated sound of compressed gas escaping as if from a punctured tire.

Then Doolin rapidly and nearly soundlessly chambered the second round, aiming three and a half feet to the left and blindly, into a dripping fern two feet from the green carpet of the jungle, fired his second round. He immediately moved his scope back toward the radio man and saw only the slight jerking of a moisture-laden group of leaves. But that was enough; his body had provided a final spasmodic end. The antenna still moved, but its casual up-and-down motion, the departing wave, slowed until it ceased, as did the life of its owner. Rising six feet from its base, now fixed in position at a forty-five-degree angle from the moist ground and the radio man's body, its stillness was declarative. Quickly, Doolin examined the area to the left of this confirmed kill shot and saw only a small segment of the leather strap of the field glasses—but it was slowly moving further to the left.

He was alive or being dragged!

Doolin again aimed, now almost seven yards away from the original site of the second shot, and between forked limbs in a tree, he refocused and fired again. This time he thought he heard a muffled sound, perhaps a yell, and then nothing. The American waited, remaining active as he scanned the entire area for a third person. Nothing. The jungle continued with her symphonic daily routine: rain pattering on the leaves, insects buzzing, and birds and sometimes monkeys calling out in their identifying harmonic voices. Eleven and a half minutes later, Doolin moved.

The radio man had been killed immediately. There was no chance of him calling for help, as was the intent. Half of his head was gone; the bullet had entered just below the left eye and exited at or near the opposite ear. The force of modern ballistics was both fascinating and horror-filled, Doolin thought. Nothing could survive the direct impact of a ten-to-eleven-gram lead projectile hurled at eight hundred to a thousand meters per second. As the bullet enters tissue, it expands and creates a cone of such force that it literally disintegrates any soft friable structures it encounters.

The man's head, or its remnants, gave evidence to the terrible power that the precision composition held by each round with supersonic velocity possessed. Manufactured in upper New York State, these bullets were quality controlled by a fifty-two-year-old mother of three, she wanted to ensure that "her ammo" met the company standard. It certainly did. A quick search of his body revealed maps and several personal items. The latter, Doolin laid back on the man's chest.

The scout had two wounds, both fatal, but the second wound advanced the finality of the first. The binoculars had been thrown upon impact of the second bullet and lay just a yard beyond the end of this man's right hand, the optical leather protective covering spattered with tissue and blood. The first round had hit him in the upper leg, tearing a nearly grapefruit-sized hole in his inner thigh almost an inch and a half down his leg from his inguinal crease; the femoral artery was severed and could not have been repaired. The second bullet had hit his chest, and Doolin did not see an exit wound during a cursory examination. Again, he quickly searched the body, finding surprisingly delicate papers in both upper pockets with several numbers—likely map coordinates—a watch, and a string necklace with a laminated picture of a young woman. This, the American left untouched.

The anticipation moments before an initial shot always filled Doolin with adrenaline-fueled focus and, truthfully, unbridled excitement. It was contact with the rarified environment of absolutes, knowing that he had the opportunity to complete his task with permanent finality. But if he failed, missed, or gave his position away, the act could very well be his last on this earth. The absolute potential of life or death cleared Doolin's conscious mind before each shot like nothing he had ever experienced since. He had to admit to himself a surreal fascination with it—there was a tangible thrill that took hold of him as he anticipated this transient sense of near-total consumed concentration.

But naturally, this was always followed by an immediate need to reassess his surroundings, to take in the totality of the environment he had momentarily disturbed with his shot. And it was then that the beginnings of terror—the fear that he might have missed other troops or alerted someone to his location—impacted Doolin. This interval also was unique and possessed its own foreseeable type of intense mental focus, but it was different, as he needed to absorb the surroundings and process his next actions.

However, Doolin was now entering the phase he hated most: regret. The feeling of seeing human beings who had no less a claim to life on this earth than him, but whose life was over because of him, his duty, his action. His mother was looking at him now; he felt her presence and knew that somewhere, she was disappointed in him.

She had wanted him to be a physician, a healer. In one of her last silent communications with Judah, she had given him the gold cross necklace that she had always kept, although he never remembered her wearing it. She had stated it was precious to her and that she wanted him to have it; now, it was Judah's. The 18 carat cross had three tiny initials along the vertical axis: MCM. Doolin had assumed they were the letters of her mother or her grandmother. She had never worn it, as far as he could remember, but she asked him then to wear it always. This took place in the last minutes before he walked away to enter the AFEES (Armed Forces Entry and Examination Station) building in Chicago, her last desperate act to protect her son. "To have God keep you safe." Ever since, Doolin had worn the gold cross every day, always hidden inside a camouflaged bandana around his neck to keep it from catching the rays of the sun, to keep it close to him. His mother was always with him, even if she was, at times like this, disappointed.

It was at this point that Doolin always felt nauseated, but he knew this, too, would pass as he again adjusted to the sounds of the beautiful but increasingly hot and damp surroundings. He needed to assess the immediate geography, then move deeper into the terrain controlled at night by the other side. This war was so peculiar, he thought, it was almost humorous. And except for the growing list of casualties of everyone involved—Americans, Vietnamese, and the civilians—it would have represented an unbelievable failed plot to any adventure story. Such a plot simply was not credible enough to be taken seriously, considering the large swaths of land marked as "Secure" by the US only to be anything but when the day gave way to night. Furthermore, the areas marked as vulnerable or "Not Secure" were inhabited by the VC or the North only rarely since they simply moved personnel and equipment through these zones as needed.

There were no fixed battle lines, no boundaries to either ensure safety or demand heightened caution. You could just as easily be killed in combat by the VC inside the US Joint Command in Saigon as you could lie, undisturbed, sunning on the beach for six hours just twenty klicks from the DMZ. The only real fixed permanent fortifications were American, such as Da Nang or the airfields, but as the Tet offensive had shown, these were not really that secure despite being heavily fortified. And of course, then there was their tunnel systems, those that Charlie had built. But even these—whether occupied or not, rebuilt after demolition or not—depending on the need, they were not truly fixed nor fortified camps.

This war was so different from Korea, from the American experiences in WWII. And frankly, the US's planning and often slow adaptation to the enemy's strategies made these disparities ever more obvious. But unfortunately for everyone stationed here, these unique characteristics were both believable and credible … and deadly.

Doolin moved deeper into their territory. The Marine sniper wore his own version of camouflage and became more like the enemy the longer he stayed in the field and the further he ventured into their domain. Doolin dressed light with no helmet, instead wearing a hat with sticks and moss and leaves, and ate rice, salted fish, and dried fruit. His most precious commodity outside of his rifle was clean water. This, he guarded, and it was the only other item, beyond military intel, that he took from his kills. Doolin wore tennis-shoe-like sandals with duct tape on portions of the soles to minimize his imprint and residual tracks. Indian moccasins would have been great, but the closed leather would not have held up in this damp, unforgiving environment; his feet would have been met with continual blisters. The tennis-shoe sandals were mostly cloth, and depending on where he was, Doolin's movement in confined areas was done barefoot. He did not mind being damp most of the time, which was the reason he could tolerate light shirts and pants.

Judah Doolin had been raised in the city but loved the old Westerns that showed the cowboys and lawmen living off the land, sleeping under the night sky. The Marine Corps had taught him how to live off this lush, fertile land, but he typically lost between seven to twelve pounds every three to five weeks he was deployed "up-country" and always developed intermittent diarrhea. He carried a multivitamin with his malaria pills and had a few chlorine tabs for water if he really ran dry, but during the rainy season he seldom, if ever, was in want of fresh water. The isolation had initially been more difficult than he had anticipated early in his tour, but soon Doolin actually craved the time alone to think, wonder, and observe. He realized rather quickly that he would never again in his life have the solitude that he enjoyed here, albeit while hiding from the enemy, completely off the grid, no one knowing if he still existed.

Any direct communication with his superiors while on assignment, Doolin had fought aggressively to prevent. It was exposure. And just like the potential of the sun's reflection off of his scope, anything that could potentially expose him, he wanted no part of. Thus, at times he duct-taped his scope, leaving only a very small aperture and thus a tiny window for viewing the enemy. In a similar vein, he demanded any requirement for field-to-headquarters communication to be as small as possible. Of course, the Marine Corps didn't like the idea of a "wild banshee" on the loose for weeks at a time, killing the enemy without being under their tight, *tight* control. And while his home away from home was the Third Marine Division at

Quảng Trị Combat Base, just off of Highway 1 along the Song Thach Han river, Doolin only went there when he was finished with his assignments and almost never ever reported to them when active up-country.

He also had no "spotter," an accompanying Marine who would sight and provide confirmation of ranges, accuracy, and kills. Doolin's extended solo status was nearly an unheard-of luxury and, in his case, often a direct violation of Marine Corps protocol. Allegedly, the presence of a two-man team helped to avoid eye fatigue and assisted the shooter in readjusting his aim, but in truth, his assigned team members were kids. Although they were the same age as Doolin, they were inexperienced and therefore a liability when dealing with talented enemy troops. Thus, early in his deployment he had arranged for a sustained absence of a spotter by providing whomever was assigned to him an excuse to leave.

Doolin provided his assigned spotter a clear understanding that if he instead wanted to go to Saigon and get some in-country rest and relaxation, called R&R, it was perfectly fine, if not preferable for Doolin's needs. The first couple of guys thought they were being tricked, but Doolin provided each of them with a small amount of cash—real money—and told them it would be their shared secret. So, while the supposed spotter visited every whorehouse in Saigon, Doolin would spend weeks alone up-country trying to stay alive. Eventually, the guys assigned to Doolin trusted him, as they knew they were going to have a great period of weeks of unaccounted-for "vacation." Command either didn't know or didn't care, and Doolin was convinced it was a bit of both. They likely had suspicions but were too lazy or preoccupied to check on him. Not to mention, he produced results.

But it wasn't until Doolin met Colonel Mallroy that he totally slipped from their intrusive grasp, and it was Mallroy's direct involvement that made this possible. The interesting irony is that this colonel was Army, not Marine, and thus this guy had to have had some serious "juice" to get his demands honored by the Corps. The only higher priority among the various American entities conducting this war, beyond their nominal commitment to winning it—and Doolin was becoming increasingly convinced this was often lip service—was to ensure that their bureaucratic legacies were held constant. So, the fact that an Army colonel had influenced a Marine mission assignment and its regulations for a Marine sniper was nearly tantamount to Ho Chi Minh lunching with Richard Nixon in the Rose Garden.

What precious few of these deskbound bureaucrats understood was that these "customary regulations" exemplified by the need for periodic contact were significant impediments to successful clandestine operations. Being able to jettison a spotter and roam completely alone decreased detection by some quantifiable measure, although Doolin didn't know what metric to calculate it by. It was just common sense: There was less obvious evidence of telltale signs that humans had been around when one person passed through an area instead of two.

Second, Doolin did not want to, nor would he usually, accept the routine assignments of meaningless acquired target range estimates, nor acquiesce to performing nonsensical reconnaissance and surveillance. Judah C. Doolin was a warrior. He was able to avoid these cupcake missions by taking some of the most dangerous assignments, with the trade-off being that he was going it alone. His logic was that he could either get killed alone as a result of his own mistake or bad luck, or he could get killed traveling around in a group with the obligatory critical mass of men who, in essence, advertised the American presence to a watchful hidden enemy. Doolin preferred the former. Casually traveling through an enemy's liar as though they were heading to a beach in Southern California on a Saturday afternoon made Doolin nervous. There was nothing nonchalant in combat operations.

Many Marine snipers operated from relatively secure environments with entry into the enemy's haunt for as minimal an interval as necessary. Other assignments, such as taking aim at enemy troops as they attempted to breach American defenses or maneuvering to kill officers, were performed from relatively safe and stationary positions. This was a standard role for many of Doolin's sniper colleagues wherein the marksman became an arm of an integrated US Marine operation. This is not to discount the inherent danger found in any combat mission, of course, but some assignments were logarithmically more hazardous than others.

The most dangerous were the uncommon requests for meaningful recon, surveillance, or termination of assets by one individual who went deep into enemy-held territory. This strategy, described as "lone wolf"—exploring and harming the enemy on their turf, so to speak—was often treacherous, yet this was the type of mission that Doolin preferred. Command bureaucrats who thought they were omnipotent in the war often preferred small mobile teams; a two- or four-man team on a search-and-destroy mission was their favored construct. But increased numbers of men on the move, unlike the lone wolf, often gave the enemy notice.

Thus, every Marine sniper's hero during the Vietnam War was the previously named Carlos Hathcock, revered due to his ability, permission, and demand to operate totally alone, although being remarkably adroit, effective, and invisible only added to his legendary status. Known as "White Feather"—his calling card left at the location of his kill—he would position himself deep in enemy territory to eliminate valued enemy assets. One such asset was an important North Vietnamese general thought critical to the enemy's operational success. Covered in mud, dealing with insects and snakes and moving mere inches every twelve to twenty-four hours, Hathcock remained hidden for over three days while inching within three hundred yards of enemy troops. Eating almost nothing, drinking water only when absolutely necessary, and urinating in his camouflaged pants, he eventually shot and killed the general as he exited from the rear of a French Citroen sedan near the mansion of an abandoned rubber plantation.

Doolin idolized the man not simply for his skill but his dedication to his mission. Hathcock often began operations with a spotter, but if deep penetration was required, he would shed his companion and move with autonomy. This is what Doolin did as well, with or without permission. But this was not usually the requested or approved mission for most Vietnam-era Marine snipers.

Doolin's activities would eventually mirror much of what Hathcock's mission parameters entailed, but it was only after Mallroy took over his life that Doolin achieved this rarified status, that of a true lone wolf. It was then that Doolin operated alone with no one knowing where he was or what he was doing. However, this also meant that he was completely cut off from Marine or friendly support—indeed, from any support. And thus, Doolin did everything he could to tip the scales of success, of survival, in his favor. Not communicating with command or anyone from deep in enemy territory simply reduced opportunity for detection.

Doolin had met with Mallroy per his request— actually his *demand*— after Doolin had handed over some intelligence material he had taken from one of his kills. Within were coordinates of planned troop locations during deployment in the highlands for the ensuing two weeks.

The problem was, however, the troop locations identified were **planned US Marine and Army** troop deployments! And the information was uncannily accurate.

Simply stated, advance North Vietnamese ground troops, or scouts, had time-specific data detailing scheduled American troop missions into the various regions of Vietnam's rural areas. The implications of such evidence being provided to the North Vietnamese raised hurricane-force alarms within the Marine command that spilled over into Army command as well. How was it possible that the enemy had detailed material outlining their proposed mission locations and the specific timing of these occurrences?

The outcome was that this unnerving discovery likely greased the operational ease by which the colonel, this guy Mallroy, was able to make successful demands across military service lines and their previously sacred administrative silos. Thanks to Mallroy's measured professional responsiveness, he quelled a panic that might have itself actually done irreparable harm. He committed his energies to uncovering the traitor(s) within American ranks, but he kept the eventual discovery so quiet that he was able to construct a detailed matrix on a select group of ranking government and military officials without their knowledge. Mallroy needed to conclusively, beyond any doubt, reveal the perpetrator, because Mallroy himself had planned all along to administer a final fitting justice for this individual—or individuals.

This "justice" deemed appropriate by Mallroy was illegal, of course. But Mallroy never even considered that he would leave unfinished the final verdict and actionable punishment for the individual responsible for such deceit. His quiet, unassuming, but very focused investigation would indeed enable Mallroy to eventually identify the culprit. Judah Doolin knew none of this at the time, but as he got to know this man, the depth of the colonel's palpable hatred of anyone who betrayed his country and put Americans at risk actually surprised Doolin, who thought it was disproportionate to Mallroy's otherwise highly disciplined and measured personality.

Mallroy's plans encapsulated a simple premise: He wanted this person to deviate from their established routines, giving away their concealed identity. Mallroy was ultimately creating a trap, but he needed to bait it at different times and with different enticements. Thus, Mallroy's activities were discrete; almost no one actually knew his real mission or that he was examining someone's outright betrayal, the silent collective penetration by the enemy within. Doolin eventually was to understand his methods and to share plans with the colonel, as he became Mallroy's principal tool in extirpating this evil. In fact, during certain intervals—in accordance with this colonel's plan, and with Doolin's approval—Doolin himself became one of the sweet but concealed enticements.

CHAPTER 2

MEETING MALLROY

Late November 1970

Hypotheses non fingo.
"I feign no hypotheses."

Judah C. Doolin's relationship with one Colonel Alfred K. Mallroy thus occurred several weeks after Doolin's initial encounter with one of the North Vietnamese teams he had eliminated. Doolin was rousted out of sleep early one morning by a "butter bar" lieutenant (second lieutenant) and rather aggressively escorted to a beat-up green-brown-and-black camouflaged jeep and ordered to get in the passenger seat. Doolin had only just returned to his base at Quảng Trị three days previously, and had been screamed at by this same junior lieutenant for failing to maintain consistent communication with his commanders.

This lieutenant must also have taken a personal affront to Doolin's appearance. To allow anyone under his command to comport in the Marine uniform and yet not demonstrate a pristine "spit-polish" appearance was unacceptable to this ersatz soldier. Doolin's presence in the middle of a tropical jungle—alone, cut off from running water, latrines, or any semblance of civilization—made this demand for a ceremonial uniform façade ridiculous, if not almost obscene. He had only shrugged that first day in response to this initial tirade from the junior officer. Doolin knew that being tasked with tracking enemy movement clandestinely and killing them covertly would trump any such nonsense in the eyes of experienced combat vets.

However, this did not stop the lieutenant from voicing his increasingly absurd concerns again three days later. Doolin had been rudely awakened because this officer had wanted to continue his "lecture" in the enlisted barracks and started by way of shouting at Doolin in front of three other Marines, waking two from their beauty sleep.

Again, this officer was furious that Doolin had not even attempted to improve his appearance despite three days having passed, and this, Doolin would have confessed, was perhaps a touch more appropriate; he did indeed still look like hell. He had shaved, of course, and his hair was cut very short, clearly within regulations, but his hollowed-out cheeks and loose-fitting wrinkled and frayed camouflaged pants and shirt looked as though he had crawled out from under a bridge after having snacks with his cousin, the resident troll. Doolin couldn't help it; he usually lost weight when in the field, and his latest case of diarrhea was only now beginning to subside. Butter Bar finished after almost three minutes of his putrid breath enveloping Doolin's head, howling a withering summation of the young sniper's inadequacies no more than six inches from Doolin's face, unevenly intermittently spraying Doolin's cheeks with phonated spittle. The young officer ended his tirade by citing Doolin's deplorable appearance and again demanded that he learn to establish a routine of reporting so command knew where the hell he was and what the hell he was doing.

Doolin just stood there, trying not to inhale his malodorous fog. He attempted to lessen the impact of the lieutenant's "suggestions" by concentrating on his uvula, which Doolin could inconsistently see bobbing up and down as the young officer's mouth opened with every other word he barked at Doolin. They were in the grouping of enlisted barracks at Quảng Trị, where Judah had begun to get much-needed rest after so many weeks up-country. The lieutenant didn't even take Doolin into the administrative area, he was so pissed, and Doolin was suspicious that this young lieutenant didn't want his senior officer to see his hissy fit, so he had decided to unload on Judah three feet from the sniper's rack. He was so close that Doolin could nearly feel the heat he was generating, and Doolin considered that the man made a ripe, if not oversized target. Doolin actually spent several seconds visualizing his brains splattering from the force of the projectile that magically entered his skull—but this was fantasy. This particular morning, though, this particular lieutenant came close to making it a reality.

However, the slightly malnourished sniper was not going to Leavenworth for murdering an officer, at least not yet. His lieutenant did not understand that there was perhaps no other way to ensure a premature and unnecessary death than by the need to "consistently and predictably" check in with command from up-country. Charlie wanted Marines to do this and looked for the opportunity to convert this needless military etiquette into a dead

American soldier. Doolin refused. Not verbally; he just refused to do it, and this infuriated some of the more pointy-headed idiots, like this lieutenant, who dressed up to play soldier in the Corps. As he finished, he demanded an acknowledgment of his soliloquy, and of course Doolin said, "Yes, sir." Loosely translated into enlisted-speak, this response meant "Fuck you, sir!"

Meeting Mallroy was the beginning of Judah Doolin's adulthood when viewed from the distant vantage point of time. But when this lieutenant roughly demanded that Doolin report to him, Doolin did not, *could* not, have known this. Two hours later, wet from the warm morning rain traveling down Highway 1 in the open jeep, the driver—who actually outranked Doolin, even though he was also a corporal—and Doolin entered the outskirts of the city. Eventually, both men traversed the multiple checkpoints and, somewhere in the bunkered structures of Da Nang naval yard, Doolin exited the jeep and passed through the first of several heightened security points to meet the colonel.

Entering the complex array of hallways, Corporal Doolin was again shown through security. This time, however, it really was a detailed search as the MP poked and padded Doolin's entire frame, looked at his identification, and checked the manifest for Doolin's name. He eventually was allowed to pass and shown to the third door down a short corridor, where Doolin ducked under a low doorframe with each of the adjoining pale-green side walls reinforced with sandbags. The room was crowded with tables stacked with papers and folders, and running along the wall opposite the door were bookshelves spanning from the ceiling to the floor lined with folders and rolled maps. The cigarette smoke cast a faint blue haze from the ceiling to belt buckle height despite ceiling fans and two overworked window air-conditioning units.

The room was uncomfortably warm, and in response to the faint lingering scent of body odor and tobacco residue, Doolin actually coughed once upon entering into the room. He glanced around briefly, gathering all of this, when Mallroy bent over the center of the largest table, spotted him, and stood up. Mallroy was tall, at least six feet two, but this was almost Doolin's height minus an inch. His armpits were wet, soaking through the tan Army office work shirt, his collar open and a dull white undershirt visible. He wore no jewelry; a beat-up Timex watch, black dial with a green canvas band, was strapped to his left wrist. He immediately recognized Doolin from his file and Mallroy frowned—actually, he almost sneered. It was not an auspicious beginning.

Born and raised in the bayous of Southern Louisiana, he was slightly odd, to say the least, but then intelligence personnel—especially Joint Force Intel, who are technically Army but work under some mind-numbing bureaucratic shared-force agreement—are people likely to be a bit weird. His physical characteristics hinted at some degree of promised eccentricity. Thin straight sandy-reddish hair, "high and tight" and receding, and nearly orange eyebrows framed hooded eyes that stared at Doolin but betrayed nothing. A repetitious facial tick, sticking his tongue over his straight and surprisingly white lower teeth, signified that Mallroy was deep in thought, and this he did often. This use of his tongue to somehow aid his cognitive process was nearly reptilian.

He was inwardly directed, as all gifted analysts are, taking outside environmental data and sifting through its possibilities in the interconnecting mental channels of thought and reflection. He had a faint sprinkling of freckles over his slightly hooked nose and maxillary area, but the intensity of his ice-blue eyes was fascinating and almost, but not quite, intimidating. He chain-smoked and, before this war ended, would have suffered a massive heart attack and likely not survived—but his life and the events within it were to take a very different and unforeseen path related to their joint efforts. Had Mallroy somehow known his own future, his personal destiny, he would have smoked even more, and worked even more frenetically. That was the man he was.

His youth had been spent exploring the bogs and waterways of Southern Louisiana, being raised by his grandparents. His dad had been a violent drunk who had driven off his wife; thus, the young Mallroy and his younger sister were removed from the tin-roofed hovel they inhabited by grandparents who were never able to understand what vital piece of humanity was lacking in their only child. As his father consumed excessive amounts of liquor, he turned into a beast characterized by a viciousness that grew in proportion to his blood-alcohol level, and he was gradually shunned by all society. Mallroy's mother had left in the middle of the night after being slapped and kicked by her husband for spending money on food for her two children that he had expected to use for his drink.

Two days later, neighbors had notified the Baptist preacher. The reverend himself had, on different Sundays in the past, attempted to modify the behavior of Mallroy's father but was unsuccessful. So, when the grandparents arrived after the reverend confirmed that no one was caring for the youngsters,

Mallroy's grandparents were saddened, but not surprised. Finding the small four-room shack in complete disarray, absent food and without heat—unfit to serve as a kennel—they had wordlessly packed up the meager belongings of Mallroy and his sister, Lois, and permanently removed them from the house and their father's life. The man was fished out of a shallow bayou tributary fourteen months later, likely the victim of his own alcohol-fueled disorientation, but violence could never be completely excluded.

Mallroy had been a remarkable student in the public schools he attended, excelling in math and literature and reading voraciously. In fact, his grandmother worried that he was going to go blind, as he was repeatedly found in the upstairs back room closet, quietly reading with the door closed, a flashlight illuminating the pages of every library book he could find on the Napoleonic wars and the Roman Empire. He expressed no interest in girls or dating, and it was only after he had procured an appointment to West Point that his grandparents seriously considered the possibility that their prodigy might not actually be attracted to women. During his third year at the Point, his grandfather died, and his sister moved back from her first year in college in Memphis, Tennessee, to care for their aging grandmother, who had taken the role of their mother.

Mallroy's experience at West Point was mixed, as he never became the aggressive, boisterous student leader destined for "stars" and command, but he did author two of the more remarkable dissertations on counterinsurgency strategies ever seen by his teachers. They marked him as an intellectual, someone who shaped policy and strategy—perhaps one who would join a charismatic leader and serve as the wise counsel, whispering in said leader's ear to ensure that careful analysis of outcomes occurred. This appeared to be satisfactory to Mallroy, for he didn't much like or find interest in the testosterone-filled matriculating pyramid of fellow cadets, their aggressive but peacock-like posturing on full display at the Point.

He was not, however, an outsider, at least not in the typical fashion. He often took time and energy away from his own interests to assist several of his fellow cadets in their expository efforts, improving their final semester projects to the point where one professor in History and Strategic Planning asked the alleged author whether he, the cadet, had received outside help. The honor code kicked in and the cadet, who would one day wear three stars, said honestly, "Yes, sir, I did." The professor knew that the work in certain parts of this guy's report was so good as to be the product of only one person:

Alfred K. Mallroy. Nothing more was said to the cadet, but he received an A for his report. Mallroy, meanwhile, received a full-page commentary in his personal file, a summary statement from this professor about the value of Mallroy's analysis. The professor, it turned out, was rather energetic in citing what he felt was aggregate evidence that perhaps only a handful of people, specifically defined as "people working for the elected American president," could have authored such a prescient analysis of Soviet intentions found in "Cadet Mallroy's report."

His eventual passing was a deep loss for the Army and, Doolin would have added, the Marines and their entire country as well. Doolin sincerely believed in Mallroy. Not only because the young sniper grew to respect this man and admire him, but also because as odd as he appeared, Mallroy turned out to be a natural and very competent judge of clandestine material related to the enemy. He was, in fact, a gifted analyst and operational leader; he just never bought into the cult of personality that underscored the popularity of a George Patton. He was much more of an Omar Bradley. Both leaders had their success and their vital roles to play, but Mallroy was perhaps even less public than Bradley and shared his disinterest in heightened public stature.

The relationship between Mallroy and Doolin was to be a unique, a very special liaison forged in a cauldron of deadly consequences, exploring treasonous behavior in America's own embedded government officials. This would ultimately link these two men together as tightly as ligament is bound to bone, each supporting and required by the other. It was also a relationship that would pass through phases wherein each of them initially suspected that the other might be engaged in his own form of duplicity, but they soon grew to understand the obligations each held for the other. But this was in the future, and Doolin could not know the twisted path both would wander, often together, searching for a traitor in their midst. He also discovered years later, through conversations with his professional colleagues, that Mallroy was gay. This knowledge was not known to Doolin at the time, and even if it had been, he would not have cared. He viewed Mallroy as a committed professional, and a pivotal influence in Doolin's life. He also kept the young sniper alive.

Mallroy's first comment was "How old are you, marine?" It was not a question; it was an accusation grounded in the disbelief that the Marines would send anyone so young out alone into the jungle, despite Doolin's somewhat older appearance.

Doolin smiled and for some reason blurted out, "Fifty-seven years old, sir!" nearly as loud as his enthusiastic responses on the parade tarmac at Parris Island had been.

For a brief five to seven seconds, Doolin didn't know whether he had just sent himself to the stockade or to an Article 15 for disobedience, since all sound immediately ceased. Doolin's response was met with momentary emptiness, a silence that must exist in stone crypts—one could hear the slow rotation of the fans, the hum of the air conditioners, and nothing else. The four other enlisted personnel in the room had become motionless.

Then Mallroy smiled slightly and stepped up to Judah, looking directly into his eyes, and from not more than five inches from his face stated, "Well, Marine, you look awfully good for such a fucking old man."

Doolin remained immobile, not responding, and he later surmised that single moment in time was the moment Mallroy had decided to examine the young Marine more thoroughly, perhaps even take him a bit more seriously, for Mallroy stepped back a bit and extended his hand, which Doolin immediately took. The colonel's eyes never left Doolin's, and Doolin did not look away. Mallroy then asked, "Do you have any idea of what you brought me?"

Doolin noted the "me" and not "us." He thought back to the delicate rice paper numbers, thinking that they indeed appeared to resemble coordinates, but not much more.

So, the younger man responded, "I brought you numbers, sir, perhaps some … coordinates?"

The heavy orange eyebrows had already begun to slide away from Doolin, his eyes searching for something on the table, but with Doolin's comment, he instantly whipped around. His eyes widened momentarily and he glared at Doolin again. Deep within his cold, calculating scrutiny was a flicker of suspicion, followed immediately by a pondering of Doolin's answer, an answer he had not expected. The Marine froze but did not blink or back away. He had been asked a question, and he had provided his best answer.

In a soft but menacing voice, the older man demanded, "How do you know they were coordinates?" Again, it was not a question, but an accusation.

Judah Doolin looked right at him. Mallroy's eyes were now ablaze with a cold smoldering fire, registering concern, but Doolin equaled their intensity as he stated, "Sir, rows of numbers conforming to typical map coordinates are not difficult to discern. I simply don't know what the coordinates identify."

And again, Mallroy just stared at Doolin. His eyes, reflecting deep pools of analytical effort, locked on to the corporal as the older man noted Doolin's choice of words. The colonel then looked up to his left for a brief second, brooding, and the tongue pushed his lower lip out—the movements associated with bringing some memory or conclusive thought into focus. His gaze reflected a calculating tactical assessment, and after a moment he motioned for Doolin to join him at the table, where a large map was laid out.

Beside the map was a partially exposed folder, noted "TOP SECRET LEVEL III," and on the tab exposed by the cutaway portion of the folder was the Marine's name, "Judah Connor Doolin." He followed Doolin's eyes and his finger tapped the folder, then he said, "This is you. There are no secrets."

Doolin nodded, then looked at the map. The coordinates he had provided were marked in red X's and circled in green. Elsewhere on the map were additional X's not surrounded by green circles.

Mallroy stated, "Each red X within a green circle is our US troop deployment assigned by Marine or Army section HQ, either to be dropped in by chopper or dropped off by vehicle. The X's without the circles are some of the additional coordinates you provided me, your gift. So, you provided exact coordinates of our planned troop deployments in addition to other sites—those not circled in green—that represent no tactical value, at least to our immediate analysis."

"What are these?" he wondered aloud.

Doolin immediately looked up from the map to see Mallroy was staring at him. Doolin did not flinch, did not move, and did not breathe. But instantly he knew the problem, and it was enough to send a cold chill into the base of the young sniper's skull. What were the coordinates of American planned troop movements doing in a VC scout's pocket? And then, of course, how had they procured them?

Mallroy's eyes never left Doolin's, and looking back at him, Doolin did not blink for several seconds. Mallroy knew Doolin was not involved, *could* not be involved, but he was examining the young man, considering his potential usefulness as Mallroy's eventual sharp-pointed tool. The older man conveyed this in seconds as he stared back at Doolin. And then Mallroy spoke.

"I would ask everyone to leave the room, please." And as Doolin started to move and follow others toward the door, Mallroy softly said, "Not you."

And this was the beginning of Judah C. Doolin's fifteen-month relationship with Colonel Mallroy.

Over the next thirty minutes, and continuing over the months of their professional relationship, Doolin was introduced to a remarkable intellect, a man able to lower the tradition-thick military barriers between a seventeen-, almost eighteen-year-old Marine sniper and a senior US Army colonel and bring this seventeen-year-old into his confidence to share his very private frustrations and doubts. He was remarkably candid, and as Doolin looked back years later, he wondered if he was not eventually trusted more with Mallroy's concerns, plans, and doubts than any other member of their common military structure. But as much as Doolin was to eventually grow more comfortable with a "bird colonel" frankly discussing potential security breaches or outright treason, at the time it was new to the younger man, and Doolin was on pins and needles. Mallroy was talking about some plan of strategy and Doolin was listening, but quietly, and finally the Colonel stopped and looked at Doolin. "Marine, I asked for your input. Please, we don't have much time."

Doolin looked up and realized a moment late that Mallroy indeed had asked for Doolin's opinion on why the enemy possessed these map coordinates. And with what the young man said over the next forty-five seconds, their relationship began to lock more firmly into place.

Doolin thought of the wonderful detective novels he used to read for hours sitting in his school library and of the fundamentals of criminal investigation, and he said without emotion, "Assuming these are purposefully acquired, it is sex, money, or shame, and our job is to narrow the choices."

Mallroy again stared at Doolin, but his face softened. The lines around those ice-laden eyes became less obvious, and he actually smiled while slowly nodding and amazingly said, "Yeah, my thoughts as well."

"Drugs or some other material that is precious, forbidden, and collectively hurts us," he softly reflected.

"I need you to get out into your designated highland zones and communicate with me on your data collection and observations; I will tell you what to look for. I am going to begin following the trail elsewhere."

Not yet fully acclimated to the colonel-corporal state of equality, Doolin requested, "Permission to speak freely."

An almost exasperated twinge of a frown began to shape the corner of Mallroy's mouth, but understanding, he instead nodded.

"Sir, communicating from the field is problematic. I work alone, seldom ever use a radio, and I do not underestimate Charlie's ability to triangulate radio signals. I am a ghost. Once they believe or show that I am in a particular sector, I am not safe, and they can flood the area with hunter-killers. Regular communications are very dangerous for me, and I think for you, they are unnecessary."

Mallroy was looking directly at Doolin, then again looked up and to the left and stared into space. Yet again the almost reptilian sampling of air occurred, his tongue darting in and out of his mouth before he replied, "You're right, but there must be a manner in which you can let me know where you are. It could become important."

Doolin had previously thought for a bit about this issue, trying to mix the need for signaling with the danger in doing so. "How good are we at scanning frequencies of radio traffic in specific areas?"

Mallroy smiled, immediately grasping the intent of Doolin's question. He nodded and then began a quick summation of US military technical capabilities.

As he talked, Mallroy and Doolin worked though the US military's fledgling use of computers in scanning radio traffic for different frequencies hoping to pick up enemy communications. By coincidence, in fact, US Joint Command had recently formed several electronic warfare units to jam and feed false communications to the enemy. This was old news to the Air Force and Naval aviators, since they routinely tried to blunt radar and radio waves out of both self-preservation and to gain a tactical edge in protecting their flying missions, but to most of the Marines and Army personnel on the ground, this was still a bit novel.

Doolin proposed a solution to Mallroy as they sat together, their knees not a foot apart, and discussed the need for absolute secrecy. Doolin wanted to be let off his leash, and to communicate only when he thought it critical. Further, he wanted to provide identification via a system that they both could endorse, but Doolin wanted Mallroy to understand that it was to the colonel's benefit to have the younger man pass information and observations directly to Mallroy. Doolin did not want to report from the field and wanted no intermediary handling the information.

There was, however, one rather troubling consideration in the forefront of Doolin's mind. Doolin did not know, and could not know, if Mallroy was somehow the actual betrayer of secrets, the linchpin to the entire problem.

So, in order to distance himself from Mallroy, out in the field the colonel would know only rather large general areas and times where Doolin would be active. If Doolin saw more hunter-killers than his senses tolerated as normal, then Mallroy was the rot in the middle of a flawed system and this Army colonel needed to be eliminated, and Doolin would do so quietly and efficiently.

To Doolin, that was not a big deal; it was war, and Doolin was, in fact, a trained American killer. Hurting Doolin's buddies deliberately, if Mallroy was the betrayer of American efforts, was unpardonable. And thus, if this Army colonel was behind such a betrayal, then Doolin's judgment would be rendered.

Doolin did not share this with Mallroy, but the colonel must have understood the ramifications of Doolin's plans as he smiled and grasped the verbal and, more importantly, the tacit implications of Doolin's proposals. Mallroy immediately approved the young man's suggestions that, in point of fact, contained these tacit requests.

"Corporal Doolin, you seem to not want me to know where you are and when you will be at these nebulous locations. Is that correct?"

Doolin said nothing and stared back into those ice-blue eyes.

"I understand," he calmly stated, "but if I tell you that we have a future mission wherein I need you to report, you better find a manner to get it done, OK?"

"Yes, sir."

"But I will try and minimize any nonsense, OK? Does that sound fair? In exchange, I will ensure that you are off the hook and completely my responsibility so you don't have to report to Marine HQ. I understand that they are pissed as hell at you anyway since you categorically disobey all requests to contact them when you are in the field."

"Sounds fair, sir."

"Just so you know, if I were you, I wouldn't check in, either. Those people are trying to get our boys killed. What absolute nonsense!"

This last bit could have reasonably been interpreted as a false peroration to quickly gain Judah's approval. To draw Doolin in and encourage his belief in Mallroy, only to mask the intelligence officer's perfidious intent. But Mallroy's manner did not suggest this. Instead, he conveyed a weary quasi-tolerance, a sad conclusive acknowledgment in the stupidity of those who told others how to behave in combat having never done so themselves. He slowly shook his head and returned to their shared task.

Doolin's willingness to communicate if absolutely necessary meant he would need to use the enemy's radio and transmit nothing but an odd band-width for seconds. But it would also occur for an interval lasting sufficiently and varying from the norm of most transmissions to be adequate for American monitoring of frequencies to pick it up. In all honesty, Doolin didn't think the American capabilities were that good and had little hope that they would spot his "messages" in a timely fashion. The byproduct of this inability to readily identify his transmissions was that it provided maximal anonymity. This, at least, was the operational plan that Judah felt best protected him.

Doolin's relationship with Mallroy needed to be validated before the young sniper would allow even a modicum of possibility for the rapid identi-fication of his geographic location by the enemy. The colonel and the enemy could be one in the same.

Doolin's plan for atypical short-interval band signaling would render it very difficult for anyone to have real-time data as to where he was operating. If the enemy did somehow triangulate his radio transmission, subsequent discovery of dead comrades would not immediately trigger recognition or confirmation that it was specifically Doolin. The communications would vary in both their interval and length with no audible human voice. All of this minimized the potential of establishing a pattern as to who was the source of the killings or the radio activity. This was important, given the fact that Doolin was almost certainly and paradoxically destined to become their "favorite" sniper—someone whom the traitor would identify as requiring immediate termination with prejudice. Doolin desperately needed to elimi-nate any tessellations that would by default finger him.

But just as importantly, the leash was to be removed, and Doolin was now able to roam rather freely for weeks at a time.

Mallroy actually made the most headway with Doolin that first meeting by telling the younger man to increase his stated paranoia regarding any future discussion with other officers of any service. As Mallroy puffed on what must have been his fourth cigarette in thirty minutes, he rested his left elbow on the map table while sitting on a metal three-legged stool and looked at Doolin carefully. He slowly shifted his gaze and looked over his left shoulder, staring thoughtfully into the distance. The young corporal was sitting on a similar stool two feet from Mallroy. The reptilian movements of the older man's tongue again were present, and Mallroy reconstructed the likely scenario that Doolin created whenever he or any Marine sniper was in an area or sector carrying out an assignment.

"Judah, you will be intervening in enemy activity, the normal hostile activities that are in themselves detrimental to our efforts to win this charade they call a war. But within these 'normal' doings will be additional operations by our dirty colleague, and it is up to you to both discover and to confirm what it is he is up to. Understand?"

"Yes, sir."

"Good. I just wish I knew what this was about. I don't understand the point of giving out our future locations and operational plans unless there is something vital that is being protected."

Mallroy got back up from his sitting position and stood by the map table, the lit cigarette in his right hand dangerously close to his hair as his fingers simultaneously touched and rubbed his ear lobe.

"A new weapon or new technology?" Doolin ventured.

Mallroy looked up quickly to meet Doolin's eyes, searching for but finding no hint of subterfuge, and then offered, "I have no idea, but certainly that would be possible. More likely it is the quantity of conventional weaponry or the numbers of troops, or something rather pedestrian but no less vital for their operational success."

"Sir, can I offer a plan and you poke holes in it?"

Mallroy looked at Doolin and carefully assessed his young Marine for evidence of naiveté or foolishness, but there was none. Doolin wanted Mallroy's expertise, no different in form or intensity than any of the other officers who depended upon Mallroy to assess their strategies and operational endeavors. Doolin did not seek emotional approval or personal acceptance, and this intrigued Mallroy.

The colonel found the young man's level of understanding and insight remarkable, if not a bit unnerving. The kid's cognitive skills were unusual, to say the least, but it was the lightning-fast understanding of Mallroy's own insecurities regarding the veracity of collected data and subsequent critique of existing hypotheses that struck Mallroy as something just short of phenomenal.

"Sure, I'm all ears." His shoulders turned to face Doolin. The cigarette dangling from the right corner of his mouth became stationary, a flagpole jutting out from a storefront on a parade day. His eyes hinted at depths of concern mixed with watchful calculation.

Doolin was up now also and standing on Mallroy's left side. He reached out with his right arm and touched the map with the index finger of his right hand.

"Looking at the map, we know where our guys will be over the next two to three weeks. So"—Doolin now pointed to the spaces representing the un-circled X's, the vacant spaces without planned American troop movement or deployments—"I should be here, or here, or ..." Doolin moved his finger to identify the interposing spaces between these naked X's as one would move to capture vulnerable positions in a checkers game.

"You will need to be careful here, Marine." Mallroy was now deliberate-ly thoughtful, extrapolating Doolin's observations. His tongue moved over his teeth again, an unsettling habit like a snake sampling the scent of prey.

"Yes, sir, that is my general intent," Doolin offered, unconscious of the obvious conclusiveness of their shared concerns.

"No, you misunderstand me. My concern is that if you end up in these spaces too often, someone on their side is going to ask how you're picking the locations so successfully. You understand?"

"Yes, sir, I do. So you want me to monitor, but not intervene at each lo-cation so they don't know I am around, correct? Thus, they won't get suspi-cious that I am always following them and possibly have inside information, which is exactly what I have. At least I now have information derived from their possession of our planned operations."

Mallroy's lips curled enough to reveal a faint but genuine smile; few people could or ever did elicit this response. "Yes, you've got it."

His left hand came up slowly to rub his chin before offering what was his summary judgment. "Let's just say, for argument's sake, that alternatively when you are around or in the area, the enemy continually discovers their dead comrades, so they know two things. First, that someone is guessing correctly too often as to their locations. Two, that perhaps it is one individual that has been visiting. And they might track this to you. After all, bodies are your calling card."

Mallroy was looking out into space staring at nothing, his eyes unfo-cused but searching, working concepts and plans. His lips parted ever so briefly and a tentative smile began to appear, but stopped as he turned to face Doolin.

"So, if you keep the body count down, then we may be able to address what is actually happening out in these areas." He retraced the map, touch-ing a couple of the same points Doolin had identified. "Furthermore, a lack of intervention—your words, Doolin—complicates any semblance of a pat-tern identifying you specifically," Mallroy concluded.

The younger man knew what the colonel meant. The time between Doolin's kills—or even the actual anatomic location of Doolin's shots on the recipients, specifically keeping the pattern of head shots and center mass shots randomized—would not or at least should not suggest any pattern portending a single operational sniper.

As cold-blooded and calculating as this all was, its relevance and importance were obvious. A lack of repetitive specificity was critical. They, Charlie, could not be certain it was Doolin killing their friends if there was no discernible pattern. Alternatively, a definite or telltale configuration could lead to quick confirmation by Charlie that the same guy was hunting in the different locations, and then they would ask how and begin to piece together data from other kills. This might trigger a reassessment of why that someone was so successful in choosing the proper areas.

Thus, if they couldn't be certain that the activity was linked to the same guy, or one single person, then Charlie collectively could not be certain how to approach these happenings. Hunting a single sniper in the jungle is very different than stalking two- and four-man teams or even patrols.

Charlie was not stupid, and if they knew it was Doolin, or any particular individual, then they could put together a map demonstrating a history or inventory of his activities and begin to make predictions of his future movement—and this could be fatal. But if Charlie thought that there might be unregistered, unreported patrols out in the jungle, this might cause them to infer that the mole or traitor in the American chain of command had not provided them with accurate information. This might protect Doolin and, more interestingly, might just add to enemy confusion or suspicions that the mole was something different than what they imagined—meaning, in fact, that their mole was not entirely their asset!

All of Doolin's variables, each one, needed to be kept fluid and deliberately random. This was important to his inherent success in masking his identity in the jungle, as old an observation as time itself. Each and every person had habits, conscious or not, and unknowingly having an objective review of Doolin's activities that uncovered routines in his line of work could be fatal. Alternatively, not being certain of who was perpetrating the activities simply made the enemy's job more difficult. Mallroy understood all of this and the implications immediately. This, and the impact of Doolin not having to communicate needlessly with HQ.

Mallroy then coughed, the cigarette never leaving his mouth, before stating, "OK, Doolin, I think you have made your point. Minimal contacts, but you do your part and make only intermittent kills, and do not develop a calling card. At least that way you can find out what is happening out there rather than become the object of their interests. We have to be on our toes here, son."

But the colonel went even further, suggesting that he begin the activity that would administratively make Doolin invisible. He was going to create the paperwork that would paradoxically make Doolin disappear.

"Corporal, I want you to remove any identification that could be used to tell who you are. But tell me something, anything, so that if you get killed or reportedly killed in action, KIA, I can at least confirm it is you. OK? In the meantime, I am going to use some of my little tricks to erase you from the manifest lists, the order sheets, and the identification rosters. Got it?"

"Yes, sir."

"It may become very important at a future date for you to be a ghost. Perhaps for your own survival."

That warm and wet morning of February 12, 1971, Doolin left Mallroy in Da Nang; he actually provided the corporal a ride back to his base camp. Doolin's head swirled from their meeting and from the implications that they had a traitor within their system, perhaps in Doolin's own Marine command. To place grunts in harm's way for personal reasons, or to be so foolish as to allow this information to become the property of the enemy, was as close to a sin as Doolin's almost eighteen-year-old intermittently agnostic mind could imagine.

But this situation was also the reason Mallroy was taking steps to simply make Doolin administratively disappear. No one would know who Doolin was or what he did. This was strangely liberating, but Doolin began thinking through the many implications of his actions, and there were many.

The young Marine was angry, but also curious. What and how was the connection between coordinates of future troop movement tied to something of value? And what was the valuable entity? He found that thinking through the possibilities was strangely satisfying, in part because it took his mind away from the awful destruction he visited on individual enemy soldiers. He found himself reinforced by the need to protect his fellow soldiers and to unmask the evil of a traitor in their midst.

Judah Doolin did not enjoy or "get off" on killing other human beings. He was trained to perform this "service" for his country in the time of war, and he did so with the belief that his actions were worthwhile. As he and the jeep driver maneuvered through the loud, busy streets jammed with cars, trucks, and people, the warm sun of the afternoon mixed with the humidity of the tropical surroundings, making this land a beautiful but heartbreakingly flawed mistress. A mistress that had begun to question Doolin's role in this unfolding tragedy.

The more time Doolin spent in this beautiful, enigmatic strip of verdant land, participating in a civil war between a single people, a single family at war with itself, the less certain he was of his role, or of his country's. It was his reading, his appetite for history that had initially triggered his growing doubts. He had not been here that long, but he had followed the war, reading its history from the French involvement to reclaim their colonies to now his own country's fear of the "domino theory" of advancing communism.

But as this war evolved, the more the implications of a soulless and amoral superpower's bureaucracy showed its face as the controlling force in an increasingly pointless conflict, and thus the less Doolin believed his efforts, or those of his nation, were of true value. This coincided with more frequent apologies to his mother in dreams linked to a growing self-recognition that he was in search of answers. Perhaps it was to free himself from the mounting belief that what he was doing was beyond futile; perhaps it was wrong.

Whatever it was, Doolin realized that he was grappling with the consequences of his actions versus the need to protect his buddies, his fellow grunts. Doolin's need to justify his actions was becoming inexplicably important. Thus, Mallroy had provided a renewal of his belief that his role was indeed warranted. It was tantamount to faith in the fact that what Doolin was doing was proper, or at least justified, against a growing suspicion within the young Marine that it actually was not.

But even this newfound comfort was transient. There was still a growing sense that Doolin's continued taking of life was an action of slowly ebbing derivative value. This inherent dichotomy was, in essence, his growing suspicion that he did not possess the same confidence he previously carried—that if his superiors said what he performed was just, then it must be.

Doolin also understood that others had previously explored this fundamental human dilemma. They, too, had wandered the timeless empty corridors of doubt. Their paths had also led to ancient steppes populated by souls who had themselves grappled with these same questions. The inherent value or justice of activity taken within the cauldron of combat, and its impact on other human beings damaged by one's own hand, were to be weighed. For many a redemption is sought, but a price is to be paid; a bill is due. Each survivor, in their own way, tries to address the elements needed for full payment. For some, they will not be successful. For others, the contents of the self-directed judgment must be tucked away in a locked box, secure but buried within the furthest recesses of the mind.

Their significance as vulnerable beings cast rootless into an imperfect, and at times ugly, violent world. Forced to take action, to allow self-preservation, but at the cost of killing other human beings. At the cost of their soul's innocence, virtue, and even honor. They understood, just like Doolin was beginning to accept, that the cost may not be fathomable.

Being adrift in a black sea of doubt without the ability to hold true to values that sustain in times of conflict, pain, or uncertainty is to enter into hopelessness. Doolin was beginning to have serious reservations about his role in this war while ironically beginning to discover a budding acknowledgement in the exegetical origins of faith. A faith that was slowly becoming personal—perhaps a renewal of what his mother long ago had provided him. The young man was contemplating a departure from his agnostic lodgings.

And thus, it struck Doolin as strange and yet somehow typical, for he was one of a "people" whose soul wandered in a broken, increasingly barren land. He gravitated toward understanding the haunting indecision and confusion that bubbled up from the depths of his young being. And thus, like others forming an endless line in time, he, too, found solace in picking up a Bible and reading, just reading it. Before Mallroy, this had never happened; after, it took root in him. For Doolin understood he must go on killing, but he needed to ensure there was a modicum of justification for his actions.

He, like so many others before him, sought an answer in a most ancient text. The seminal anthology reflective of the vital relationship between God and human beings. Doolin's tasks were not over despite his dwindling faith in the overall mission; in truth, it reflected a quest for closure in Vietnam.

This occurred in between assignments, when he was alone in the barracks for three to five days. He took a small scruffy, beat-up brown leather-bound Bible from the guy three bunks down as this GI always laid it out on the stand next to his bunk. Doolin always returned it to the same place and tried to make sure it was in the same position as when he took it, but he found himself reading it more and more often, especially the Psalms.

One day as Doolin sat on the edge of his bed with his back to the main door, he was deeply engrossed in reading and felt rather than heard or saw someone looking at him. Doolin had completely missed the footsteps, the presence of the guy from Indiana, the owner of the Bible, and he was standing at the end of Doolin's bed looking at him. His tanned face, with a thin, slightly hooked nose and cleft chin, registered no anger. His gentle brown eyes were somehow accepting, almost knowingly placid and calm.

Doolin expected him to be upset and accuse Judah of appropriating his personal items without consent or agreement, yet he smiled when Doolin looked up. Doolin must have had the look of complete guilt in his eyes as well as astonishment that he, a well-trained and generally acknowledged very competent Marine sniper, didn't even register the Bible owner's presence. But the book's owner nodded slightly and simply said, "Just leave it where I can find it when you're done, OK?"

Doolin immediately got up, and holding the Bible, extended his arm to give it back, but the young GI held both his palms vertical to stop Doolin. "No, it's OK! It's fine, go ahead. You were really reading that, Doolin. You didn't even answer when I called your name."

It was then Doolin realized that he had been completely absorbed without even a trace of sensing that the Bible's owner was present. He smiled stupidly, his forehead wrinkling and eyebrows lifting. Doolin must have looked the fool, but again the other man was relaxed and stated, "Talk to you later." He turned and left, walking out of the barracks and quietly shutting the screen door.

Perhaps this had been His plan all along. Years later, Doolin remembered this incident and felt that it was his beginning of asking for help, in a sense, but the journey was not going to be straight, simple, or easy. Then again, it never was, at least for most. This was both the beauty and challenge of life.

Doolin simply found he could not escape dreaming of his mother, always linked to her enduring disappointment in his chosen line of work. When he could eventually drift off and settle into a disturbed sleep, she voiced concerns about his "work," and this always troubled Doolin as he awoke with remnants of these imaginings.

CHAPTER 3

HIGHLANDS OF VIETNAM

April 24, 1971

Hic manebimus optime.
"Here we will stay most excellently."

J udah Doolin was now at almost two and a half weeks by himself in the dense green foliage encompassing the beginning of the Central Highlands, the home of the ancient Montagnard or Degar peoples. These folks were fiercely independent and resisted any and all forms of centralized non-Degar government. He made a point of avoiding their villages and small hamlets. His current location was near the plateaued beauty of Tây Nguyên bordering the high mountain ranges of the Annamite Range, each peak climbing skyward but covered with lush, dense growth that provided a protective habitat to various species including the gray-shanked douc langur, the banteng, and the rarely seen Indochinese tiger.

The young Marine was near the Vietnam border, closer to the lower part of Laos, looking for Charlie in the fading day after the sun had left the sky. A blue-black canvas with faint high-altitude gossamer clouds had replaced the sun-streaked orange and red dying light. His ever-alert continence did not prevent his near intimate stumbling over one of these rare Indochinese striped feline hunters. He had to move quickly and carefully to an elevated position downwind as this beautiful massive cat trailed or more precisely hunted a midsize gaur.

This was an Indian bison, one of a group of eleven. The beautiful elegant predator was very large, probably almost 410 pounds, pure muscle and just about nine feet in length. Smaller than Bengal or Siberian tigers, and their orange fur coloration was a shade or two darker, almost a golden hue with multiple beautiful short and narrow single dark-brown, near-black stripes. Doolin couldn't be certain of its size, and no one would have believed him anyway if he had described the beautiful animal as being that large. Even today he knew what he had seen, but anyone else might have doubted his story's veracity.

He watched through his night scope downwind from this stunning, graceful hunter as it moved efficiently and silently, perfectly made for its nocturnal stalking activity. The moon began to appear, climbing and changing the inky blackness to a faintly lit dark background showing filmy cotton-like clouds, scudding to partially obscure the waning lunar sliver. Use of his scope easily picked up the rippled muscles of the animal's powerful front legs and shoulders, the rhythmic activity of its biceps and triceps bulging from beneath its flawless coat with each step. It was totally silent, but then Doolin was no closer than 160 to 170 yards and had no intention of getting any closer. The gentle breeze was inconsistent but pushed into the Marine's face, allowing him to take in the damp tang of the forest. Doolin was surprised; he had thought tigers had disappeared from Vietnam, but then this big boy—judging by the size, it was likely a male—could travel vast distances in search of its meals if necessary.

And then the animal stopped, raised its head slightly, and turned slowly but deliberately to the right. His ears pitched up and its head stilled, and as Doolin watched, curious as to what scent or sound it had encountered, it sank suddenly to its strike position, ready to pounce but also listening and heeding any change in the fragrance of its tree-filled surroundings. Doolin scanned the area to its right, looking for clues, and then his night scope caught the very slight asynchronous movement of small trees and bushe 325 yards ahead and to the right of the tiger. The animal must have heard that something that the sniper could not or simply was unable to perceive.

The cat resumed its stalking posture, back arched slightly before silently padding forward two or three steps, neck extended. It held its powerful head in a sniffing position, testing the wind. Its large paws moved quickly but without sound as its muscled silhouette brushed up against the undergrowth and was swallowed by the night, and then it was gone. Apparently, it had no intention of engaging with whatever was out there, but the disjointed movement of the distant highland vegetation persisted. Intermittently, the brief but chaotic movement grew closer to Doolin's position. It must have been humans, he surmised, as there was a rippled incongruity that outlined the undergrowth. It grew steadier, slowly, carefully advancing toward his position with no sound.

No animal was that clumsy or careless, hitting low tree limbs and distorting the natural curves of the foliage. Yet, the absence of sound continued—another clue that while this was likely human, it was also assuredly someone not wanting exposure. *There!* Silhouettes of shoulders and a neck, a head with a leaf-covered canvas helmet. *How many? Come on,* thought Doolin, *show how many ... Gotcha!* One hundred and fifty-plus yards away, two individuals moved between trees but brushed the smaller limbs enough to announce their presence. *Shit,* thought Doolin. One trailer, and yes, a "comm guy" or radio man. That made three.

So Mallroy had been correct: the region that Doolin occupied, the area where his sniper nest was located, did, in fact, represent one of the areas marked by the naked X's on the map. An area void of American troop involvement, and thus a source of mystery to Mallroy and Doolin. For the last two weeks, the Marine had been traveling on foot into the areas that they had identified, and Doolin had seen VC scouts on three nights of the seven thus far. Tonight made four. The only reasonable conclusion was that the enemy was sending scouts into regions on the map wherein American troops were not scheduled to conduct operations, but where Charlie had something of value. This made enough sense to Doolin; if you didn't want to confront the enemy, best to stay away from them.

Their ability to avoid American troops or circumvent engaging their forces was only possible through the possession and subsequent use of the Americans' operational patrol schedules. Now, it looked as though the enemy indeed had both this data and these goals! This was the reason Doolin had gotten involved in this nonsense to begin with—someone was supplying the other side with valuable, and supposedly secret, American tactical schedules for troop and patrol movement, and the Vietnamese were going where US personnel were not. This was the hypothesis they had formulated after discovery of the map coordinates and Doolin had now confirmed this, because here they were—again.

Why ... what the hell were they doing in these areas that was so critical that they wanted to be outside of American circumference for tactical engagement? Doolin was both fascinated and deeply troubled as he wrestled with this question. The North Vietnamese knew, as did US troops, that with American near-omnipresent use of helicopters, the areas accessible to American troop movement encompassed a much greater radius than if these same troops were limited to activities reachable only by truck or foot. Thus, it was a given that any area of value was penetrable by our flying metal machines.

But these areas now being investigated by Doolin at Mallroy's request had been identified by the captured confidential coordinates specifically showing no American presence. Mallroy had asked Doolin to investigate the regions that were far from planned American activities on specific nights. The North Vietnamese knew US troops were not going to show anywhere near these areas. The question again was: Why was this important to Charlie? *Why?* What were they trying to hide?

The three scouts were picking their way along what seemed to be a predetermined path. Doolin really wanted to know two things: First, of course, was what were they actually trying to accomplish? Second, did they have copies of the American troop movement coordinates on them? Doolin reflected that his other three encounters early in his four-week deployment were purely observational, but tonight, he might just engage the enemy and try to lift some intel from them if he was successful in overcoming whatever they offered as resistance. Doolin desperately wanted to see if there was a telltale map with coordinates like the one that had started this whole project. Naturally, "overcoming their resistance" was a euphemism for eliminating them and searching their bodies; thus, he accepted that he was either going to kill three people tonight or be killed in his attempt.

Not for the first time, he had to ask himself what it was about his species that allowed for the simultaneous holding of beliefs that condoned purposefully ending life while worshipping a superior being acknowledged as responsible for that very same existing life. Another aspect of the imperfect species called Homo sapiens. This had always intrigued Doolin. Further, in his case, this "sanctioned" killing of others of his own species was conducted for what amounted to philosophical differences. Communist versus capitalist—as if God really cared about these bullshit human definitions.

Why did anyone think his species would survive or thrive on this planet if they continually lacked the understanding that simple variance in appearance, belief, or custom was sufficient reason to end another's life? It always struck Judah as paradoxical that the very biological reason humans existed as a successful species on this planet lay in adaptability, which at its core was a heterogeneity in human responsiveness to the environmental challenges they faced. That, over millions of years, humans had adapted to the environment underwritten by this changeability, and yet it was this very thing, this heterogeneity, that caused humans to kill one another. Whether it was difference in appearance, religion, philosophy, or customs, differences were frequently and repetitively anathema to peaceful coexistence.

Such philosophical discrepancies were then difficult to grasp as a justification for the murder of scores, hundreds, or even untold numbers of human beings. But the Nazis, or Stalin or Mao or even Doolin's government and their treatment of Native Americans, exemplified that this pattern was all too common. Doolin just found this entire reality a bit bizarre—that the very source of our sustainability as a species was the same reason humans tried to kill one another. And here he was in his own personal bubble, engaged in the very same hypocrisy. He was performing his duty by killing these three, and if he did not do this here and now, well, his life would end tonight. He concluded that, indeed, he was a member of a strange species.

Doolin's rifle—a significantly modified Remington 700, called an M40A1—had an enlarged and retooled ejector port, a fiberglass stock, and a foam-filled leather pouch strapped to the buttstock that served as his cheek rest. He tried to keep this from becoming too caked with dirt or camouflage paint. The total length of his barrel was twenty-four inches with a rifling that was not customized, as it had a 1:12-inch twist, not including his self-made nine-inch sound suppressor. Doolin's issue was that he had to hit three targets quickly and then, per Mallroy, ensure that they were alone before he came out from hiding and searched them for intel.

The simple routine was to make sure that he was alone, search them, and evaporate into the night. This was the plan, and it was paramount that Doolin get all three done in proper sequence to avoid a radio distress call being sent. Mallroy had warned him that these scouts were very smart; they did not need detailed or even brief audio communication into their mic. In the case of trouble, they might only double-click their mic, for example, and with the recipient 1,000 to 1,500 meters away they would come fast, bringing sufficient numbers of men to disperse into the area and hunt down the source of the distress message. So, he had to plan the attack based on several variables, but quick lethal action was essential.

Then, upon searching them, if Doolin could also set the dead radioman's bandwidth to an uncommon frequency monitored by Mallroy and leave it for ten to twelve seconds, then set it back and disappear, he would be done—a successful mission. This was his signal to Mallroy that he would have to identify.

Doolin's predatory feline friend roaming around out there was both an unexpected benefit as well as a potential problem. He might come back to "taste" any available meal, and this, of course, would confuse the subsequent evaluation of bodies by the North Vietnamese troops. It might also drive any "rescue" party away! But just as concerning for Doolin was the fact that he couldn't be sure this tiger might not consider *him* part of the menu. Truthfully, he wasn't even sure that the big cat would consider indulging in human flesh.

Doolin smiled in spite of himself, thinking how far he had traveled from his suburban high school both in miles and experience. He wasn't absolutely certain, but he would have wagered not many other seventeen-year-olds were addressing similar variables, such as whether subsequent decisions might get them eaten by a real tiger, before finalizing their course of action.

Doolin waited until he had two of them seventy-five yards ahead of him and the radioman about eighty yards. He tucked himself under a highland rocky overhang, squeezing ever so slightly into the earth before he started his routine: focus, finger, touch and caress the trigger, inhale, exhale, and then the release point—with the kick and simultaneous gas expelling, he would rapidly reload his precision 7.62x51 mm NATO round. Same sequence again, and then again; with the third and final shot, he would be done.

The first shot was the most challenging. Doolin wanted to hit the radioman, but not the radio—center, one inch above the nose, through the forehead into the skull. He was probably 3.5 millimeters to the right, but it was nearly perfect, and the man collapsed behind his two comrades. The second man, Doolin hit in the back at the base of the neck as he was turning to look at his buddy. The bullet entered through the center line of his neck near C7, the exact area of his cervical vertebrae, and he was done. But the first man was moving out of sight, and now Doolin's shot would be blind.

He adjusted his body to realign his sight and as he prepared his shot, he saw the North Vietnamese soldier's foot plant and hold for a second. Doolin shot and hit his right leg just below the knee. He cried out, and that was enough to confirm to Doolin that he had hit the man. Doolin then rapidly fired a fourth shot two feet above the leg and his right foot was suddenly in the air, joined by its companion, boots flipping up fourteen to eighteen inches off the ground with a slight tremor in the right leg, and then both landed softly on the wet carpet of leaves and ferns. All movement ceased.

Doolin quickly moved to his prearranged secondary position, not taking his eyes off the surroundings of the kill zone. He moved silently, avoiding limbs, brush, and any higher branches that would signal a person's presence and, ducking under a broad green three-leaf fern, controlled his breathing and waited. His night vision scope's optics provided a somewhat indistinct soft green outline of the various forms he examined, but as he continued looking, sweeping the floor of the jungle systematically, Doolin did not see any movement other than the gentle motion of the multitudes of black-green outlined leaves swaying in unison in the soft night breeze. After almost twelve minutes he began a circuitous path, slowly picking his way to the bodies, making almost no sound and remaining low. His head and hat were never truly perpendicular to the ground, mostly parallel as he made careful side glances and then moved forward. Doolin closed his eyes and listened and smelled; there was nothing different, but his internal alarms were on high alert.

The rain was beginning again, slightly harder now, creating a background noise that efficiently masked the sounds associated with animal movement as well as the telltale acoustics of human activity. Doolin had to be aware that his motion was not, in fact, running headlong into a patrol of seven to thirteen troops, because if this were the case, he would most certainly not survive. Three or five yards at a time, he moved with his torso bent forward, close to the ground, listening when he stopped and surveying for scattered atypical movement of limbs or bushes.

He enjoyed the patter of drops cascading down though the layers of the green-leafed canopy; a pungent earthy aroma rose from the green-and-brown carpeted floor. The forested acres, with its nearly countless branches and leaves, delayed much of the rain as it traveled slowly through each verdant stratum. His skin was soaked, but Doolin really didn't mind, for the water cleansed his skin, removing the sweat, oil, and the aroma of his humanness. Doolin was really becoming one with this land, traveling silently and respectfully within its boundaries, yet he had to honor his mission and duty to abstract canons imposed by men sitting in Washington assessing its geopolitical value. There, official tenets had demanded that this young Marine sniper kill other people deemed to be the enemy, and so he had.

Each man was dead, and a quick search of their pockets was disappointing: nothing. The radio was intact and of Chinese origin. Doolin couldn't entirely comprehend all of the symbols on the various knobs, but he discerned one was the control for bandwidth. He turned it a quarter turn to one of several predetermined frequencies, clicked the mic on, and held it for exactly twelve seconds. Then he positioned this mic, a scuffed cubelike hard plastic object, within the dead man's hand. No one would be certain this open mic was not a terminal action. The bandwidth dial was returned to the original position, or close enough; again, who could ensure that it was not altered in the last seconds of the decedent's life, or that his falling to the ground was not responsible?

As Doolin returned to the last man, he again found nothing in his canvas satchel. He was about to move back into the night when he reluctantly looked at the effect of his shot to the dead Vietnamese soldier's leg. Doolin had unconsciously begun to limit his analysis of his created wounds, as he had seen enough over the last months to understand the trauma caused. It was not that he was squeamish, or even unsettled in giving a professional, dispassionate assessment of his work, but his work with the rifle had begun to disappoint him, as he knew his mother would have also been disappointed. This, after all, was the summation of his life's work thus far. Judah C. Doolin killed other human beings for his soldier's paycheck and had become fairly adept at the entire process.

While it was fair to state that a paycheck for his work was the furthest thought from Doolin's mind, in truth he received little of this money; it represented the collective summary of what he performed that provided value to his employer. He was a soldier and killed enemy soldiers. Doolin was a human being and killed enemy human beings. The eventual derivative philosophical or explicative argument became depressingly hopeless if one were arguing the value of his activity before God—at least that was what Doolin concluded. *Yes, Lord,* he thought, *I repetitively kill Your creations because they believe in something different than me, or more accurately, something different than the beliefs of our government, whoever the hell they are!*

Doolin already knew God was not going to rule in his favor here, and this was becoming a bit of a problem for this young man with special skills with a rifle. His self-described inconsistent agnostic perspective was becoming a bit tenuous the more he was asked to destroy other living beings. As much as Doolin wanted to intellectually dismiss his parents' influence on his personal beliefs, killing and the finality of it was paradoxically weakening his self-assurance in the agnostic viewpoint. His purpose on Earth should be tied to something more than simply becoming efficient, if not really good, at killing other people. But he needed to let this go if he were going to survive this complex land of beauty mixed with incalculable despair called the Republic of Vietnam.

As it pertained to Judah's pay, almost the entire cumulative amount was still being deposited in his mother's account despite the fact that she was dead. His name was jointly on the account, and the government had not moved to change anything, as far as he knew, and wouldn't as long as he was on active duty and far from home. Judah's father had dropped dead at age forty-six exactly twenty-nine months ago—the combination of what in a later era would be called post-traumatic stress disorder, but amongst WWII vets, it was called alcoholism, tobacco abuse, and morbid obesity. These variables and their determinative impact on his heart had resulted in sudden death in his mid-forties. His gentle, loving soul had been so traumatized by the events seen and experienced in that war that although he clung desperately to Judah's mother, she could not save his father as he slowly and methodically killed himself, taking twenty-four years to accomplish the job. His father had never missed a day of work, but at home he spent most of his time silently sitting in front of the TV consuming cheap vodka, eating chips, and inhaling packages of Camel cigarettes.

His death had sparked a financial crisis. There was literally no money coming in, and thus it was an understandable and actually quite easy decision for Judah Doolin to enlist early and provide both his mother and younger brother with the security of some income. His parents had been lovely people, truly considerate and caring people, and they had done their best to raise Judah in a home with palpable Christian values, aside from the liters of vodka his father consumed. But Judah's father was a gentle drunk, and he had effectively conveyed his love for Judah, despite wildly elevated blood-alcohol levels, in many tender nonverbal ways. Neither of Judah's parents had been stingy with their emotional support or withheld their visible happiness regarding any of his young life's activities. Whether it was baseball or track or the chess team, Doolin's mom and dad were all in for him. And although neither had ever attended college, both insisted that he was destined to go on to college and were certain he was to attain even greater levels of education.

Judah didn't feel right about the dismissive attitude that other better-dressed fathers of sons on the baseball team had taken toward his dad. And at times it was more than an attitude, a snarky smile communicated silently to a friend as Judah's dad walked past, a bit red-eyed and stepping carefully to avoid an embarrassing fall. But this had never altered his dad's sincere happiness at seeing Judah pitch in a game or get a line-drive single or double on a Saturday afternoon. They were great parents. After all, both his father and mother had chosen to take Judah into their home, and for this, their son was eternally grateful and would become even more so the older he grew. Yet, as time passed during his Vietnam tour, he felt the disparity between what he did versus what his parents had hoped he would accomplish. Instead of a healer, he was a US Marine sniper. What he did was not exactly shameful, but could one call it purposeful?

The point man's lower leg was nearly completely severed from the more proximal thigh at the knee, where Doolin's first round entered his leg. As the metal expanded on impact, it formed a lead-based scythe, shearing through tendons, muscle, and artery. The bottom of his leg, from the knee down, lay at an odd, unnatural angle; it was disconnected from the upper bone, the femur, and the thick red-brown, almost black congealing liquid was soaking his pants and the leaves underneath. Taking this in, Doolin turned his head, readying to leave, but his eye noted a tiny incongruent change in the continuity of outlines farther down the leg, near the top of his boot. Protruding just slightly from beneath the cuff of his uniform's pant leg was a triangular piece of plastic. Judah almost missed this, as it was fairly dark, but there was just enough light in the sliver from the lunar reflection to see it poking out from inside the dead man's uniform: a clear plastic bag or container, and there was something inside.

Doolin reached down and felt this object, and yes, it was plastic and had the composition of a lunch bag. These bags were becoming popular with moms back in the States, who used them to pack peanut butter and jelly sandwiches for their kids. But this was a bit heavier plastic, and although similar in that it was clear plastic, like sandwich bags, it was shaped into a gentle curved sheet small enough to fit snuggly into a uniform pant leg. He pulled gently, then a bit harder until it dislodged from the cloth; adhesive tape had held it into place. It was easily deformable, and Doolin unfolded the lip over the top and examined its contents.

The thin paper within had writings that, as Doolin examined them with the green light of his flashlight, were enough to cause a chill to creep up his spine despite the eighty-degree night, followed by intense anger. Here in front of him, yet again, were groups of numbers consistent with map coordinates, and next to five of them were dates. Four of the dates were yet to come, but they were in the near future, and all of them were no more than two weeks away. However, there were two additional columns of numbers next to these and they, too, had the appearance of coordinates. Knowing what Mallroy and Doolin had discussed previously, he began to have a sinking feeling. Could this be US troop future positions next to their corresponding dates?

Quickly, the young sniper memorized one set of coordinates and wrote the others down on his own tiny paper notepad that he pulled from his left upper chest pocket. On his 2x3-inch notepad, he carefully copied the dates and the coordinates, writing as small as he could and checking again to ensure accuracy with the originals. Then he repositioned the papers back in the plastic and reinserted it into its original position within the uniform of the dead scout. The plastic had been clean, and Doolin ensured there was no evidence of blood on it now. As he repositioned the adhesive tape a final time, he checked to satisfy himself that the material was free of any of the now brown-red congealing material. The upper leg was shredded where the round had impacted with its deadly force, but the unnatural position of the man's leg had left it free from the resultant hemorrhage.

Doolin left the bodies otherwise undisturbed as they lay, moving quickly deeper into the jungle toward the Laotian border. He and Mallroy had agreed that he should not remove material from his kills—let the enemy think that their precious coordinates carried by some of these scouts were safe. Mallroy had told Doolin than any competent enemy commander would not assume that any of the data was safe, but they both knew that competence was not universal in any nation's military. Thus, allowing a superficial or lazy commander to be lulled into a false conclusion that his coordinates were untouched and safe was preferential to the knowledge that they had been compromised.

The rain had started again. Doolin wondered if it was God's attempt to cleanse him of his recent sins, the taking of three more souls who would be forgotten memories to all but their closest relatives and friends. Statistics in a war driven by metrics—body counts and precise weights of explosive tonnage dropped on the Northern cities by the Americans' modified B-52 strategic bombers. It was almost as if the government accountants had discovered a novel field for the application of their skills and were enthusiastically demonstrating their aptitude to US leaders by presenting graphs and pie charts showing the incredible successes of their military efforts. The only problem was, of course, that America was losing this war, both here and at home.

Of all of the tectonic surprises in Doolin's life, few were larger than the painful awakening of his consciousness after reading the starkly different views of US actions in Vietnam within contrasting narratives of *The Stars and Stripes* and *The New York Times*. The frank propaganda of *S&S* was as absurdly enthusiastic of American goals as the nightmare-like denunciations of the same by the *NYT*. Sounding almost like a deranged primary school teacher lecturing a child, the *NYT*'s editorials thematically drifted into condemning not only the war, but also the actual soldiers, pilots, and seamen who were fighting it. As if these man had a choice, unless they ran for Canada. It was as naïve as it was disingenuous and hurtful. Doolin did enjoy the tight, efficient editorial writing style, but for many of the editorial staff, hearing and pontificating about the daily "atrocities" committed by American troops without having ever placed a foot on the soil of Vietnam exposed them as frauds. Nothing more, nothing less.

But it was while on leave—dressed as a civilian, sipping a cup of American coffee on a Saigon street in an open-air café, reading this material—that several mental pieces had clicked into place for Doolin. It was an emotional as well as an intellectual epiphany as to the level of support that members of the Armed Services could expect from his fellow citizens upon returning home. Unlike the heroic and warm embrace for vets from WWII or the stilted silence awaiting those returning from the Korean "conflict," the stature of those returning from Vietnam would take a far more ominous turn. Doolin's generation were the "baby killers," and so neighbors and strangers would see them in that light, at least for a period of time. It is one thing to feel that you have been asked to do a difficult, dirty job for your country. It is quite another to be spit on by peers for having the conviction to step up and complete your nation's requested task. But this was the reality that would be waiting for many of the Vietnam veterans … those fortunate enough to return home.

Yet despite his growing sadness over this national waste of human resources and fracture of loyalties, creeping into Doolin's being was the fact that North Vietnamese troops had access to classified American information and were efficient enough to get it out into the field and to their troops. And this fact was putting Doolin's fellow grunts and him at risk—a potentially cataclysmic risk. He couldn't let it go. No—more to the point, he was *not* going to let it go unanswered. Doolin was going to find out what and who were responsible.

CHAPTER 4

THE PEN

May 7, 1971

Cui bono?
"Who benefits?"

A s Doolin would look back through time and his maturity, his anger at finding important and secret material in the hands of the enemy was disproportionate, for there is a predictable ebb and flow of such events in war. Each side steals, misleads, tricks, and is, in fact, proud of the subterfuge it inflicts on the other party. But this dispassionate discourse is for historians to make and categorize in forgotten essays and monographs gathering dust thirty or two hundred years after the fact. For those living or simply trying to exist within the confines of war, these actions of deceit and betrayal represent potential impediments to their very survival—the so-called "existential threat."

And thus, Doolin was determined to understand how and why these co-ordinates were of value to Charlie and his collaborators. How were they being used? What purpose did they facilitate? Yes, they had American positions and could inflict sudden and devastating harm to a platoon of unsuspecting American Marines or Army grunts, but so far this had not occurred. No one had laid waste to an American patrol; no ambushes had occurred, as far as anyone had reported, using this specific data. And this was part of the fundamental excitement growing in Doolin: the knowledge that they were apparently sitting on this information. Or were they? What the hell were they doing with it?

The month of May was the official start of the rainy season. Peaking in June, July, and August, it was not uncommon to have drenching showers every day for weeks, beginning and ending in the early or midafternoon, yet it was the humidity that could be exhausting for newcomers. It simply sapped your energy as you experienced beads of water piling up on your forehead, neck, and arms even while sitting. But as Doolin traveled light, with only his rifle, water, and small amounts of food, moving back into the highlands through the jungle, the terrain showed the effects of the life-giving water on the foliage and surrounding wildlife. He had grown to love the harsh yet incomparable beauty of the jungle, and as it transitioned into the more open terrain of the highlands, even the sunlight took on a different character.

Shifting from the soft dappled cones of illumination seen in the dense ecological growth of the jungle to a more direct and uniform presence, the light nonetheless gave evidence to the unique and continuous beauty of this land. Humidity-laden haze would hover over and coat the ground early each morning, making any visual inspection of the surroundings impossible, but by midmorning the gauzy-white vapor would be gone, burned off by the sun and its energy-containing light, before the midday rain began. Doolin would ultimately smile at the lost opportunity he had foreseen early one morning, thinking at the time that he was becoming just a bit soft, if not stupid.

But twenty years from now, Doolin would indeed look back and shake his head at his sudden idea of bringing tourists to this land to witness the indescribable majesty of its vibrant emerald-colored topography, this slice of geography called Vietnam. Yes, Judah would actually acknowledge the incongruity of these feelings, though nearly twenty years into the future. But like Patti's smile regarding her father's abandonment of her and her mother, it would also hide the pain that only those exposed to Vietnam's tragic beauty during the war could feel.

Doolin had decided to begin "visiting" the listed numbers found on the paper he had discovered in the pant leg sealed within plastic. He realized that he was scheduled to reappear and meet Mallroy within the next nine or ten days, but Doolin wanted more information. He assumed these to be additional map coordinates, and he needed to understand their significance. While this was not approved by either Mallroy or the perfunctory ersatz "command" who still believed they controlled his activity, Doolin felt strongly that Mallroy would approve. At least he hoped he would.

Following these newly acquired coordinates would take him on a journey deep into the land bordering Laos and heavily infiltrated by the North Vietnamese regulars. This was the area they used as they brought supplies down from the north via the infamous Ho Chi Minh Trail. It would also delay Doolin's reappearance to Mallroy by nearly thirty days, enough for him to conclude Doolin was KIA. But the sniper was fiercely driven to understand why this written material was being carried by scouts and patrols from the North, and thus more evidence needed to be procured.

Doolin moved almost exclusively at night, mainly after eleven p.m., and napped during the day in the shade of rock formations or uprooted trees, but never in abandoned huts or buildings. It was well-known that both the Americans and Charlie booby-trapped many areas where protection from the incessant rain could be found; thus, the wet, humid environment outside of human comfort was his zone of safety.

His biggest worry, besides being seen by Charlie, was snakes. They were abundant in the Vietnamese countryside, with some reports suggesting that 30 of the 140 snake species were poisonous, including Asian cobras, king cobras, coral snakes, kraits, and other vipers and pit vipers. It was not uncommon for GI docs to have bitten children brought to them, and although not widely known or reported, many of these young victims died. There was also the mythical "two-step," so named by Doolin's GI brethren, as you were allowed two steps after you were bitten, then you were dead. Doolin thought this was a bit of hyperbole, but then he was not interested in testing the issue. He was careful of where he stepped and where he was willing to let his head and torso rest. But he did rest, and sometimes he fell completely asleep, drifting off to the rhythmic patter of rain and the repetitive sounds of animals announcing their presence to one another. Doolin was alone, completely self-sufficient and separated from the orderly brick houses and manicured green lawns of his native Chicago suburbia.

Doolin had arrived at the third group of coordinates and waited an additional forty-eight hours beyond his arrival. The new day had started. He watched as light slowly pulled away the amorphous gray shadows, transforming them into a clarity of trees and surrounding brilliant-colored forest topography. Nothing really transpired until he saw two figures, both mountain people, come near dusk from the West. Not military, and both moved with purpose but were not threatening. The presence of any human beings in this area was surprising; this was a rather substantial distance from any populace. So, Doolin watched as each individual entered his line of sight and moved silently in and among the trees and plants, separated from each other by seventy-five yards, neither paying attention to the other but listening and moving as though inspecting.

This alone piqued Doolin's interest. He was looking for clues as to what these two were doing, and why here? They continued, each man bent over with their heads individually sweeping back and forth while making quick strides, and then unpredictably stopping and raising their faces from examining the floor of the forest, looking hurriedly all around, before beginning again. It appeared as though they were working together to efficiently examine the entire area spread before Doolin.

The American would have liked to dismiss their activity as incidental and his need to assess this as wasted effort. But the more he examined their very careful movements, the more Doolin understood that they were performing their own version of reconnaissance. They were moving within familiar territory, in proximity to their tribe or extended family structure, and were extremely cautious, almost suspicious, in their systematic visual inventory of the surrounding dense forested hills. Doolin had to move twice to avoid detection, and he was lucky the second time, as he needed to relocate just as one of the men was almost on him—he was quick—before Doolin recognized his stealth approach and fortunately successfully pulled out of his view.

They were being very careful as they continued their movements. Doolin realized that they both had been examining the ground and surrounding vegetation for evidence of broken branches and flattened grass. One of them had picked up several objects, and when finally they met, standing side by side, they communicated with hand signals; they did not speak. Only one of the objects picked up was something Doolin could make out; it appeared to be discarded paper. Yes, thrown away food wrappers in the form of oily light-brown paper. Troops had recently been here—this was what these men were confirming. Doolin was at the correct location, only too late.

Doolin stayed in the area after the two tribesmen left, also examining the terrain and looking for discarded evidence that troops had been here. He found two objects. The first was a crumpled light-blue packing wrap of Gauloises Caporal, French cigarettes. The second item was a crushed cigarette, and before Doolin had finished, he found a total of three. Troops had been here, but what were they doing?

Doolin sat in a copse of trees and passed the morning and then afternoon hidden, sitting at the center of a natural V-shaped tip of two fallen trees. The trees formed an enclosed triangular perimeter, shielding Doolin, with the larger one on top of the smaller. Beyond this natural apex were several other trees that prevented anyone from casually passing through this area.

Someone would have to go around these saplings, and Doolin would easily remain hidden unless they already knew he was at the apex of the wedge-shaped barrier. He sat and looked up through the branches, to lightly clouded blue sky, and thought through the events of the day. He felt he was missing something, but what? What were the mountain tribesmen looking for?

After waiting for four or five hours, night had begun to fall, and he began moving to new coordinates taken from the last two columns listed in his discovery of data from the North Vietnamese scout's pant leg. The location was four klicks to the northwest, just under two and a half miles away. It would take him the night and then some if he was efficient and pushed himself. But time of arrival mattered less than maintaining his invisibility, so he did not set out to walk a straight line; instead, he took a bending arc with several acute angle redirects as he approached the new target area. This area was at or near the Laotian border, and Doolin couldn't actually confirm to himself that he had not left Vietnam, potentially straying into its neighboring country. But no one was going to voice an objection—number one, they didn't know he was there, and number two, if Doolin was detected, either by the enemy or by a tribesman, he would almost certainly be killed.

As the last hour of starlight approached, their faint luminescence was fading, the distant points of light quickly becoming invisible. The clouds had broken into gray cotton balls with thin tails. The moon was missing as it traversed its cyclic journey of renewal. Absence of the white lunar orb within the inky, shadowed sky had provided safety, yet now the darkness gave way to the gray ambient twilight just before sunrise. As Doolin approached the specific coordinates, from five hundred yards away he could discern shards of artificial light flickering between the trees and undergrowth. Judah also noted engine noise caught on the gentle breeze drifting over the hilltops. This was coordinated activity, and it was occurring at 5:37 in the morning.

Doolin approached slowly. He knew there would be sentries positioned discretely along some ill-defined perimeter. Using his night scope, he easily detected the two soldiers closest to his position, but these two, as well as their companions, were engaged in various forms of activity that diverted their attention. The American moved to obtain a location that would offer safety from them and a clear view of the proceedings.

What he found was not surprising, but he was still missing essential details to explain this activity in the middle of nowhere. Boxes—or, more precisely, wrapped packages—were being moved into trucks from covered bamboo-rimmed stacking platforms. The sort of objects that lined most factory warehouses, the normal wooden-raised pallets facilitating forklifts to slip their two metal arms under and then lift and move the material were present on the forest floor. But these wooden structures were not exactly the same, as they had thick bamboo limbs that formed the perimeter edges of a 4x4-foot square with the center composed of leather strips or rope netting. Under each of the corners of the bamboo were nearly six- or eight-inch blocks to keep the bamboo platform off of the ground. Along the side of each, along the opposing parallel sides of the square, were two additional bamboo limbs thicker and longer than the platform, obviously used to lift the entire construct.

The most interesting feature, however, was not the wooden structures, but that they sat next to squared dugout pits—not round—that appeared to be slightly larger than the bamboo pallets. These holes and bamboo structures were off the forested paths. Those that Doolin could see appeared to be placed within hidden areas, such as a triangular grouping of densely packed ferns or low scrub bush that formed an irregular but effective masking vegetative copse. Doolin could not see how deep each excavated area was, but the three that he could examine from seventy-five yards consisted of the hole, the platform, and the rapidly receding amount of wrapped packages being moved from the pallets' surface into trucks.

Equally fascinating was the near panic of one of the senior ranking soldiers; he appeared to be the commanding officer, but Doolin could not be certain. His activities were animated as he rapidly moved from platform to platform, examining the packaged material and the ground nearby. He darted among each bamboo pallet, stooping as he looked underneath each, shining a flashlight between roped platforms. He was talking in an exaggerated and certainly amplified fashion, as fragments of his voice could be heard from Doolin's hidden location. Several of the men quickly joined him in this same task, looking and examining the surroundings with equal intensity. Scanning the ground around the bamboo pallets, looking into the dug-out areas, they were hunting for something important, but Doolin had no idea what had brought on their coordinated behavior. This continued alongside the steady loading of the plastic packages into the trucks until the bamboo pallets eventually were cleared of all material.

Doolin watched for about fifty-five minutes. After this time, more interesting still was the fact that the bamboo platforms had been carefully placed back into the dug-out square recesses and covered with a leaf-stick mesh so that only the most intense inspection would reveal any disturbance to the earthen forest floor. Doolin watched with fascination as the three military trucks lumbered off, each with troops in the rear who stood along the sides in two rows, holding on the railings. The same man who had been emphatically searching the ground must have been an officer or at least a leader of this group; he took the front right seat in the lead truck after conferring with two of his men for almost three minutes. There was something else about this man—he had gray hair that showed beneath the back of his military canvas baseball hat. He was definitely the leader and the senior man.

The tops of the green canvas cloth covering the truck's rear bumped up and down with their cyclic appearance in and out of Doolin's sight, corresponding to the rise and fall of the uneven rutted path. The sound was muffled by the vegetation and growing distance; it rapidly diminished, and then it was gone. Alone once again, the light was beginning to rapidly increase, and the surroundings quickly took on a beauty characteristic of the highlands.

Doolin waited and carefully approached the area where he had witnessed the bamboo platforms and their corresponding holes. He wanted to examine these camouflaged pits, but Doolin also did not want to accidentally step into one. Falling into one—unknown in depth and possibly having punji sticks at the bottom—might be an unrecoverable mistake. These little devils were sharpened bamboo ranging between one to two feet in length and often fire-hardened by the enemy and smeared with venom, animal waste, or even human excreta. They were positioned or fixed in the soil at the bottom of holes, trenches, or pits, pointing upward so that the force of a person's own weight while falling would result in impalement.

They did not usually cause death but resulted in a GI being injured, bleeding profusely and needing one or two buddies to drag him to safety. This was the logic behind putting these in defensive positions around Charlie's camps or strongholds; these pits could easily reduce the attack force by multiples of two or three and impact the odds of an outcome during a firefight. But out here—alone, and miles from anyone—falling onto these punji sticks could prove to be fatal. Thus, Doolin was careful as he picked his way along the floor of the forest. In his right hand Doolin had his rifle, the shoulder strap wrapped around his forearm, loaded, round chambered, and all he had to do was aim and pull the trigger.

His left hand held a thin 5.5-foot-long bamboo branch, fitted with his K bar—his US Marine-issued knife with a seven-inch blade—with the 4.75-inch stacked leather "washer handle" tightly wrapped with vine. He did not use rope or string, as Doolin didn't want to have any of it discarded or left in the environment to announce to the enemy someone had been present. Using the branch, he repeatedly probed the path in front of him, waiting for the knife to pierce or at least detect false coverings of potentially deadly holes.

As he moved around a large tree, Doolin stopped. His nostrils encountered the all-too-familiar scent of a dead human being and blood, the musty, sour odor of protein decomposing and the trace of iron from a huge amount of blood being unceremoniously exposed to the atmosphere. Doolin then saw a right arm clothed in the traditional light-blue cotton jacket of a mountain tribesman lying awkwardly along the outline of a tree trunk. The figure was lashed upright to the tree and as Doolin moved carefully to view him better, the man's limp body hung on frayed rope under his arms that circled his chest, holding him in place. His exposed throat showed a vicious deep gash; the bone of his spine was exposed, the deep cut nearly decapitating him, and his abdominal contents lay spilled onto the earth, covering his worn short boots. Insects were already buzzing and feeding. His eyes stared motionlessly ahead and his skin had a tallowed color, his life gone. Doolin saw markings on his left hand of burns; they had tortured him and then ended his life, but not before leaving an unmistakable communication to any of his people. "Do NOT Interfere!"

Doolin couldn't make sense out of his anger; after all, he had killed more people in a week than this single human being, who had apparently been killed by these troops for interfering with them or committing some infraction. But Doolin killed quickly and tried to minimize any associated pain. The Marine closed his eyes in anger. He couldn't logically argue his perspective that his mode of killing was somehow "more humane" than what he witnessed before him. His logic was a comedy of satire, and Doolin knew that he was not rational in his intense visceral anger. But at this point in Doolin's tour, torturing was not something that he was comfortable with, but who knew if this also would change. Doolin was slowly beginning to descend into a Nietzschean perspective after previously asking God so frequently how this environment, the killing zone of Vietnam, could exist.

Without any of His answers, at least absent those answers to Doolin's desperate pleas, the blackness of nihilism began to take hold and value and reason became empty vessels, ghost ships on an endless sea. Judah had lost the moral compass so carefully and tenderly implanted by his beloved parents, and their absence had undoubtedly released the brake on his descent into radical skepticism and the denial of epistemological value. Seeing this thirty-something-year-old tribesman broken, violated, and dismembered did nothing to restore confidence in anything other than man's inherent potential for cruelty. And Judah C. Doolin was a card-carrying member of that club.

But he was still trying to confirm what the troops had been loading into the trucks. He suspected, but he needed evidence, something that he could take back to Mallroy. It had to be drugs—opium or heroin or something. There was nothing else that could be packaged in plastic wrap and would be important to bring into the South. This was the North's international currency, and Mallroy had discussed this newly minted coinage. He had, in fact, provided Doolin with a contextual understanding of why importing drugs into South Vietnam was so vital to Charlie's success, and although Doolin had been a bit underwhelmed by the colonel's reasoning, as he thought through Mallroy's argument more carefully, it made sense.

And it was with a growing sense of frustration that Doolin realized that every weapon is to be used in war. To allow or draw artificial boundaries around activities in war is to ensure that you will lose. It is that simple. And it was becoming increasingly apparent, even to Army grunts fighting this war, that the Americans represented a nation layered in bureaucracy and politics, a nation unwilling or unable to let loose its warriors to achieve victory. This massive nation was ultimately fighting for a stalemate, doing it by the rules—a "clean war." But this was Charlie's home, his land. His history was his most precious investment, and his victory was naturally more important to him than America's was to its bureaucracy.

The totality of the North's war strategy was to corrupt and divide the political, military, legal, and religious infrastructure in the South. Mallroy had explained this to Doolin inside of the colonel's smelly, cramped glass-and-plywood "office" where the young sniper had first met him months ago. Mallroy had said that luring vulnerable lower-level police with the drug money and working simultaneously down from the upper echelons of officers of Saigon's notoriously corrupt law enforcement leadership served several purposes.

First, looking the other way and ignoring shipments of illicit drugs offered immediate opportunities to expand the "normal" drug contraband to include weapons and explosives. This made arming Charlie within the large busy Southern cities much easier and made terror activities more likely to be successful. Second, for these "police on the take," existing political alliances might be corrupted. If the Saigon police were being paid more hard currency from the drug trade than from their legitimate employment, they might begin to become de facto neutral as they began to question who was going to win this war.

For many, it was already a fight challenging the flow of history. On one side stood those allegedly wanting unification of their country, and on the other side were those wanting a stalemate and Euro-American maintenance of an outside culture's status quo. This "outside culture" was a unique recruiting tool, invoking the nationalism of the Vietnamese people and their ancestral homeland, scrubbed clean of foreign dominance—of which, the North argued, the US was simply the latest in a long line, including the Japanese, Chinese, and French.

The ineptitude of the South's leadership in their insistence that Vietnam must be two separate countries, closely aligned to Western values, and maintain an established (but seen as intrusive) presence of European religious influence angered traditionalists. It left the masses vulnerable to Charlie's skillful propaganda that the South's leaders were puppets to foreigners. This, combined with their failures in combating the drug flow and its dirty money, only reinforced the perspective that leadership was out of touch, if not incompetent, and mere stooges of the Americans, and thus illegitimate. The more money flowed into the lower levels of Saigon's law enforcement, the more malleable some of these same police were to the tacit, near outright active support of Charlie's activities. Drugs were simply another tool in Charlie's art of war, one that was proving to be quite effective.

Doolin recognized that his own interests were very pedestrian: He simply wanted to prevent injury to his fellow grunts and get home alive. At this point, Doolin found the strategic and tactical arguments of why the drugs were flowing irrelevant to his sense of immediate danger for him and his buddies in the field. Judah was searching for proof that these packages were indeed filled with drugs, and then would let the command structure of this massive military organization decide what needed to be done. Yet, in truth, he was already forming his own plans as to interdicting in the Southeast Asian drug trade. His mind had snapped shut with decisive anger when he saw this unnamed tribal inhabitant of the highlands butchered and left to rot tied to a tree.

Doolin moved to the first hole and examined the perimeter of the nearly invisible covering, strewn with leaves and sticks of fallen branches. He was not going to lift the "lid" without knowing that he was not prompting either detection or destruction. And … *yes!* As he looked along the edge of the bamboo-cloth covering, there was a momentary glint of reflected light along a thin linear structure. It was easily missed unless one was examining the surroundings and light struck it at the correct angle. This was a trigger mechanism, similar to a nylon fishing line, and as Doolin followed it along its path, he saw the small clump of leaves and branches at the base of a nearby tree. Brushing these gently away, Doolin saw a variant of a claymore charge—designed to blow out a wide arc, including the entire area where the top of the hole lay and three feet to each side. The charge—neutral green, about 9x6 inches, and tied to the tree—carried deadly shrapnel in the form of pellets and sharp needles. *Yes,* he thought gravely, *this would be certain death if detonated.*

Doolin had not seen them plant these, but then he presumed they had been set up earlier. Perhaps days or weeks earlier, as there was a thin layer of dirt covering the grooved edges of the small explosive container. But this finding reinforced that Charlie wanted these holes—or, more correctly, these ground-storage pits—left alone, and anyone examining these out of curiosity or ill intent was unwelcome. Doolin carefully unhooked the firing pin that transmitted the change in tension to the explosive charge and re-examined the remainder of the perimeter one last time.

It was not uncommon for duplicates or some form of redundancy to be used in booby traps, but seeing nothing, Doolin lifted the covering. He did not remove it completely but shined his flashlight into the darkness of the pit and found nothing except the platform resting at the bottom of the square grave-like hole. As he moved to reposition and recover the pit, he glimpsed a reflection at the bottom in the distant corner, furthest away from his position. His minor movement had provided a different line of sight and as his head again retraced its change in position, he saw the glint again. Stuck under the stout bamboo leg at the corner of the platform was something reflecting light back to him. Doolin had to get into the hole to get a better view, as it was almost four feet deep, and once down there he saw a torn plastic wrapper. The earth provided a pungent musty odor, and the air in the pit was cooler than above.

Two of the corners of this square excavated tomb had cut bamboo limbs that reinforced the edges to prevent the sharply demarcated perpendicular walls from gradually eroding or caving in. One of the other corners used a tree and its roots as its natural reinforcement. Doolin did not turn around to examine the corner immediately behind him but squatted, using the right-angled bamboo perimeter of the pallet to balance his weight and carefully lean over the empty leather straps. This allowed him to see the contents of the earthen ossuary-like structure. The reflection turned out to be a plastic wrapping material—a remnant of the previously seen package coverings, still with tape on its surface, but at last Doolin smiled as he saw small accumulations of white powder in the tiny folds of the 6x8-inch irregular remnant sheet. But the tape was adherent to the plastic partially and irregularly wrapped around a slender linear object of soft yellow metal.

Its partial covering was unintentional, as the metal protruded from the plastic in a haphazard fashion, yet the object was smooth and finely tooled—he could now see it was a pen—and as Doolin slowly pulled the tape and plastic off of it, it was an 18 carat gold Cross mechanical ballpoint pen. Along its seven-inch barrel, embossed in the soft metal composed of 75 percent pure gold, were the carefully inscribed initials EWH. English letters—not Chinese, not Cyrillic.

Certainly, they could be Vietnamese. The use of the Latin-based alphabet, Portuguese and then modified by the French, was but another of the inherent objections that Vietnamese nationalists in the North voiced, a hatred stemming from the loss of their unique Vietnamese language and script, a blending of ancient Chinese and their de novo unique Vietnamese modifications. The North and Charlie had successfully influenced the young as they railed against the French imperial Occidental culture. Labeling them a cesspool of inferiority characterized by superficial cognition, lacking grace or elegance, they demonized the Europeans, and now they saw the new colonialists as irremediably worse. The plastic programmed replacement nature of their American Coca-Cola mindset typical of California had supplanted the hated French.

But for now, Doolin had what he needed. He meticulously folded the plastic into a 2x4-inch rectangle and stuffed it into his upper left shirt pocket. The pen, he slipped into his zippered pant leg. *Got it.* He was excited, as he now needed to get this stuff to Mallroy.

Doolin was about to exit the hole when he heard sharp voices. They were not speaking English, but there was no doubt that the speakers were not just angry but very upset. Mountain tribesman had just discovered the dead man. Doolin was completely hidden, with the only real danger being that one of them might fall into his temporary quarters! He did his best to locate the exact origin of the sound and then pushed up the corner of the bamboo and cloth covering about an inch as he examined the surroundings. Nine or so yards stood between Doolin's position and the body tied to the tree, and he could see, hear, and smell the three newcomers.

Doolin was fortunate that he had not left any belongings outside the hole. He was also pleased that his diet was almost identical to the mountain tribesmen's cuisine; all senses were heightened in combat, and smelling the presence of an outsider was often easy. But these tribesmen were busy cutting the rope and lowering their friend, perhaps their relative, down onto a frayed and patched blanket of sorts. They were absorbed in their loss. As Doolin momentarily saw the nearest individual's face as she turned, tears were streaming down her otherwise handsome slightly tanned face. There was also anger, even hatred in her eyes, but it was a preeminent deep sorrow that was most visibly expressed as they gently lowered the body onto the blanket and wrapped him in it, allowing them to transport him. They tied the ends of the blanket with worn gray rope and lashed each segment over the ends of a nearly six-foot bamboo pole. Quickly, each man picked up opposite ends of the bamboo, carrying the body between them, and without sound all three departed.

Doolin watched their departure, each of the three moving quietly and continuously surveying their surroundings. A bigger, somewhat stocky man took up the rear position, shouldering most of the weight. The woman holding a rifle was three meters ahead of a smaller man making the front of the two-person team, one at either end of the pole. All had weapons—rifles — but they were old with wooden stocks, no scopes, and beaten worn leather shoulder straps. Doolin glimpsed that the woman's weapon had a simple rope strap as she moved out of sight into the dense growth of the forest.

The American waited ten minutes and then exited his earthen hiding place, moving quietly to a vantage point near where he had previously watched the soldiers. So, he now had what he needed. Doolin would have wagered almost anything that what he was about to confirm in the residue of fine granular powder clinging to the folds of the plastic sheet would prove Mallroy correct. Within the discarded plastic tucked into his pocket was heroin, ready for the Saigon street market. This was the totality of the enemy's war strategy, no stone left unturned. And Doolin almost admired their effort; he certainly respected it. Yes, the Americans were going to lose this war since they were not willing, and perhaps no longer able, to engage in the philosophy that "anything is fair in love and war."

As Mallroy had emphasized, Charlie would do anything to free his homeland of the filth and contamination of foreign overlords, and the Americans were just the newest in a long line of arrogant dissemblers believing that the slender and often delicate-featured men and women of this Southeast Asian strip of land were incapable of governing themselves absent the "wisdom and guidance" of outsiders.

CHAPTER 5

PROVENANCE OF A PEN

June 1, 1971

Hannibal ad portas.
"Hannibal is at the gates."

I t took Doolin two and a half weeks to get back to his basecamp, where there was an active discussion of a general court martial—Judah C. Doolin's! His immediate supervisory officer, now a different second lieutenant, was furious with him. Doolin had overstayed his assignment for what the lieutenant thought was at least three weeks, perhaps four, and he didn't even know Doolin's name since the data from command concerning the young sniper provided no identification. All this lieutenant knew was that his senior commander, a major, had also been looking for Doolin and simply referred to Doolin as "the kid" or "Mallroy's kid" who would be coming out of the bush.

This senior officer, a Major Sumter, had—in accordance with rather high-level orders—told the lieutenant to also start looking for Mallroy's kid a month ago. Even the major was nonplussed by the label given to Doolin, a label without a name. The major had summoned the young lieutenant and explained that for reasons that only higher command knew or endorsed, an unnamed US Marine sniper was coming out of a prolonged assignment up-country, alone and outside of the normal chain of command. The fact that the lieutenant had had to spend his time trying to find Judah, this unnamed phantom, for almost four weeks nearly drove this butter bar insane.

He was simply astounded that once Doolin actually appeared in the flesh, he didn't have a name tag, dog tags, or carry orders; he had absolutely no identifiers. Doolin would not tell the lieutenant his name, which culminated in this young officer nearly suffering apoplectic hysteria. Doolin's response to the request for self-identification was to say, "Sir, I am under orders to not divulge any identifiers regarding me or my mission."

The lieutenant's summation to all of this was that Doolin's conduct, appearances, and status were absolutely unprecedented, probably illegal, and, above all, in his words, "completely fucked up!"

The butter bar had never, and would never again, experience anything like this: a virtual apparition appearing out of the bush. Finally, and almost more troubling to the lieutenant, more than all of the irregular, if not unanticipated, extreme variances from the norm was the fact that this guy called Mallroy's Kid appeared rather young. Too young to have so much freedom, too young to be so experienced. But the lieutenant saw and felt that this guy, with the somewhat sharp features and hollowed-out cheeks, was in fact both young and extremely experienced.

Doolin actually almost smiled back when the lieutenant started shouting at him. It took all of the officer's discipline not to grab him and physically let him know who was boss. This self-restraint was aided, however, by the fact that Mallroy's Kid actually looked dangerous. The young lieutenant was not stupid, and he recognized a combat soldier and this guy, whatever his name was … well, he looked like he was used to killing!

Lieutenant Upset had just been exposed to Mallroy's subterfuge in making Doolin administratively "invisible." The young lieutenant really was beyond words trying to understand what his commander, the major, had saddled him with when Doolin finally did report after his weeks up-country.

Still, this didn't prevent the young officer from toying with a suggestion that Doolin had gone AWOL and had hung out "smoking dope and screwing the Vietnamese whores" in Saigon or Da Nang. Who knew "where the fuck this disheveled joke for a buttoned-up Marine" had been? The lieutenant didn't for an instant really believe this—Doolin reeked of combat engagement, danger, and decisive action—but the young officer certainly let Doolin know the extent of his frustration with the entire situation.

So, when he took Doolin into the administrative section of the base camp, the butter bar was quite hopeful that Doolin would hang by the neck from the tie beam of the galvanized steel top panels of that very building! Unfortunately for the young officer, this was a dream never realized. Sumter, who had communicated directly, albeit briefly, with Mallroy took the lieutenant aside and—slightly out of earshot from Doolin and others in the large administrative room—had a rather one-sided conversation with the young officer.

Doolin stood there. It must be said that he appeared remarkably relaxed after being dragged into the Command Center. And while the two officers talked—or, more precisely, while the major lectured the young lieutenant for over two minutes—Doolin sat without permission, causing the lieutenant to glance in his direction. Doolin was only partially interested in the verbal exchange between the two. He actually was trying to ensure that he didn't have to run for the latrines to empty his bowels of the watery mix of partially digested food and malaria meds he had ingested. He really didn't feel well, as was the norm after so long up-country.

Slowly, the junior officer's facial expression transformed from one of indignation to suspicion to near intimidated disbelief. Over the nearly two and a half minutes of this rather one-sided discussion, the anger and confusion registering in the face of the younger Marine officer melted into a pensive acceptance of his commander's narrative.

As he left the room, the lieutenant glanced over and nodded to Doolin, briefly conveying acceptance and even a bit of newfound reluctant respect. But he left the room shaking his head; he couldn't believe the major apparently didn't know this guy's name, either.

Doolin had lost twelve pounds, exaggerating his sharpened features and an already slender, wiry body. He had not been allowed to dress or change his uniform, having been unceremoniously dragged in front of the command officer of the day, and thus his field garb, not Marine regulation or proper military, emphasized his position as someone conducting deep penetration into the enemy stronghold of Vietnam's bush country.

The major approached Doolin with a thick dull-green canvas binder about the size of a legal pad with a zipper at one end and a small locking mechanism that secured its contents. He then ordered Doolin to follow him. They entered a room immediately off to the left down the narrow hall of this sheet metal structure with separate partitioned spaces. Once inside, as Doolin stood at attention, the officer looked at Doolin and shook his head. A part of him was exasperated, but Doolin also sensed a seed of respect mixed with unease. Doolin did not appear as the picture of health, but professionalism seeped from every pore of his being.

And while his appearance suggested that he probably belonged in the kennel with the military police canines, Doolin knew he communicated efficiency at his trade, and his vocation was that of a trained United States Marine Corps sniper—a hunter-killer of men. This unnerved his current acquaintance, as this Marine major spent most of his career inside offices processing paper chits regarding deployment status and discipline issues of lower-ranking troops. A paper pusher looking into the eyes of a killer ... but a killer needing a long hot shower.

Doolin's uniform was objectively a mess, torn and unwashed. It was actually filthy. The Vietnamese red dirt had blended into the garb's faded brown, gold, and green. It was earth-stained and sweat-soaked. These camouflaged rags were without identification as to its occupant's name, unit, or country. Both it and its resident provided an odor that was not pleasant. It was even absent any identifier as to its tenant being a Marine.

Doolin, upon completion of basic training, was nearly a poster child for a US Marine. Clean-shaven with a regulation haircut and perfectly fitting regalia that announced to viewers of his graduation photograph that he was "Semper Fidelis." He now was almost unrecognizable in this version of the livery, but the difference between Doolin's appearance and that of the officer in front of him was a statement of "finality of purpose" without excuse. In this, the language of his appearance was universal and uncompromising. The major did his best to accept this affront to his military bearing and deal with the problem that Col. Mallroy had dumped in his lap.

He handed Doolin the bag and asked, "Anything for the colonel?"

Doolin took out the plastic taken from the hole in the highlands two-plus weeks ago and placed it in the bag along with the pen. As he reached for it, Doolin deliberately zippered the bag and locked the mechanism, securing its contents.

The major started to bark his objection, glaring at Doolin, but Doolin's eyes caught his. Doolin looked directly at him; the young sniper's cold stare immediately conveyed terminal intolerance to any of his concerns.

"Orders, sir. Contents from me to him through this." Doolin pointed to the bag. He handed it back to him, locked, and considered the possibility that the major might be able to open it at any time after he was alone if he had the combination and the key, but Doolin already knew he did not possess either.

Mallroy wanted this chain of evidence uninterrupted . . . and safe.

The major stared at the young Marine a bit longer, appearing to decide whether to lecture him or understand that Doolin's inviolate orders superseded the major's concerns. Four seconds passed and then his face softened, and he led their exit from the smaller room.

They returned to the larger room and the officer surprised Doolin when he asked, "When did you last get a hot meal?"

Doolin looked at him coldly. "Six weeks ago … sir."

The major literally flinched, his brow furrowing, thoughts deepening as he processed what this likely meant. This kid was important, or at least his activities were beginning to earn an air of importance. So this was Mallroy's kid!

The word had begun to seep, but only slightly, from under the edges of a hermetically sealed intelligence operation, a hidden effort that Mallroy himself had constructed to protect this kid. Mallroy wanted Doolin off the books. He wanted Doolin safe. He wanted "his kid" to live. The Marine major knew then that he was dealing with something substantive, perhaps even singularly determinative, in a war that offered nothing but administrative detritus, but he had no idea of the specifics. And then, if one was looking at his face, it was almost as if he came to a realization and reached a sense of peace with this ambiguity, this uncertainty, and this significant deviation from the norm.

His features relaxed, and his voice softened in both decibel and tone. "OK, we are about done here." And then in an even softer voice, he suggested, "You need to get some rest and get presentable, Marine. You look kinda like shit."

This last bit was stated almost with affection, as perhaps he had come to accept the nature of, if not in details but in theme, the understanding that Doolin's mission, per the colonel in Da Nang, was actually important. The corners of his eyes elevated just a bit … a smile almost appeared, and then vanished.

But this fact did not protect Doolin from the palpable hostility emanating from Gunnery Sergeant Kinkade, who glared at him from behind a desk in the back of the administrative section. He had not placed himself in the direct line of discipline regarding Doolin or Doolin's lack of Marine oversight, but the very fact of his apparent freedom to roam for weeks on end off the leash was a violation of everything this gunnery sergeant felt sacred. He was what the guys actually fighting in the field not-so-affectionately called a desk jockey, or rather a "desk turd." Overweight, with his belly pushing at his tan webbed belt, bushy light-brown eyebrows, and early jowls, a sycophant to the officers who outranked him. He would have lasted thirty seconds during an actual firefight.

He had carefully positioned a wad of chewing tobacco in his cheek, his teeth a hazelnut brown, his hair cut high and tight, balding at his crown. He was the personification of the perfect clerk. Paperwork on time and collated to an exactness for anyone who might be remotely deserving of his "blessings," one could set a Swiss timepiece by his scheduled workday.

His appearance was immaculate. Even here in the humidity and heat of Vietnam his uniform was starched, but this did not prevent the growing bilateral stains of soaked armpits. Yet, his creases along both the pants and shirt were knifelike. From his perspective, to have Doolin, a young Marine, without proper respect for the uniform or command stirred a deep anger that was beyond rational. Unknown to Doolin was the fact that this overweight "gunny" would ultimately attempt to share even the paucity of available specifics regarding Doolin's highly classified orders with Vietnamese nationals, not thinking, or perhaps not caring, that they were riddled with informers and Charlie sympathizers.

But even more troubling, if Doolin had known, was his Vietnamese girlfriend. He supported her in their dingy gray-stucco-walled apartment just off base, his noncommissioned officer rank providing him the privilege of residing off base—"living native," as it was called. One look at her and immediate suspicions should have surfaced. She was a beauty, with her jet-black hair, prominent high cheekbones, and almond-shaped coal-black eyes. A supple figure, the hint of her shapely legs hidden but whispered at through the sheer silk of her white *áo dài*. Her teeth near perfect and white, lips full and soft.

She was at least five grades above this dude's AI, or "attractiveness index," that Doolin's high school classmates had used to rank relationships during their four-year matriculation. And while Doolin had at the time considered their prioritization scheme a rather insensitive reflection of teen ego—one self-perceived hottie deserving another self-perceived hottie—ironically, throughout Doolin's life, the principle of this index has been remarkably accurate. Supermodels generally didn't date or marry convenience store workers, and wealthy CEOs didn't generally select fast food workers as their significant others. Doolin himself was not voicing an opinion as to moral or cultural wisdom, sensitivity, or even correctness; he was just acknowledging this truism was rather consistent! European history supports the fact that "royalty begets royalty," at least publicly.

And thus, alarms should have gone off, as this gunnery sergeant did not match with this beauty. She was refined and gorgeous, and well, he really had little to offer … or so it seemed.

But she herself was a soldier, too, and totally committed to the removal of the foreign presence from her country of beautiful fields and mountain villages. She was asked to do the unthinkable and she accepted her fate, as her desire to achieve the goals asked by her commanders was never in question. Yet she drew a hard breath and asked her ancestors to understand, for she had to sleep with this ugly, foul-smelling American to gain the information that he processed on a daily basis as the overweight clerk in the combat chain of command. This nobody-of-importance Marine office clerk, sleeping with a genuine and remarkably beautiful young woman, routinely ticked through paperwork involving US Marine tactical planning. Of course she would memorize the names, the wisps of information that this porcine-eyed clerk would discuss after he had emptied his seminal vesicles into her while clumsily pawing at her firm, generous breasts. She hated this Michelin-bodied American, his bad breath and unclean toenails.

The woman had stalked him for six weeks, gradually working to "meet" him in the commissary where she initially worked stocking shelves and avoiding the undressing eyes of every GI who entered. She already knew he was assigned to an important administrative position, cutting orders for those men coming and going through this Marine camp, and astutely felt that he was an easy target for her predatory charms. Of course, she had been correct, and a simple direct communication over his purchase of shaving cream and deodorant had initiated a steady trail of talk one afternoon that ultimately led to his asking her to dinner.

The rest had been almost too easy as she accepted her role; her ancestors would not have approved, but they would have respected her remarkable commitment to victory. Two weeks later and only two almost unbearable penetrations of his small masculinity, she had been asked to move in with him. A last spasm of disgust was pushed aside as she remained obstinate in her assigned role. The information slowly started coming, and as she was naturally patient, deliberately erecting small delays to any "shop talk," he initiated as the pieces were set up on the board for truly significant data collection.

It was Hanh Nghiem's willingness to sacrifice her self-esteem and position in Vietnamese society that underwrote her commitment to victory against the foreign occupier. She had been raised in a traditional Vietnamese feminine cultural role, and she knew that simply comporting with American servicemen was actively condemned. To sleep with him without marriage was a stain on her and her family that would never be erased. But then, she had no family left: all had been killed in this war, their embers, the memories of her ancestors, scattered without delicacy, thought, or purpose by the invaders who thought they brought prosperity when in reality, they often effected pain and disfigurement to her ancient culture.

If the "gunny" had been marginally alert or minimally objective, he would have questioned the eventual odd persistence of her questions regarding his work. Or he might have at least grasped that her recurrent interest in his ideas on his latest office gossip that invariably contained restricted, even classified information was unnatural. He might have even looked in the mirror and realized that the odds of his corpulent, overbearing, self-absorbed ego could not account for him enjoying this beautiful woman's affections. His allurement was as hollow as her smile, its specious happiness masking contempt and treachery.

She knew that her actions, allowing the physical intimacy with this American, would eat at her very soul. Her willingness to prostitute her body had to be justified by a higher, purer goal, and for Hanh Nghiem, this ultimate goal was to rid her land of the foreigners and take back their nation. Her father's generation had battled the French and won, only to have them supplanted by the Americans. Now it was her turn to join the struggle.

Most of the moms and dads in the United States sending their sons to Vietnam had been told that the war was one of limiting Communist aggression, and the mantra at the time was to invoke the potential devastation of the "domino effect" of losing Vietnam, Cambodia, Laos, and all of Indochina, which might have been followed by loss of the Philippines and Taiwan. They had been told that as Americans, they had to stop the scourge of Communism before it crept around the globe.

Trouble was, the US government—being no different than history's list of other once-dominant powers—failed to understand that the broad swath used in understanding geo-diplomacy, a lumping under the banner of "Communism versus Western democracy" was as simplistic as it was wrong. Each nation had nuanced elements that made such an American one-size-fits-all approach to unfriendly forces ridiculously naïve. Doolin could not have known this, nor could Hanh Nghiem, but her country would in fact welcome travel from Americans within twenty-five years of the fall of Saigon to the Communists, and the Vietnamese would be using American influence and military presence to offset the real threat: their age-old nemesis, the Chinese.

Had she the prescient understanding to envision these upside-down future changes in alliances, she might have thought twice about her willingness to allow the porcine-eyed Marine to periodically flatten her against the mattress as he spread her legs. But such foresight was absent, and even if accepted as the future, it did not facilitate the needed outcomes of the moment. Hanh might not yet have been wise, and she was no philosopher, but she, like many people, intuitively grasped that even awareness of future outcomes cannot address present demands.

Thus, when looking back, those rendering judgments of past actions now adjudicated against current social, legal, or ethical standards must tempter their views. The unrestrained use of evolutionary optics without past context is a futile, if not malignant process. Hanh hoped her decisions now to allow this uncouth foreigner to empty his seed in her would not be used to condemn her by future generations. Her efforts were an important conduit with their straightforward goal of picking up any information and passing it through to the Viet Cong, and these efforts were among the countless sacrifices of her people enabling victory.

Most of the collected material was useless, but a tiny portion would indeed be critical. Eventually, the gunny himself provided her with appropriate vetting to procure employment as a low-level clerk on the same Marine base. She did nothing requiring security clearance but was always within earshot of gossip—and such chatter is the life's blood of intelligence. Such morsels led to the important identification of Vietnamese agents working for the Americans, and the foreseeable subsequent assassinations of these agents, often along with their family members, would for the most part go unsolved by Saigon police. But they originated in the collected intelligence from efforts throughout Vietnam exemplified by those similar to Hanh's.

She and others like her stole, viewed, or enticed material like bees, forming a complex tessellation of the American war machine, its treasure leaked drop by drop to penetrating agents of the North. And for the American colossus, these drops ultimately turned into a hemorrhage of information, and events subsequently perpetrated by the enemy were reflective of this pilfered information. One such event was the assassination of someone Doolin knew well, but that event was yet to come. Yet sources such as the gunny's soft-eyed, petite twenty-eight-year-old girlfriend were indeed part of the complex data-gathering system that Charlie employed. It was Kinkade's inability to fathom his contribution to her activity and tendency to involuntarily assist the enemy providing fragments of intelligence that, when pieced together, enabled retribution against those deemed necessary by the Viet Cong to eliminate.

His role, the blood of fellow Americans that stained his hands, and the violation of the code he swore to uphold underwrote an unpaid personal bill itemizing his stupidity and arrogance. And while he would eventually pay for his lack of awareness and his inadvertent self-absorbed incompetence, most would argue the payment was too little and too late. He was in arrears for this personal account, clouded by his own delusions of self-importance and ego, and unfortunately for him, the only viable currency left was his miserable life. But even this ultimate payment was inadequate for those he had inadvertently silenced. Doolin would ultimately forget this hostile but inept Marine, but not his lady friend who had fleeced nearly all the valuable intel from this contemptible excuse for a solider. All of this was unknown to Doolin at the time but would germinate future events planned to terminate his life.

However, in the present steamy Vietnam morning, Judah Doolin simply registered the gunny's continual stare. His contempt was only partially concealed, the rage reflected in his body language; those unspoken but communicative signs of unbridled resentment were discernible. Almost as waves of radiant heat from indignant embers, it was pure vehemence. The major called the gunny over to facilitate orders for Doolin to Da Nang to meet Mallroy. Kinkade pushed back from his desk and immediately walked to Doolin and the major.

"Who do I cut them for, sir?" he asked crisply.

"Under 'Name,' put an *X* followed by Mallroy, Colonel, USA." The major looked at the gunny, his eyes blank, nearly as empty as those of a dead fish, but silently emphasizing his statement was an order. The gunny frowned, thinking about commenting that this was very irregular, but then stopped, inhaled his objection, and returned to his desk.

He complied silently, yet his eyes betrayed a malignancy that triggered Doolin's instant heightened alertness. He could already sense a deep ferocity of hate brewing in the gunny, and somehow Doolin knew even then that more was to come from this guy. The sniper just had no idea of the form, timeline, or if Doolin himself was to be the target.

Mallroy greeted Doolin with a bit more casual friendliness than the young American was accustomed to, from him or any other officer, yet there was a seriousness in his face that suggested problems were at hand. Since they were in the middle of a war, Doolin wondered what had prompted the colonel's troubled expression, given the fact that their chosen profession—or, in Doolin's case, his assigned one—gradually but systematically desensitized any human being to a variety of unthinkable horrors on an hourly basis. What could be troubling Mallroy that he had not seen countless times over the past three years? The requisite cigarette dangled from his lips, and his brow was furrowed with a light sheen of perspiration misting the skin of his temples.

Doolin greeted him, "Sir," and saluted smartly but not dramatically. He sensed Mallroy was not in the mood, and he seldom ever pushed the military etiquette.

He grunted in response. "Sit," he commanded.

Doolin did.

"You brought me very high-quality heroin."

Doolin remained silent and Mallroy stated, "Marine," then his voice softened. "Judah, I need your input here, and we must work as a team. A bit of an unconventional team, but let's cut through the military crap, OK?"

It was the first time he had addressed Doolin by his Christian name, and Doolin was a bit startled but did his best to recover quickly. "OK," he replied.

"Good. Now, how many of these packages would you estimate were present when you were observing them loading?"

"It's a bit hard to say definitively. Maybe equivalent to five bamboo pallets."

"What does that mean in packages?"

"Sort of like two hundred to three hundred shirt box packages, perhaps two kilos per package. I don't really know—three trucks plus troops?"

Suddenly, as the winter wind on the Northern plains can chill the bones, a deep, troubled look emerged as the colonel lifted his head and looked directly at Doolin.

"Judah, we have a problem."

"Sorry, sir?"

"I mean us—you and me, and the Marines, and the United States—we all have a problem."

Judah looked directly into his eyes and registered confusion, but also a growing sense of alarm. "What?"

Mallroy opened the brown folder marked "Top Secret-Level II" that had been sitting at his left elbow and pulled out a single piece of heavy paper bearing the same classification. He handed it to Doolin, and as he glanced at it, Doolin realized that he was looking at a highly classified document.

At the top of the paper was a picture of man in his early thirties, handsome with blond hair, high cheekbones, light-blue eyes, and thin lips, clean-shaven in the classic graduation or promotion pose showing from mid-chest to face. He wore a burgundy tie, powder-blue shirt, and a navy-blue three-button suit jacket. Nearly unbridled arrogance—but just beneath the surface. Below the caption read "CIA Station Chief, Cam Ranh Bay, RVN, Eric W. Haney." Doolin froze as his mind shuddered to a full stop.

"EWH."

The 18 carat gold pen. Found in the bottom of an NVN/Charlie heroin storage pit in the middle of the Vietnamese highlands. The enemy officer's madcap activity prior to leaving the area.

This officer lost the pen.

A gift ... a trophy?

Yes, perhaps this made sense now. Were there other explanations? Of course, but then coincidence is a lazy man's excuse for analysis, thoughtful examination, or any ruminative activity, and to allow it to encumber one's perspective is to invite an untimely death.

As Doolin looked back to Mallroy, their eyes met.

Mallroy stated softly, "Officially, I have made you vanish administratively. No one knows you now exist. At the very least, no one could know you are working for me, but I think in reality you have become vapor, OK? You are off the books, not found anywhere in the system as of five weeks ago."

Judah barely nodded. "Permission to speak freely, sir?"

He raised his left eyebrow, having already given permission and wanting efficiency, not military ceremony. "Yes," he stated wearily.

"Can we try to fill in some dots, sir?"

His intensity and smile returned immediately.

Not knowing where to begin, but intuitively understanding that his choice of words was critical, the younger man asked, "You don't think the pen was stolen?"

Mallroy smiled again. "Do you? Or more appropriately, do you *want* to?"

"Then my next concern is simply … motivation?"

Mallroy shook his head slightly and looked down at his knees, the weariness again nearly palpable. "Money?"

Doolin just spontaneously blurted out, "… What?!" the anger and frustration coming quickly to the surface and then disappearing almost as fast.

Looking at Doolin registering his anger that someone would put their troops in danger for money, Mallroy nodded. "Yes, Judah, some people don't have the same moral anchors of the group, or of you."

Suddenly Doolin understood what was happening to him. He, too, felt adrift. Doolin felt as though someone had sliced through his tethering ropes, freeing the large hot-air balloon and the undercarriage, his moral anchors, were adrift.

Every 10.7-gram metal projectile supersonically leaving Doolin's weapon and entering another human being took him further away from any semblance of morality.

Colonel Mallroy must have seen it in Doolin's eyes as he slowly shook his head and asked, "Judah, how old are you?"

"I can't remember, sir. Almost eighteen years old, I guess."

The older man nodded and then sighed slowly, shaking his head from side to side. "God forgive us, son—we have stolen your blissful, indulgent youth. Taken it without even considering it was not ours to possess and justifying our actions with …" His voice trailed off before he almost whispered, "Divinando mendacium."

For what seemed an eternity, he simply looked down at the floor until Doolin broke the silence. "Respectfully … English, sir?"

The colonel raised his face, half smiled, then almost winced, a sad gesture. "We lied. And it was a bullshit lie to justify our actions."

He said nothing but immediately realized Mallroy was correct. But they had not only stolen Doolin's youth; they had violated his life, and yes, his soul, uprooted any trace of decency that Judah's parents had planted within him. And such it was for every man-child coming of age in war, where the moral edifices assembled within by parents, relatives, by society and culture, the still-wet and hardening ethical concrete that buttresses our societal values, were ruthlessly torn from their foundations and casually scattered over the earth.

Doolin's mother's hopes for her son—a doctor, a healer of people, a force of goodness. Instead, he represented the harvest of the tornado's howling, deafening winds clutching a flimsy mobile home. Its deadly fingers gripping and then tearing apart whatever form of nascent shelter stood in its path, leaving the exposed helpless, terrified, defenseless lambs facing a heartless predator. They had taught Doolin how to become an efficient killer, a force so disruptive to his innocent youth that recovery might not be possible. It was in the first twenty seconds of combat that these still-maturing social ideals implanted in youth were destroyed, their souls permanently stained and then scarred by the inherent horror, cruelty, and desolation of war.

And for those survivors, it left a black emptiness, a wanton, craven hopelessness that sought redemption, a soul which must be reborn if it were to survive. There must be a renourishment of life's inherent beauty, or the revenant will search eternally for meaning and find none. It was then—perhaps this very moment, Doolin realized years later—that his moral wandering and the foreseeable ambiguity began.

Doolin asked, "What do you want to do?"

"I need to ensure that you are anonymously buried deep within the bureaucracy, but you will continue in the field. I will begin to assess our friend's background and movement."

"You really think he may be involved in this enterprise?"

"Judah, we've moved beyond the gray fog of war, past good and bad or right or wrong. We are in shadows of deception itself, and no good can come of this. We are in a highly compartmentalized war effort, and this means that someone may be ultimately paying off or employing the same people who are killing our soldiers, either directly with bullets or indirectly with heroin. I don't know, but my gut says this is bad. You tell me how a personalized pen from a living, healthy CIA station chief ends up in a VC field commander's possession?"

Doolin again asked, "Why don't you find out if he reported the pen missing, stolen, or gone?"

Mallroy nodded. "A place to start, but if this guy's any good, that will have long ago been covered with a solid explanation."

Doolin then smiled inwardly, and unfortunately it transformed his lips. Mallroy looked at him and asked, "What? What is it?"

"Well, let's bait a trap, Colonel. Let's do something that causes him to expose himself, even if such a response is masked within his web of lies and deceit. Let's pluck the fibers of whatever delicate web he has created and watch him crawl out to respond. He must be under pressure also … to prove or to remain above suspicion as he deals with an enemy who is likely looking for his betrayal of them, as he has already betrayed his own people."

Mallroy looked at Doolin and not for the first time paradoxically realized that he was dealing with a young man, but a man whose youth did not disguise the insights and judgement of someone much older. Mallroy was between astonished and proud, for he realized he had a worthy partner and felt that they might just successfully complete this investigation and the justice it merited—and it was likely to be hard justice. He was working with a man-child who was transforming before his eyes, and watching was both fascinating yet worrisome.

He looked at Doolin and smiled, almost with affection. "Sherlock Holmes one of your favorites? Trouble is, son, we don't have much time, and we don't have many resources at our disposal that could be of assistance in ensnaring this character. But what you propose has merit."

Doolin frowned and looked at Mallroy thoughtfully. "Will you lay a trap?"

Mallroy never moved his lips, but his eyes confirmed he had already set the game afoot.

The colonel just chuckled and as Doolin was preparing to leave, Mallroy again became serious. "Judah, it now becomes important for you to remain completely anonymous and for the record to identify you as a nobody, perhaps not even a Marine sniper assigned to a forward recon platoon. No talking to anyone, no name tag, et cetera. There has been talk of you being mine, you know … 'Mallroy's kid' or boy. You realize that the bureaucracy cannot stand independence or spontaneity. They have labeled you but do not officially know your name. I have to get rid of you for a while. I will not allow anyone to know, not even my superiors, what you are doing, who you are, or where you might be … understood?"

"Sir." Doolin nodded and slowly began to grasp the enormity of what he had just been told.

The Marine was to remain a ghost, but he had moved into the realm of nonexistence. Now it meant that if something happened to him, no one would come looking; no one would care. With his adopted mom and father both dead and only his brother by law alive, there was no one who would ever know what happened to Doolin—no one who would really care if he did not come back from Vietnam.

He was alone, totally alone, and yet Judah found a comfortable familiarity in this, as it was almost a sense of fulfilling his true destiny. He had never been deemed worthy of claiming. At birth, his biological father had rejected him, and his birth mother had let strangers have him. And yes, these strangers, the Doolin husband and wife, were beautiful people, and he would be forever grateful that they had stepped in, but it was a fact that they were initially strangers. This is the paradox that adopted souls experience, accept, and endure. Judah was alone, again. It was a replication of the story of his origins and his life.

Mallroy looked at him. The colonel's eyes questioned whatever expression Doolin wore, and then Mallroy slowly nodded.

Doolin had been dismissed.

CHAPTER 6

THE ASIAN FLOWER

June 1971

Pulchra Femina
"Beautiful Woman"

As Judah walked out of the Naval complex, he passed through the last security checkpoint. A white-and-green-trimmed fortified guardhouse surrounded by faded green sandbags announced its compact but reinforced terminal position. As the young American left the compound, he nodded to the Marine guard as he stepped into the open street, teeming with people, and was enveloped by the tropical humidity. The sweat immediately beaded up on his forearms and paralleled a thin line of moisture appearing on his upper lip. He had acclimated to this climate, but it took time and had required an understanding of his own body's requisites for comfort. Whether in the city or out in the country of this beautiful land, the heat and humidity no longer troubled him. In fact, he actually looked forward to the afternoon thunderheads that rolled up from the coast, and even the monsoon season with nearly continuous rain had its own pleasant rhythm.

One simply had to dress appropriately, but of course the basic Marine uniform compliant with regulations was anything but "climate-friendly." It also advertised the young man as military, a Marine, and if Charlie knew the uniform badges or identifiers—which they did—it could aid in identifying Doolin as an expert with a rifle. So, with Mallroy's approval, Doolin had changed into a typical white short-sleeved shirt and khaki slacks and wore his beat-up tennis shoes, which were originally tan but now displayed a faded dirt-laden brown. The loose-fitting baseball cap couldn't hide that he was a foreigner, as his height made him tower over the average Vietnamese, but one couldn't immediately be secure that he was military. He might be government, press, or even a French national. All precautionary moves, as

Mallroy had insisted that Doolin minimize any unnecessary advertisement regarding his "chosen line of work."

In the rural highlands of Vietnam, he also dressed in thin loose-fitting garb, without combat boots. He was comfortable, but Doolin was unquestionably "clothed" in the livery of lethality to anyone with knowledge or experience. As the young exasperated lieutenant who had exhausted himself yelling at Doolin had sensed, causal appearances may indeed mask predatorial intent. And Major Sumter himself had felt Doolin radiated danger, confidence, and combat experience.

Mallroy had insisted Doolin must avoid unnecessary interest or attention at all times. Thus, walking these streets in a proper Marine uniform would be an act directly announcing his presence; perhaps to those informed, it might even hint at his professional expertise. So, instead of a foreigner profusely dripping with sweat soaking through his military attire, he looked like almost every other person in the busy metropolis. Only his height identified him as different, but Judah was comfortable as he walked, watching his surroundings.

Judah knew he had entered into a tangle of deceit and self-interest. As there were a few hours left before his mandatory return to base, he needed some time to think, and this often was easiest when he was moving. One part of his brain watched the environment and the other floated within his thoughts, looking for patterns or connections that were not casually evident. As he walked slowly away from the heavily fortified security checkpoint, he considered what he understood and what both Mallroy and he really knew about the spectrum of facts confronting them.

Point number one was the reality that drugs—hard-core, high-purity heroin—were pouring into the Saigon market and other points in the country at an astonishing rate, almost unchecked—demand being served by excellent supply. Someone was making an enormous amount of money in addition to the weakening of traditional alliances, the loyalties of police to commanders, commanders to officials, and officials to the government. If Doolin was to examine this objectively, if he were a senior official, he would be tempted to take the money and run, as the South's government was corrupt and unsustainable without firm and enduring American support. And judging from what Doolin was hearing in the news from home, the support was hemorrhaging.

But something else was nagging at Doolin, a single wooden sliver embedded ever so marginally into his subconscious, causing but the tiniest irritation and thus unavoidable re-examination. Could Mallroy be orchestrating a sophisticated ruse? With the amount of money in play, was he pulling Doolin in to entrap him? Was Doolin just one of Mallroy's many pawns? Would he be easily eliminated, and could this young American become the fall guy? While he did not think so, and his inherent analysis *felt* that Mallroy was not a problem, red lights were as yet smoldering, although not quite blinking, in his brain.

Doolin wanted to dismiss this notion and emotionally endorse his feelings of loyalty for the colonel, yet almost immediately, out of discipline and training, Doolin found he could not. Feelings without analysis and re-examination could get you killed. Doolin could not become sloppy and certainly not sentimental, even for the weird orange-eyebrowed colonel. It was of interest to Doolin that people drifted toward areas of human endeavor for a nearly infinite number of reasons, or for no reason at all. But often, those seeking "careers" leaned toward areas they either enjoyed or were comfortable with; the pursued activity that ultimately occupies their zones of personal security also characterizes their formal work-related efforts.

Those in the intelligence business were puzzle-solvers, game-players, and these were mental games—the human chess game where sophisticated strategies countered equally erudite defenses or offensive tactics. Mallroy was such a person, and perhaps so was Doolin. He had to acknowledge that Mallroy had the ability to plan, and yes, to execute such a complicated labyrinthine game. But there was a singular difference between the colonel and the young sniper: Doolin also loved action, but not the romanticized cowboy "good vs. evil" sophistry that appeared in all of the Marine recruitment films. No, Doolin loved the action that completed the task, good or bad, right or wrong; it was the finality that he often craved after playing the chess game himself. It was almost the pronouncement of the sentence and the foreseeable sentence carried out that Doolin needed to mentally and perhaps spiritually close the door.

Judah C. Doolin, however, even approaching the age of eighteen, was already aware that the neat, tidy rooms within his mind might not be sufficient to ensure permanent closure. Would there be a future of self-acceptance? These rooms housing the facts, actions, and events of his last months in this Vietnam killing arena, these closed-off memories, might not so tidily store away his own sins. These ghouls might still rise from their assigned closed coffins and haunt his life in ways that he could not presently imagine or prepare for.

Doolin presently, however, could not fully appreciate these troubling reflections. Only years later would he begin to understand more completely, yet even now he sensed he was not finished with these buried memories, as countless generations of soldiers could confirm. Collectively, they would ruefully and knowingly acknowledge the coming sleepless nights that legions of combatants have experienced, the torn and fragmented memories of combat, snippets filled with terror and remorse that layer one's life like morning fog across a field. And as Doolin was considering these options, or more correctly *because* he was deep within these thoughts, he missed or did not initially observe a set of eyes intently following him as he strolled along the Parisian-style boulevard.

Doolin passed along the shops, some of them appearing to be made over into stores catering to Westerners. The city was teeming with life, an enthusiastic racket joined by the smells of spices from the numerous outdoor restaurants. Innumerable men and women around him, almost all with onyx-like black hair, had that characteristic delicate frame accompanied by hidden strength and an at times superhuman commitment. They dressed in white cotton or silk shirts, blouses, and *áo dàis,* dashing in and out of establishments, waiting on customers sitting at sidewalk tables. A steady flow of bobbing heads from individuals of varying heights flowed as a stream along the perimeters of these populated outdoor cafes and patios laden with small tables and chairs. A small lane for this pedestrian traffic to pass widened and narrowed like peristaltic waves.

Doolin sensed that rain was imminent, and the canvas umbrellas in the center of the outdoor tables were already fully extended. The automobile exhaust formed discontinuous blue-gray layers of hydrocarbon clouds lingering just over the wet, slick red-brown brick and concrete road. He was enjoying the near-frenetic activity associated with the open storefronts on that sticky Da Nang morning, but something told him that his wandering was of interest to someone as he negotiated street and sidewalk traffic. To this day, he never could point to what it was that alerted him to danger or to the reality that someone was watching him. But a steady discomfort began in his scalp and neck, and with his muscles tightening ever so slightly, Doolin began to feel more than objectively discern alarms being activated.

Hanh Nghiem watched from the opposite side of the street, sitting at one of the outdoor tables that populated the fashionable boulevard set out by an unnamed French bureaucrat nearly sixty years earlier. As did most European colonial powers, the French envisioned their "French Indochina" as a chance to impress the native culture with their "advanced" ideas of urbanity, and thus a surprising number of the restaurants were similar to or modeled after the world-famous French cafés of Paris. She had been alerted to a strange series of events at US Marine command by her doughy "lover" whom unintentionally served as her source of continuously updated military information. He had been angry that some young US Marine had recently returned from a rural or isolated assignment, being gone for weeks alone without proper surveillance. Further, this lone "two-striper" was a "disgrace to the Marine uniform" but was being protected by someone up high in the chain of command. No one really even knew this kid's name.

"In fact, can you imagine cutting orders and putting X in the name box?" he had ranted.

To her pudgy gunnery sergeant, this entire situation was unacceptable. Accompanied by his squalid breath, he had provided that when this "bullshit excuse for a Marine" returned, he had provided something—"some evidence or whatnot"—in a sealed bag that had been delivered to a colonel named Mallroy. This same Marine corporal had then been summoned to meet individually with this Colonel Mallroy, who was known to be "some sort" of military intelligence officer, or "spook."

Yes, this young man was unknown by name, which was troubling to the network of data gathers working for Charlie and the North Vietnamese. She had received orders that actually surprised her, as they required her to move quickly and be at a location in Da Nang ready to watch for someone. She had had to arrange to leave her ever-jealous gunny and provide a cover story that she hoped would suffice. She was told to position herself to observe the traffic coming out of the Da Nang Naval complex that particular morning, and she had been given a fairly precise description of what this "kid" looked like.

They had told her that he was tall, close to six feet, three inches, and that his tightly cropped hair was a dark brown that had the strange natural curl found in Westerners. His face was actually handsome, they said; she would actually find it surprisingly attractive. His bright hazel eyes failed to mask a fierce intelligence shadowed by thick eyebrows, high cheekbones, and a slightly angular appearance of his midface but with a very square jaw. He had an indentation in his chin's midline—not as prominent as that

Hollywood actor from the fifties, but it gave him an interesting look of being sturdy but sharply defined. His lips were generous, but his mouth was, if anything, unobtrusive. He was deceptively fast, quick, and yet the courier had carried the information that Doolin moved with a fluidity that almost obscured an intense assessment of his surroundings. The fact that he was not known by name to her gunnery sergeant drove Kinkade nearly insane; according to him, it was an affront to his "position of stature."

She wondered, not for the first time, if this nameless and apparently very young man could really be anyone of importance. Logic dictated that his youth made him a low-ranking Marine. Thus, how influential could he be to anything of value? What could this man of such low rank be up to that might be so imperative? The same man that her foul-breathed gunnery sergeant had ranted on about couldn't be that important, could he? The possibility intrigued her.

Hanh had made notes on two other people passing out of the naval complex but had decided they were not close enough to the description. Too short, although they each looked superficially like the individual she sought. Again, all she had been told was that he was a tall man, very young, had sharp features, was handsome, and moved with the authority of someone much older. She had laughed at the information and its intended use. Like it helped her even minimally, she sarcastically thought. How was she going to be able to identify this individual?

She wore a conservatively cut white áo dài and left her large rice hat in place so as to hide her eyes and mask her beauty, which sometimes became a cumbersome nuisance. It was a simple fact that men from any culture could recognize beauty, and this often, or at least more often than she wanted, created interest from men of all ages and cultures. But to address this, she sat with a fellow soldier, a young fifteen-year-old runner for the Viet Cong who provided her with her requisite male chaperone, posing as a "cousin" watching over his beautiful family member.

She had desperately tried to get her balloon-shaped Marine gunnery sergeant to provide additional information on this young Marine, but he was frustratingly unhelpful.

Oh! Wait a minute—who is this?

Was it the man of interest who now exited the Da Nang Naval complex, walking on the opposite side of the crowded street?

Her gunnery clerk himself had voiced to her his antipathy for this eighteen-year-old "affront to the uniform" and his rage over his inability to get either the major or the lieutenant to tell him anything substantive.

Kinkade had puffed out his chest before derisively declaring that this was a "bullshit mission" since he was not in the "need to know." Thus, Hanh Nghiem could not get the information she needed, and she was uncertain that the man she was now watching was really anyone of importance. Hanh had almost dismissed her gunnery's hostile narrative until her leadership had surmised that perhaps this individual, said to be nameless, had raised their collective suspicions. The fact that he was nameless, bearing no identification at all, was distinctly unusual, if not completely unique. Could this man somehow be connected to the killing of their scouts?

But as Hanh observed him, she was indeed struck by his youth, yet she also sensed that this man was a confusing mixture of unsettling inconsistent characteristics. Young, but purposeful. A relaxed, flowing rhythm to his movement hiding deliberate trained skillsets. An unusual degree of competence? *Could he be important?* Could he be the one she sought?

These impressions were further heightened as she continued to watch this tall, wiry but muscular youthful American effortlessly navigate the communal chaos of the street, moving with a degree of authority belying his age. He wore sunglasses and a Western cap, but she could tell that he was visually inspecting everything around him. He stopped at a bookstore that also served coffee and sweets on the other side of the wide boulevard, and while she could not see the actual book he picked up, she knew that the store and that particular section of reading material was not the typical comic book or adventure magazine characteristic of so many of the American soldiers. She also began to feel a growing unease as she realized he was carefully and methodically inventorying his surroundings.

Hanh was a trained operative and recognized immediately his systematic and continuous assessment of his environment, moving with ease yet deliberately positioning himself in optimal defensive and observational locations. He was good, and this both puzzled and troubled her. Was this the man, and what was his role? Who was he?

Moving a bit deeper into the open storefront, he drew out a thick book. He opened it but read only briefly, using his actions to facilitate further careful surveillance. As he looked up, his gaze held firm; she suddenly felt a cold chill tickle her spine and crawl up to her scalp.

He was looking directly at her!

As she registered this, she casually reached over and patted the hand of her young colleague, and he nearly jumped at her touch.

She said in a command tone, but just above a whisper, "I need you to respond to me by talking and smiling and nodding your head."

This he did immediately, and she responded by smiling and nodding herself and then saying in Vietnamese, "I am not certain, but we are likely being observed by someone we are supposed to be watching."

And he nodded in confirmation, again smiling.

She tilted her head as to "listen" more carefully to his "comment," and in doing so she was able to shift her eyes back across to the storefront … and he was gone! She nearly flinched, moving enough for her companion to say, "You OK?"

She quickly searched the adjoining storefronts with her eyes. She even stood momentarily to look both ways down the sidewalk that passed in front of the stores, extending her examination sideways to her left and right along the opposite walkway.

What she could not see, or simply did not observe, was that Doolin had crossed to her side of the street, joining the countless other white-shirt or blouse-clad citizens of Da Nang, invisible in the crowded walkways as he feigned some issue with one of his shoelaces to bend at the waist just enough to disguise his significant height. Doolin moved quickly but casually before he stopped to observe her from thirty-five yards off of her right shoulder, tucked into a neighboring store entryway hidden from her view.

And although she did not see Doolin, she felt his presence. Instantly, she understood that he was not some flunky drafted kid from America's heartland looking for a McDonald's in the middle of Da Nang. He was something very different, and this frightened her in spite of her professionalism.

She subsequently dared to casually ask her fetid-breathed gunny if it was unusual for him not to be provided details or some degree of information regarding another Marine, especially someone who was of lesser rank and would normally be part of his daily clerical concerns.

He had responded with a self-inflated description of how important it was to have "precision" in all of the paperwork to ensure that troop movements and tactical planning could be "ideally coordinated." Not only was this unusual, but it was also, at least in the gunny's opinion, unprecedented for him to be screened out of the chain of clerical documentation as to who and what this guy was about. What was even worse, in the gunny's sanctimonious perspective, was that this guy was disgracing the Marine uniform and the Marine way of life, probably due to his being the "bastard offspring" of some general.

But unbeknownst to him, Kinkade had added to Hanh's growing discomfort when he stated that "curiously, this kid" just disappeared. All traces of him—paperwork, any notes or orders—just … poof! Gone!

But Hanh knew simply by observing Judah C. Doolin for thirty seconds that he was something special, and that meant something troubling. She did not know his name, but she knew she was correct in her assessment. He possessed a degree of competence that belied his youth, he was a trained asset, and this suggested that he indeed might be this "Mallroy's kid."

But who *was* this young man?

Watching him and reflecting on his actions, his ability to vanish in front of her despite her trained observational skill, alarmed her. Perhaps he was important—perhaps his mission or presence was even critical.

And thus, it might be similarly important to nullify this "kid" for the benefit of her movement's success. But how was she going to get additional information regarding him? Alternatively, could they just track the Marine when next they saw him and kill him?

CHAPTER 7

THE MORAL VACUUM

Four Weeks Later

Proditor
"Traitor"

She was indeed beautiful: her lithesome body; shimmering straight, thick coal-black hair falling softly around her delicate face, just touching her shoulders; her curves flowing in her favorite native garb of a white silk áo dài. Hanh Nghiem turned heads of both women and men routinely. In fact, this was at times a problem, and thus she often dressed very conservatively and wore a large Asian rice hat, deliberately obscuring most of her face. If anyone would describe her, they would readily admit that her femininity and features were striking. Yet there was a fierce sadness, almost a trace of sorrow, in her eyes. She was a survivor, but there were times when she wondered if her troubled nights, often spent in restless sleep and violent dreams, were worth the price of survival. She had often contemplated that she might have rather embraced, even enjoyed, a premature eternal rest.

She meticulously took note of the handsome man with captivating yellow hair exiting the dull military-green Ford Galaxy from the passenger door. Hanh observed him carefully. She had done the same looking and observing with Doolin, although she did not know this latter man's name. She had not forgotten this brief visual encounter—his seemingly easy, almost lax navigation along the walkway to the bookstore, disguising purposeful movements, his falsely detached yet intensely watchful purposeful inventorying of his surroundings.

She had reported to Duc Lien, her superior, and conveyed her abstract concern over this man. Duc had initially shrugged off her trepidations until the intensity of her unease caused him to pause. He sensed her disproportionate apprehension and he, always a professional, sat with her, asking what about this man made her uncomfortable. Her responses were carefully framed; she offered little that could be classified as hyperbole, and Duc knew her well enough to weigh her feelings with prudence. He later filed her responses in his memory and then passed his own thoughtful inferences on to his command. There was something about Hanh's young Westerner that required follow-up.

After all, Hanh had been ordered to watch for Doolin from colleagues of Duc, but as Hanh had dutifully reported through her gunnery sergeant, this young man had virtually disappeared. All administrative and knowledge of his whereabouts had somehow been erased. Hanh and her people had failed to locate him, and this alone was problematic for Duc. Why would a lowly Marine have been made to disappear? And what sort of training would be required by this man to extend such an outcome?

Presently, Hanh was seated comfortably in a cushioned Western-style captain's chair, her legs crossed at the ankles adorned with delicate white sandals. She was positioned three feet back from an open waist-high window, its view framed by delicate previously white but now grimy gray drapes. She was in the office of one of those iconic rice hat makers—a buyer who was also of her cause, a patriot who was virulently but tacitly anti-American. He had opened his office to her and left her alone.

She had received orders from her cell to observe and report activities regarding this yellow-haired man. She had thought it unusual since she would only be able to observe him for minutes, if not seconds, in the open parking area behind one of the Da Nang-run CIA "substations," but her orders were clear. Hanh was to establish his habits and note the times, so she did. She was unaware that Duc was using her in cross-checking the movements of the object of her surveillance.

She had told her corpulent ever-jealous American lover—Gunnery Sergeant Kinkade, Third Marine Division at Quảng Trị Combat Base—that she needed to see her mother's sister, her aunt, as the elder lady had taken ill. She wrinkled her nose in spite of herself, her disgust palpable as she remembered the exchange. The audacity of the man … he had volunteered to accompany her, but she knew it was not out of compassion for her relative. No, it was to ensure that she was not seeing any other man besides him. His suspicions, she thought, reflected his ignorance of Vietnamese women, or an inherent American cultural bias that all woman were unfaithful. This itself infuriated her.

That she would allow more than one man to enter her! Were all American women so inclined? The reality was that she was forced to provide him, this malodorous American, with her beautifully sculpted body, her supple, toned frame and silky skin. *This bubble-headed man should thank his undeserving ancestors for his good fortune*, she concluded. His hygiene was revolting, forcing her at times to hold her breath as he whispered his affections to her, his weight pinning her to their undersized bed in the cramped dingy apartment.

These were the explicit instructions from her sector commander, and she had complied. And even though she lived with the Westerner, it did not prevent this fleshy Marine from being suspicious of her. But his suspicions were entirely pedestrian, related to her gender, her body, and his need to ensure his exclusivity, instead of what might have been entirely appropriate concerns or suspicions: her professional activities. As if Hanh Nghiem would be intimate with more than one man. She was repulsed by the American and all that he represented.

But his suspicions reflected an irony that hung over her like the early morning mist blanketing the Da Nang harbor. She was, indeed, intimate with another, and she longed for his embrace, a situation causing as much bitterness as the hostility she kept under control regarding the American.

In fact, "her Marine" was not wrong, for she was in love with her commander, Duc Lien, a married senior Viet Cong officer running multiple prongs of penetration into the American war effort. His wife lived with her parents in the rural northwest, not far from that fateful field of dreams Dien Bien Phu, the place of his nation's true birth and hope for self-governance and independence. Duc himself revered the name, and his wife and her parents lived not twenty kilometers from this site. His efforts in the South were beginning to pay dividends, although he would not have used that term. He was beginning to see results within the chaotic, deceptive world he inhabited in spite of his longing to be in the peace and rhythm of the bucolic setting, waking to the smiling eyes of his wife.

He had not seen her in ten months. His responsibilities grew and he, in truth, enjoyed his work: contributing to and watching the American war effort fail. His clandestine efforts to burrow into the superpower's war machine were remarkably successful—but then, the Americans were not very good at security. In fact, one might objectively argue that collectively, they were appalling. For starters, the fact that they would let native Vietnamese work on their combat bases, in their civilian-run government offices, and even in their classified military work areas never failed to amaze him.

They were careless, as they thought that a person's word was to be taken at face value. No detailed or real checks, no cross-checking to ensure loyalty to the South. But even when they had attempted a meager validation of an individual's political provenance, their efforts would have been wasted; the Vietnamese culture simply did not allow any degree of certainty in the establishment of partisan commitment or loyalty. Unless a Vietnamese American-employed embassy clerk arrived at work wearing a North Vietnamese Army uniform with accompanying identification, little real scrutiny was ever performed. The infrastructure of the American war effort was thus worm-eaten with betrayal.

Of note, the present debate between Duc Lien and his staff was whether Hanh Nghiem was best positioned in her current hated role or if she should instead be offered to procure a position in the American embassy as a typist and work her way into a trusted position. With her beauty and personal intelligence, they felt that she could come to occupy a crucial position rather quickly, but they could not wait. They needed data now—something was happening to VC scouts, and they had no idea who or what was causing the destruction of their carefully orchestrated activity. They had thus deemed it a time-sensitive need to get potentially relevant information from Marine commands in different sectors of the country, and so she had been requested—she had actually *volunteered*—to endure the affections of her obese, ill-kept gunnery sergeant with deplorable dental hygiene and filthy toenails.

Hanh had not infrequently felt a wave of nausea rising from her gut at the thought of Kinkade's amorous attempts to impress her. But her role had been almost too easy, as he tried to demonstrate his latent, if not under-appreciated importance by sharing tidbits of information on the American Marines' intentions from his role as senior clerk at the Command Center. Her commander, Duc, had noted that important patriotic activity required advanced planning, and this was carried out by scouts that often were regular army from their Northern divisions.

Trouble was that over the last four months, several of the scouting teams of two and three men had been killed by what appeared to be a single sniper, as there was no evidence of telltale enemy troop residue. Investigations revealed that there were no signs of existing or associated crushed or deformed fauna in the area of the killings, no betraying food or American detritus left in the area. The areas were, in fact, eerily sterile. Further, the impact of the responsible high-velocity projectiles accomplishing the killings suggested a competent sniper, or perhaps snipers. Finally, what was perhaps the most concerning was that Northern command had taken careful steps to ensure that the activity was conducted in remote areas, far away from American or South Vietnamese patrols or encampments.

She had ventured a question to Duc Lien as to whether perhaps there was the inadvertent coincidental arrival of both parties, American and their Northern troops, in the area at the same time. Could it be coincidence? Duc had looked at her, assessing whether to provide her with additional information. She really had no need to know, and he decided that he would not supply her with the knowledge that the Northern divisions had been provided precise locations in advance of both American and South Vietnamese troop activity.

However, she had surmised the answer from his polite yet evasive response, his circumferential monotone allowing her thoughts to immediately grasp the reality of concern over these killings. His talking points—"those possibilities were exactly what he considered" and were "being investigated"—cemented her correct assessment that treachery was suspected, not coincidence.

She knew from reading his face and his eyes that their forces must have had access to enemy logistics and yet, in spite of this, they were being killed. This was the foremost concern. Was the North being fed false information? Or perhaps someone on the American side had independently discovered that data was being surreptitiously shared with the North and then had decided to "crash" the party? The commanders in the field had reported that they had found no evidence that the bodies of their scouts had been disturbed or searched; they had conclusively stated that nothing was reported as missing from the remains. Duc had smiled somewhat cynically at this deduction, hoping that his commanders would respond to the potential that in spite of appearances, the information was in the hands of the Americans—again! But he had kept his mouth shut, as his superiors were marginally tolerant of being told how to perform their tasks. Such is leadership in every army throughout time!

Thus, Hanh had accepted that her role of obtaining as much information from the swinish-eyed gunny actually was important and might even be critical. She remembered the young handsome man in the bookstore and could not help but wonder as to whether he somehow fit into this complex puzzle. But with all of her gunnery sergeant's inadvertent betrayals in his continued attempts to impress his Vietnamese beauty, she was unable to learn anything confirming that the young man she had seen at the bookstore was indeed "Mallroy's kid."

She had once even admonished her sergeant to be careful with his information, shooing him into silence as he began to clutch her breasts, his small erection desperately trying to come to full posture. He became more aroused and, as she had foreseen, his protective filter regarding his classified position and its relevant material simply evaporated as his eyes wandered over her near-perfect skin and smooth shapely breasts. She rapidly memorized his shared excessive information, at times timing her giggling and cooing to extend his dialogue if the information was especially valuable, clasping his hands to redirect his movements, gentle touches instead of his rough pawing.

She simply shut down her emotions and mechanically adjusted her body to accommodate his grunting entry into her. A small consolation was that the duration of the infrequent episodes lasted less than ninety seconds; he would reach his physical pleasure quickly and then roll off of her, sometimes falling asleep within an interval less than the time spent in her. As awful as this was for her, during these events she mentally conjured the image of her commander, embracing the compliments he provided as to the respect he and others reserved for her.

In truth, Duc Lien felt she was little better than a common whore. His "respect" and even his forced rare intimacy with her was another of his many professional military responsibilities reluctantly embraced to ensure that the information continued to flow to him and his senior officers. That any respectable Vietnamese woman would share her body with an American under any circumstances, even the threat of death, was anathema to him. His views originated in a near-fanatical perspective formed as a child, knowing his mother provided her French rubber and cinnamon plantation employer with more than her cleaning duties in his colonial mansion. His greatest joy as a young man was the realization that Dien Bien Phu had destroyed the French and the owner of the mansion was forced to leave and return a pauper to France. His mother's shame, however, was shared with her son, and he used this internal persistent growling ache to fuel his efforts for his beloved country.

Duc had recognized the talent in this young beauty, and her efforts had yielded important, if not pivotal actionable information. Apparently, there was an American sniper, or more than one, working within a very odd, almost unique operative logistical unit—but the early hints at information had gone completely dry. Duc had argued with his leadership that this sniper or perhaps several snipers were active, but despite Duc's and Hanh's efforts, the names, information, and missions of said snipers ceased to exist within the military chain of command. The paperwork, the orders, the summaries of activities—all of the normal mindless bureaucratic requirements that impeded spontaneity and thus often eliminated the success of American efforts were absent regarding the activities of anyone involved in the targeted killings of VC scouts. Duc Lien trusted Hanh Nghiem professionally, and he shared her disquiet in being unable to identify anyone associated with the specific actions taken in killing the VC scouts.

This fact was then linked to the truculent commentary of Hanh's gunnery sergeant, who had noted some "kid" had deliberately been de-identified of both name and rank, followed by all paperwork of his existence vanishing. This same gunny bemoaned his being shielded from any involvement in this individual's missions. Such conduct was opposite to his typical entitled knowledge regarding this corporal, as would be customary given his "status" as the chief clerk. Even the sergeant was nonplussed, if not alarmed, at the total paucity of documentation surrounding this individual. Someone was going to extreme lengths to obscure the entity or those persons involved in a clandestine mission or missions, and it was not a quirk that the timing of these events corresponded to the elimination of Duc's VC comrades.

Hanh had properly noted the initial description of a man previously in the presence of her gunnery sergeant. According to this same fat gunny, this mystery person had stood with a Marine officer, a major, when the officer had ordered that the name in the orders were to be marked X, and the X was followed by Mallroy's name. This allowed Duc and his people to surmise that Mallroy, who was military intel, was working with this young man, his "kid," and perhaps others. But then the entire paper trail and intel from the gunnery sergeant went dark. Duc was uncertain as to whether this Mallroy was running parallel operations to Haney or whether they might be working together.

What Duc needed to know was whether the *đầu vàng*—"yellow head," or blond-headed man—was playing both sides against the middle in this fluid environment. Was this yellow head giving aid to his countrymen while pretending to support the drug trade controlled by the VC? Thus, he needed to begin by establishing timelines and activity profiles for this đầu vàng to allow them to form a composite of his workday extending to his week.

Duc and his superiors did not know whether the young man Hanh had seen was significant. Was this man, seen exiting the naval complex in Da Nang, part of a sophisticated effort to impact their drug-running activities and the hard currency it won for the Viet Cong? But Duc knew several disconnected pieces of information. First, that Hanh felt strongly that this man, briefly observed, stirred an unease in her. She reported her belief that he was someone of importance. He was possibly connected to the second point: that their scouts were being killed at various locations. Locations that should have been removed from American interference, because this yellow-headed man had provided the map coordinates of prospective missions; thus, other areas should have been secure. Three, they also knew that a Colonel Mallroy, someone high up in Army or Joint Command Intelligence, was using someone loosely referred to as "Mallroy's kid." But here was where the transition between knowledge and speculation began.

Duc had no idea as to whether Mallroy's kid was also Hanh's young man in the bookstore. Was there a direct linkage between this young individual, an apparent soldier, and the targeted elimination of their scouts out in the field? Even if this guy seen at the bookstore did work with Mallroy, it said nothing conclusive or specific about his involvement with this colonel or his potential involvement in targeting their scouts. These were but a few of the unanswered questions, and Duc felt more than knew that there was validity to Hanh's concern. It was an almost paradoxical existence of youth linked to experience, witnessed by her in the man who had casually walked but then disappeared as he traversed the Saigon boulevard. But repetitive attempts to gain additional information regarding who he was had since been a failure.

Data linking this tall young man to Mallroy's kid was simply absent. Duc was even uncertain this individual was the same man that the gunny had initially described to Hanh. Any paperwork or data on this individual, or individuals, was air-sealed, and this fact alone was the single defining aspect that troubled Duc more than any other. Such expertise in making someone disappear was rare; it implied expertise and commitment. Duc Lien was unaware of any previous effort or apparent success in maintaining this level of blackout on information. There was even uncertainty that he was actually pure military. Could he be CIA? Was Haney, the yellow-headed man, that remarkably treacherous?

Worse still, that idiot lover of Hanh's was of little or no assistance. They were playing a new game, and the typical American sloppiness was nowhere to be seen. Was the young CIA station chief slowly readying an operational coup? Was Haney directly pulling the strings of a complex puppet show to entrap the North Vietnamese? Was Duc himself one of the prizes?

The đầu vàng was allegedly a man of some actual importance in his government. He was a minor chief among spies working in the vast American espionage corporate structure called the CIA. What was known to the Viet Cong was that this man sought out corruption and countermeasures to allegedly assist the American war effort through efforts in the South Vietnamese forces, but with a rather cynical twist. Haney had eventually identified General Nguyen Trong Ang, a three-star officer in the ARVN who both possessed significant money and lived a lifestyle of breezy relaxation. Money and a relaxed attitude in a war zone where South Vietnamese officers were often the targets of assassination was of interest to anyone paying attention, and the young CIA station chief was. Both variables foreseeably raised suspicion, and thus the đầu vàng had targeted this man for full assessment.

In truth, Haney was good. He had cornered Nguyen Trong Ang, establishing beyond doubt that the general was an established conduit to the VC and their debilitating drug trade in the South. But what had initially astonished Duc and his superiors was the offer made by the American to the general. Haney made no pretense; he simply informed the general that the price of his continued freedom and lifestyle was a piece of the action for Haney in the drug business. Ang's drug profits were to be skimmed as part of Haney's "expenses," and, if done in accordance with what Haney explicitly requested, this straw-headed man stated he would ensure that the general and his most valuable assets within the established network moving the illicit material into the South would be "alerted" as to impending "busts," as he put it. They would be "protected" from efforts to impact their business for a slightly higher proportion of the profits.

Even more remarkable to Duc was the fact that Haney had forced Trong Ang to revise his personal habits, changing both his ostentatious display of wealth and his lifestyle, which could not reasonably be supported by an AVRN general at risk of assassination by elements of Charlie—unless, of course, he was not at risk. This lowered the general's profile and brought less potential for random interest by other American investigators, like the reported interest of a certain military intelligence colonel called Mallroy.

Haney had heard that this Mallroy was good, and he wanted to reduce the profile of their illicit business to avoid detection by this colonel or other like-minded patriots. Haney ran a tight ship, and the corrupt AVRN general complied. At first reluctantly, but then somewhat more enthusiastically as he realized that, indeed, his shelf life would be prolonged. But was this all part of this American's ruse?

Haney further demanded that he meet other key players in the Viet Cong's drug trade. This was vigorously resisted for multiple reasons, including that, of course, Haney could in fact be setting up an elaborate sting operation in an attempt to take down the entire network—not only of the drug trade, but of senior VC commanders in the South. But on the threat of exposure by Haney, in the end General Ang did supply two individuals. These two, while not at the very top of Charlie's officer corps, were important members of the enemy's Southern officer structure, and all relevant parties met to discuss the proposed business opportunity.

As it turned out, Haney demonstrated that he was as ruthless as he was greedy and made good on his pledges that the drug trade would be reasonably protected from his position in knowing the workings of the American drug enforcement efforts, which included American military deployments that might also harm the drug trade. These were the real threats, people like this Mallroy and other American investigators, as most of the South's other officials investigating the drug business were, in truth, VC operatives. But here Haney had created a nearly perfect scenario, as he knew it was likely that at some point in the future, other American assets would look into or perhaps already were looking into his activities. Who could know? Perhaps the VC were penetrated by American double agents or assets that would expose him.

But Haney knew that if this was the case, his escape hatch was the identification of Ang and all the people who were under him involved in the transportation and cooperative business ventures with VC in the South. Further, Haney recognized a consistent human habit: people became sloppy the more familiar and accustomed to each other they grew. Thus, over the weeks of working with Ang and his subordinates, Haney took detailed notes identifying and categorizing the members of their collective effort in the heroin trade.

As Haney continued to observe, he burrowed deep into the operations of the VC effort to flood the South with heroin, but he was frustratingly aware that he was still not close to being familiar with the highest level of directorship. There was a level of organizational control, a powerful group of phantoms, that directed overall strategy and ultimately approved the most critical decisions. These were hidden from him, and his surreptitious efforts to unmask any of these individuals had thus far been unsuccessful. But he knew they existed.

He thoughtfully considered the reasons that he had been cut off from the most senior VC and North Vietnamese military leaders controlling the strategy of the illicit drug trade and understood there were many. Most simply revolved around basic security logistics, but Haney intuitively accepted that there were higher-ups who made the most important strategic and tactical decisions. Haney took note that there was always a delay in finalizing critical decisions, even when he had given his counterparts in the VC firm, almost de facto scenarios. This included discussions of planned elimination of individuals who were causing problems, such that when critical targets were discussed—perhaps a rival member of the Chinese Triad, a Chinese version of the mafia—there was always a delay. Then, within three to four days, enough time for communication, meetings, and decision-makers to approve or reject a decision, the final ruling or decision occurred. And notably, it invariably was never brought up for discussion again.

Thus, although Haney had never met anyone he could affirm was at the most senior level of control, this circumstantial data suggested that higher levels of leadership within the military-narcotics empire existed. But this did not impede him from constructing a detailed schematic with all known names and contacts. The final result was an impressive list of midlevel and quasi-senior officials involved in the business of trafficking heroin, and most importantly, Haney knew that almost all of these people either tacitly or actively worked for the North. Those who might claim they did not were nonetheless facilitating the North Vietnamese strategic goals of destabilizing the Southern government, law enforcement, and the military infrastructure.

As such, if Haney really needed to or ultimately intended to lower the hammer and eliminate these enemy agents and VC sympathizers, he actually could cause a major degree of injury to the North's war efforts expressed via the illicit drug trade. What he did not know but actually repeatedly considered was that the entire operation was being directed by very senior intelligence forces in China—a fact that would have eventual far-reaching ramifications for Haney himself.

Haney toyed often with the potential of gaining as much personal material wealth during this activity as possible, then lowering the net of American authority onto his VC "colleagues," depending on who was actually going to win this war. It might have been shocking to his superiors in the CIA to realize that one of their own could be so ruthless as to build up a level of influence with the enemy and appear, for all practical purposes, as a valid source of enemy penetration, a co-opted asset, only to find out that he was positioning himself to be even more effective in destroying these same individuals. This was classic double agent tradecraft. It might actually have won the respect of the "old guard," as they often had run similar very risky operations during WWII.

He smiled at the setup he had created; it afforded him several opportunities, choices, and protection. Haney was making vast amounts of money cooperating with the VC and the North's war strategy, but he had an escape hatch in that he could actually severely cripple their efforts if he chose to do so. And he just might if he was cornered by someone like Mallroy.

He could imagine the older generation of clandestine warriors comparing him to those forerunners of the CIA, the OSS operatives who had managed successful efforts in WWII behind German lines. They would raise their eyebrows at the requisite level of audacity and skill employed to successfully conduct such a tightrope operation over months. They would see Haney's results and, even though several among the old guard might wonder if there was a deeper, more sinister aspect to this Haney fellow, his ability to claim "scalps" of the enemy if needed would probably shield him from any significant rebuke or harm. Paradoxically, such results might just elevate his stature rather significantly.

Within this complex theater of Haney's deceptive operations, there was only one impermissible act: the killing or targeted elimination of an American who came too close to apparent disruption of his and his Viet Cong partner's drug trade infrastructure. Haney realized that with the Americans investigating the illicit narcotics activities of the VC and North, their efforts rarely caused even momentary slowing of the brisk trade, let alone serious harm to the overall illegal trafficking or profits. Thus, absent some existential threat to him personally, these American drug interdiction efforts did not represent real danger. Haney thus considered the likelihood of any meaningful disruptive event remote and the need to kill an American to eliminate a threat to profits as unnecessary as it was unwise.

Because of this, Haney took it upon himself to aggressively discourage his VC counterparts from killing any Americans involved or associated with narcotic trafficking investigations. It was not that such an event or targeted elimination would be immediately linked to him, but it might have been, and this would have been ruinous. Thus, NO ONE was allowed to kill or sanction the murder of an American without explicit agreement from all parties involved. This took into account how "necessary" or how "important" such action was deemed by street operatives, as they often only had fragmentary information. Only if and unless actions were combat-related or concomitant to the immediate timely termination of VC assets was such action reasonable; otherwise, leaving Americans alone was prudent. In essence, it was a bright-red line that should never be crossed.

Any murder of Americans broke the red line and created unwanted enhanced interest in the illicit trafficking market. This interest might establish a linkage to Haney and the targeted American killing, placing him in an unrecoverable position. All the work he had done, his orchestrated ruse on both sides of this venue, would collapse. You couldn't demand the respect of American supervisors for your tightrope-walking and penetration of VC operations, claiming that you were a double agent all along, if you killed fellow Americans! That had never and would never be allowed.

Further, there were too many loose ends. Too many discoverable facts that could, to the trained investigative eye, form a pattern of Haney's taking money directly from VC enemy leaders. Thus, Haney needed to control any such investigative efforts if they were to occur. He had to manage the information and scheduling of when any such data were released to ensure maximum safety for his continued role in working with the North Vietnamese and Charlie. Unscheduled unmasking of Haney's activities basically would demonstrate his complicity, and this was treason.

The killing of a fellow American related in any way to drug-trade operations was thus taboo. Even peripheral involvement in such an act was the destruction of a career, along with ten years to life in prison. This is what the legal community looked for when they brought charges of conspiracy, and such activity could only raise the level of complicity to an undeniable, firm connection.

So, over several very profitable months, Haney had worked in concert with the VC and Ang to avoid any of this unneeded activity. However, the same standard was not enforced for South Vietnamese personnel. If loyal

South Vietnamese came too close to Haney or the VC-directed drug distribution through investigation or incidental discovery, they were eliminated.

Duc viewed Haney's activity with a surprising degree of parallel expert judgment. A de facto sanctuary against targeted murder of Americans was a logical position for the đầu vàng to take, yet it also might hint directly at his duplicity if he was truthfully setting up a double-cross to take down Viet Cong assets. One doesn't kill Americans if one is, in fact, working within the American clandestine system to harm or destroy the North's attempts to flood the South with illicit contraband.

But Haney's argument for his repeated objections to murdering or killing any Americans was that such activity would refocus very deliberate specific energy on their business and harm it.

Haney had stated, "Let the cancer grow undetected."

He meant that if no cataclysmic events took place to alarm or arouse the Americans, they would only pay nominal attention to the drug trade. And to date, no real interruption of business had occurred; their operations were very successful, and money was being made—a lot of money. So far, the very senior leaders in China were accepting the skillful đầu vàng's strategy.

Duc, however, was suspicious of the events surrounding the ill-defined and unexplained killing of VC scouts in the field. He viewed this as a troubling inflection on the barometer of their future success, but Haney had already taken an additional step and conferred with Duc's superiors, offering a simple and direct observation.

Haney noted that until recently, several of the more corrupt South Vietnamese officials such as Ang—and there were others—were simply too obvious in their lifestyles and naively displayed a level of wealth difficult to miss by anyone observant. Patterns of ostentatious lifestyles attracted the attentions of many people, and not just Americans. Haney felt that rather than some sophisticated American anti-drug interdiction or operation, it was far more likely that Ang's competitors within the Vietnamese underworld or even combined Chinese-Vietnamese underworld might be eliminating scouts to steal product and sell it through their own competing networks.

And in fact, there was an element of rational truth to this explanation, although Haney was never completely convinced of its actuality. He had effectively argued for a focused approach, to begin to systematically deliver a message to competing underworld networks that it was time to join the eight-hundred-pound gorilla, meaning the VC-North's network, and to cease any and all attempts to continue independent fully autonomous business operations. In this way, the various underworld activities could be joined to the North's overwhelming dominant position, providing security and money for all. Left unsaid was that the money for the underworld would simply be less than they had previously enjoyed, yet despite this convenient and potentially valid explanation for the elimination of the VC scouts, Haney secretly worried that some other force was responsible. But by his proposal, creating an all-encompassing umbrella of illicit drug trafficking allowed him to begin to eliminate alternative scenarios responsible for the death of the VC teams. It might also, he thought, allow him to pinpoint who actually was responsible.

The approach Haney suggested was viewed as inherently reasonable. In fact, it was almost identical to what had taken place in the American mafia in the 1950s and '60s as the more business-minded gangsters in America tried to stem the often wasteful and fruitless internecine bloodshed resulting from competing interests among those involved in illegal activities. But what Haney argued, and what most senior leadership in Hanoi and Beijing concurred with, was that it also provided the cover of "gangster or underworld" activity masking a direct military strategic front in the war against America. The American government allowed the underworld to operate rather freely, but if the activity could be tied to a military objective, resources would be allocated by the Americans to actually destroy the distribution of narcotics.

Of vital interest to Haney, and incidentally judged correctly by North Vietnamese leadership, was that this strategic vision provided Haney with yet another layer of deception as to who was really controlling the illicit material. After all, he could easily convince his American superiors that he was using the underworld to identify possible links to North Vietnamese activities since this was what the American government had done during WWII with Sicilian mafia facilitating and aiding American war efforts in Southern Italy. Finally, it provided a practical mechanism for Haney to both prove he was not behind these targeted eliminations of Northern scouts, a fact that tacitly disturbed him, and to potentially identify who actually was behind the killings.

Thus, to further cement his alliances with Ang's superiors and relevant subordinates, Haney cleared the important pathways for Ang's partners while impeding any other freelancers, and this rarely, but demonstrably, meant killing other Vietnamese military, civilian, or government personnel. Anyone interested in the lucrative business of illicit drugs who might be working with the Asian mafia, separate from the North's efforts, had to be eliminated. Haney wanted the major players to join together, and in doing so he could eradicate another potential source that might be killing his scouts.

Haney knew that the Asian underworld couldn't have cared less who won the war; they were out to make money. But in making them join the Northern military efforts, everyone got paid and the potential for violence might be lowered, along with unmasking whoever was killing his people in the field, if indeed the underworld was involved. And finally, if Haney could get the various parties to all sit at the same table and see the potential for enormous profitability, he could also reduce the inadvertent killing of any Americans, and by default reduce the potential for a subsequent obligatory investigation into their illicit activities. He actually was euphoric over his plans; the Northern leadership observed his efforts with cautious cynicism.

The Vietnam War, Haney believed, was to be viewed in history largely as a struggle of independence, pitting two sides of a family against each other. For those who wanted close ties with their former colonial masters, adopting a measure of their more open governmental structure was a realized promise. This was opposed by those who wanted a complete break in this form of pseudo-dependency, as they viewed it, but who also advocated authoritarian hegemony. While this was obviously an oversimplified assessment, there was much truth to it.

For those true believers—those in the South who were virulently anti-colonial, thus both anti-French and anti-American—the sacrifices entailed were to rid their land of foreigners. This did not ignore the hidden actors buried within the struggle between two different ideologies; existing within camps were those who simply wanted to gain power and control events. They worked assiduously, lacking any true belief or commitment to a particular political ideology. Yet for many in later generations, including Haney, the war was seen as a family at odds with itself.

As such, the killing of these "yellow men" by others of their same race was all too predictable, as it reflected the divergent views between the Northern and the Southern leaderships. To the temerarious hubris of the bureaucracy of Washington, DC—such as Haney, a card-carrying member—it simply was emblematic of these "immature cultures" being unable to reasonably solve disparate visions of the future. How quickly these same US experts on foreign policy forgot their own nation's history and the tragic Civil War fought in the nineteenth century. This seemingly ancient war also involved family members on different sides of the Confederate-Union vision.

But it was not surprising that Asians killing Asians was not weighted the same as the killing of Americans by those within the US clandestine services. This presumptuous attitude had always been a bright-red line within the CIA that meant deliberately sacrificing Americans to gain operational success was unforgivable, save some existential threat to our nation's future. But it quickly evolved into a series of both articulated and unspoken regulations within America's covert world that even putting American operatives at undue risk was a nonstarter. At its core, for many, this was the acceptance that "yellow men" were simply not worth the same as "white men."

While the aforementioned conceptual and emotional separation between American assets and those composed of yellow men was inherently racist, it nevertheless was a reality that CIA officers inherently understood. Most unquestionably agreed with this tacit perception. Haney certainly did, and he knew the prevailing winds of the CIA culture. Thus, Haney understood that those Vietnamese who were not members of his business ventures were expendable; their disappearance was not likely to trigger the same degree of focused attention as the murder of an American. Finally, supporting the elimination of these independent Asian gangsters who complicated the VC strategic vision to degrade the American war effort went a long way to proving his special value to his VC "business" counterparts.

But despite Haney's inherent worth to the VC—and, in truth, his remarkable track record in furthering the success of the drug trafficking in the South—there is one essential rule in espionage and certainly in war: Never trust, EVER! It was almost without thinking that Duc had Haney followed, investigated, and observed to construct his daily routine. The vital need was to assess his vulnerabilities and to catch him in any inconsistent or incongruent activity that might clearly establish that he was a double agent. And thus, Hanh Nghiem sat in her chair, leaning forward, still within the shadows and not visible to the outside world, and watching the handsome yellow-headed man. Times and activity were carefully noted—and she was but one of a tight nexus of observers that Duc had procured for the đầu vàng.

Haney stood as he exited the car and breathed in the aroma of Vietnam's kitchens, open sewage, and humidity. He had initially rebelled when he found out that his assignment was this fertile green ribbon of land consumed by a war, pitting ideologies and the proxy control of one global power against the other. Long a French colony and now an American frontline in the global resistance against alleged communist adventurism, his assignment to Vietnam had initially struck him as a career-diminishing disaster. But as he explored the opportunities and researched the legacies of those who had served here, he began to reconsider. The more he investigated, the more he saw what his grandfather must have witnessed at the turn of the twentieth century in America. Vietnam was a land much like the younger United States where one could amass enormous wealth, as the laws and regulatory demands had not yet caught up to the creativity of a sublimely corrupt mind.

Eric W. Haney was the third son of a wealthy New York family. Two generations removed from the driving ambition of a young, equally handsome man in comparison to his eventual grandson, Eric's grandfather had excelled in "numbers" but had no college or advanced education. But what Eric's paternal relative had possessed, beyond a valid mastery of basic mathematics, was the ability to understand what wealth respected. He rose through the fledgling banking system in New York City quickly, always dressed in an unimaginative but well-made conservative suit and tie, almost an iconic caricature of the mid-nineteenth to early-twentieth-century "man of stature."

And the man had worked hard to copy the language of his educated affluent rivals that occupied the highest levels of corporate rank. He despised them but also took note of their mannerisms, tastes, and nuanced pronouncements, along with their self-serving habitual perspectives; these, too, were emulated. He took it all in and blended these into his own mannerisms, and he also learned to be falsely deprecating in his routine—a necessary attempt to mask his steadfast simmering hostility to any and all whom life had blessed with either greater material wealth or stature.

And thus, the resulting success of Eric's grandfather was, not unlike Eric himself, found in an ability to modify his appearance to appear as if he had already achieved a privileged status. Hiding his desperate need to climb to success, to attain influence and material prosperity, his grandfather rose steadily within the nascent banking operations of the day. And along the way, he plotted and schemed to injure or at least slow all who might challenge him. The concept of a level playing field was reserved for idiots, or those who could afford such luxuries.

In the end, Eric's grandfather had succeeded, perhaps even beyond his driven ambitions. Robert Eric Haney had left behind nearly twenty-five million dollars that his son, Eric's father, had turned into nearly one hundred million, and now his two older brothers were on their way to making it somewhere in the vicinity of three hundred and fifty million. Their expertise was in law and banking, and in the construction of financial instruments reserved only for the individual and corporate giants exploiting time-sensitive critical information and opportunity not available to anyone outside of the exclusive "club."

Eric was the "additional" son, as he was five years younger than his next oldest male sibling. There were four children, including one girl who was two years behind Eric. Attempting to compete with his two older brothers, who were separated by fourteen months, was a virtual impossibility. They were driven nearly as much as he, yet they were the focus of their father's generous and indulgent support. In truth, had Eric been an only child or even an only son, perhaps even the oldest son, he would have loved his father more than words might have expressed, as his father was a giving, encouraging man. He was also a firm disciplinarian. Unfortunately, these aspects of the older man were almost exclusively reserved for Joseph and Scott, his two oldest boys.

As such, Eric grew up resenting the near adulation lavished on his brothers and yearning to find something that allowed him to shine brighter than either of them. But again, regrettably, this was objectively difficult, as these two were highly driven and quite successful in academics, sports, and then in the business they inherited. Eric was not, however, void of talent. He attended Harvard, following his brothers, and was being prepared for the family business when he came to the conclusion that he was not interested in the role of being the perpetual third wheel in the family dynasty for the remainder of his earthly days. He thus sought out and joined the CIA immediately after graduation from college. There, he rose somewhat more rapidly than his peers, as he spoke French and German and sought a posting in Europe to participate in the clandestine activities that underpinned the Cold War. But it was not to be, and his assignment to Indochina, Vietnam, came as a cold slap in the face.

But as he carefully examined this catastrophe, possibilities arose, and he realized there was a potential in Vietnam that simply would not exist in Europe. For in Europe, many of the senior near-legendary intelligence officers were still rotating in and out of numerous embassies and running assets from the Eastern Bloc. Few wanted the turbulent environment of Indochina and the civil war that existed there among the parties vying for supremacy. So, Eric began to study Vietnam and arrived in country with his eyes open and his moral boundaries absent. He was perfectly configured for the environment.

Eric Haney stood at just over six feet tall with thick blond hair, and while not curly, it was unruly and wavy. As such, he bore a superficial resemblance to an actor in Hollywood who was to make a movie in 1969 about two outlaws, Butch Cassidy and the Sundance Kid. However, Haney had light-blue eyes, the color of faded washed jeans, and blond eyebrows. The chin was similar to this actor's, square and full. His lips were thin, and he had a slightly prominent aquiline nose. Haney was a magnet for women, and he knew it. He used his assets to full advantage, mentally rating his numerous sexual conquests, categorizing each within his private ranking system. He registered no emotion to their reciprocal interests and provided only cold silence to their voiced hopes of establishing any continuance in a relationship. One might have said objectively he was self-absorbed, but this was a marked underestimation of his pathological desire to achieve whatever he sought.

As Haney slowly walked to the rear exit, heavily guarded by four Marine sentries, he contemplated the irony in the fact that he was potentially worried about an Army colonel or a lower-ranking Marine interrupting his very lucrative enterprise. Beyond the flow of money, however, was a more serious concern that this specific Army colonel—Mallroy, yes, that was his name—might expose him as an opportunist and traitor.

He was not yet certain, but in trying to fit the disparate pieces of the puzzle together, he had confirmed that this colonel was making serious headway. Haney was recognizing that Mallroy had begun to absorb and congeal various indicators wherein Mallroy was successfully beginning to understand the players and structural hierarchy of the illicit drug business. Over time, this colonel was certain to unmask the "powers" behind the opaque screen. Haney's exposure would not only cause his lucrative cash flow to dry up but also identify him as the American source providing the North Vietnamese with classified information on American troop deployments. That could not be allowed to occur. Was it possible that he, Haney, could sanction the elimination of this Mallroy?

In pondering this, Haney considered, not for the first time, that this US Army colonel might have employed someone to cause disruption to the rather smooth operations that had previously characterized the VC-North's drug trade. Haney was desperate for information if this was true, and if so, needed to know who specifically this someone (or someones) was. What were the circumstances by which this colonel had engaged this person inter-fering with Haney's successful heroin partnership? Yes, apparently someone or some persons had hit several of the North Vietnamese scout teams, and Haney's business partners were increasingly upset by this activity. But were these Northern scout eliminations connected to the odd-appearing Army colonel?

Haney understood that these outcomes had cast some doubt as to wheth-er Haney himself was really who he said he was. These were wisps of ru-mors and concerns as to who was Haney's true employer. This last concern had been voiced by the leadership of the Viet Cong's heroin trade through General Ang, and the general had conveyed this directly to Haney. The smirk on his face had irritated Haney almost as much as the implicit threat had chilled his bones.

It was becoming more obvious to Haney that he might be forced to sus-pend his prohibition on eliminating Americans. He probably needed to get rid of Mallroy and cut off the head of the snake. Would a sniper, possibly more than one, be rendered ineffective if leaderless? That implied that they were directly connected to Mallroy, but Haney could not be certain of this. Or should he go after the sniper as the optimal solution? Or both Mallroy and the sniper(s)?

The key, of course, was knowing that Mallroy was the one directing the sniper. And if that were the case, it was also possible that there were two or three riflemen that Mallroy was using, and yet killing Mallroy might create such a vacuum as to render any further near-term trouble for the People's Army of Vietnam's scouts moot. But to get rid of Mallroy's sniper or snipers, US servicemen? This might be the equivalent of kicking the hornet's nest.

Haney would have considered such a thought an indication of personal psychiatric instability not ten months ago, but now he was seriously weigh-ing the pros and cons. It was also alarming to Haney that someone had been examining his "dark money" accounts. Haney was no fool; he employed watchers, with generous retainers, at several of the financial and banking in-stitutions in the countries he used to shelter his hidden accounts. His network of sources had alerted him to only a couple of inquires that, on the surface, appeared entirely routine. Yet within the present context, such activity could only mean that someone was sniffing around these accounts. Haney immedi-ately targeted Mallroy as the suspected offender.

He had considered that Mallroy, in his capacity as a senior overseer of

Army intelligence, was simultaneously involved in multiple operations. This colonel was talented and, by reputation, motivated beyond the norm. Both of these characteristics were of concern for Haney. Thus, despite his past prohibition on eliminating Americans, Haney now had to rethink his proscription.

Potentially assisting Haney was the high likelihood that Mallroy simultaneously controlled multiple ongoing clandestine ventures, which meant that any number of parties might potentially be interested in the elimination of this Army spook. The larger Mallroy's operational menu, the more numerous the stakeholders interested in his demise. Was this enough to fully mask Haney's treachery? If so, no one would know that this linkage to Haney was the trigger that ended Mallroy's life.

It was still risky, but risk was part of the game. Yes, this made sense to Haney—his response would be the elimination of the "shadow puppeteer." In his mind, this was no different than the US's very successful efforts to assassinate VC and PAVN's high-ranking officers. In fact, the legendary sniper Carlos Hathcock, aka White Feather, had also been a Marine sniper. Hathcock had killed a PAVN general in hopes of delaying or impeding this talented adversary's activities. So, killing the colonel might not be such a singular act that would prompt a full-scale investigation leading to Haney, any more than this killing of the PAVN general had caused the North to assume a traitor was in their midst. Because Haney surmised that technical advancements rather than direct human intelligence were the weak link exposing the PAVN general's supposed secret location, the North would as well. Haney reasoned that the North had most likely concluded that communications had been intercepted by US electronic eavesdropping.

Unfortunately for him, Haney was wrong. He was unaware that within four days of the PAVN general's assassination by White Feather, a definitive response commenced. The general's personal guards, driver, secretary, and radio communications specialist each suffered hours of torture and then were unceremoniously lined up and shot in the head in front of a full brigade of North Vietnamese regular army troops. The message was simple: no proof beyond a reasonable doubt was required. Lose a leader, and all who might be responsible were eliminated.

Even without this knowledge, Haney knew the American investigative protocols were inherently different, and thus perhaps largely ineffective. A targeted assassination of Mallroy would not immediately point toward participation of a corrupted or traitorous American. US investigators did not adhere to a binary code of guilt absent firm proof of innocence. In contrast, VC or PAVN investigators operated absent due process. Even the opportunity for treachery germinated distrust, yielding suspicion culminating in termination. This was yet another not-so-subtle demarcation as to the disparate commitment to victory that existed between the North Vietnamese and the Americans; there was no forgiveness, only victory. But Haney reasoned that given the twists and turns of this war, it might seem foreseeable that this Mallroy might be targeted. At least this was Haney's logic.

These thoughts occupied Haney's mind as he exited the Ford and slowly walked toward the fortified secure rear entrance of the CIA substation. His rigid enforcement of protecting Americans from assassination or murder in order to avoid the winnowing of his plausible narratives and options for operational success had always been his priority, but now, it was perhaps more important to deal with this Mallroy. Haney's confidential financial source overseeing one of his hidden accounts in Taiwan had warned him that while very minimal activity existed regarding one account, such activity in the form of requests for verification of balances had never previously occurred. Was someone checking?

Haney had immediately suspected Mallroy was using this standard fiscal tool, ensuring accuracy in business transactions, to verify and then potentially expose this dark money account. Haney knew he could not fully explain the existence of this account, or much of his phantom fiscal activity, to his superiors, and he felt that Mallroy was also likely the best suspect who could directly harm movement of product by elimination of PAVN scouting teams. If Haney could take advantage of the multiple dangerous muddy waters that Mallroy functioned in, perhaps the operational pots were numerous enough to sew confusion; so many possibilities, in this case, were advantageous. To anyone investigating Mallroy's death, the spider web of Mallroy's activities clouded any direct line tied directly back to Haney and the narcotics trade. Mallroy's interest in the narcotics trade and those involved would be but one of the many operations this colonel oversaw. Thus, Haney's alleged involvement would likely never surface.

The morning rains had been brief, but the humidity was almost the equivalent of droplets as it hung dense like a blanket of vapor, almost visible. Even while walking slowly and expending minimal effort, Haney was uncomfortable. He had perspiration beading up on his upper lip and the back of his neck as he submitted his briefcase to the guard, who gave its contents a cursory examination. The expensively tailored cream-colored linen suit provided a tolerable attire, but Haney's was still overheated for much of the day. Even the overworked air-conditioning window units were ineffective in cooling his office, and he showered twice a day.

Hanh Nghiem lost sight of him as he ducked into the metal-reinforced security covering extending out from the rear entrance of the building. She noted the time, what he was wearing, and his mannerisms to the extent that she could after such an abbreviated interval. She wondered again why her superiors had asked her to monitor this man's activities and submit her notes to her commander.

Of course, she was unaware that the very concerns that Haney had about eliminating Mallroy were also being voiced in China and the upper echelons of the PAVN war council. The higher-ups wanted to ensure that this đầu vàng was theirs, and theirs alone. They needed to definitively limit Haney's ability to double-cross or harm them, as they, too, were aware that he was talented. Those who worked with him had concluded that Eric Haney enjoyed and actually wanted the money linked to their lucrative heroin trade. He obviously did not desire responsibility or accountability for his actions in assisting the North's war efforts as he prepared to return home; his self-aggrandizement was that of a seasoned veteran of clandestine activity in a war zone. Returning home with hidden unspeakable wealth—real wealth, independent of his family—would allow him a degree of career-enhancing freedom to take risks, to voice his opinions and care less about the responses from ossified bureaucrats running the CIA. He also would never have to ask his brothers for support or financial assistance. Eric would be the one child to have made his way outside of the family's ordained money-making profession. His father might even take notice that his youngest son had actually done something that his older brothers could not. His Indochina experience would thus have been transformative for Eric—personally, and professionally.

The Vietnamese were less intimate or immediate in their concerns, as their focus was strategic. They simply wanted to ensure that Haney could not harm their efforts in the South. The Chinese amplified this strategy but added a significant future option: Beijing's council of leaders had carefully assessed this man and wondered if they might groom someone able to assist them in coming decades as their nation's stature grew to rival this American leviathan. Many now might scoff at such potential self-importance by this Chinese consideration, but then were these Asian technocrats not descendants of the oldest, most venerated source on the successful waging of war: Sun Tzu?

It was to these distant relations of this ancient general and military historian from Wu, of the Zhou kingdom, that careful preparation for decisive victory often meant not having to endure the sacrifices of the actual conflicts associated with war. At times, one could beat an enemy before the first shot was ever fired. Such planning typified the Chinese mind as their nation rocketed from an illiterate agricultural backwater to a twenty-first-century superpower, and such planning also accepted the low probabilities of future success. But the efforts were encouraged, as rarely indeed did such planning succeed beyond even the most ardent believer's dreams.

CHAPTER 8

THE DORMANT VOLCANO

July 22, 1971

Aut neca aut necare.
"Either kill or be killed."

The Mekong Delta, also known as the Nine Dragons River Delta, was a biologist's paradise, home to a remarkably diverse fauna spread out over the southwestern area of Vietnam comprising twelve provinces. This mighty river emptied into the sea through a diverse and ever-changing network of distributaries. Its topography was flat, consisting of flooded fields save for the Black Virgin Mountain standing at 996 meters—an extinct volcano shaped as an almost perfect cinder cone save the northwest side, where its slight bulge and saddle-shaped surface provided a gentle sloping descent. This mountain became the center of Judah Doolin's life for a little more than a month in the wet season of 1971, July through early August, until Mallroy and injuries pulled Doolin out via helicopter almost at the height of the rainy season.

This mountain commanded an uninterrupted view of the entire surrounding landscape, and thus was of both strategic and tactical value and home to the Special Forces Third MIKE Force. It also was the site of some of the most intimate, but less publicized vicious combat in the war. Its legacy was one steeped in the blood of both sides, the heroics of young men from countries with differing political viewpoints thrown together with individualized outcomes so savage as to recreate the horrors of clearing the caves of Japanese warriors at Iwo Jima.

On the night of May 13, 1968, the base was attacked and overrun by Viet Cong. The dead American and VC numbers, while relatively low in comparison to other actions in the war, could not convey the absolute barbarism of the confrontation that characterized the assault and eventual successful retaking of its boundaries. These were very intimate encounters, typified by sharpened steel in the form of handheld bayonets forcefully rammed into Charlie's mouth, puncturing his skull as he in turn discharged his last rounds into his adversary's chest. It was now three years later; the base had held, and American forces still maintained radio and communication assets on the mountain, as its strategic value had not diminished. But it was plagued by sporadic but quite frequent, if not nightly, effective probing of its defenses by VC and, more recently, by elite professional North Vietnamese Special Forces.

Mallroy had previously considered moving Doolin out of the business of tracking heroin shipments for a period of time. The discovery of the pen linked to the CIA station chief and Mallroy's own investigative results were troubling. The colonel's efforts had demonstrated corruption within CIA and South Vietnamese government elements and collaboration with North Vietnamese-run heroin distribution, but Mallroy recognized that there were too many potential weak links in the chain of command that could expose Doolin despite Mallroy's objectively remarkable steps to nearly erase his identity. All it took was one careless error by some junior or even senior officer in the vast military hierarchy. Doolin would not only be exposed, but eliminated by those stakeholders looking to limit the economic fallout from his part in the disruption of the heroin trade. With this in mind, Mallroy finally made his decision and acted quickly.

Mallroy's actions initially triggered some degree of suspicion on Doolin's part, since the colonel had not explained the specifics regarding this fluid and malignant environment. This somewhat cryptic posture by Mallroy regarding the escalating danger and why Doolin might need to pause in his heroin interdiction missions left the young Marine to suspect numerous possible reasons. Most were nefarious. At the time, he considered that Mallroy might be hiding something from him. Was the colonel setting up the young corporal?

But Mallroy accurately read the suspicion creeping up into Doolin and explained to the young Marine just how perilous continuing these missions could be. Mallroy was very nervous that a traitor might strike quickly and kill his young sniper; thus, his hesitation in continuing what was in itself somewhat of a predictable pattern of Doolin's roaming the countryside looking for these VC scouts. The North's leaders were not stupid, and a subtle but effective counter to Mallroy's interdiction was to bait a trap. Using known future locations—as identified through Doolin's own actions, the "lifted" coordinates from killed scouts—the North could harm or terminate Doolin. The PAVN could, in effect, reverse the use of these locales, drawing Doolin to one such location, hiding large numbers of PAVN troops, and flooding the area once Doolin was spotted in the area. Doolin would almost inevitably be killed, or worse, captured.

Mallroy surprised the young Marine by offering him a choice. He could continue these heroin-tracking missions but not engage the enemy, or Doolin could temporarily alter activities with an entirely new mission. Mallroy had realized that Doolin's skills made him immeasurably safer in the wide-open terrain of the highlands or the jungle compared with almost any other environment, but this did not prevent Mallroy from offering to send Doolin back to Hawaii for some phony boondoggle training session that would last forty-five days.

The colonel relented when Doolin rolled his eyes at the mention of some bullshit training and thus offered him one other option. This was not a choice that Mallroy was entirely comfortable with, as it had real risk, but he again understood that such an environment was more likely to provide Doolin with inherent security from any planned assassination. This last, less favorable option was also linked to the fact that Mallroy had to call in a favor from an individual he knew and could request the importance of hiding Doolin. The colonel was assured, to a degree, that at least the leadership was therefore vetted. Of course, Doolin immediately chose this very option: inherent danger or not, and Mallroy's comfort be damned, Doolin chose Black Virgin Mountain.

Doolin recognized quickly that Mallroy was indeed offering him protection of a sort by sending him into a combat area where easy access to clandestine-based harm would be difficult. Further, he understood that Mallroy himself, as well as the enemy, could not easily control or plan specific targeted outcomes in such an area. While not impossible, this harsh environment was enough to quell Doolin's suspicions. While Doolin considered that Mallroy could indeed hire an assassin and murder him in any area at any time, the fact that he was going to a Special Forces base run by people Mallroy personally knew realistically limited Mallroy's potential for nefarious input.

Truthfully, if the colonel wanted to have Doolin killed, he was already a dead man walking. But the somewhat eccentric colonel's actions did not comport with someone who was covering his tracks or setting up his "favorite" sniper. He either was extremely adept at concealing his intentions, incredibly patient, or both. Candidly, thought Doolin, Mallroy was capable of all of the above, but then this was war, and everything was in play. Doolin had to trust his somewhat peculiar army colonel.

Black Virgin was a geological relic, a dormant collection of piled cinder and stone pushed up from the earth's deep magma through fissures reaching the surface and stacking to a height of nearly 3,300 feet. What made it so important was that it was situated in the otherwise flat and flooded plain of the Mekong Delta. It commanded a remarkable view of the surrounding lush, fecund soil, these flooded fields forming large rectangles demarcated by a latticework of raised dirt borders that also served as walking and bicycle paths. Its strategic value as an observation and radio transmission site was simply that it was the only high ground in the entire delta.

The top of this cone-shaped tree- and vine-covered structure was occupied by the Special Forces, and the saddle-shaped hump on the one side was actually a mini-plateau leveled off to make a near-perfect helicopter landing pad for airlifted supplies and manpower. This landing zone was not particularly large and thus required seasoned chopper pilots, not "newbies," to touch down safely. One had to come in either in a straight line and stop before descending or ring the top of the cone and drop to the treetops before the last twenty-five-to-thirty-five-foot descent and a semihard stop. The landing zone, or LZ perimeter area, was heavily fenced with manned dugout reinforced defensive firing positions, or DFPs, and spaced claymores pointing down its sloping topography. The trees and underbrush had been cut back fifty yards to create a clear empty space that ensured optimal targeting of anything attempting to cross through this defensive zone, intended to slow Charlie during any firefight as he tried to get up the hill.

During any such firefight, Doolin still couldn't imagine how these chopper pilots and their crews got in without getting shot to pieces, and indeed more than a few were killed or crashed with predictably life-ending results. In fact, remnants of charred metal flying machines and bent "helo" blades were strewn throughout the dense fertile greenery of the mountain's base. These relics were pushed off the plateau and down the mountain, sliding for variable distances. Some were bunched together, some were cast off, all representing individual broken memorials, alone and silent—a testament to man's determination to assist another in harm's way.

The major problem was that while the American forces occupied and commanded the top of the mountain, Charlie occupied the bottom, especially when the sun went down. The middle areas were contested on a nightly basis and had been for nearly five years. Plus, what US troops *and* Charlie knew was that the mountain was riddled with caves and tunnels. So much so that during one of the near-cataclysmic almost successful VC attempts at overrunning the camp a second time, enemy heads popped out of spider holes, the terminal ends of enemy tunnels. Charlie had burrowed deep into the mountain and came up within the American camp.

This resulted in a counterattack that could only be described as something from Dante's *Inferno*. Aviation and cooking fuel were poured into the spider holes, sloshing down into the burrowed caves before flare guns were fired into the partially sealed openings, causing erupting plumes of fire reaching fifteen to thirty feet in the air. The Fourth of July had come to Vietnam, but these were not innocuous store-bought Roman candles; they were gasoline-petroleum fuel explosions shooting up from the ground, as if a dragon's breath from childhood nightmares had returned to claim the village maiden.

The first American to discharge his flare directly into a gasoline-soaked cylindrical hole during the height of one of these fights for control of the base demonstrated ingenuity in the face of overwhelming enemy numbers. He also immolated himself, as the backblast of fire instantly roasted him alive. The end result was a pockmarked lunar surface throughout the perimeter, including scorched and now-sealed earthen excoriations within the confines of the base proper. This, along with the permanent stench of gasoline, JP-40, and cooked Homo sapiens, clung to the base as a reminder of what was, and what was to be.

It was into this lush "vacation" spot that Doolin arrived as a single passenger on a HU-1A, dropped along with several crates of ammunition on a humid morning on July 22, 1971. He had long been hardened to the costs of war, or so he thought, being by himself in the bush and watching the daily killing and reciprocating in kind. But he had not visited this outpost of Special Forces, chosen to defend this strategically valued base, and now found himself looking into the eyes of dead men. Hollowed-out faces, thin bodies, noses discharging a thin clear mucous, with skin sun-baked but tallowed, insect-bitten with crusting scabs. Many had straggly hair that was anything but regulation, and several sported ponytails. It was almost as if

Doolin had entered a camp of zombies. But what he realized almost instantly was that there were camps within this camp. These guys—assigned here against what they thought was fair or right—made up the initial group that Doolin encountered as he exited the chopper.

Doolin jumped down from the side door just in front of the mounted 7.62mm M134 Miniguns, one on either side. The derivative models of the UH-1, along with their affectionate monikers—frogs, hogs, guns, and slicks—did not belie their design as perfected killing machines that fly. No other symbol came to represent the American experience in Vietnam more than these nine thousand or so flying machines made by Bell Helicopter.

One of the gunners, with crooked teeth and a wad of tobacco tucked into his cheek, lifted his chin, suggesting Doolin get away from the "bird" as he initially crouched beside it, blades spinning over his head. Taking the gunner's advice, Doolin headed quickly out of the downdraft, just in case the Bell UH-1, affectionately called Slicky-1, was hit and the blades became a massive shearing tool to everything within its radius. Doolin had his rifle with him, equipped with scope and silencer, and this immediately drew twelve pairs of eyes. They locked on to him as he crouched and scurried away from the whirling beast.

The Huey lifted up and away, veering sharply when it was less than forty feet off the pad. Doolin was buffeted by the rotor-created air blast as it pushed everything toward the ground, and as he watched the bird move away, Doolin caught several of the men staring at him. The "helo" moved rapidly, creating distance from the LZ before accelerating directly out over the delta, randomly changing course every two to five seconds while putting distance between it and the "cone." Doolin turned his head back toward the group of men and shouted a question at the nearest guy. "Where's our XO?"

He was met by a combination of silence linked to an intense inspection of him and his rifle. Doolin had worn his combat camouflage uniform, registering his name and rank as corporal. Now, he even wore dog tags. Mallroy had said it was important to be within all regulations starting out on this mini-tour to ensure that there was no gossip regarding a sniper who was not wearing rank or identification. Thus, they would deprive prying eyes and ears any clues as to who Doolin was and prevent them from connecting any dots as to his past escapades.

Doolin waited, but the silence continued. He shrugged and moved off the LZ and up the mountain, following one of several well-worn footpaths.

As he neared the first set of buildings near the top of the cinder mountain, Doolin could see the change in topography, and the view was actually spectacular. In all directions, the flooded fields were being cultivated by men and women bent over, pant legs rolled up to mid-thigh, wide-brimmed cone-like straw bonnets or sunhats covering their heads and necks as they worked the fields. His attention also increased in response to the change in appearance of the uniformed troops coming toward him; almost all were clean-shaven. For a remote base on top of a mountain, these folks appeared to have that "military bearing" that troops had drilled into them during the first weeks in the Corps.

Doolin acknowledged an approaching large man over six feet three, around Judah's height but much broader in the chest, with powerfully thick forearms bearing tattoos of snakes coming out of human skulls. His shaved head and face fit his intense small nearly black eyes, his uniform well-fitting, wrinkled but clean. He eyed Doolin warily, registering recognition.

"Sergeant?" Doolin asked. "I was told to report to the XO."

He smiled. "Follow me. You are a bit of a mystery. It's Doolin, right? You suddenly popping out of nowhere to join our little paradise here on the hill. What did you do, really piss someone off? Fuck the colonel's dog?"

"No, sir. Asked for it."

His head immediately whipped around, his eyes conveying disbelief and genuine surprise. His focused stare registered concern, confusion, and almost a trace of gathering apprehension. Not quite fear, but something close had crept into those coal-black eyes. It was the look of an experienced warrior, an uncomfortable look—a look found in the muted seconds of absolute silence immediately before anticipated combat actually began. The look of uneasy expectation.

Doolin was immediately on guard, but steadied himself and stated evenly, "Did I make the wrong choice, Sergeant?"

His eyes softened a bit. "Son, I'm not sure. We don't get many requested transfers … well, more like that has never happened before. So, I don't know if this is a good omen, or the beginning of a shitstorm." His smile partially returned, although traces of concern lingered. "Come on, I'll get you to the XO."

They walked a short distance to a half-sunken bunker structure, its walls reinforced by sandbags and concertina. This was a wire used as a barrier composed of numerous small knifelike blades intertwined in the wire, and it was wrapped around the entire structure save the step-down entry into the main room. From the outside as Doolin approached, the roof was a foot below his chin and heavily reinforced with logs, some standing upright three to four feet high. More sandbags with additional concertina were layered across the roof, making any attempt to run over it impossible. Jumping across the structure would challenge a cheetah at full speed. The roof of manmade impediments would prevent suicide bombers or tossed packs of explosives from transferring the full force of a blast directly into the sheets of corrugated metal covering the structure.

Where windows were supposed to be, there were slits of open space; some were covered with the same heavy corrugated steel slats. There were mounds of dirt, rather large collections of rock, and cinder and soil at seemingly random intervals spaced along the perimeter of the clearing that housed the fortified structure. For the guys who lived in these, life resembled that of their Neolithic cave-dweller ancestors. Doolin thought that he really had screwed up this time. The officers were living underground, and Doolin wondered what he, a lower-ranking enlisted, could expect to experience. But it was for only six weeks, he told himself, and anything could be endured for six weeks. That is, of course, assuming he didn't get KIA in the first night of probing enemy fire.

But then that was why he was here: to pick out a place each night and probe the middle of the hill for unwanted guests in the space between the American-held base and the flat enemy-controlled rice fields. The command, while happy that they finally had the sniper they had requested, ironically lost some of this enthusiasm when they realized Doolin had requested the base. They became immediately suspicious of him; why would anyone have *asked* to come to this place? And Doolin almost regretfully grinned internally, as he could not really disagree with their collective logic!

As Doolin walked down into the half-sunken room, he saw immediately where the mounds of ecological debris deposited seemingly randomly outside the structure had originated. Inside, this central room was filled with roughly constructed plywood tables serving as work desks; it was but a transition point into several deeper tunnels that ran directly into the mountain. Each was large enough for a man to pass through, if willing to crouch a bit, and emptied into other rooms, smaller but hidden completely under the earth.

The cinder cone was similar to a pyramid of ancient Egypt with cut-out passages leading to a variety of rooms and antechambers, only here, Army engineers had designed them as a semicircle of spokes on a wheel. The spokes directed into the mountain proper so that during an attack, if this larger outer room was threatened, the other rooms and their inhabitants might survive intact. And looking more closely, Doolin was surprised to note that a staff sergeant entering one tunnel came out of another completely separate passage, confirming that the deeply seated rooms within the mountain were also interconnected. The Americans in effect were duplicating the infamous tunnel systems of the Viet Cong.

The XO, part the Army Special Forces, a Major Stein stepped from behind a plywood table and motioned for Doolin to approach. Doolin's eyes quickly grew accustomed to the reduced light coming from the slats and reflected from cage-covered bulbs lining the passages. An electric fan dispersed damp, earthen-scented air. The odor of the room was not that different from what Doolin had previously experienced: a combination of a freshly dug grave and an unclean toilet, too many male bodies having gone unbathed, and the ancient, heavy scent of the cinder-laden dead volcano.

The major had short light-colored hair and a deep scar along his right cheek, dropping from the corner of his right eye and curving like a reverse letter *C* that ended at the edge of his jaw. It was purple, meaning it was not that old, and Doolin knew looking at it that his face would likely require some of that fancy plastic surgery eventually, as there were already little tendrils of scar tissue pulling at the edges, distorting the smooth curve of the healed larger wound. The net effect was an altering of the natural alignment of the right corner of his mouth, the beginning of a wicked clown's smile. But his eyes, even in the darkened room, conveyed confidence and a calm acceptance of whatever awaited him, not to mention curiosity. Why was Doolin here, and why voluntarily?

He offered, "This is a Special Forces base, son. We welcome you to our humble abode."

"Thank you, sir."

"Why?"

"Why, sir?" Doolin asked.

Immediately after speaking, he knew what the major wanted to know, but before Doolin could add his answer, Stein asked, "Why us, Doolin?"

"I thought I might help, sir."

"Indeed, you may, actually. You are needed, soldier . . . I mean, Marine."

He glanced briefly at his two companions. "We have unwanted visitors almost every night, and these visitations have grown both in frequency and violence. Most of us feel they are fucking planning something, and I would like to toss a new piece of shit into their plans, and that is actually you!" He smiled. "That is not to say you are shit, Marine, but I hope they view you as equally unwelcome."

"I get you, sir."

"Yes, I hope you do." He glanced at Doolin's rifle, the modifications hidden to all but the most experienced eye. He surprised Doolin by pointing out one immediately. "Does the end-barrel notch for the suppressor hinder accuracy?"

"Not within four hundred seventy-five yards, sir."

"Really? I'd have thought … well, I gather from my end that guys hate those damn things."

"I made my own, sir."

And with this statement Stein raised his eyes, lifting them up from the visual inspection of Doolin's silencer to meet the gaze of the young sniper. They shared a silent visual scrutiny of each other, and then Stein slowly nodded his head. Perhaps an acknowledgment of professional respect, perhaps an indication that a decision had been reached.

"Well, folks,"—he turned toward his two subordinates—"we may have someone here who actually might help us."

He then did something unexpected—he turned to one of the tunnels and motioned for Doolin alone to accompany him. As he crossed the earthen floor to the mouth of the passageway, he turned his head and tossed back, "You folks continue. I'll be back shortly."

The two men each individually crouched, entering the tunnel, and moved into a small but surprisingly comfortable subterranean room thirteen feet from the main bunker just exited. Major Stein again looked Doolin over in the stark light provided by the hanging naked bulbs and spoke softly but deliberately.

"I'm not in the habit of speaking informally to enlisted, you understand, Marine," he began. "But I know Mallroy from stateside, three years ago, Joint Command. He is good, and he has endorsed you." He could see Doolin's genuine surprise and added, "Yes, Corporal Doolin, he endorsed you almost *too* much. He thinks you are one of the good guys, and talented." He looked down at his boots and said, "It seems he would like you to live, to get past this shit," as his left arm made a sweeping semicircular motion, conveying the totality of their current situation.

Doolin was nearly holding his breath, fascinated at the paradigm that had leapt into his young brain. Learn special skills, and you are a sought-after commodity. It was the first time he had ever articulated this reality; it was a meaningful moment in time, and its message would serve him from this point forward. But he was also waiting for the other shoe to drop, which it then did.

"Corporal, Mallroy has asked me to let you do your thing, absent my or anyone's interference. That I would seriously entertain such a bizarre request is either a sign that I'm quickly becoming a proverbial shit-for-brains or that I think he trusts you, and since I trust him—well, it's done. Don't make me regret this, son, and you do not need to answer.

"Second, the guys down on the pad are barely controllable. Most want out, most hate me, and most might turn around and fire into our compound, not out at the enemy, if given half a chance. So, don't expect any help, assistance, or support from them. Watch your back around them. Finally, tell me what you need. I'll likely laugh in your face, but who knows, I may be able to help. By the way, they"— he pointed back to the main room—"are working on the defensive mission to secure our base during attack. A new plan, or more realistically, a modification of an existing one. Dismissed, Corporal."

Doolin got up, standing as straight as he could with the low ceilings, and left the bunker. It was obvious to him that the ragged group of misfits down at the pad were smoking reefer. More than smoking, they were living it; some were in a constant state of being stoned, and this likely led to the fall in discipline, morale, and quality of soldiering. But Doolin did recognize in his exchanges over the next week that not all were weirdos. Most were quiet, some hid under the veneer of being an oddball, but all were still alert, aware, and adherent to a semblance of military discipline, if only for improved self-preservation. Being stoned sometimes just took the fear away.

The young sniper discovered this because he began his activity immediately after Stein had dismissed him. Doolin took one of the four footpaths down to the LZ and started examining the terrain, looking for spots where he could blend into the rock-wood montage found on the mountain's rising slopes. There were numerous irregular outcroppings of rock, ledges, and pointed half-buried gray-and-black stone pseudo-cliffs that would provide excellent cover if he was able to insert himself into the underside of these formations. The bushes or scrub brush debris facing down the hill would further conceal him, and in addition, scattered tropical copses rose at various heights and densities to further screen him from prying eyes. But many of the best areas were actually outside the base proper and likely would be vulnerable to quickly overwhelming enemy numbers if he got unlucky.

But as Doolin inspected the area, exploring with movement just outside of the perimeter fortifications, a young skinny Army private popped his head up from a sandbag-reinforced firing position. "Careful, you're close to the mines."

Doolin immediately froze in place.

"You're OK where you are, but don't go any further to your right."

Doolin slowly turned his head toward him and asked, "How would I get up there?" pointing to his first good position overseeing the barren area, a strip of cut-back tropical growth serving as a defensive perimeter.

"Let me show you."

"I'm OK, but sure, thanks. Thanks a lot."

He came toward Doolin with his helmet and flak jacket on, no shirt under it, and a dull silver chain carrying a small cross hung around his neck. His M16 was in his left hand and his right was used for balance as he climbed around the firing position fortifications and up the path to meet Doolin. The man strode up with short and sandy cropped light-brown hair, blue eyes, and acne extending over his forehead and chin. His teeth revealed a slight overbite; his thin lips and slightly hooked nose gave him the appearance of being older than he was, except for the acne and traces of a desired mustache.

The stranger extended his hand, which Doolin took immediately and vigorously shook. "Hey, I'm Jason Bird. Call me Tucker."

"Hey, Tucker."

"Why are you here?" he asked, and Doolin decided that he would control the information flow to the rest of the troops through Tucker. The simple truth, or at least portions of the truth, was in order.

"Like I told your Major Stein, I was told you might need some additional support. Thought I could help. Is that true?"

"You bet it is. Shit, every night Charlie wants to get his fingers into our business and do damage. One by one folks are getting zapped, and we usually get one or two of them, but it's not an even trade, and it shouldn't be that they get the better. We're getting a little thin with our patience, if you can understand that."

"Yeah, I do."

"Yeah, the guys are spooked. It gets fucking crazy here at night sometimes. Guys are freaked 'cause we watch the zone—you know the area," he said as he pointed to the cut-back defensive strip. "And one second we're clear, the next we got two gooks coming across real low. So, we fire on them and perhaps get one, but then they coordinate and concentrate heavy fire on one position, often zapping one of our guys. Fuckers. So it's like we're just waiting for our turn, sort of."

Doolin watched him grab the barrel of his M16 and twist his hand around it in a worried writhing motion.

"Really think you could help?"

"Yes, I do," Doolin answered.

"OK, what the hell, you got my vote. What do you need ... hey, what's your name, man?"

"Doolin. Just Doolin."

"OK, Doolin, what's the deal?"

"I'm going to see you guys tonight, around oh seven hundred, and move into one of three positions, all above you and to your left. Try not to shoot over there or you may kill me, OK?" Doolin said with a wink.

Tucker loved it and laughed. He turned to his buddy in the DFP, a guy named Sebastian Lopez, and said, "You hear that, Lopez? Can't shoot over there or you will kill our fucking protection!" He laughed again and so did Lopez, a young Latino kid who was smiling at everything Tucker said.

Some guys actually just hit it off, just as certain couples matched for personalities or their sense of humor. One could not actually be sure of what the variable was, but these two guys were like long-lost brothers, and while they couldn't have come from more disparate backgrounds, they actually were well suited for each other and had become pretty close during their weeks on the mountain.

Tucker responded, "Yeah, OK, got it. Hey, want a beer?"

"Can I take a rain check? Want to get situated." Doolin needed to address his gear and get ready for tonight, for without mentioning this to Tucker, Doolin sensed there was something in the air. Something evil, a menace, and when the sun went down it would be unleashed.

"Sure, catch you later."

"Thanks, Tucker. See you in a bit."

Doolin wandered back up the hill using the footpath from the LZ closest to where he had originally found the first site of opportunity. But suddenly, for no reason other than not wanting to be predictable, even to himself, he shifted to the next one a bit higher with a better view of the barren strip. In truth, this defensive perimeter around the LZ provided only a modicum of security for the young guys in the fortifications that were sandbag-reinforced firing positions. These numbered twelve and extended around the LZ. The mountain itself started to rise immediately in back of these DFPs so that the LZ plateau became a steep slope less than twenty-five yards behind them. An additional eight were up on the mountaintop so that the troops situated lower, near the LZ, did not get hit from the back side, allowing enemy attackers to overrun them.

The very top provided a little of its own natural barrier, as the thinned-out ecological growth near the apex served to expose anyone but still required a similar cutback of some vegetation as was done down at the LZ. In like fashion, the area was reinforced with claymores, concertina, and mines, which might not prevent a full-scale attack from a company or an enemy brigade, but the losses would be extreme. Thus, Charlie must have judged it adequate strategically to harass the Americans each night in hopes of eventually making the cost associated with the defense of this geologic oddity too high, forcing eventual abandonment.

Doolin later discovered that the back side of the base had a brand-new device that ultimately would be found on the shelves of all hunting stores in America some thirty-five to forty years later. Since the potential harm from the enemy approaching from the rear of the dormant cinder cone was judged to be much more difficult due to the steepness of the rock-faced cliffs, fewer men were deployed at the apex overlooking the near vertical terrain. Yet, because there were fewer men, potential successful incursion from this side immediately created more of an existential threat, as the enemy would be hitting the Americans from their vulnerable back side.

To this effect, the Special Forces had employed these electronic devices and found that they were actually remarkably effective. Very similar to a camera, only using early infrared technology, they cast a narrow invisible light beam across a segment of ground to a receiver that is a tiny bulb-like structure. Each of the components, the transmitter and the receiver of the infrared light, was tiny and could be attached to a tree by a strap. If the light beam was broken, it registered an alarm to those monitoring, providing sufficient warning.

As it turned out, this was one of many technological advancements that occurred during the sixties with military applications that eventually made their way to the consumer market in peace time. These things were the forerunners of various models of popular hunter cameras that increasingly populated patches of fields or forests for detection of game. The seminal development during the 1960s was the miniaturization of these devices. Ultimately, taking them out of laboratories where researchers had long appreciated the phenomenon of interrupting or "breaking" a light beam allowed it to be quantified and provide contextual data useful under a variety of circumstances.

But instead of taking up the space of an entire laboratory room in the basement of some university, the devices now were slender, compact 9x6-inch boxes, battery powered, and could be easily strapped to a bamboo trunk. Containing a beam aimed at the receiver ten feet away, they provided 24/7 monitoring of an uninhabited but potential infiltrative portal. These devices—coupled to a few DFPs strategically positioned on the back side, each with two-man teams—created a level of redundancy that safeguarded this sector. The belief was that this was adequate protection for the steeper back side of the mountain.

Each of the DFPs was fortified on the sides by sandbags and reinforced corrugated steel slats, and these provided the sleeping quarters for the guys. They often enjoyed a gentle breeze climbing up from the surrounding delta, holding the mosquitoes and flies at bay. Some of the DFPs had three men, though most had two, and each man took shifts watching the perimeter of the LZ.

It was 18:30 before Doolin had actually unpacked his gear in a small triangular wedge-shaped natural fissure in the cliff's face twenty-seven feet above the LZ, directly overlooking the six o'clock end of the semicircle of DFPs. He was positioned above the nearest "foot" of a letter *C*, with the body of the letter composing the perimeter line of the evenly spaced positions of the DFPs. The area within the perimeter was the actual LZ and the very top of this flattened letter *C* was somewhat elongated, bending with the curve of the mountain. Doolin's view of the last three DFPs was thus limited due to the natural conical shape of this dormant volcano. He had been told that two of these last three DFPs apparently had heavy machine guns aimed directly down the slope of the cinder mountain.

This natural triangular wedge in the massive stone was, in fact, a crevice and was bordered by a separate large ancient boulder. It jutted out two feet from the natural contour of the cliff's surface and was shaped like the bow of a modern ship of war, allowing Doolin to crawl out along its surface just enough and view the LZ and surrounding area with clear lines of sight. He spent some time checking over his rifle and ammunition with extra time allotted to ensure that his scope and night vision were operational. He then swallowed some candy bars after some lightly salted fish, spitting out a few bones, and Doolin was ready to tuck himself into his new nest.

Doolin settled in, taking time to arrange smooth rocks along with natural foliage that would almost completely eliminate any visual identification of him, especially since the enemy would have to look up at a rather steep angle to even see his nest. He'd chosen well, for this was a crevice that extended laterally into a rock formation almost too narrow to accommodate the thickness of his torso's front-to-rear dimensions as he lifted up on his elbows and positioned his rifle next to his right cheek. But Doolin had just enough room, as long as he didn't bring his head up too quickly within the enclosure. His head would be protected during a firefight, but he could still emerge to assess the surroundings and perform his skills as needed.

He sheepishly considered that staying within the geometry of this jagged scar in the rock required that he not lift his head too quickly in the chaos of combat, or else he would suffer a rather significant contusion to his skull. It would be quite a spectacle to "introduce" himself to his fellow soldiers on this rock pile by knocking himself out in the first minutes of combat. He was certain they wouldn't approve, although they might be entertained! But contemplating his survival, he realized he could rapidly slide back into this stone enclosure to protect himself; Doolin just wanted to ensure this "fortuitous" sliced defect in the mountain's surface wasn't going to also serve as his grave. He would take his chances as to whether he would be impressing his newfound colleagues or embarrassing himself; only time would tell.

Looking up, sideways, or down, Doolin felt confident that he was invisible. The end of his rifle barrel was hanging outside of the natural boundary and outline of the cinder mountain, but the foliage would mask it almost completely. It was rather obvious no one could see him. The left side of his body was snug against the cool stone surface; the right was ringed with small irregular rocks but was open. He had an excellent view of at least two-thirds of the cut-back barren perimeter and an even better view of the down-sloping forested area beyond the perimeter's distant boundary.

Doolin had a large plastic bottle with him for urine, a second larger bottle containing his water, and he had packed three candy bars and dried lightly salted fish wrapped in rice paper in an inside pocket. Now he waited, and as the sun went down, slowly he began a systematic scan of each sector. The purple and pink wisps of cirrus clouds set against the fading robin's-egg-blue sky provided a magnificent reflected beauty seen on the surface of distant flooded rice paddies. The rich, deep brown and lush green geometric earthen boundaries of each suggested a West Virginian quilt, a natural tapestry. Birds circled above, catching the warm updrafts of heated air, gliding effortlessly, rising and falling, before banking and disappearing, their paths now below Doolin as they moved out along the twisted path of the Mekong River. It was at times like this, as he prepared himself and his set of skills perfected over months of his journey through this beautiful land, that Doolin directly asked God, "Why?" No answer was yet forthcoming.

He settled in for a long night, his first here on the mountain, and knew there was going to be a problem. The night would be black; the lunar orb for the new month had yet to start. It was a night for mischief, a night absent light, a night cloaking movement. The last remnants of sun's fading rays left the area at 21:10.

At 22:45, Doolin's night scope picked up movement 275 yards from his position and 70 yards beyond the farthest perimeter fence down the hill. Doolin had been told that any movement beyond the cut-back area was a viable target; American troops were not out there, and anybody knowing anything, including surrounding villagers, would not innocently traverse this area. They had been warned not to walk anywhere on the mountain at night. He waited, however, as he wanted to see how good this person was or if it might in fact be an animal. Doolin did not have to wait for long, as soon the outline of a hardened cloth-covered pith helmet came into view.

Oh God, no! His bowels froze; his pulse accelerated rapidly. Doolin suddenly had visual confirmation that this helmet was the head of a snake-like formation with seven, eight, or even ten more helmets behind him—and this column was one of perhaps a dozen. All were moving slowly, crouched or squatting with crab-like movements, but advancing toward the perimeter fence. They were holding rifles—AK-47s—with their characteristic banana-shaped clips, long tubelike structures with a handle midway or so between the ends, and a distinctive pinecone-shaped attachment with a formed nipple at its end: rocket-propelled grenades.

Shit! Immediately, Doolin's brain screamed, *This is the leading edge of a huge attack formation!* While he wanted and needed to get this information to the guys down there at the LZ and the command, Doolin also knew that he had no time, and the optimal expenditure of his energy was in killing the enemy advancing on their positions. He had already made the mistake of not being able to effectively communicate with his side; this was going to prove costly, but in retrospect, one additional but fortuitous "mistake" was that he had nearly all his ammunition with him in two separate backpacks, nearly four hundred rounds. Normally he traveled light when he was on the move, with only fifty to seventy-five rounds. He instantly made a decision that he was not moving from his perch—he was going to live or die here tonight in dealing with what appeared to be a rather serious attack force. As he mouthed a silent curse, Doolin also became remarkably calm, the paradox he had felt often just before decisive action.

Doolin refocused, aimed, and quickly let the first round fly almost before he was ready, but he had been trained well. The round connected with the intended second man in the line, entering just above the left eye, piercing his skull and cutting a jagged path though his cerebral cortex that exploded out the posterior half of his head before entering his buddy's shoulder. This second victim let out a muffled cry; the first dropped without a sound, and Doolin realized that he needed these bad guys to make noise, an alert to the Americans in the DFPs.

He then focused his second-round firing into the upper leg of another man moving quickly to the front, and the round hit its mark. It tore through his femur, splintering the bone into minute fragments and vaporizing a connecting segment of his femoralis profunda before deforming it, yet carrying enough energy to burst through to his inner thigh. A raw mass of tangled, shredded meat spewing a ruby liquid instantly replaced his smooth, muscle-laden thigh, and he screamed involuntarily. A split second later shouts, screams, and tracers filled the night.

A blast filled the black evening sky with orange-white light originating from the fortified perimeter. Then the claymores started going off, and silhouetted against the moments of explosive white light and force were portions of bodies flying into the air and the shocked screams of young men. What little Vietnamese Doolin understood did not obscure a terrified scream of "*Cha!*" or "Father!" and a body absent a left arm and on fire soon staggered and fell in plain view near the fence. Doolin could intermittently make out the crackle of his burning flesh and was certain the soldier's horrific demise caused satisfaction in young, terrified eyes on the US side of the barrier.

Doolin closed his eyes, looking through his night scope to avoid momentary blindness, and as the claymore activity diminished, he looked again and found a runner behind a man crouched on the perimeter. He was carrying a long tube and Doolin aimed chest-high, center mass, and squeezed his metal hook. The rifle kicked slightly as the gas expelled. The Vietnamese took but a half step and then stumbled. As he fell forward, the tube and the pinecone-shaped explosive grenade scraped the ground and his hand lost control, inadvertently pulling the trigger. A blinding light instantly erupted, and although relatively small, Doolin again closed his eyes. Reopening them, he saw remnants of a uniform; legs severed above the knees lay on the ground. They had remained aligned, almost in parallel, but lay alone, the hips, torso, and arms gone. Curling smoke rose from a small basketball-sized divot in the ground.

Three runners in pith helmets streaked across the cutback, reached the first fortified firing position, and in a beautifully choreographed moment, two fired their clips into the steel-sided sandbag structure while the other tossed in a satchel. Doolin got the lead man, again center mass mid-chest, who went down after a short burst from his AK-47. A moment later, the fortified position vanished in a large fireball with its sand, stones, and metal debris raining down on the LZ. This tactic was as serious as it was successful, and Doolin wanted to prevent any repeat performance. He removed his suppressor; there was little use for it other than reducing the end-barrel flame and, in doing so, providing a bit of additional cloaking of his activities. Someone down there was calmly viewing the progress of this fight, and a repetitive telltale flashing light from Doolin's rifle would ultimately invite a response, but this was a risk Doolin had to accept. His troops needed his best effort, and it was needed NOW.

Next, he concentrated his rounds on the satchel carriers. Immediately from the corner sector came two runners, one with an AK-47, the other holding a large package and pulling on the detonation cord immediately behind him. A single round into the base of his neck and he collapsed and rolled a single time, the dropped charge stopping his movement. His companion must have felt his fall, and he in turn stopped and reached for the satchel. Within an instant a large white-yellow light ignited the entire area, momentarily turning night into day, and then it was black again, but the concussive shockwaves were unexpectedly vicious. Through Doolin's night scope he saw no bodies—just a five-foot-wide hole in the ground, smoke slowly pouring out from its base and then disappearing as it caught the night breeze.

Again, another duo sprinted through the damaged perimeter fence toward the fortification situated nearest the opening of one of the footpaths. As the carrier slowed and struck a football quarterback's pose, Doolin's bullet caught him just above the sternal notch, severing his spine as it plowed through his trachea and superior vena cava. He instantly fell back, limp, and dropped the satchel, a telling vapor curling from its fuse; it hit the ground. A second later, another large red-yellow light illuminated the area.

Doolin sought out other targets and successfully hit many without too much trouble, but gradually the shots became more difficult and opportunities began to fade. Immediately, he realized that someone on the other side must have given the order to pull back. The unexpected failures of these suicide satchel carriers surely perplexed their side, and they wanted to study and counter this novel development. Doolin couldn't help himself; he smiled, as he knew that their failure was in large part his doing, but his smile was also a rueful acknowledgment that Charlie would be focused on ending his contribution to the defense of the Special Forces MIKE Force.

Both sides were nineteen minutes into the fight, and then suddenly it was over. Doolin fired five or perhaps seven more rounds and probably hit four enemy troops. Three were likely instant kills; one might have lived but would never walk again. Through the battle he had fired rapidly but always with purpose, likely hitting 60 to 70 percent of his targets, and used seventy-eight rounds; he had arranged his ammo to allow instant access and accurate counting. Of course, that also meant that forty-nine to fifty-five souls had departed this life based on his set of skills. Doolin had, however, unquestionably saved American lives. Either way, it was done.

Seven minutes later, "Puff, the Magic Dragon" appeared over the delta and emptied 6,200 rounds into the base of the mountain below. A converted C-130 Hercules cargo fixed-wing aircraft, this machine was fitted with a surprise package that included 20mm rotary autocannons, and its 40mm Bofors cannon configuration detected departing unfriendlies and successfully targeted them. The American inspection at dawn revealed the tangled wreckage of human bodies trying to exit the battle area. The rising stench of dead and decomposing flesh was now beginning to attract indigenous wildlife, and of course the insects were already nesting in remnant body parts. The

Americans knew that Charlie would be back, but it would likely be a longer interval than the Vietnamese had originally planned.

MIKE Force's leadership conservatively estimated that nearly 197 enemies were lost that night in nineteen minutes of combat. But the vast majority of their losses, perhaps 115 to 120, had been secondary to the prompt arrival of Puff, which, they later found out, had been up in the sky monitoring frequencies when their call for assistance originated. This accounted for its rapid response, much faster than Charlie had anticipated, and because the VC had not successfully overrun the camp, Puff was free to indiscriminately unleash its terror into the base of the mountain since no Americans were exiting the playing field.

As Doolin climbed the scarred footpath back up to the perimeter fencing of the base, careful to follow the engineer's well-marked path through the mines and newly implanted claymores, he found the major standing at the site of the demolished fortification. American losses were remarkably low; they had counted a mere seven KIA with sixteen wounded, only two of which were serious and they were already gone, lifted out earlier by medevac UH-1 teams. Unfortunately, one of the seven was Tucker, caught in a sweeping crossfire of AK-47 rounds as he stood his ground and stopped three VC from entering the LZ. A single round had entered his neck, and crawling back toward protective cover, he had died alone, his blood soaking the ground beneath him.

And while Doolin couldn't have known the full extent immediately, his buddy Lopez was devastated by the loss of his friend. He sat in the shade of the partially damaged DFP steel-slatted structure with his knees tucked to his chest and his arms wrapped around his legs. His dirt-covered face was lined with furrows of skin washed clean from the downpour of tears. He sat quietly, motionless, staring off into the distance, a St. Christopher medal previously owned by Tucker held in his white-knuckled hands. He was oblivious to his surroundings, having mentally retreated into a compartmentalized sorrow that immobilized him both physically and emotionally.

Doolin could not know yet that Lopez would eventually play a meaningful role in his life some years later. But as Doolin looked over to Tucker's friend, he saw the profound emptiness in Lopez's eyes, the sadness and the grief that follows meaningful loss. For two kids thrown together in the middle of a strategic political struggle between nations, they had shared an instant and natural bond of friendship: easy, light, and fun. But it was forged on a cinder cone in the rural desolation of Vietnam, 8,400 miles from their respective homes. They had shared mutual enjoyment of each other, even affection. Nothing physical, but something much more—the excitement for and interest in another person. They liked each other and respected each other because somehow, it fit. And now Tucker was gone.

Doolin would spend some time with Lopez over the next several weeks, slowly going over the events and emphasizing the young man's duty to carry on, minimizing the guilt of his survival and slowly trying to assist as he decided whether to even attempt to rebuild his life. He did eventually carry on. He never lost his effectiveness as a soldier, but all of it was without enthusiasm; his own life's energy had temporarily, perhaps permanently, been altered by the sudden death of his friend.

Such a profound need for philosophical adaptation and soul-searching at such a young age, directly brought about because some Washington, DC, bureaucrat had demanded that this place was militarily important. One understood why some of the older guys never developed close relationships; they were terrified of grief, both the process itself and the self-harm or real destruction that it might cause. Doolin also needed to tend to his fragile psyche to recover from his trained effectiveness as a killer of other humans. He needed to face his mother's image, and until he did and could answer for his actions, Doolin could not reasonably give support to Lopez; his spiritual vessel of empathy was empty.

Doolin stopped to survey the cutback area, the site of the most intense activity only ten hours ago. He had long wondered what emotions had been felt over the centuries while standing on a battlefield, minutes to hours after the fact. The bodies being cleared but still present, the air uncommonly still, the noise of the jungle and fields uncannily and respectfully silent. Did others feel as he did now?

Doolin imagined being connecting with the souls of those deceased, those honorable combatants. The mist still held to the surface of flooded rice fields along the Mekong River, its vapor slowly rising as the morning sun grew. He sensed their souls were still present, unwilling to leave, yet to dissipate even as the light grew more intense. Some were pondering their sacrifice, simply curious to understand if they could join with other souls from either side. But Doolin clearly felt their presence, as clearly as though someone had brushed up against his arm. Perhaps, Doolin thought, it was the Creator, viewing with sadness the destruction of His life-giving efforts.

Pressed into the still-moist earth, wet from the morning fog, soaked from the blood, urine, and feces of those so recently swept away in the recent carnage. God stood in mourning. Doolin knelt, his head bowed in homage.

After a moment he felt someone looking at him. As he turned slowly away from the battlefield, Stein was staring at him with two of his trusted NCOs standing at his side.

Deliberately, respectfully, he asked, "Doolin, would you come over here for a second?"

The fact that he remembered Doolin's name and that he had asked him rather than ordered him was a bit of a wake-up jolt this early in the morning.

"Sir."

"I was able to watch some of your work last night, son." Doolin anticipated a rebuke, a quiet but direct condemnation regarding his unwillingness to get down into the fight, to go down to the actual LZ and surrounding cutback. But instead, "You saved a bunch of lives, Marine. Thank you, son."

Doolin stared at him with his mouth partially ajar as the major then smiled and said, "I would gather you were not expecting those particular comments?"

Doolin actually stammered a bit. "W-well, I'm not sure what I expected, but no, I didn't expect that."

"How many rounds fired, Marine?"

"Seventy-eight."

"How ... many?"

"Forty-nine to fifty-five, sir. Can't be certain."

Both of Stein's companions looked up quickly, their eyes searching the face of Stein and then of Doolin.

"I saw both the RPG runner ..."—Stein pointed to the area with a small depression in the soil where Doolin had killed the second runner carrying the RPG, triggering the discharge and explosion as he fell—" ... and the guy trying to take out Sanderson's DFP number five. That was a timely shot— would have killed three more guys and potentially allowed a partial overrun of that sector." Stein moved his arm, pointing to the area that had been at risk.

Yes, indeed, Doolin thought, Sanderson and his guys in "defensive fire position #5" had very nearly joined the occupants of DFP #7, meeting together in the hereafter.

But Doolin frowned and answered, "Yes, sir, had to stop him."

Stein looked at Judah for a long moment, surprised and perhaps somewhat intrigued. Had he expected a mindless "rah-rah" response? He couldn't mask his startled expression, made even more obvious by the contemplative nature of Doolin's response, which was involuntarily linked to the corporal's frown. Both had framed a slender reed of Doolin's own personal pain.

Stein was perceptive. Again, it was Doolin's mother's enduring influence; he could not take too much credit for any "success." In Doolin's mind, her concerns still were fresh, as if she had spoken them yesterday instead of communicating from her grave. Her disappointment was underscored by the actions of her son. *Was it "success"?* thought Doolin. In nineteen minutes, plus or minus a minute or two, he had killed upward of forty-nine or more people. She would have lowered her eyes. This was not her definition of achievement. She would have shown a paucity of enthusiasm, and thus Doolin was enveloped by her sadness.

Stein registered a moment of perplexity grounded in a creeping realization that this kid actually might represent more, much more than he had anticipated. It was a feeling uncommon in life, that opponents or colleagues occasionally, perhaps rarely experienced: that naked and immediate understanding that the guy opposite you is simply better at what he does than you are at what you do.

For some, it is crushing; for some, it engenders fear or jealousy; for others still, it is a release, as they intuitively surmise that while they cannot match their opponent's skill, they are free, truly free, to try. To give it their best. Stein at this point understood why Mallroy had wanted this kid treated fairly, as an asset to be valued.

"Doolin, we owe you. You may have been the tipping point in this little affair."

"Sir, we all did our part. Permission to get some shut-eye?"

Inwardly, Stein smiled. "Yeah, get some rest."

As Doolin saluted and moved up the footpath toward his fortified lean-to, he heard the closest sergeant ask Stein, "Forty-nine to fifty-five, sir? Isn't that bullshit?"

Stein in turn said something that Doolin couldn't hear, but he shook his head, his negative response causing the other sergeant to immediately lock on to Doolin. The young sniper felt his gaze for the next twenty yards up the path.

And so it had begun. For the next several days Doolin kept to himself, joining the other guys when they needed to work the defenses and restore the DFPs, planting or positioning claymores, and even helping the engineers lay down some mines. It was obvious something had occurred with the guys; even the most obvious "zombies" would begin a task, such as wiring a claymore, then turn and say, "Hey, Doolin, think this is a good place for this bad boy?"

And when Doolin didn't, he would stand up, walk over, and ask them to examine one or two other choice spots with better kill potential or coverage to harm Charlie and then let them decide on either spot. Invariably, they would comply, which really surprised Doolin; there were no issues, no anger. Just a simple exchange, and then they did it. When he did agree, Doolin was direct: "Yeah, that looks good." Oftentimes he would offer an explanation of why it likely was optimal, showing them the defensive position covered and the benefit of their chosen location.

This sort of honeymoon and mutual love affair was great, but was a bit stressful for Doolin. He had grown accustomed to being alone—he *liked* to be alone. Doolin imagined Stein had discussed something with them, but he was wrong. The sergeant, one of Stein's closest and most trusted NCOs, had meticulously but rapidly studied the enemy kills, those that had not been carried off by their side, and examined the wounds closely. He even made some notes. He had performed what would someday become an entirely new field of study, a new expertise within the hallowed field of medicine: a battlefield autopsy. And while he was not anything close to a medical doctor, from growing up in the hills of West Virginia he was a natural hunter and tracker, and he likely had more experience examining gunshot wounds than all but a select group of Army surgeons. His rapid but thorough assessment of the LZ enemy casualties left him to conclude that of the twenty-four bodies examined, an astonishing sixteen had wounds consistent with those conferred by ammunition that Doolin alone used.

He prided himself on his skill, experience, and objectivity, and he did not have any predetermined interest in either giving Doolin or taking from him any credit or criticism. Thus, when this sergeant reported his findings to Stein, both looked at each other, intuitively grasping the weight of these data. Doolin had inadvertently made his mark, and in doing so had cemented his value to a group of crusty veteran warriors. Doolin was the newest weapon in their arsenal, and they were going to treat him with special care. He not only was a member of the team; he was a revered shiny new object causing interest in all quarters of the base.

Stein even took time and asked for Doolin's input regarding firing positions from high above the LZ. Doolin took this as a sign of support, but Stein also believed that his perspective may offer a new set of eyes to analyze and to potentially hold off any enemy approaches. It was during one of these professional exchanges that Stein became quiet as they talked, just the two of them, near the perimeter at the apex of Virgin Mountain, well above the LZ.

He looked at Doolin and asked, "How long you been using that rifle, Corporal?"

"Going on eighteen months, sir."

"You know you are good, right?"

"I'm OK ... there are better."

He smiled. "There are always people who are better, think they're better, and tell others they're better, son. For my money, you are about as good as I've seen."

"Thank you, sir."

"Yeah, but you find your work ... ?"

"Troubling at times ... sir."

He turned and looked directly at Doolin; his interest had grown exponentially in a simple fraction of a second. "How so?"

Doolin had to decide whether to engage and finish this, shrug and not answer, or simply ignore his question and move to a safer subject. But at that moment, he decided to tell the truth. The blunt, naked, horrible truth.

"My mothers wouldn't approve, Major."

While Doolin had expected him to laugh, or derisively hoot in humorous or even satiric dismissiveness, Stein grew quiet. The major became motionless as he looked out over the delta to the Mekong River.

"Mothers?"

"I have—or had—two, sir."

He frowned for a second, but continued his gaze out over the flooded delta. "You know, my wife left me. Told me I was a fool, that I really must enjoy killing people and that she couldn't love a guy or love me knowing that was who I was ... you know, a killer—a baby killer. A fucking deformed baby killer."

Doolin sensed that they had left Vietnam and entered neutral ground, a sanctuary where each did not have rank, authority, responsibility, or judgment. Doolin only partially understood Stein's despair and his hopelessness, but even for his youth, he was one of a few who could. How do you serve a government that can't decide whether or not it wants you to win and measures success in "body counts" that it publicizes for all to view? To ensure that the entire world knows how many human beings its military is killing on a weekly basis? This metric became an ominous substitute for a strategy-less war without definitional victory; the absurdity of this practice was beyond understanding. How does one justify the lives taken, lost, destroyed, or scarred when half of their own country's people spit on them when they return home?

"Perhaps she is not the most important judge, Major. My dad told me the guy you face in the mirror every morning is that individual, sir."

Stein had turned away again, his unfocused gaze out over the delta, reliving the images and memories known only to him. He nodded slowly.

"Yep, your dad's right, Doolin. But it makes me crazy to know that she's fucking someone else now."

"There will be other women, sir."

"With *this* face?" He absently fingered the scar on his face, slowly tracing it down to his jaw.

It was a sudden reality that hit Doolin, a truth so plain that he almost flinched, but then it just tumbled out of his mouth. "One day that will be a most precious and revered characteristic, sir."

And again Stein turned toward Doolin, a bit quicker than before, and just looked at him, a perplexed gaze registering a degree of wonderment. Then he shook his head slightly, not quite sure of how to respond.

"Doolin, you need to survive this war. You need to live to tell others what we dealt with here. May God protect you."

And with that, he abruptly walked down the path back toward the command bunkers. Silently Doolin stood, watching him depart.

It was sadly foreseeable, almost uncanny, for not twenty-five years removed from Europe's darkest hour, the horror of intimate desperate conflict was again being forcefully relived. And for the precious surviving participants, their main preoccupation found in the surprise of survival was to communicate their history, *so as to never allow this catastrophe to be repeated.* Major Stein was in some ways also such a victim—someone who had lost his way, or perhaps who had had it taken from him. His voiced concern was for Doolin to live to communicate the harm done to human beings, both friendly and hostile, by governments collectively unable to understand the personalized consequences of their respective actions. Doolin hoped and even offered a prayer to God, although he was not certain He cared, that Stein eventually would find solace, meaning, and purpose beyond the entanglement of Vietnam.

Doolin knew then, at the age of just eighteen, that history's most noble causes are frequently seen and often defined through the optics of the survivors. It is the average soldier or citizen, simple men and women, children, and the infirm, who pay for the time-honored superlative narrative that ultimately encases justification for the blood spilled and the price paid. Doolin's father had been a WWII vet, and one of his mothers, his biological mother, a WWII Army nurse. The horror of war, no matter the honorable or noble reasoning for the conflict, stains the soul of all who partake of its bitter taste. But Doolin had also realized firsthand, by tasting the blood and dirt, the sorrow and emptiness of war, that great even righteous governments can make mistakes as to the need for armed conflict. And by *default*, that same "greatness" may certainly describe the magnitude of their misjudgment.

The ensuing days at the mountain had been relatively uneventful. One might even say confining, as it was the first time that Doolin had had to stay within a specific geographically limited area. Wandering about in the Mekong Delta was suicide. Tasks were minimal on the mountain during the day, with the exception of helicopter-delivered supplies and planting increasing numbers of claymores and mines. This was primarily done by the engineers, but for some reason Doolin was fascinated by their articulated strategy and technical concerns. He joked with one of the Army engineers that when one of these explosives went off, the entire side of the LZ might collapse since it would trigger the remaining mines and claymores. Little did Doolin know that the corps of Army engineers had met twice in the last four weeks back in Saigon to discuss the untoward density of ordinance and its potential for geologic remodeling of the mountain. In other words, the possibility that the mines might actually make the damn cinder composition of the 3,300-foot structure "settle"—i.e., collapse or break down.

The inhabitants of the dormant volcano had since seen Charlie three to five times a week, and the engagements were minor by the standards of Doolin's very first night in camp. This did not mean that they were not associated with real harm, however, as several of their guys had been injured in various probes. Two weeks prior, one of their guys had been killed when a mortar round landed directly outside his DFP. While there was some debate as to what really happened, Doolin thought the isolated motor round was a lucky shot and simply plummeted into the earth, wedging in between the tightly positioned sandbags and the corrugated steel slats positioned to be the last line of defense. Doolin's best guess, and one that he discussed with Stein, was that the mortar round had had such a trajectory that it landed between sand and steel, partially burying itself just below the base edge of the steel with the sandbags, in effect directing the full force of the explosion into the DFP structure.

Their guy, Jenson, had been sleeping or at least trying to, his head literally inches away from the steel, and when the charge detonated, his head took the full force of the concussive force. Forceful impact with metal, wood, or really any object was unnecessary if the concussive force of sound waves tore blood vessels away from their attachments in the skull and ripped the brain apart.

They were initially confused as to what had killed him since he had no real wounds, just a bit of blood in his right ear. Both that ear and his face were swollen like a beach ball, but they weren't sure this hadn't happened after the fact. Doolin dismissed this conclusion; he had no idea what the proper medical terminology was but knew intuitively that such sudden and forceful motion to a human brain would result in traumatic tissue injury. His head was probably snapped back away from the wall with the same force as being hit by a car, only the force was sound, not metal or wood or anything the men were used to seeing.

The troops spent the next two days reconfiguring their sandbag-steel protective walls around the DFPs and extending the slanted roof structure an extra eight inches to make it impossible for any round falling from the sky to get in between the sandbag and steel interface. Doolin thought they would have already taken care of this, but apparently there was a small chance that a forty-degree arc for a round coming in *could* actually get in between this bilayer and cause exactly what had happened to Jenson. All too often, humans respond or react and do not anticipate, a very costly habit in war. The best generals always anticipate and attack.

While Doolin was not an expert in history, it never seemed to him that this quality of successful leaders versus the average joes was ever that difficult to understand. Doolin believed that defensive positions, or trying to defend them, was a recipe for disaster. And this was his existential concern for the American strategy: Despite being the most powerful military on Earth, the US's decisions, both political and military, were predicated on defending the ground in South Vietnam. The colossus military might of the United States was not ever going North over the DMZ to hurt the enemy, and this was a strategy inviting failure. He did not think it was that difficult to understand, but Doolin was not a college professor, a general, or any high-paid CIA analyst. Doolin was a "nobody," a sniper in the US Marine Corps sitting on a mountain in the Mekong Delta, defending an Army Special Forces communications base thought to be of intense strategic value in a country where the average rural citizen thought a candle was consummate technology. Could it get any more bizarre?

Doolin's relationship with Major Stein was never really the same after that first night and the subsequent discussion they had had on the apex of the mountain. He never said a word to anyone about Stein's marriage, or the major's crazy idea that his scar would, in the future, somehow limit interested females. But his actions, to Doolin, were meticulously professional; questions were raised, discussed, and resolved as they moved on to the next concern. Doolin acted more deferentially to him than he had to any officer before or since—even more than Mallroy. Doolin understood what internal searing pain felt like, and in his estimation Major Stein was compartmentalizing well, but someday his day of reckoning would come when the internal hurt would overwhelm his core defenses. It would come for Doolin as well.

However, despite his intentions for a sterile professional continuation in his relationship with Stein, Doolin had a weird little habit, and he inadvertently shared this with Stein. Doolin's routine was to examine events and replay them with changes in key variables. He liked to assess, to think through whether such vicissitudes introduced would also result in different outcomes. Thus, looking repeatedly at the early evening attack of five weeks prior, one of the variables Doolin considered was the timing and the calendar. So, as simple as it sounds, Doolin pushed one of the attack scenarios up to early in the morning, at dawn, and got rid of the requisite black night, a night without lunar reflective lighting.

In doing this, he was strangely but completely convinced that Charlie was actually doing exactly the same thing, going through the same exercises and tactical explorations, and doing it in present time. Thus, Doolin shared these concerns with Stein at 05:30 one morning after getting up to empty his bladder. Stein was crouched near the edge of a sandbag bunker wall, resting on one knee and staring off toward the down-sloping hill beyond the LZ.

"Major, I've been replaying alterations in their attack strategies, sir." He laid out his concerns directly—no hiding, no residual options left, allowing him to save face. Doolin told Stein his concerns quickly and concisely.

And once again, Stein startled Doolin. Having thought Stein might have been previously embarrassed himself for exposing himself a bit too much to a nobody like Doolin, the young Marine would not have been surprised if Stein had irritably dismissed Doolin's apprehensions and walked away, or simply laughed at Doolin. Instead, he instantly took two rather remarkable actions.

He quietly but quickly, with pressured speech, added one more variable.

"What if they were to distract us down there again?" he spoke, pointing now to the LZ. "And then hit the top behind us, willing to sacrifice some in a narrow corridor, but get twenty to thirty VC up there through the mines and claymores?" He now was pointing up the hill. Looking at Doolin for a second, there was that strange serenity-before-a-battle look. And then he sounded the alarm for imminent attack.

And then the attack actually began.

As US troops flew out of sleep, he shouted at Doolin, "LZ, now!" and pointed down the hill. "I've got to get to the top and stop these fuckers or find where they are trying—!" But he never finished the sentence as he raced up the footpath toward the perimeter with his rifle in hand, slapping his helmet on his head. Doolin noted that Stein, like himself, was wearing his flak jacket even though it was five thirty in the morning. Stein had given strict orders after the attack five weeks ago that every American troop had to eat, sleep, and shit in their body armor, and at all times they were to have their weapons immediately ready for full use: cleaned, oiled, and fully loaded. While this was not something new to Doolin—he never let his rifle get more than six inches from his hands—Stein's orders had now likely saved countless lives and prevented their massacre.

Doolin raced down to the LZ, going directly to DFP #5, and began to seek out targets using his night scope. It was at this moment that an explosion went off up the hill and rained down rock on the men but did no damage, as they were in their sand and steel-fortified cocoons. But then Doolin looked back up the hill and he momentarily froze; the perch he had used the first night was spewing smoke, and a noticeable defect in the stone comprising one of its walls verified that an RPG had successfully hit its mark.

"Son of a bitch!" Doolin yelled.

"What's wrong, you hit?!" screamed the young private next to him.

"No, I'm good—you look out that way. Kill anything that moves!" he called out, pointing to the LZ and the cutback area. "Just give me a second."

Doolin knew the effective range of an RPG, and he also knew that this man had to be up there near his old perch, closer to it than his comrades down here at the LZ. But where was this guy?

Two things happened simultaneously. Doolin saw the PAVN soldier moving slowly coming from behind a tree, moving over to an area with a clearer shot into Doolin's old perch, and almost without taking a breath, Judah aimed and fired. The round caught him in the lateral chest in what they call the axilla, the armpit, and tore through his chest into his lung, ripping the left subclavian vein apart, a huge vein just inside the collar bone. He was dead in thirty seconds. Concurrent to this was Doolin's absolute certainty of what Charlie had in store for the Americans. Doolin grabbed the radio and called out to Stein's most trusted NCO, who Doolin knew was over in the bunker backing up the semicircle of DFPs.

Doolin shouted, "I need to speak to Sergeant Linker. Now!"

Linker's voice came over the radio. "Identify." And then less professionally, "Who the fuck is this?"

"Doolin, Sergeant!" Without waiting, Doolin gave him what he knew was going to happen. "Sergeant, don't use the claymores until we see the bulk of Charlie. They want us to use the claymores, and then they're going to hit us with everything. I say again, wait on the claymores until mandatory!"

"Fucking Doolin, you giving me orders?" an exasperated metallic voice came back at him.

"Damn it, Sergeant, shoot my ass tomorrow! Just tell the guys to fucking wait on the claymores, OK? They want to form a corridor after we use our ordinance—don't let them do it. Doolin out and going up to Stein on top. They will be up there as well."

"What? Wait, how the fuck … Doolin? How the fuck do you know that?"

"Shit, Sarge … just tell the guys about the claymores, OK?"

And then Linker did just that. Over the radio the metallic, somewhat annoyed Linker stated, "Ladies!" and gave the quick coded verbal response to verify that it was him and the order was authentic. "Hold off on claymores until I give order. I say again, do *not* detonate the claymores in your sector until I give specific order. Now, ladies, do not lose your cool!"

Doolin was already running, crouched low, up the footpath to the apex and Stein. Judah had to get there. He knew that if they got three guys through, all of the Americans would die. Their plan was simple and yet beautiful, and Doolin knew what it was.

They were going to sacrifice four or five people to get through a narrow path up the hill. The electronic surveillance would be worthless in the middle of an ongoing firefight, and once topside, the perimeter claymores would be detonated. Then they would bring ten to twenty troops through the path at the apex and charge down the hill toward the LZ. At some prearranged signal, the bulk of Charlie waiting at the LZ would simultaneously storm the perimeter, and without residual claymores—assuming they had already been detonated—Charlie would simply overwhelm them. Puff would not be able to be employed effectively since the tight mixture of US and PAVN-Charlie within the camp would make casualties extreme. Doolin needed to get to Stein and help him, and he also needed to ensure Puff was coming.

Doolin spotted Stein firing into the wired apical perimeter and yelled as he came up from behind, "Major, Doolin here to help, sir!" Without moving his head or altering his rhythmic firing with each sector scanned, he shouted, "Left shoulder, four to six VC trying to flank us!"

Doolin moved at light speed and suddenly felt searing pain in his left shoulder. *Shit*—he was hit, but the pain was localized, and his arm responded normally. Doolin ducked behind a rock, and through his scope he saw his targets one hundred yards out and closing on the perimeter barrier. Two of the DFPs up here were positioned behind the razor wire fence and had already been destroyed, as evidenced by the smoking ruins of their former structures and body parts strewn across the surrounding area.

A gaping hole in the camp's perimeter defense was now open for the enemy to plow through, with only the remaining concertina wire to slow them. Heavily armed VC regulars, too—these guys were likely Special Forces themselves. Doolin attached his suppressor and aimed. He hit the lead guy in the neck, just below the chin, and he fell after one additional step. This caused the second man behind him to stumble, and as he regained his footing, Doolin's second round entered his chest just left of center to his midclavicular line. He spun as the force of the round tore into his chest, and he fell.

Then Doolin saw it.

A fourth guy in the residual of this five-to-six-man column was carrying a large pack and pulling on a cord. A satchel charge, and a big one. Doolin fired at the same time that rock chips exploded near his head, stinging his left cheek, pulling the shot down and to the right. Somehow, Doolin still hit his target, left upper thigh.

Someone in the column had seen Doolin and was targeting him.

The PAVN ordinance carrier screamed from Doolin's round entering his left thigh and his upper body twisted as his leg buckled in an awkward motion, causing him to lose control of his satchel.

Doolin watched with both fascination and building dread as the man stumbled but righted himself. Another shower of rock fragments rained down on Judah's neck as the wounded soldier picked the material up and began stumbling toward the last impediment, the razor wire. Doolin's next round entered his chest, and he fell. He must have already been in the motion of throwing the canvas bag, as it alone continued forward, slamming into the base of the fence before its motion stopped for a split second. Blinding light, even at five fifty in the morning, preceded a thunderous explosion, erupting and carving a seven-foot gap in the razor wire barrier and shearing away the lower limbs of nearby trees now intermingled with the concertina wire. The concussive force threw Doolin four feet back, even seventy-five yards from the blast and behind a ground-imbedded solid boulder.

Five PAVN soldiers rapidly appeared from hidden sheltered positions and moved to pass through the breach into the inner portion of the perimeter. Doolin killed two with successive rounds, but the third guy was on him, and his AK-47 radiated fire as the emitted rounds crashed all around Doolin and the stone and dirt halos from these tiny supersonic missiles carrying deadly kinetic energy covered his face and neck. Doolin could not recall the exact sequence that transpired, but the PAVN troop actually had a bayonet on his automatic weapon, and as his clip emptied, the smaller, almost delicate-boned man was on Judah.

Doolin smelled his rice-fish breath and body aroma as the canvas-helmeted silhouette charged into him. Suddenly Doolin was looking directly into the man's fire-breathing eyes as the bayonet blade obliquely entered the left side of Doolin's belly. He knew that he screamed or roared, at both the pain and the rudeness of this small man's actions, just before he grabbed the K bar strapped to his own right leg. The recognition that this man wanted to hurt Doolin upset the young American more than the reality that this North Vietnamese intended to kill him.

As they tumbled to the earth, in one swift adrenaline-charged motion Doolin buried the blade deep under the enemy's rib cage, cutting through his uniform and skin and severing the anterior wall of his heart in addition to his aorta, piercing his lung. The forceful motion opened an eight-inch-deep life-ending gash in his upper belly just below his ribs, and Doolin's hand and wrist became warm and wet as fluid poured out over both of them. The enemy combatant's eyes looked directly into his, and they instantly widened. He attempted to scream, but no sound came save a horrible sucking bubbling noise. As he died in Doolin's arms, his head rolled back, his sightless eyes fixed in a terminal position.

But Doolin had no time to assess their struggle or to be embarrassed, as he had promptly emptied his bladder, peeing himself. Doolin grabbed the Vietnamese's assault rifle and gently but quickly pulled it away from his torso, first removing the smaller man's dead hands still gripping the stock and barrel before pulling the gun and bayonet out of his pierced belly. Doolin was incredibly fortunate. The blade had entered his abdominal wall tangentially and penetrated only the skin and superficial layered tissues; it had not gotten into his deeper abdominal cavity. Although Doolin did not know the specifics, he knew that it was not that bad.

However, its sharp point had reappeared four inches distant to the entry point, exiting his skin like some giant needle, creating both an entry and exit wound. Its shiny tip was covered with his blood congealing around the blade's grooved surface. It was clean, and Doolin smiled almost comically as he half thanked his dead "dancing" partner—the Vietnamese had apparently not covered it with human feces or poison. Doolin was bleeding, the thick coppery-red liquid dripping off the tip, but it was already beginning to slow; it was not gushing.

The entire struggle, its results, and Doolin's assessment had taken seven seconds, and as he reached for a second banana clip from the dead man's belt, he heard another man approaching from the other side of the large rock. Simultaneously crouching and snapping the clip into place, Doolin rolled from behind the stone. With his finger pulling hard on the trigger, his injured arm ached as he directed the AK-47. It responded, kicking its disapproval as rounds moving at 715 meters per second sprayed in the direction of the sound. The approaching enemy was carrying an RPG-launcher and Russian Makarov PM sidearm, aimed at Doolin, and he fired only once before Doolin's haphazardly discharged bullets ripped into the charging man's chest and belly. They hit him slightly off-center line, their force creating angular momentum and spinning his body.

Looking like a green-clothed child's spinning top reaching terminal precession, he soon collapsed, hitting the ground and landing on his back. Doolin had momentarily felt the air expand and then collapse near his left temple before the man fell; the bullet discharged raced by Doolin's head and harmlessly buried itself in the dormant volcano's cinder. The dying soldier twitched slightly, and then became still. The RPG and Soviet Makarov each lay silent by his side.

Doolin was wounded. He hurt, and he was already exhausted mentally and physically, but Doolin also sensed that if he didn't get these last guys before they got down the hill, the Americans still might not survive. Doolin turned to see Stein. He was on the handheld radio directing fire from the remaining two apical DFPs, and thus far no one else was entering the newly created opening in the fence.

Doolin yelled at him, "Got to get down there!" while pointing down toward the LZ. "Two got through."

And as he finished his last word, two more men—one carrying an RPG and one with an AK-47—rushed through the fence opening directly at Stein. The guy with the machine gun fired at Stein, causing him to involuntarily leap up as the bullets narrowly missed him, followed by his body crashing down to the dirt and leaving him resting on both knees.

Stein was only slightly protected by a large rock. Doolin immediately recognized Stein was a bit disoriented and thus was exposed, about to die right there. The major was almost, but not quite shielded by the large stone as the guy with the Kalashnikov kept coming toward him. The distance between these two was shrinking, and yet Stein was in the field of fire between Doolin and the approaching North Vietnamese.

Doolin screamed, "Major, down!"

He immediately flopped and lay prone as over his chest and head, at the very level where his torso had been seconds previously, Doolin laid down a whole clip of 7.62×39 mm rounds from the AK. This killed the man with the Kalashnikov machine gun immediately but only wounded the other carrying the RPG, his right arm shattered above the elbow. Using his good hand, he grabbed for his Makarov just as Doolin reached for the one dropped by the man who had just nearly shot him in the head.

Doolin was up and running toward the last man. Their actions became a race, each of them hoping to cross the finish line.

The North Vietnamese was up and running also.

To kill Stein, to finish what his companion had started. This wounded man attempted to unholster his weapon, using his good left hand as he ran, closing the distance.

Doolin ran directly toward him, holding his belly and firing five times as he, too, closed the distance to point-blank range. Two bullets hit the wounded enemy.

He died before he could control his handgun.

Stein had already recovered and looked at Doolin, wide-eyed and clearly stunned. But ever a professional, he immediately began reassessing their surroundings and got on the radio to shout a command to the apical DFPs to be ready with the claymores in each sector. He now fully understood Charlie's strategy.

Doolin sputtered, "Got to get down there—two or three got through and they will trigger the LZ overrun!"

"Easy, Doolin …"

Speaking into the radio, he stated clearly and remarkably calmly, "Stein here. Two or three unfriendlies on the loose from up top on the hill, your back side. Get your people from the bunker and take them out. Ready your claymores down there, gentlemen. They are coming now. Doolin in behind the intruders—do not kill him, OK? I say again, our guy Doolin coming behind these unfriendlies. Stein out."

He turned to Doolin. "OK, go."

The sniper raced down the footpath carrying his reloaded Kalashnikov and an RPG. His biggest worry was getting shot by friendly fire, as Doolin's silhouette was framed by two weapons Americans did not use, but Doolin was going to do his job. As he rounded the bend before the footpath opened to a flat area housing the bunkers, he saw Charlie, a satchel charge being readied.

Oh, shit! Doolin wailed inwardly.

He skidded to a stop, wincing as the newly acquired holes in his skin were pulled back open and started to bleed. Doolin shouldered the Kalashnikov at the very moment a small, almost feminine-looking North Vietnamese troop swung his arm back, ready to launch this aerial satchel bomb. Doolin's rounds showered down on him, hitting rock and dirt and landing in the right chest and shoulder. This did not eliminate the forward progress of the enemy's throw but thankfully minimized its effective range. The troop collapsed, cut up by Doolin's rounds, dying. Unable to move, unable to complete his assignment.

But his buddy, a slender man coming from behind a tree into view, locked eyes with Doolin and raised his rifle to fire. But then instantly he hesitated, moved his head, and redirected his focus, taking in the position of the canvas pack that had hit the earth five feet in front of his dead colleague. It had rolled another four feet, now sitting between his dead comrade and him. The man saw a thin curl of smoke rising as the fuse burned toward detonation. He looked back at Doolin, and the last image Doolin had of this combatant was his weapon shouldered to fire, but with a look of accepted resignation.

Doolin was on the ground behind a large tree and a sarsen, a geological remnant of the volcano that had been in place some fifty thousand years. Doolin was ignorant of its geological history, but it saved his life—with his fingers in his ears, the blast of the satchel charge lifted him fully off the ground. A fragment of stone tore through his exposed right boot and broke the fourth and fifth metatarsal bones in his foot, but he was lucky. Two of the American troops seventy-five yards from the blast had been killed. One had a small piece of a tree branch slam into his eye, piercing his brain and ripping apart the delicate vessels inside of his skull; he bled into his cerebral cortex and was dead within five minutes. His companion was sliced apart by three pebbles traveling at supersonic speed from the blast, colliding with his neck and face. His carotid artery was severed in two places.

The second part of Charlie's plan never happened. They must have understood that the Americans had held the top, since only this blast was noted, and thus they did not attempt to overrun the perimeter at the LZ.

Oh, and Puff came after all. Someone—which turned out to be Linker—had had the foresight to get the flying fire-breathing dragon into action. Doolin could hear Puff's engines, and the beast made fourteen runs until they were out of ammunition; they had emptied everything they had into almost identical coordinates as the fight five weeks before.

Charlie really suffered. MIKE Force found 356 bodies below the LZ and near the base of the mountain later that afternoon. Stein initially refused to tell his command the actual number out of fear that they would accuse him of exaggeration and grandstanding. He also thought the idea of body counts was abhorrent and spoke of an arrogance and unfounded hubris typical of bureaucrats. Like this was a surrogate for a winning strategy ... typical of these fucking administrative pseudo-warriors! He despised them.

One of his sergeants wanted to line up the dead VC on the LZ and let the UH-1s take a picture from the air. Stein was furious with this suggestion and forbid it. Doolin reflected that Stein had come to the end of his tolerance for killing. He yelled at the guys all morning and nearly came to fisticuffs with someone in response to properly securing loose ammunition. Even his trusted NCOs looked at each other with acknowledgment that Major Stein needed some R&R. But the "party" with Charlie was over, and most of the Americans were alive. They had lost eleven people that day and an additional fourteen were wounded, including Doolin and Stein.

Doolin was standing on the foot path, about fifteen yards from the back side of the command bunker, when Linker came out, spitting dirt and cursing. They took some heavy fire in the bunker, but it held. He was shouting orders to his guys to secure the perimeter, rearm, and ensure that the residual claymores were still charged. Doolin was still carrying the Kalashnikov, his light camouflaged green top was soaked with blood from mid-chest down, and his pants were completely soaked with blood and fluid and caked in dirt. He was hobbling a bit. His boot was torn and his foot broken; he was lucky that the rock fragments had not opened up the skin on his foot. His left shoulder had a minor but intermittently bleeding superficial wound. Infections were frequent here, and once started, they could actually be deadly.

Linker slowly walked toward Doolin, looking him over carefully, as Stein came down from the top on the same footpath. Doolin started to salute, but he was in pain. Stein saw this and waved Doolin off.

Linker was still intently taking Judah in. Stein was the first to speak.

"Doolin, thanks. You saved my bacon." It was a statement—not really warm, but factual, accurate, and it brokered no dissent.

Doolin responded, "Yes, sir …"

Then he asked, "How bad is your belly?" and pointed to Doolin abdomen.

Linker hesitated, then asked, "What happened?"

Stein grunted, "Took a fucking bayonet to the belly, you believe it? Like we're at Gettysburg or something."

And then Linker surprised Doolin. "Is it deep, kid? You have to watch out for a belly wound."

Doolin observed that Stein even smiled at the concern registered in Linker's query.

"I don't think so, Sarge; pierced the skin and came out three to four inches from the entry. Hurts, though."

Linker then asked, "Doolin, you get that guy carrying the charges?" He pointed up to the new depressed and scarred surrounding area of earth where the explosive charge had detonated.

"Yeah …"

Linker turned to Stein and what came next nearly did kill Doolin, he was so astonished.

"Major, I want to put Doolin in for … to receive the Cross."

Even Stein was momentarily shocked, but slowly looked at Linker and nodded. "Yes, I think so. Sergeant, let's make it happen, please."

And then both men looked at Doolin. The Distinguished Service Cross is awarded for extraordinary heroism that while not justifying the Medal of Honor, the nation's highest combat honor, involved acts of heroism so notable and involving risk of life so extraordinary as to set the individual apart from his comrades.

Doolin looked back at them and slowly shook his head. "No." *How do you give medals for killing other men even though you saved the lives of your comrades?* Doolin didn't want that recognition.

As if reading his thoughts, Stein said gently, "No, Corporal, you're wrong here, son. I'm not doing this for you. I'm doing it for us."

Linker then added, "Go get those wounds attended to, and if there is an issue, we will chopper you out of here."

"Sir … Sargent."

Weakly, somewhat painfully saluting the major and nodding to Linker, the conversation ended. And with that, Judah C. Doolin walked back over to the command bunkers in search of their medic who would examine his wounds. Twelve hours later he was in Cam Ranh Bay, never to return to "the Mountain."

CHAPTER 9

A VISIT UP NORTH

September 22, 1971

Abundans cautela non nocet.
"Abundant caution does no harm."

Entering a complex lattice of hallways one hundred fifty meters from the Cam Ranh Bay docking facilities, Doolin was shown to security, where the MP searched him. The man's body odor was nearly suffocating. Doolin wondered if this guy had ever taken a bath; his forehead was covered in a sheen of perspiration with droplets forming at his temples and some running down into tightly trimmed sideburns that barely reached beyond his hairline.

As he searched the young Marine, Doolin winced and the military guard straightened instantly, looking at him. "What's the problem?"

"Just got out from the sixth CC," Doolin stated sourly, indirectly advising him both that he had been wounded in combat, recovering in the 6th Convalescent Center, and that Doolin was not some guard dog in a safe zone of this huge deep-water port facility—unlike the MP.

The MP half glared at Doolin. "Sure, Corporal."

Doolin instantly decided he hated this guy, but only stared back and said nothing.

He looked at Doolin's identification and checked his manifest for his name, then frowned. The MP hesitated as he looked again and checked Doolin's military green-and-white laminated ID. He then motioned with his right hand with a "gimme them" flicking of his fingers, and Doolin pulled out his newly issued dog tags from beneath his light camo top and showed the MP the embossed information, not removing them from his neck.

The MP examined Doolin's ID card, the tags, and his face and then called to his senior sergeant.

"Hey, Smitty ... come over here for a sec—"

The senior NCO ambled over, belly just beginning to protrude over his canvass webbed belt, his uniform immaculate but his face scarred around the right eye socket. Two deep thin white lines, one running back into his hairline above his ear, distorted the natural evenness of his two eyes, the right being pulled up and laterally, giving him almost an Asian-appearing epicanthal fold.

Mr. Smelly said, "This guy ..." and again looked at Doolin's ID and then his manifest. "Doolin ... this guy is supposed to be cleared for 3 Section ... that can't be right. He is a corporal and has no provenance." He said this last word as though his intellect and ersatz education would remind Doolin of his less-than-enamored standing and put the Marine sniper in his place.

Doolin smiled in spite of himself. The guard caught it, and this was not appreciated by Mr. Malodorous. He immediately redirected a hostile gaze at Doolin, but Smitty said, "Let's take a look ..."

Sergeant Schmitz examined the manifest carefully, positioning his head so that his left eye was used as the only source of visual inspection. He studied the typed coded reference alongside Doolin's name and looked up at the Marine, registering immediate recognition and something a bit unexpected: a degree of respect.

"I'll walk him back." Schmitz motioned for Doolin to follow him.

Smelly stood there with his mouth open, confusion and slowly accumulating anxiety surfacing in his eyes, but he said nothing.

Doolin passed by him wordlessly and fell in behind Schmitz, who then slowed and allowed Doolin to accompany him as they entered 3 Section. The two men turned down the hall and were waved through a second security checkpoint at the entry to the highly classified region of US Army intel.

Doolin could not have known, but the Cam Ranh Bay morning brief had informed this senior NCO that among the various important visitors, both civilian and military, entering the tightly secured 3 Section that morning was one Corporal Doolin: a candidate for the Distinguished Service Cross, a combat warrior who had likely saved countless lives in recent action at Black Virgin Mountain. He had just turned eighteen years old, celebrating his birthday by recovering from several wounds received in a vicious fight for control of the Special Forces camp. For some reason, this Doolin was an important individual, participating in the gray amorphous activities of 3 Section.

Schmitz looked him over from the corner of his good eye and saw an eighteen-year-old kid. Muscular, a bit thinner than advisable, tall, reaching nearly six feet three, with developing coarse hair along his upper lip. Not quite a full adult—a man-child, but with premature deep crow's feet and sharp eyes that missed nothing and a gait that was strangely deliberate, almost premeditated. A strange compilation of youth and professionalism ... someone Schmitz knew intuitively that you would want by your side when the balloon went up.

Sergeant Schmitz walked in a nonchalant manner, pulled his chin up, and slightly turned his head toward Doolin. "He's not a bad guy, but people like you make him nervous," he said, indicating Mr. Smelly. "In fact, I imagine you make most of these guys nervous."

Doolin watched him carefully.

"Difference between actual combat and combat tour," he said. "You? You reek of actual fucking combat. Makes people uncomfortable."

"But not you," Doolin guessed out loud.

He slowed, stopped, and turned to face Doolin. He smiled. "Can't really see out of this eye," he said, imputing the right eye, the one with the scars.

Although the globe of the eye was intact—in fact, it did not appear harmed—the damage to the tissue around the eye had injured it, somehow decreasing visual acuity, and thus he was now in security. "Can't aim to hit anything but the side of a barn. Satchel charge blew a door into me. Killed my XO."

Doolin said nothing, but the bond between the two was cemented in place; nothing more was needed.

He asked, "You healing up OK, Doolin?"

"Yeah, I'm OK, Sarge."

"Good. Here's the office. Have a good day, Corporal." He turned and was already walking away, nothing else needing to be said.

Doolin approached the whitewashed door. There was no window and only one sign saying "Three."

Doolin knocked twice. From inside, he heard a clear "Enter." As Doolin turned the handle and pushed through the door, he saw Mallroy at a table with an AVRN three-star Army general, a General Nguyen Trong Ang. Both men rose from their chairs on either side of the small table between them.

Clear glass tumblers half filled with melting ice, condensation running off their sides, and a small plate of cut limes lay on the table. As they rose,

General Ang turned to face Doolin and briefly frowned ever so slightly, and then it disappeared. Turning back to Mallroy, he extended his hand and shook Mallroy's briefly before walking toward the door.

Doolin stepped aside and Ang exited through the door, turned into the hallway, and headed back to the security checkpoint. He followed him with his gaze for a brief moment before he returned his focus to the colonel. Mallroy motioned for him to come join him and Doolin walked over to the general's empty chair, looked at the colonel, obtaining confirmation, and he nodded. Doolin sat.

He had changed, aged—Mallroy looked nearly ten years older than six weeks ago. Doolin did not avert his eyes out of respect, but the younger man was shocked. Beyond any metric imaginable, Mallroy indeed was a decade older. He simply looked exhausted. His thin lips had darkened, his skin now gray and splotchy. There were deep cheerless pools of flesh beneath his still-intense eyes, but his face had fallen. His ashen skin appeared pasty, and the hair near his temples had actually begun to whiten.

In just six weeks, his appearance was no longer that of a man in his late thirties—a "burner," or a rapidly ascending officer within the US Army Intelligence branch. He looked as though the quizzical interested youth, once characterized by his nuanced and contemplative aptitude, had died within him. Only a remnant shell was left, an ossified brittle fossil. His very soul seemed to have departed, and his life's spark looked as though it was preparing to leave as well.

Mallroy looked at Doolin for a long moment and then softly spoke, "Been keeping tabs on you over at sixth CC. You appear no worse for wear, son. All healed up?"

"Almost, sir."

He looked at Doolin, concern momentarily clouding his eyes. "Is there a problem? Something not going well?"

Doolin quickly responded, "No, sir, just tired. Fatigued, actually. A bit more than I would anticipate, that's all."

He looked at Doolin carefully, assessing his face. "Yeah, well, you had a pretty interesting time out at Black Virgin. I told you to be careful and keep off the radar, and what do you do? You get yourself nominated for the Cross." This last part was said with pseudo-admonishment, a light sarcasm that actually conveyed his approval almost as much as his pride. "Try not to get yourself killed with this next plan of ours, OK?"

"Sir ..."

"I want you to go up-country, Quảng Bình."

Doolin knew most of the provinces in South Vietnam, and yet this was not a familiar name. He began to worry that perhaps he was more ignorant of this land than he thought, a terrain that Doolin had endlessly trucked through. Or perhaps ... *shit, no.* Perhaps he was being asked to go into the forbidden land—the North.

It turned out that Doolin actually did know his Southern provinces, and thus his latter concern was validated. Quảng Bình was a province in central Vietnam, North Vietnam occupying the land extending from Laos to the sea south of the Gulf of Tonkin. Within this region there was a geological oddity that was unique, beautiful, and very useful to Charlie, as it was home to one of the world's two largest karst regions.

These are areas with a unique topography formed from the slow and steady erosion of soluble limestone, dolomite, and gypsum. Time, water, and gravity work on these surface minerals to create spectacular carved-out caves and sinkholes that are often interconnected beneath ground, making it a remarkable natural storage area for anything needing to be hidden from prying American surveillance.

There also was frequently a distinctive natural underground drainage system that removed water from the surface, and as it dissolved through the limestone and other indigenous rock it then formed a network of subterranean water flow, creating buried river systems and even underground lakes. It was the North Vietnamese province bordering the DMZ, making it is a perfect intermediary staging site for the Golden Triangle's heroin en route to anywhere in the South, Saigon, or its surrounding municipalities.

This name, Golden Triangle, had been coined by the CIA itself and represented a region where the borders of Thailand, Laos, and Myanmar met at the confluence of the Ruak and Mekong Rivers. The illicit production of opium was the principal export and had been so since the latter stages of WWII, second only to Afghanistan in opium harvesting. From this assembly hub, the Triangle's product was then moved over numerous routes using multiple transportation modalities to supply Western Europe and the United States, its two dominant customers. It was also the Republic of South Vietnam's main supplier and formed the foundation for the strategy of undermining the South's government with bribes, treasonous cash, and crossed loyalties.

Doolin looked at Mallroy and carefully considered his next set of questions. "And Colonel, what is it that you want me to do?"

"Doolin, what I am going to tell you is again obviously for your ears alone. You have risked your life to support this mission. And more than guys who are in the field, because we order them to go; you have volunteered to undertake crazy risks to uncover something so malignant in our government that I am ashamed to share its common lineage.

"And you have done this because you—and I share this with you—have a belief that we owe our total commitment to those same guys who are, in fact, ordered into the field. You literally bristle anytime I or anyone else makes a statement that is remotely condescending or insensitive to our grunts. I will never be able to make you understand how much I respect you for that, Doolin. It is your most remarkable quality. I think you have earned the right to hear where we are and what I want, the bigger picture. So, I am going to share information with you far beyond your pay grade.

"Also, in case something happens to me—and I could not be more serious—you and you alone will have to decide what you are going to do with this information, and your derivative actions will also be yours to make alone … and unfortunately, potentially without any support."

Mallroy paused and rubbed his forehead slightly with the fingers of his left hand. For a moment, his familiar reptilian glossal structure appeared, moving out over his teeth; his tongue looked as though it was almost scenting the air before his mouth closed. He then took his glasses off and massaged the bridge of his nose, slowly concentrating while seemingly trying to relieve the discomfort, if not outright pain, from a headache. In the end, he simply looked down and shook his head ever so slightly, wiping away the demons, the doubts, and the filth.

"I am a colonel in the greatest military of the greatest country the world has ever seen. I believe in the chain of command, and until last week I believed it was inviolate. I no longer feel … I no longer accept this. I guess I must confess that I still do in most instances, but when we deal with the weasel-civilians, especially the CIA, I neither trust them nor, frankly, respect them. They are the bottom-feeders, the opportunists … not all, but all it takes is one.

"In combat, cowards are miserable failures as soldiers, and they often impact others more than themselves. Their failures influence those close to them, their immediate buddies, but also their command. Their cowardice may, in fact, make a successful mission fail. But traitors, especially spook-traitors, may bring down a country. There is a force multiplier to the consequences of their action … for good or evil.

"The chain of command becomes a liability that these sorts of people can exploit if they need to in dealing with naïve idiots like me. I just had that three-star general officer in here and was telling him there was no evidence of any rats in his immediate staff, which is a blatant lie—and he knows it is a lie, and he knows that *I* know it is a lie. Three of his subordinates and the general himself are receiving drug money directly from the North, and he is in bed with Haney."

He looked directly at Doolin and said softly, "But I told him this and thus, in not so many words, that I am for sale. Understand?"

Doolin nodded and realized he was watching the disassembly of a man's core faith. He was in the process of asking and trying to answer if he had taken the correct action after a potentially life-altering decision; he still was uncertain, and now he was spiritually adrift. In this, Doolin and Mallroy were similar.

"Why? Because I know he is bought and paid for by the North. We have evidence that he is accepting money in the form of gold, literally gold coins and bars, for his silence and shielding of VC activity in Saigon and other municipalities. And our general has lunch with EWH every Thursday afternoon. Forty-five to ninety minutes of wine and food, fine china, and watercress … money and treason …"

Mallroy was now looking away, his tongue once again between his lower lip and his teeth, deep in concentration. And then he slowly returned his gaze to Doolin.

He knew Mallroy well enough now to understand that he was formulating the seeds of a trap. So, Doolin looked directly at him and stated, "When you get confirmation that you are a player, that you have been accepted, how do you tie it back to EWH?"

The man's head shot up, his eyes connecting to Doolin's. He thought he had made a sophomoric mistake: ego. Doolin's ego had seeped through, trying to impress—uncommon but, well, it had happened, and now he waited for admonishment.

Instead, Mallroy grew pensive. Then, as if some internal bridge had been crossed, he nodded once and spoke.

"EWH will never be so sloppy as to leave even ghostly traces of his involvement. No, I am going to ask you to intervene—for one person to transiently impact their remarkable economic success in a manner that will cause him to respond. And if he does, I am going to kill him."

Doolin sat upright. This last statement shook him.

Looking intently into Doolin's face, Mallroy's eyes registered disappointment, acceptance, and a trace of bitterness. Doolin understood that Colonel Mallroy, too, had crossed the line and entered into the land of no return.

Doolin asked, in the same manner as if asking his Little League battery mate on a Saturday afternoon to frame a curveball on a three and two count, "And what specifically are you asking me to do?"

"Up-country, you will have an opportunity to deduce for yourself what you can do—something you can do one time, a single time, that will be maximally disruptive to their shipment of product."

"And what if I don't get a chance to do anything?"

"Then this is not going to happen and I end up killing a person who may be innocent, although I doubt it. Perhaps the bad guys win. But if you can do something, EWH will respond with one of several specific actions. He might try and leave the country, call a meeting of other traitors and either eliminate the general or require some form of redemptive action on the general's part, or … deduce that I am the new variable and have me eliminated."

Again, Doolin locked eyes with Mallroy.

He wasn't sure how his own actions would cause, facilitate, or assist in any of this, but he knew Mallroy wasn't crazy. Doolin also knew that if his colonel was going to kill EWH, the CIA station chief in Cam Ranh Bay, this wasn't war; this was murder.

"I want you to be as deliberately messy as possible up there. Eliminate the protection, destroy the material, and burn the trucks, and make it look like a mole in their outfit hijacked the product and killed the transporters."

"So, you want me to kill the men transporting this material, whoever they are—military or civilian, despite their lack of hostile intent or action? Just shoot them and conduct a pseudo-hijacking of the cargo?" Doolin was about to tell him to "Yes, Sir," which in enlisted speak is "Fuck you," but he did not. Instead, he remained silent.

Doolin was looking at the shell of an individual that only nine months ago, he had cowered before. Mallroy's twin "eagles" pinned to his uniform's collar, his bearing that of a senior experienced and committed officer … confident, assured and patient. He had looked as Lincoln did sitting in his memorial, dignified and solemn, eyes searching through the passages of history. Nine months ago, he was the epitome of the American military's best.

Doolin sat now before a man humbled by the personal loss of his most fundamental and intimate guiding principles. The ruin of all that he had valued, believed in, and revered, all that had allowed him to swim in the river of shit called the Vietnam War. An experienced warrior in dedicated service to his beloved nation, now he himself was fragmented waste strewn about his feet, his beliefs the cold embers of an extinguished fire.

Doolin shared much with this man; the loss of a moral infrastructure topped the list.

The young American paused. And then he said, "I will do whatever you want … whatever it takes … not for me, but for all the mothers of all my guys who will never again go to see Fourth of July fireworks. Kill him if he is dirty, and let God decide your innocence or guilt, Colonel."

He looked at "his kid," Judah, and through his eyes he saw not an eighteen-year-old grunt, not an immature man-child soldier, but an equal partner—a fellow living being who understood the countless ambiguities and impediments found in war … and decided to continue forward. He had found both a friend and a trusted colleague.

"Doolin, you must survive … perhaps I should send you home."

"With respect, sir, I will not go."

He nodded gravely, saying, "I know … I know."

But he looked as though the weight had been lifted, the cloud had passed, and his eyes slowly began to brighten. "OK, son. Let's get started."

He then proceeded to share his plan. If he was killed or was gone by any means, Doolin was to hunt down EWH and kill him. Mallroy had someone in the Cam Ranh Bay CIA station, someone who had very limited access but would and could provide EWH's daily schedule. He provided that name and Doolin realized only later, years later, that this was Mallroy's male lover. If Doolin needed this man to provide information and Mallroy was gone, he was given the detailed protocol to follow to activate the office mole. Doolin had no idea if this was even remotely realistic, but Doolin would proceed as his colonel asked and, in fact, had ordered.

Doolin's last order, his last duty to Mallroy … and then Doolin was to either disappear or to fetch the repository of material that was accessible only to him, kept in a Taiwanese bank in a safe deposit box. Classified material demonstrating to any JAG officer Doolin's orders and the context of his actions. It might help; it might keep Doolin out of thirty years of prison.

Here he was, a US Marine Corps sniper trained to follow binary orders: shoot or don't shoot. And now, he was involved in an intricate espionage chess game crossing wits and swords with the CIA, the US's own military, and the senior officers of the AVRN and Charlie. *Great.* Doolin briefly considered leaving Mallroy to his own isolated fate by asking for a transfer to somewhere—Khe Sanh, or some other place where his odds of returning were nearly zero, but perhaps better than his current situation!

But EWH had his schedule, and although it varied during each fourteen-day interval, segments were repeated and thus predictable. This allowed Mallroy to spot-check him, to ensure there was some absence of variation, and of course it provided a baseline to assess responses of this man to adversity or troubling information. And deviation brought scrutiny for cause, and Mallroy knew EWH's repetitive activities almost intimately.

This, however, did not address the major flaw in Mallroy's strategic approach: his resources were in essence totally committed to surveillance of EWH. If there were other explanations or if EWH was not involved, Doolin's colonel had made a serious mistake … both career-wise and potentially even regarding his mortality.

Haney, when viewed by his countrymen, was nearly the prototypical midlevel CIA employee on the rise, ego-driven for institutional approval and acceptance, but this did not make him stupid. However, in his most private moments, Haney could not quite admit that he actually sought refuge from being "average" and the youngest son of three brothers, relegated to an also-ran within a hypercompetitive and very successful family. His two older brothers sucked all of the oxygen out of the room and, by any objective metric, were very talented individuals.

Eric Haney had never been able, at least in his own mind, to win more than limited appreciation of his self-absorbed father. And he desperately wanted more, even as an adult. Yet, once he donned the mantle of a clandestine warrior, he was the embodiment of their creed. He exemplified their finest: good looks, snappy, quick answers, and breeding. A disquieting superficiality mirroring the caricature of Hollywood's popular 007 secret agent, only brought to real life. The poster child of how a clandestine operative ought to look and act—at least for those doe-eyed middle-aged women confined to their homes and using soap operas to expiate their future.

He was the new look, the big man on a unique campus. Eric intuitively understood this and continued to exploit his shallow veneer of professionalism at each office get-together and at every semiannual performance review. But even more important to Haney was the fact that the clandestine service offered him the opportunity to act in a manner consistent with his life's view. To do anything—no matter how illegal, unethical, or immoral—in pursuit of satisfying his own needs and walk away not just free from justice, but celebrated as a valued member of our nation's protectors.

All that was necessary to ensure his gallant endorsement could effectively wrap his actions within the veneer of "service to country" so the wise men would furnish a moral waiver. It could not be doubted, then, that in Haney's mind, employment in such an organization offered everything that a smart and morally bankrupt individual could hope to achieve. He knew, as would anyone who carefully observed him, that he was a dressed-up used-car salesman who worshiped at the altar of his own ego-driven oracle. In fact, psychologists note the absence of a conscious understanding of "right or wrong" as prime elements in defining a sociopath. Haney's internal hardwiring routinely strayed across the boundary identifying him as such.

Haney was also a natural predator. The weak, the vulnerable, and those in need of assistance or reassurance—he could sense their liabilities as a fox sniffs the air, taking in the aroma of fear, dread, intimidation, and need. In many ways he was a natural spy, but his employer was not the CIA, and it never would be. It was only EWH himself, and this would not change throughout his life.

Mallroy had seen this all before through his years in the numerous briefings held often in conference rooms of pretentiously large office buildings within Washington, DC, or closed rooms in military facilities. The arrogance of the recent Ivy League graduates, now official spooks, with gratuitous smiles hiding their pedigree of disdain for the "blunt instruments" of American military might. "We use our wits, not our brawn, Mr. Army Man." Yes, he had seen their special hubris along with the groupthink that often accompanied and at times ensnared their national strategic decisions.

The Bay of Pigs nearly brought down a president, but perhaps more importantly, many believed it later triggered the Cuban Missile Crisis that nearly resulted in the initiation of a nuclear war. Mallroy had difficulty respecting these people, but he was not so naïve as to dismiss their cunning or their potential for wickedness. Thus, he carefully cultivated his information on EWH and waited patiently for Doolin to spring the trap.

The beauty of his teamwork with Doolin, from Mallroy's perspective, was that even he didn't know exactly when Doolin would strike. The Army colonel knew what constituted Doolin's basic plan of action, and he also knew the strategic value of Doolin's intervening to disrupt the narcotics business of Haney and his compatriots. Mallroy loved this ambiguity, this lack of knowledge regarding specific actions, as it made this remarkable young man safer, less vulnerable to the treachery of betrayal. Because frankly, if even Mallroy didn't know, then *no one* knew the details of Doolin's activities—only the primary operative! This was not a watertight op; this was airtight, hermetically sealed with only Mallroy and Doolin generally aware of the desired outcome that was set in motion. Only this eighteen-year old Marine sniper knew the specifics, the tactical outcomes on his end. And this was as it should be.

It was remarkable, he thought, for within the hallowed ground of America's clandestine services was a veritable cadre of people who had access to top-secret information. Breach any one of these cogs in the human chain of data flow and you would have access to some level of a plan's operational life. But not this one—no, Mallroy had been careful to the point that if something happened to him, virtually no one else, save Doolin or Mallroy's lover, would know. And even his Steven, within Haney's office, possessed a minimal understanding of what Mallroy was up to in needing EWH's daily schedule.

This level of secrecy would also protect Mallroy ... should he have to eliminate EWH. But now came the hard part: reconciling the need to spring the trap, using an unusually dedicated eighteen-year old kid, to extirpate treachery in the hallowed grounds of America's war effort. But Mallroy inherently understood that Doolin had been transformed by this war, as all the men were—in plain fact, as all human beings who encounter war are altered. Doolin would not accept a lesser role.

Mallroy had dug into Doolin's past, carefully examining his strengths and weaknesses, his record, and his character to understand as much as possible about this individual. There was much to like, but Mallroy had grown hesitant as he came upon the earliest comments of the Parris Island drill instructor and the psychologist who had examined Doolin as he volunteered and was selected for the Marine Sniper School. Mallroy sensed through his reading that Doolin and he shared a common need to mask their backgrounds and fortify their present lives by eliminating any public exposure of their past. In Doolin's case, this psychologist had candidly stated that Doolin was reluctant to discuss his parents or his childhood, including friends and teachers. It was almost as though he was trying to protect them, but it was a characteristic that went beyond the norm; he simply did not easily or volitionally share personal information.

And while this struck the psychologist as a bit weird, since most people given an opportunity to discuss themselves nearly bring their audience to tears of regret for asking, Doolin provided minimal information. His most common responses were "I'm not really sure" or, interestingly, he would state, "I can't remember because it really didn't seem to matter at the time …" And this, from an individual with a nearly perfect eidetic memory.

These polite but repetitive dismissals of probing questions created a cloudy patchwork of information about Doolin's childhood and early years, but there were known events. It even prompted one headshrinker to recommend *against* assignment to the Corp's sniper elite, as he felt Doolin might hold traits consistent with a developing sociopath. When Mallroy read this, he was both incensed and simultaneously nearly doubling over with laughter. Obviously, this pencil-neck psych wunderkind had little understanding of what Doolin's country was asking of him! Objectively, what psychological terminology would be used to describe a human being who voluntarily submitted himself, and actively sought, to become a trained assassin of other human beings?

Doolin was adopted, but there were significant gaps in this part of his background. When personal history checks were repeated—after he had applied for the sniper school and additional information regarding his psychological stability were required—noted inquirers had found that Doolin's biological mother was a decorated Army nurse from WWII.

Someone who would now be called a gifted child, Margaret Catherine Mahoney O'Brian had demonstrated a rather remarkable intellect, matriculating through her school years quickly. But this was the 1930s and early 1940s, and women had minimal outlets for whatever their promise of prodigious intellect, so nursing was her choice. And thus, she graduated from Vanderbilt School of Nursing at the age of nineteen, more than two and a half years ahead of her classmates. By the end of the war, she was a captain within the Army Nursing Corps, and by 1940s standards this was a rather significant rank, made even more impressive by her relative youth. Just prior to the end of the war, or immediately at the end of the European conflict, she married an Army captain. Of course, he was in the Army Intelligence Corps, a solid man—also smart, but not at the level of his remarkable young bride. The two left the service, as did nearly everyone within three years of 1945, and began their family.

Judah Connor Doolin was the last of three children, but there was a problem. The young intellectual prodigy Margaret C. Mahoney O'Brian was now the chief nurse for the emergency room, and assistant director of all nursing in a large, busy, and highly regarded Chicago hospital. She was also the walking epitome of an Irish beauty, with full red lips, wavy auburn hair, and pendulous breasts, oversized for her small-boned petite figure, catching every male's attention. But it was her eyes, perceptive, quick, and responsive to her environment, that drove some men to distraction. And unfortunately, Margaret was also rather more book smart than wise.

While she honestly enjoyed what she viewed as the innocent attention of men, she also mistakenly assumed the boundaries established by her marriage with Frank would restrict any and all inappropriate contact from her many admirers. She was wrong. And it was also Margaret's misfortune that for however intellectually gifted she was, she was a vulnerable woman emotionally and socially. She never quite understood why her ability to instantly grasp the patterns in numbers or in the science of biology or medicine did not enable her to just as rapidly identify the hidden perfidy in those around her.

Even among her male colleagues, who were almost exclusively physicians, she saw clinical signs or symptoms often before all but the most talented of these men recognized them. Thus, it was not long before several of the most highly regarded surgeons and physicians often discussed changing conditions in their patients with her, to explore the clinical possibilities or simply to confirm their judgments. She was careful in this arena of shared knowledge; she understood the male ego enough to allow the surgeon to derive a conclusion, suggesting that he had already found the correct diagnosis, or when in her judgment he hadn't, she gently and incrementally led him to whatever concern she thought was more apt to be important. And for those men in whom an intelligent, if not brilliant woman did not intimidate, but was instead an enhanced attractiveness, wrapping it within her soft, lush feminine Irish beauty pushed them from respect to near adulation. But it also unmasked naked desire in some, if not lust.

Margaret could also not quite understand, as was common, the repetitive banal games played by her female nurse colleagues and many of those same physicians, done so obviously to attract each other's attentions. She lacked patience and acceptance of what she felt were the same social conventions first witnessed in her schoolyard in Tennessee in second grade. But slowly she came to accept that for many of her female nursing colleagues, baiting the trap might just ensnare a good man in the form of a husband who was also a physician.

In this, she rapidly connected her chosen profession and its incumbent environment with the newly blossoming TV shows called "soap operas." She found it ironic but humorous, as the settings of some of these melodramas were in identical hospitals involving the same types of men and women surrounding her on a daily basis. The inferred sexual activity of these snippets of American life was unfortunately not lost on her husband, Frank, who grew to resent his inability to keep a 24/7 watch over his sensual wife. He both badgered her and, nearly to the point of physical violence, accused her of recurrent infidelity.

Frank O'Brian had experienced what many who served in the war found in the transition from military to civilian life. The end of the war and his service stripped him of what minimal title and rank he had possessed, and he ended up selling insurance. Despite the fact that he was reasonably successful at his occupation and certainly made a decent living, he transitioned from being an officer with twenty-five men under his command to being a worker reporting to a boss overseeing twelve other salesman identical to him.

He put on fifty pounds over three years and continued to smoke and drink while becoming ever angrier at his wife's growing responsibilities and stature. He simply couldn't accept his new role as a mere worker and his lack of intrinsic societal importance, or his failure to progress in promotions in comparison to his wife. And although he was not stupid or even average intellectually—he was actually a clever man—he undeniably knew he could not come close to matching his young bride's cerebral capabilities. It was foreseeable, if not understandable then, that he ultimately found a replacement for Margaret—a rather dour, notably less intellectually gifted surrogate—to reestablish his maleness.

The marriage ultimately ended bitterly, with Frank's refusal to accept that their youngest child—or more specifically, *Margaret's* third child—was in fact from his seed. There was a footnote at the end of the page suggesting that Doolin's true biological father was not O'Brian after all. The inference was that a visiting surgeon of Jewish ancestry, whom his mother actually did have an illicit affair with, was Judah's true father, suggesting that Frank's anger was not entirely misplaced. This would make Doolin at least half Jewish. As Mallroy had reviewed this information, he actually winced as he continued to read what had transpired over the first year of Doolin's life. Mallroy saw parallels to his own disrupted childhood and unconsciously shook his head at the chaos surrounding this kid's arrival on the planet.

Margaret O'Brian, suddenly absent a husband and with a newborn and two older daughters, five and ten years of age, experienced three of life's more unpleasant events simultaneously. First, she presented the certified blood type of her infant, confronting her soon-to-be ex-husband and confirming the origins of this new life as belonging to him, at least consistent with his blood type. She felt this was enough to undermine his mantra that she was a "loose woman." He slammed the door in her face and retreated into his new house with his new woman. As it turns out, Frank's anger might have been justified, as the blood type alone is not conclusive under many circumstances. The test simply has inherent limitations; a pivotal constraint is that it cannot distinguish between two men with identical blood types. But O'Brian's actions were also meant to emotionally injure his soon-to-be ex-wife, and in that, he was successful.

Margaret was devastated. It is likely, but unprovable, that her subsequent "mental collapse," as noted by authorities, was greatly exaggerated and was in fact a common condition known as post-partum depression. But apparently, its onset was so "severe" that the State of Illinois formally and legally moved to remove the newborn from his mother, as there was concern that she might harm the infant. Whether this was true or exaggerated at the behest of her soon-to-be ex-husband so he could more easily proclaim veracity as to her infidelity, and thus not have to support this third child, was not present in the record.

But this caused the thin ice that Margaret was treading upon to crack, and she then fell into a deep, inky-black dysfunctional mental state. She was hospitalized for nearly nine months after her delivery of infant Frances O'Brian, our Judah Doolin. Mallroy knew that this was a legal way of stating she had been mandatorily "institutionalized" for severe depression. In other words, she was committed to the nuthouse. Her daughters were stripped from her, and the two sisters moved in with relatives for almost twelve months as their mother was unceremoniously deprived of her liberty, her freedom, and nearly her future life.

The remnants of Margaret's family eventually got back together after Margaret was released, finally being judged as no danger to herself or her two female children. Frank was long gone; new wife was already pregnant when our Doolin was born. But this infant son, Mallroy learned as he grimaced—his very own sniper—was gone from Margaret's life, apparently mandatorily put up for adoption. She never saw him again, and he never met his sisters.

Had Margaret agreed to this? Was she coerced? Did she feel that she couldn't provide a home for three children? Was she secretly aware that this child was not O'Brian's? The record did not speak to these concerns, to Margaret's ultimate logic or thought process in releasing her son to be raised by strangers. A motherless soul had entered the world, a biological father's unwanted soul. The record went on a bit more, but details were limited to informed speculation.

Apparently, Doolin had actually lived in the hospital for some time after his birth. The duration was not clear, but it appeared to be anywhere from six weeks to nine months. Mallroy smiled to himself, shaking his head in near disbelief at the report's inherent hubris as the author editorialized that in the 1950s, nurses were members of a de facto religion. In the years immediately following WWII and during the Korean conflict, the report opined that the nursing profession was composed almost exclusively of women who were deeply committed to each other based on shared beliefs and common experience. Mallroy briefly looked up, his gaze becoming unfocused as he considered the veracity of the anonymous author's expressed opinions. His head tilted slightly, his thoughts focused but ultimately acknowledging the legitimacy of the narrative.

When RNs were morally incensed, when their hackles were raised, no male—not even a male of legal authority—could safely challenge them. It was almost a comical outcome, as these women, different nurses working each shift in the hospital, each took turns caring for young Doolin as though he were their own infant child. Mallroy smiled as he read over this part, actually pondering whether God had purposely intervened and watched over this newborn. From the time he inhabited the neonatal and then the pediatric wings of the hospital, Doolin had had multiple surrogate "mothers" who were totally attentive and committed to him. *Talk about neurodevelopment in the setting of a potentially gifted kid ... shit ...* Mallroy chuckled to himself at this point, as he understood that his impression about the young man's intellect was accurate. He was certainly not of limited intelligence.

But the smile faded immediately as Mallroy reflected on what he was asking this "kid" to undertake.

The remainder of the record was pretty standard, save for the fact that Doolin had eventually been adopted by Virginia and Jack Doolin. A couple who provided young Doolin with a home and a life as close to an ordinary upbringing as possible, save for the fact that neither parent had quite known what to do with a child who, by all accounts, was as intellectually gifted as his biological mother had been. The record showed that Jack and Virginia Doolin had graduated high school, neither had attended college, and Jack was employed as a midlevel organizational clerk in one of Chicago's growing corporate payroll companies. Apparently, the federal taxes involving payrolls had become so complex and burdensome for midsize companies by the 1950s that they were looking for and finding companies that would accurately calculate these values for a reasonable fee. There was a lot of running and organizing of data, and Jack Doolin ensured that material handed off to the company found its way to the correct section for timely processing.

Sounds impressive, and it was, but it was almost identical to Jack's previous job in the military. He had also joined during WWII. During his time in the Army, he was responsible for bringing material to specific sections to ensure their operational tasks would be correctly allocated and done in a timely fashion. He simply had a knack for processing information, and organizing it in sizes that other people could digest and successfully act upon.

Luckily for him, the liters of vodka consumed in the off-hours did not diminish his ability to perform, and few people at the company would have suspected he drank. In fact, there was very little of this in the record; most of what Mallroy knew concerning Doolin's adoptive father's alcohol habit was from passing comments from Doolin himself. And these remarks were not bitter or angry; they were objective dicta about the human cost of war that his father had likely experienced. In fact, it was only a person closest to his father's desk at the company, the middle-aged woman who took most of the calls before handing some off to his father, who noted the progressive nature of his shaking, tremulous hands that had become much worse just before Jack Doolin's fatal heart attack.

After his father's untimely passing, young Doolin's response was to assume control of the family. His emotionally shattered mother took time to heal, and then there was concern over being able to live; there was no money.

And so Doolin enlisted, leaving high school and the promise of becoming one of the very people that Mallroy hated: an Ivy League-educated know-it-all. Although in truth, Mallroy didn't think Doolin would have ultimately succumbed to this sophomoric temptation. He had undoubtedly lied about his age, joining just before he turned seventeen, but since fewer and fewer able-bodied men were now volunteering for the service, he had instantly been taken in. Doolin was immediately recognized as good, rated "exceptionally good," in fact. And remarkably, in an era where it was becoming harder to handle the pushback and bitching from young recruits, Doolin responded with only seasoned, almost veteran compliance.

Unless, of course, someone did something that crossed over his razor-sharp line of fairness or decency. This he would not tolerate, and compliance then transformed into hyperaggressive behavior. And thus, a disagreement at the Marine Induction Center in Parris Island, South Carolina, that escalated into a serious altercation between two recruits, one black and one white, exposed Doolin's aggressive sense of evenhandedness.

Apparently, the white kid—while correct in Doolin's eyes—had belittled the less educated inner-city nineteen-year-old black recruit, and Doolin intervened to politely ask the Caucasian to ease up on the other young guy, who may not have fully grasped the full ramifications of the situation. This Caucasian, instead of accepting the friendly input, attempted to punch Doolin, at which time Doolin savagely kicked his legs out from under him and pinned the guy to the floor with a chokehold that, if continued, would have fractured several cervical vertebrae! The guy cried for help and for Doolin to stop, and Doolin complied—but not before the recipient absorbed the knowledge that this Doolin guy played for keeps.

Doolin then turned to the inner-city kid and told him to rectify the problem, as he was in the wrong. Apparently, the level of directed violence shown by Doolin convinced the African American recruit to comply. Both guys were unhappy with Doolin, but he simply stared at them and nothing else transpired. The facts surrounding this were conveyed independently by three recruits before graduation from Parris Island. The colonel in charge had laughed at the NCO who conveyed this information; the NCO wanted to discipline Doolin. In fact, the colonel was the very same man who had written a lengthy letter to the Marine Sniper Training Center in Quantico, Virginia, to ensure that Doolin was selected; this senior officer knew quality when he saw it. Mallroy watched Doolin exit his office with a wistful smile.

Doolin was escorted back through the security checkpoints before returning to his temporary lodgings, a barracks in part of the Cam Ranh Bay 6th CC rehabilitation and recovery complex. Doolin was on "temporary duty" status; the TDY was actually for treatment of his wounds and to build his strength back up. It was ideal for Mallroy, as he wanted to see Doolin a couple of times during his stay that was now rapidly coming to a close.

Mallroy would then have new orders cut for Doolin that would move him to Saigon and administratively bury him in a bogus unit enforcing the Cam Ranh Naval Base security, sort of a police force to protect the Naval facility. The fact that Doolin was a Marine did not matter; there were growing casualty lists and recovery of personnel enabled makeshift authentic units, cobbled together from not only different units but also sometimes different branches. So, it was not a big deal that Navy and Marine personnel within these units were serving together. Individuals were rotated out as they recovered, then sent back to their original units or sent home if recovery did not go well or if the "time in-country" for their tour expired.

Mallroy would continue his monitoring of EWH and begin to address how and where he would finalize this guy's termination. His source had made it clear that EWH had at least another nine months of duty in-country, but there would be gaps, as Haney would fly to Hong Kong, Clark AFB, Japan, and even South Korea for meetings. Mallroy might just pay EWH's office a visit in civilian attire—a visit using one of three slightly modified identifications Mallroy possessed—and examine the surroundings.

While Mallroy knew this was a touch risky, what with security checks and the possibility that someone he knew professionally might recognize him, but he also felt that the more he knew about Haney, the better. There was always something that could help in ways that might not be foreseeable but could, in fact, be a critical determinant in the success of a mission. *Mission*, Mallroy ruefully thought. *Yeah, my mission ... the successful murder of a CIA station chief, a US citizen allegedly working for our government.* He slowly shook his head.

His mind slowly refocused, and he began to plan.

Incredibly, Doolin returned to the 6th CC and it was as though someone had injected him with a happiness potion or serum of energy coupled to enthusiasm. He almost cursed himself, but the hunt was on again, and he was excited. Yes, Doolin was truly electrified in a manner that took him back to a time in Michigan while at his uncle and aunt's house with his parents on Christmas Eve nearly fifteen years earlier, knowing that his father had spent his hard-earned money to get his son several gifts that Judah had deemed "important" in his young life. Doolin smiled at the memories. The gifts were now hard to remember, but the emotion of lying in bed at nine p.m., wide awake and thinking that he could *not* possibly successfully wait until four thirty or five. The next morning, Judah did spring out of bed and explored the gifts under the tree, exultant, as his father had given him exactly what he desired. The memories were as clear as if it had happened seconds before.

How could he feel this way about the upcoming mission? The not-so-subtle irony of lying in bed as a child, memories of vibrating with excitement on the observed celebration of Christ's birth, dreaming of presents under the tree, to now be matched by his anticipation of a mission that almost certainly involved killing innocent men and perhaps women—all in an effort to trigger a fatal confirmatory response in a treasonous CIA employee. The sad irony was not lost on Doolin. But he had descended voluntarily into a snake pit where these choices and their outcomes were the only metrics by which he could value his worth as a man.

Would God care? Doolin had begun to suspect that his soul was lost. He didn't want to consider what his mother's opinion of his "occupation" would be. Doolin imagined that God would leave him to his own sad end, believing he was now simply wandering as though within a horrible, violent dream set in a foreign country, void of friends, companions, or family. Judah felt truly alone and likely would die alone … totally alone.

CHAPTER 10

CAUSING CHAOS

October 7, 1971

Ab Irato
"From an Angry Man"

T he rhythmic thudding of the blades moved them forward, their rotational force caught the air suspending the helicopter's passengers above the green canopy of the lush jungle below. They moved in a seemingly random path, turning and banking in accordance with the whims of the pilot. The UH-1 was traveling light to conserve fuel, with only the two pilots and no loaded unmanned side-mounted fifty-caliber machine guns. However, they had Doolin. In point of fact, the chopper was always making distance directed north in spite of the curves and arcs, flying through a spectacular orange-and-purple sunset and catching the reflections of clouds and the tangential light below as it bounced off the flooded rice fields. The air was heavy with moisture, the heat just beginning to dissipate from the uncomfortable cloth-soaking temperature of hours before. This land was so beautiful, and yet it barely hid the scars of its inhabitants and their repetitive attempts to harm each other.

Call sign Golden Flower-223—which, to Doolin, sounded like a mobile float in a high school football homecoming parade—was their bird's identification, and it was a clandestine mission. Its job was to drop its package, Judah Connor Doolin, nearly forty clicks into North Vietnam, in Quảng Bình. Satellite, U-2, and F-4 reconnaissance had identified remarkable truck activity in what was otherwise a mountainous region principally made up of the karst cave system. The roads were horrible, but it made sense that Charlie would use these, along with the beautiful geologic formations, as a natural storage depot for its illicit material destined for the large municipalities of the South. The major concern that Doolin had, and it was a growing worry, was the methodology of his exiting this area.

He would be in North Vietnam alone, a single US soldier looking to temporarily disrupt the illicit drug routes, create a momentary panic, and thus elicit a response at the other end of the supply chain. He thought that the entire idea first outlined by Mallroy was a bit loose, but it became completely disconnected from reality when Doolin began later to consider how he was getting out of there. As he ran through the last-minute checklist and review of his operational parameters, he had almost maniacally focused on this phase of the plan: his extraction. Doolin worried that he had failed to properly consider this component of the plan, the literal near insanity of its potential for success dawning on him too late.

Mallroy had stated that he had not wanted to preemptively alert anyone to the need to transport an American soldier out of North Vietnamese territory. He stated he was risking enough to have Doolin transported there by chopper, but he had apparently handpicked these two guys and they were hardened professionals who were also completely loyal to the orange-browed colonel. Doolin's concern was that there were only about a million aspects of this entire plan that could go wrong. But then again, life in many ways mirrors this nearly infinite set of challenges and, well, Judah just had to either accept these limitations to potential success or not go. And he was not sitting this out.

The thin wisps of cotton-white clouds rippled across the sky high above them, their undersides radiant in oranges and pinks; the sunlight was ebbing rapidly. There had been no radio noise. Doolin was allowed to wear a headset, but it served mostly to dampen the noise inside of the UH-1; there was no talking. Then suddenly they were in the North, identified by the copilot turning back and signaling to him. Doolin sat in a makeshift canvas middle seat behind but in the center of the two pilots, and they stopped making their soft arcs and random turns and raced in a straight line at treetop-level toward their preselected coordinates. The copilot, Chris, held up a hand with three fingers: three minutes till Doolin's target, the drop site. Shortly after they were there, searching until they found a brief opening in the rocky ground formations.

Against protocol, the copilot had left his seat and grabbed Doolin's explosives, located in an insulated light-brown bag. Fuses were in a separate smaller satchel within this first bag, and the additional ammo was also in a thick canvas duffel already attached to a rope; both went out. Doolin's training at Parris Island came back as he pulled his gloves tight and grabbed the rope, preparing to rappel down to the surface. His right hand lightly gripped the thick cord while simultaneously his left hand became his bottom brake, held at the small of his back, to manage the speed of his descent.

Moments later Doolin succeeded in landing in soft brush, avoiding impact on the rocky surface. He rapidly untied both his ammo and explosives while the copilot quickly hauled the rope back up into the hovering metal beast. And before Doolin had run even ten feet, his transport was already moving hastily back toward the South.

He was alone. Doolin was in North Vietnam, and no one save Mallroy and his two pilots even knew where he had been dropped off. Moving rapidly into a copse of trees surrounded by low scrub, Doolin checked his map coordinates and gear. When out in the bush, his major concern was always fresh water. Unknown to his pilots, Doolin had placed three additional liters of water in large plastic containers and wrapped them in towels, and thankfully they had survived the nearly seventy-four-foot fall. Doolin was in good shape; his gear was intact.

His other worry was that he had packed several timer detonators that could potentially be damaged and, although less likely, could be made unstable. It was a relief to confirm that his meticulous—some might even suggest neurotic—attention to the details of his gear and ammo had ensured their survival during the drop. It was likely to have been a long day with altered outcomes if his ammo had been damaged, or if he had ended up with no water to drink. Even with the satisfaction of confirming that his supplies had survived, Judah would be on a strict water rationing and still needed to take more from the enemy when an opportunity presented itself. His rifle, scope, and sound suppresser had been strapped to his body and were more important to him than either of his feet; one does not drop into enemy territory defenseless unless you want to become either a corpse or a prisoner. Doolin wanted neither of these options.

Moving rapidly, he carried his gear and ammo, covering the almost three kilometers to the coordinates that Mallroy had chosen: a location near the perimeter of the beginning of the karst rock formations. It was an easy 1,250 yards from a barely visible, by satellite imagery, tire-rutted road. The conduit was large enough for a single vehicle, however, and thus it was felt to be a good starting point.

It was night, and Doolin felt he was making too much noise. Every twenty-five to fifty meters he checked his scope and confirmed that he was alone. As he came within four hundred meters of the coordinates and the road, Doolin chose a temporary hiding site for his gear and reserve ammo. Judah stored his water in two separate locations in case he was on the run and couldn't get back to the primary site. It was now 22:00, and Doolin selected an overgrown crag in the stone face of a cliff that ascended almost vertically for 1,100 feet not 140 yards from the side of the truck path.

He looked at the wear on the rutted path and yes, it was eroded more than a cursory inspection would suggest, and certainly more than any satellite image could convey. Someone was spending time on this mountain "highway." Doolin walked along its path, hugging its perimeter for thirty-five to forty yards until he came to a minor clearing that extended sideways into the forest. There were the telltale signs of human activity, including the vapors of human excrement. Troops, or someone, had used this as a gathering or rest place.

There was little more that Doolin could discern within the shrouded darkness, but he had confirmed that Mallroy had picked a reasonable starting place. As he backed away from the road, Doolin took a circuitous route, checking various footpaths as best he could before reaching the site of his chosen perch, the overgrown crag in the cliff face at 23:40. Without his night scope, Doolin's movement within the stone formation would have been impossible, but Doolin had been trained well and carefully picked his way safely to his nest. It was an excellent location for watching and firing upon anyone using the road 45 feet below and 175 yards from his position.

It provided Doolin an excellent view of the clearing with only one small perimeter interval partially hidden. Everything else was rather easily observed using his night scope optics, even during the moonless night. At Mallroy's insistence, the mission had been scheduled when the lunar orb was absent, as he demanded that Doolin and the crew were not going to be outlined against the plant's white glow while traveling in their UH-1. Every North Vietnamese with a rifle would enjoy using the American helicopter as target practice. Now, Mallroy's decision was welcomed by Doolin, as it had been earlier by the two pilots of the metal flying machine.

Looking out into the clouded but patchy night, Doolin could see stars intermittently, but the light level was very low. *A good night to travel.* Doolin sensed that he might have company by early the coming morning, and he wanted to examine his surroundings more carefully in the early morning daylight to ensure rapid access to escape routes. Unfortunately, he would not be afforded this opportunity.

The first headlights appeared at 02:30 and swelled to at least ten trucks and about thirty people—troops mixed with simple peasants or village inhabitants, as there were both those who wore uniforms and those who donned traditional clothing. As best as Doolin could discern, the first fifteen minutes were consumed by their leaders discussing the appropriate storage sites, and it turned out that these were two grottoes tucked into the base of the same cliff face as his position, only forty-five or so feet directly beneath him. While Doolin was almost fifteen meters above them and slightly to the right of their activity, if one was facing the nearly vertical wall of stone, they repetitively disappeared beneath Doolin as they moved the bundles of pack-ages that he assumed contained heroin or some other illicit material.

Doolin could clearly see their movement, as their path was lit by flash-light-carrying troops that lined a route or corridor slightly curving away from him and descending rapidly. The villagers did the bulk of the lifting and transporting of this material, and it was remarkably efficient and quiet. So quiet, in fact, that Doolin was hesitant to move for fear of loosening some rock and causing a cascade of stones betraying the presence of another hu-man being. He had not explored any of the terrain in the area of their activity, either the pathway or the deeper structures surrounding the grottoes.

Doolin concluded it was fortunate that he had waited. He would have needed a light, and he had no idea if there were semipermanent guards or scouts that had been sent earlier; any movement could have again demon-strated his presence. From his perch, he knew that he was safe—that these folks would never suspect some insane American was taking in their ac-tivities, assessing strength and planning tactics. Doolin knew that he had no chance against a force of this magnitude, but he was eager, if not a bit fearful, to learn how they would exit the area. Would all leave at the same time? Would only some depart, and if so, what was the configuration of the individuals left behind?

The Marine had already emptied one of his smaller bottles for water and used this to urinate in as he lay flat in the wedge-shaped stone crag in the mountain face. He knew that he could have changed his position and crouched or stood up to urinate, but in truth, these were the types of rookie errors that got men killed. Doolin played by the rules of extreme discipline and focused risk versus benefit for every contemplated action.

He watched the process of unloading and transporting the cargo before him for a total of forty-five minutes and then, using his scope, he began to evaluate whether he could identify the ranks of any of the men who appeared to be in charge. These leaders were the ones directing the others and were so obvious in their minimal physical effort, Doolin had to smile to himself; military structure and culture were consistent throughout the world. It struck him that the remarkable leaders, the effective leaders, were the ones who, at least during their early days, actually worked and suffered beside their troops.

The great ones were the men in history who slept, ate, performed the grunt work, and shared the risk of death with their lowest-ranking men; they did not stand and observe battles from behind safe lines. Yes, over time the responsibilities of these great leaders evolved, and the more successful they became, the more they exited the above routine and the proximity of the foot soldier. But it was a given that within the history of great military command-ers—from the Egyptians, Carthaginians, and Romans through to WWII and men like Patton, MacArthur, and Bradley—the truly great commanders were never far from their men, whether in spirit or activity.

At 04:15, the leader, whom Doolin had now identified as a regular North Vietnam army full colonel, was directing all but one of the trucks away from the storage area. And as Doolin counted quickly, it appeared that only seven troops did not reload back into these green canvas-hooded military vehicles. The trucks then restarted, plumes of exhaust visible in his scope. They began to pull out, slowly lumbering down the path and forming a steel-and-rubber-wheeled caterpillar, undulating as they moved in unison out of earshot and finally out of sight. This was a critical moment for Doolin, as he desperately needed to ascertain the number of troops remaining.

Of particular interest was the fact that none of the people dressed as villagers remained; they had been loaded into three of the trucks and were among the first to leave. But Doolin had taken precautions. He had very quickly and as precisely as possible counted the numerous individuals when they were first exiting the vehicles and then again as they loaded, accounting for the total number of people who had returned to the trucks prior to leav-ing. This left seven people, unseen but presumably still present. He could not be certain, as there was a small chance of an error in his counting or that there were additional people who had already been in place when the trucks arrived earlier. All it took was miscounting by one, and he was potentially dead.

Doolin still had about an hour and forty-five minutes before dawn and the resultant light that would strip him of concealment. He needed to either move now or to wait until a full day passed and night again fell. He decided not to engage, but to explore the surrounding environment carefully in hopes of finding any potential advantage. If he was actually going to face odds that were not in his favor, Doolin wanted to know as much as possible about the surrounding terrain. Understanding the topography to formulate plans and gather as much information on activity in the limestone cave structures below was essential.

And so he left his new temporary home, this triangular stone divot that extended back from the cliff's face, open on one side and rapidly narrowing as it extended deep into the rock itself. It was almost nine feet long, three feet high, and four feet wide but quickly narrowed as it extended into the rock to a slit. Seen from a distance facing the cliff, this slice into its monolithic face was a minor interruption to the side of solid stone, having the appearance of an isosceles triangle, with the long hypotenuse side open to thick scrub brush and ferns. The crag thus formed a shelf with a slightly uneven floor, nestled in the side of the giant stone's monolithic surface.

The entire structure, if viewed from the air, was that of a 150-meter pale sheer white-gray cliff rising from the forested floor, reaching a solid stone apex rounded and somewhat smoothed during eons of wind and rain. It formed a natural cap over what in essence was one half of a pyramid structure, cut vertically from its top through its base in a straight descending plane and forming a triangular right-angle mass of stone. The vertical cliff was the exposed surface of the symmetrical triangular shape, with the grotto opening at ground level. The sloping hypotenuse portion of this triangle was its back and its sides.

Adding to its unique configuration, when viewed from the ground facing the rising almost perfectly vertical stone cliff, was a flat, somewhat scooped-out fertile area. This area had trees and bushes in front of the rising cliff, enclosed with two nearly identical semicircular stone walls that formed a rounded perimeter not unlike a lobster claw. These had the appearance of matching curved stairways in a mansion dropping to the reception room, which here was a dense vegetative floor of the forest leading into the caves of this karst structure. These curved seven-to-eighteen-foot walls did not quite enclose the area, as they ended before completing their circle, and thus the entrance to this geological structure was easily accessible.

The back side, as seen looking from the apex toward the rear, formed an irregular descending slope. Within this descent, some portions dropped rapidly, others less so, but collectively they comprised a series of interrupted naturally formed channels or rifts, almost like claw marks, in the solid stone surface covered with vegetation. Some fissures were very deep and short, others elongated as they traversed the general incline, and viewed from the air, this rear topological surface resembled a lion's unbrushed mane. Many of these cut channels were themselves strewn with stones, some of them massive structures creating often deep, irregular clefts and linear scars. Several of these gray-white crevices appeared interconnected like tree limbs branching into smaller narrowing interstices.

It continued its downward descent until forming a nearly symmetrical retaining wall of limestone nearly ten feet high marking its most posterior boundary. The length from apex to this boundary was nearly six hundred yards, and the terminal portion of this soft-sloping lion's mane then abruptly dropped to the floor of the surrounding forest. The wall was nearly four hundred yards in length, and its curved demarcating structure gradually decreased to less than two feet in height at its furthest point from the central rear location. This back wall was also covered with vines and lush green plants, partially obscured by trees at certain locations.

Doolin had entered from this relatively unobstructed rear side, the natural back half of a pyramid, climbing slowly until he saw the front. Now he moved back down this same way, carefully picking his path along its uneven rocky forested terrain. Moving with deliberate slowness but without difficulty over an almost natural footpath that wound down from the top of its densely tree-covered surface, he began to direct himself toward the extreme right. He attempted to descend toward the right-sided curving wall, finding the juncture between it and the cliff's surface as he continued very cautiously looking closely at the terrain. Doolin examined the surrounding areas for any other preformed passages to the floor of the jungle near what he assumed were openings to the grottoes and caves at the cliff's base; he did not want to trip over a sentry.

He had changed his boots for his modified tennis shoes, as they were less noisy and gave him better traction as he picked his way among the loose stone and embedded large boulders, deliberately moving from one tree to the next. Finally, he had a clear view of the openings to the grottoes below, not more than twenty feet below and thirty degrees off his left shoulder. Using his scope, Doolin could see men sitting at the cave opening, smoking and talking. Normal conversations with absolutely no evidence of heightened awareness of their surroundings or that they could conceivably be in danger.

Doolin waited and took a mental inventory of the contour of the cave's opening, the number of men, and understood that surprise linked to ruthlessness would be his two major advantages. This was the phase wherein adrenaline began dumping into his system and his senses had heightened focus. Doolin wanted three or more of them to come out into the open, and he wanted to ensure that they did not have a radio to call back their recently departed colleagues. Finally, he needed to silently eliminate at least four or five of them before getting into the unknowns down in the cave. Unfortunately, reality then stepped in.

Judah slipped. Incredible ... a stupid-ass mistake, but he slipped on loose gravel, fell, and slid nearly four yards toward the sheer vertical drop of the twenty-foot-high wall, only saving himself from plunging over it because he became entangled in the roots of a tree. Now, he had super-charged levels of adrenaline—he had thought he was going to die immediately. The rocks and pebbles cascaded down to the floor of the flat enclosed area, communicating a strange intermittent cacophony as he struggled to regain a proper position. Instantly, three men were aware of the falling gravel and up and moving quickly toward his location. Two things happened that, in retrospect, made a fortuitous series of events. First, they did not shout alarm or commands to anyone inside the grotto; second, they were deliberately quiet as they were intently listening, trying to figure out what had made the sound.

Doolin later came to conclude that they must have initially thought this was an animal or some natural event, something that triggered the slide of rock, but they had no reason to even remotely consider that it might be an American soldier planning to attack them. The chagrined Marine had become twisted in roots and vegetation, but this concealed him as he righted his body. He heard rather than saw the men quickly closing the distance to him. Fortunately, he had not lost his grip on his rifle, the suppressor still securely attached. Doolin examined their individual positions as they approached before he pulled the trigger. His first round caught the second man in the face at the ridge of the nose and he fell, almost totally silent. Whatever requisite sound that should have been released was suppressed by the cushion of leaves and moss on the forest floor.

Immediately, Doolin saw the lead man not ten yards from his position at the perimeter of a small clearing near the base of the vertical stone wall below and fired at a near-perpendicular angle, firing into the top of his forehead at his hairline as he looked up. His surprised expression briefly framed his face, as it was instantly replaced by an exploding tattered scarlet-colored mass of ripped and dripping tissue, and he dropped.

The last man was still unaware of the fate bestowed on his companions as he approached the juncture of the circular vertical wall and the floor of the forest. But as he entered the same small clearing he saw his fellow soldier motionless, a blood-soaked body lying on the green forest floor, and immediately whipped around, racing to retrace his steps and escape at the same instant Doolin's final shot hit him. It landed below the occiput, dead center through his posterior cervical spine. He never uttered a sound as he collapsed. There was a brief spasmodic movement of his legs, and then all went quiet.

The near-catastrophic rookie-like slip propelling Doolin's body toward the edge of the rock cliff may just have resulted in a "fortuitous" initial probing into his enemy's strength. Even so, Doolin knew he had to act quickly to get to the bottom and examine the mouth of the cave and the deeper interlinking system of grottoes. As he moved rapidly down the slope, hugging the perimeter edge of the natural stone wall, he approached the rutted single-lane truck path. Doolin saw that the cliff system was like a giant horseshoe, with the rather flattened forested surface tucked inside its perimeter.

As he approached the road, there was a remaining five-foot ledge to pass. He jumped down onto the rudimentary vehicle pathway and moved rapidly along the perimeter of this portion of the stone barrier to the opening at the front of the entire karst structure. Doolin then retraced his previous descent, hugging the curve of the wall, but now in the lower plane on the actual surface of the enclosed inner region that gave entry to the caves, bringing him back to the clearing now occupied by two bodies. He rapidly searched each, and on one he saw the outline of a handheld short-distance radio, looking almost like the vintage communications gear that American GIs had carried onto Normandy beach twenty-five years earlier. Doolin listened carefully and was quickly able to turn the volume down; no communication was discernible.

Next he moved down remnants of a footpath toward the pale gray surfaced mouth of the cave system, carrying one of the Kalashnikovs lifted from the lead man. Encountering the third body, he pulled him off the path into the denser vegetation. Doolin's own rifle was now slung over his shoulder; he ignored this last man's weapons, specifically this individual's sidearm. Doolin had his own, a Colt .45 caliber clip-fed semiautomatic, a weapon used by US forces since the early part of the twentieth century, a potent and effective man-killer at close range. If Doolin needed another weapon because of reduced ammunition, he hoped he would be able to return for any dropped arms and ordinance.

He rapidly closed the distance and was at the larger triangular opening to the interconnected cave system in eight seconds, where he stopped and waited. Like every other predator in the jungle, Doolin inventoried his senses, straining to hear any sound of his quarry, smelling the air, and visually inspecting the surrounding lush growth for any human presence. It was a disturbing stillness that met his ears, that of a gentle breeze, but otherwise? Silence. Doolin knew that unaccounted-for troops remained, but how many was a calculation based on incomplete data. He worried remaining soldiers could have entered a deep labyrinthine system within the underground grottoes and might even have exited from another point, potentially nearer to him than he wanted to consider at the moment. Doolin waited and slowed his breathing, focusing on sound and sight.

Almost thirty seconds passed before an interrupted fragment of a human voice carried through the air to the surface where he was standing. Doolin tensed and once again checked the Kalashnikov's ammunition. This was followed by a faint but telltale light that bounced on the opposite cave wall visible to the young American, just beyond the far side of the entry. Were men climbing … *a staircase*?

Then, suddenly, the light was extinguished as they reached and approached the entry to the underground system from below. A couple of laughs, and then a sarcastic tone. Three men, or two, or four—Doolin could not be certain—and then they were coming out. From his position, he had three or four seconds of their movement exiting the cave opening before accurate targeting might no longer be ensured. If they came further, someone could hustle off the pathway into the woods, ducking behind a tree, and Doolin would have a firefight and likely a call on the radio for reinforcements on his hands, perhaps those just recently departed troops. These reinforcements could be closer to his position than the time he needed to get out of here and be safe.

All of this raced through Doolin's head as he watched from twelve meters diagonally across a footpath with a clear line of fire. Three men were now standing and looking for their friends. Waiting just a bit longer until he could be reasonably certain the group exiting was the entire remaining force, the lead man's remnant smile at his buddy's last statement suddenly faded; he must have sensed trouble. Doolin stepped out and pulled the Kalashnikov's trigger.

Thirty rounds at near point-blank range tore into all three of the men. The first man with the fading smile was hit twice in the chest, and his nearest companion suffered a round to his right shoulder and neck. The third man was attempting to hit the ground, but the arc of Doolin's projectiles followed him, and he was hit with three separate injuries in the chest and back and rolled over. Doolin had already thrown the AK-47 to the ground and had his Colt out of its canvas holster, running toward the men, when he heard footsteps and a metallic crash inside of the cave.

Oh, sweet Jesus ... there are more!

Instead of running back for cover, Doolin stormed into the mouth of the cave. In the dimmed light, he saw movement down and to the left and instantly emptied the entire seven rounds from his Colt. A scream, or more accurately a yelp, only footsteps away from him. Doolin pulled a flashlight from his pants pocket and illuminated the area emitting the sound. Makeshift steps carved into stone descended rather steeply from a short entryway, leading to a narrow-tunneled hallway. Doolin saw dark, almost brown liquid splotches—a blood trail, and it was significant. The brownish-red cherry-amber liquid formed nearly a continuous line; this individual was moving, although making virtually no sound. He reloaded the Colt, pulled back the slide silently, and chambered the first round. He had one clip remaining.

Doolin hustled toward the tunneled opening, holding the light shoulder high and off to the side. The cool pale gray stone was damp nearest his right side. He could actually hear water faintly hitting a stone surface somewhere ahead of him as the passage curved, creating a blind area beyond the bend not too far from his position. The tunneled structure was not quite four feet wide and almost five and a half feet high in its most generous dimensions, but dropped to just over four feet high for varied intervals. Doolin briefly considered the wisdom of continuing his advance, but if there was more than one individual, he was going to have a difficult time anyway. He put the battery-powered torch or flashlight carefully on the floor of the passageway to illuminate along the far wall as he hugged the near wall, the lesser curvature in this winding tunnel. Let them shoot at the light he was giving them, he thought—a chance to see how many and if they were armed.

If they were able to contact the recently departed troops, Doolin's chances of survival dropped even further regardless of how well armed these people in the cave were. The light shone upward along the opposite wall, allowing him to move without forming a telltale shadow. If he or they were going to fire, perhaps they might miss Doolin and hit his electric torch, but then the ricochet might get him anyway.

Doolin abruptly came to a stop, and listened. The recent noise of seven discharged rounds from his Colt had nearly deafened him, but slowly his hearing was coming back. He really was listening for a radio call for help, as this meant he would not survive, but nothing. Silence.

Again, he could make out the patter of water hitting stone, stronger and louder now; it masked all other noise. This was effective auditory camouflage, for each party.

The Marine suddenly considered, *Shit, they might have already called for help*.

He waited again, reaching back to turn off his light. Standing perfectly still, he strained all of his senses toward analyzing the blackness of the deeper structure. But as his eyes grew accustomed to the near-total darkness, Doolin realized that there was some other source of light ahead.

Doolin slowed his breathing and focused on seeing any movement. Very slowly, he crawled on the moist rock of the tunnel floor, feeling with his left palm along each and every inch in front of him. He moved silently; the electric light was now secured in his pocket. Now it was only his handgun in his right hand, hammer pulled back, ready to fire. His rifle, parallel to his spine, its scope turned on its side, was also touching his back. Doolin inched along with caution, and as he rounded the curve in the tunnel, very carefully picking his way along in small increments, Doolin felt he was descending the further he moved into the cave. The light was growing, but he could not see a source yet, just a weak but slightly brighter shadowed glow.

Finally, as Doolin rounded enough of the gentle passageway bend, he was able to peer into a large space with an indistinct but steady stronger glow of orange-white light. Then it flickered and he was looking at a gas lantern, either partially covered or blocked.

As his eyes were now accustomed to the inky black surroundings of the cave, this incandescent glow looked like a searchlight and illuminated a giant natural cavern set deep inside the surrounding structure of the cliff's face. Doolin could not see the ceiling but could make out a distant wall, its irregular surface ill-defined as light reflected off the interstices of countless stalactites, forming bizarre ethereal shadows. Slowly, he reached the subterranean mouth of the tunnel. Moving into this underground room, he partially shielded his eyes from the brightness of the soft glow of the gas-driven light. And then he heard him.

Or rather *her*, a rather slender young woman in traditional peasant garb, a blood-soaked short waistcoat. Her chest wound bubbled slightly as she struggled to breathe. She was unarmed, and Doolin could see already the fine sheen of sweat covering her evermore pale skin. She was dying, but this did not stop her eyes from widening instantly as she recognized his dirty American uniform.

"*Người huê kỳ?*"—*American?*—she gasped.

Doolin nodded.

She looked momentarily confused and then closed her eyes, and her breathing became raspy. She gurgled and then the movement of her chest slowed, diminished, and stopped. Her eyes were open but saw nothing.

Even in her bloodied, traumatized condition, she was quite beautiful. Her features were delicate, with high cheekbones, shimmering black hair, and dark alluring eyes that were now forever sightless, directed toward some distant point over Doolin's right shoulder. Suddenly he was sick to his stomach and retched once, turning away from her so as not to contaminate her with his stomach's contents. But he quickly hardened his thoughts and looked at the source of light while listening intently for any other movement.

Doolin got up and retraced his steps, climbing the short but steep carved steps to the surface and examining the scene. No one was alive; all was quiet as to human activity. The birds, however, were beginning their morning chirping, and the natural sounds of the forest were rapidly coming alive.

Doolin moved quickly back to the cavern and examined it and the source of light. It was a liquid fuel-fed camping light, similar to the recreational models used by the growing number of campers and hunters in the States, but it emitted enough light to survey the surrounding boxes and crates stacked neatly everywhere around it. This light, in effect, was sitting in a natural minor depression with small rocks or stones surrounding it, forming a cylindrical barrier. It appeared as though it was protection from a fire hazard.

And then—*yes*.

Doolin understood, realizing that a majority of these crates were ammunition. Any risk of fire and the mountain might explode, from the inside! So, for about three minutes he examined all of the crates that he could. Among the neatly stacked RPGs and boxes of ammunition, he found crates of what the North Vietnamese termed *dap loi,* smaller mines. These were both MD-82 copies of the American "toe popper" anti-personnel ordinance. Used not to kill but to maim and slow advancing enemy troops, these were among the cruelest of the American inventions … not that anything in war used to kill, disfigure, or permanently disable other human beings could objectively be assigned a relative "ugliness value." Doolin also found the same precision in the packaging of wooden-crated containers of plastic-wrapped heroin. He instantly understood that the amount of material inside this natural cavern could easily supply a regiment of North Vietnamese regulars for more than a month in a heavy firefight.

What he needed was to find the stored fuel for the gas light and see if there was enough for a good old harvest moon bonfire. He searched around for another two minutes before finding just what he was looking for. Back along the side wall of this massive stone cathedral-like open space, just seven yards from the opening of the tunnel, was a grouping of five rather large green-painted transportable fuel cans. Two were nearly empty, but the remaining three were full. Doolin immediately began to pull apart the wooden crates to create kindling and dumped the gallons of fuel over the crates containing heroin.

A thought was forming in his head—he wondered if he could get away with making this look like an accident, a horrible, perfect storm accident, instead of an incursion by hostile forces. A dramatic mistake that had led to the destruction of all their carefully stored materials. But this would require getting all three bodies from the cave entrance in addition to those three at the base of the cliff. Doolin instinctively knew that this would take far too much time and effort … but what if he stripped the first three of all their belongings, uniforms, and materials, brought the items back here, and allowed them to burn? Made it look like the other three had robbed and then killed them?

No, stupid, there are too many unknowns.

There was too much Doolin didn't know about the relationships between these people that might make any staged killing look exactly like what it was. Perhaps they were cousins or even brothers; he had not examined them closely, so this was possible. But as Doolin considered his options, he realized there was probably not going to be enough time for them to conduct a detailed forensic assessment.

Slowly, another idea began to take shape, to solidify ever so incrementally. As he continued to stack the remaining wooden slats from the dismantled crates, he hurried back through the tunnel, using his light briefly to ensure that he would not knock himself out by striking his head on the unyielding stone surface of a ceiling or stumble. Doolin got to the top and again quickly examined the surroundings—no sound but the beauty of the morning. He hurriedly began pulling the three bodies back into the cave and down the stairs, trying to ignore their placid facial expressions, fixed, unchanged since the instant their life's spark departed.

He actually spoke briefly to one of the bodies, apologizing for his requisite actions and sharing with the corpse that war was no longer some descriptive state or nebulous noun but was, in fact, a compilation of human souls too quickly departed from existence. Doolin was efficient in his actions and movement, but his mind also needed to express its regrets, his latent sorrow for what he had done. But he also acknowledged that he was involved in a trade that demanded no less, and his future would not allow any remorse; this was for later.

With all three corpses randomly placed within the cave, Doolin then looked around and opened an RPG crate, removing two RPGs. He then opened several crates and grabbed several mines.

These anti-personnel metal canisters were essentially explosives with a pressure plate linked to a trigger. Doolin knew how to open them and carefully studied the lower metal seal, a pie-shaped circular plate. He carefully pried open the metal latches regularly spaced around this rather thin round sheet-metal barrier that formed the bottom of the mine and exposed the neatly packed explosives. He did this as quickly as reasonable for a total of four mines and placed them around the ammunition stacks. As he departed, Doolin scooped up two more containers of drinking water previously attached to the bodies and exited through the tunnel, carrying one of the fuel canisters. He began dumping generous amounts of the fuel as he scurried back along the length of the underground passage and was relieved when he came to the stairs, as the entire underground structure had begun to emit petroleum vapors.

Before Doolin climbed the stairs, he took one of his two timer-triggered detonators and set it for thirty minutes, the maximum time. Doolin set it down in the mouth of the fuel can and moved rapidly up the stairs. He had never completely trusted the engineers and the consistency of their timers, so he did not want to be within a mile of the cave when it blew.

He raced back near the site below where he had slipped, causing gravel and rock to spill over the stone ledge. He then quickly stripped the bodies of the three men who initially had come to investigate his almost catastrophic mishap, dragging each of them to the lip of a jagged crevice that originated at the base of the fifteen-foot stone wall. Doolin was breathing heavily as he rolled and pushed them into the deep natural stone fissure. He left the two RPGs neatly stacked nearly fifty meters away from the mouth of the cave—not in plain view, but discoverable with any search of the area.

The distance between the small cleared space where he had encountered the first three individuals and the mouth of the cave was a little more than 150 meters. Enough to create meaningful separation? He doubted it, but perhaps. He carried the clothes and boots into the cave and tossed them next to the half-filled fuel drum. There would be little left intact after the fire and explosions.

He did not know the skill sets of those who would find the destruction in the cave. The potential lack of forensic analysis or detailed systematic investigation might render these three bodies wedged into the stone fissure permanently hidden. While they might provide enough of a malodorous decay to announce their presence, they might also interact with the porous karst limestone and gypsum and actually go unnoticed. It thus might also create confusion for anyone suspecting that perhaps these three individuals had targeted their comrades in what might be interpreted as a drug-related struggle for control of a lucrative product. As long as they were not discovered, any conclusion was fine. As long as they were not closely related, as long as they were perceived as potentially interested in drug money. Too many "as long as" issues, and Doolin knew it.

Finished setting up the scene, Doolin left, retracing his original semicircular route ascending back along the top of the stone wall. It formed a remarkably symmetrical perimeter for the forested green within its encircling wings, the mouth of the cave, now emitting that vaporous petroleum odor, getting smaller as he climbed. Where his path joined the face of the karst's vertical wall, he turned and proceeded down the back side of the limestone structure. The wind had picked up slightly, a pleasant breeze, but the temperature was climbing.

Doolin had effectively killed seven people—the last one a woman, a villager working simply to maintain the supply depot and cook for the men. He wondered if this might even be judged a murder. He had shot and killed her without even waiting to assess, query, or examine if she was armed or a threat at all. But this was war, and he was under orders from his government in the form of Colonel Mallroy to get the job done. *The end justifies the means!* God only knew how Doolin hated that expression! No one would ever know, no one but him … but this also really didn't matter. Doolin had been *excited* at the prospect of disrupting their supply of heroin into the South, if only for a transient amount of time. The human price to pay associated with this delay was simply an inconvenient reality of war. She was on the wrong side, and it had cost her. Tough!

At least this was what Doolin tried to will himself to feel. But he had no time; he needed to get out and put distance between this place and one Judah C. Doolin.

As he quickly picked his way along its edge, Doolin moved efficiently from the peak down the gently curving back slope, working his way between boulders and carefully avoiding the jagged crags in the stone. No twisted or broken ankles! He moved rapidly to the back edge where a second seven-to-nine-foot stone wall composed the furthest back boundary of the entire geological structure. This was where the mountain met the beginning of the continuation of a forested plain, a beautiful rocky landscape similar to plateaus in Colorado and Wyoming.

He was nineteen minutes from the inner semicircle and the cave's mouth, exactly thirty minutes from setting the detonators. He was pushing hard and fast into this plateau region when a low rumble, almost a sustained growl, could be heard. Doolin looked back over his right shoulder and came to a full stop. He had actually made good distance. As he stopped to view the area he had just traversed, a sense of incredible force suddenly pushed against the soles of his feet. The sound lasted for nearly four minutes, and eventually Doolin saw white wisps of smoke rising above the tree-topped peak before being wafted away as it caught the breeze.

With that, Doolin turned and continued to hurry further South toward the DMZ, knowing that he soon would exit the hills and the rolling rocky and forested plains to encounter flat farmland and rice fields. Open and devoid of any helpful cover, he would have to move at night. The closer he moved to ultimate freedom, the DMZ, and a form of safety, the more treacherous his journey would become. He rested after walking almost five kilometers. Doolin again consumed a minimum of fresh water and started searching for a place to sleep. In the distance, he heard nothing; no planes, no vehicles. He wondered how long it would take them to return to the charred remains of their underground storage system.

In all likelihood, his previous target was only one of several natural storage depots and might, in fact, make little difference to them strategically. But anyone with any analytic skills would be alarmed by the suggestion that someone within their ranks would be so corrupt as to kill their own people to steal or destroy heroin and whatever else they found missing. Doolin found it strangely comforting that by being inside of North Vietnam, he probably was as protected as he could be. Given that few of the enemy troops would consider that a single American would be the source of this destruction, he likely would be relatively safe. They would be looking for a Special Operations incursion made up of dozens of US assets, and even this would be very unusual given that the Americans almost never ventured into the North, at least on the ground. Nevertheless, Doolin also realized that his highest risk of getting killed was from an accidental discovery of his presence by some farmer or village inhabitant leading to the North Vietnamese troops being alerted, and he was not going to become a prisoner of war. Nope, that was not for him.

That afternoon Doolin dozed until almost 21:30, and then he was up and looking through his scope along the various line of sight corridors that the trees and stone would allow. Most villagers would be asleep by nightfall; electricity was uncommon for all but the busy metropolitan areas, and even there it was at times sporadic except in American military establishments. Even Saigon had areas repetitively losing power. Doolin had already accepted that if he was identified by anyone, he would immediately kill them. He wanted no witnesses and no possibility of capture by the North Vietnamese. Deciding to kill "them" might include a defenseless farmer or even a village child, but then Doolin would do whatever it took to survive.

The young Marine thus began to acknowledge that he had drifted about as far as he could have from the precepts of his parents, those gracious and lovely souls who had raised him. He was a killer, and now not just a killer of military combatants, but of anyone who interfered with his mission, or what was loosely perceived as his ordained and self-approved activity. But he latently discovered that he was not immune to the self-loathing that had claimed so much of the serenity, if not the lives, of those he had served with.

Doolin contemplated his discussions with Major Stein; this man was going to be lucky to get out of here alive. His spiritual being was immersed in a terrible struggle, his actions self-adjudicated as "just or evil." Attached briefly to a young wife, she whose juvenile perspective could not grasp the complexity of the byzantine and often difficult moral choices inhabiting Stein's existence, he was attempting to resurface from the cesspool of self-hatred and guilt, and it was not yet clear if Major Stein would succeed. This ultimate exegetical debate would decide his fate; its verdict would predict whether Stein would be a survivor or a living but broken casualty of this war. Doolin sheepishly smiled to himself that he just might join Stein, or even surpass him in his self-condemnation and spiritual brokenness. But these reflections rapidly faded, as his self-preservation was still important enough for Doolin to at least try and survive.

It was night, and the surroundings were motionless. No moon existed in the sky and the clouds were a low-hanging amorphous gray blanket without the faint reflected moonlight of the surroundings. Yet, there was some light from the stars, and remarkably the human eye can recruit even minimal amounts of visible energy to see outlines and shapes. The textures of the terrain surrounding Doolin were distorted in the pale blue-gray pastels that continued down an uninterrupted slope to the beginning of cultivated fields below. He started his descent, moving slower than in daylight, as he needed to avoid unanticipated impediments that might trip or injure him. He had been lucky so far, not only in overcoming the opposition forces, but in managing to minimize any accidental injuries. Both were potentially deadly—some sooner than others—but each carried exponential risk for every day he was within hostile territory. Doolin took but a measured comfort in the cloaking of darkness, as he knew all it took was one curious villager, one farmer trying to check on his stock or look out on the water-filled rectangular fields while relieving himself. But the young American was fortunate.

Nine days later Doolin crossed into South Vietnam, not certain as to the exact location where the southern boundary of the DMZ ended and the formal line demarcating South Vietnam began. At present, he was more interested in avoiding the infestation of toe poppers and larger buried pressure-activated landmines. He was now traveling very light, obtaining drinking water from the afternoon rain showers, having become an expert at funneling the runoff from vegetation into his canteen using leaves and stems of plants. Doolin had his Colt, his rifle, and scope, and he must have smelled like a wild animal. He had bathed twice, once in a stream and once in the rain. His shoes were not boots but the cloth-rubber tennis shoes that he had taped with thick uneven layers of packaging tape on the soles.

His preselected rendezvous point was the Rock Pile, more formally known as Elliott Combat Base, approximately ten miles from the southernmost boundary of the DMZ and sixteen miles west of Dong Ha. This was another cone-shaped structure, another ecological karst, and although its geological origins were different from Black Virgin Mountain, the two shared many characteristics. It had been labeled by some of his Marine buddies a "toothpick-type" mountain, with almost perfectly vertical sheer cliffs situated in the middle of an open flat farm and vegetative region not far from the DMZ and the intersecting five valleys at its southern border. By mountain standards, it was more of a hill. It was not that impressive, a mere 790 feet tall, but stood one kilometer from the vital vehicle transportation artery Route 9. While it was unquestionably the highest peak in the immediate area, there were much higher hills in almost all directions if one looked out on the more distant horizon. Still, it was critically important as a strategic observation post and forward support base, a FSB able to effectively observe and inflict injury to Charlie coming in from the North and through the DMZ.

The problem, Doolin had always realized, was getting back alive and safely reintroduced to his own command. Both Mallroy and Doolin had known this particular issue was inherently dangerous when they planned his return previously; he did not want to get shot and killed by his own side. Appearing out of the damp, misty jungle, an amorphous shape, a moving apparition with a rifle—he was a rather tempting target for some fellow Marine sniper. So, the closer to the region of continuous observation by those in the Rock Pile, the more he moved in and out of the minimal cover that the flat topography provided. Doolin had an idea of what day it was; he thought he was in the middle of the preset time zone that Mallroy had dictated was Doolin's return date. This meant that Mallroy should have alerted another of his Army or Marine colleagues that he was due to come into camp, but of course, Doolin had no way of confirming that his colonel had provided such information.

Doolin also knew military personnel rotated rather frequently. There was a natural turnover within these camp locations over time, and he just didn't want some young itchy trigger-finger to claim his initial notoriety as a consequence of Doolin's scalp being pinned to the man's belt.

It was 6:35 in the morning, and an uneven blanket of mist hovered over the partially flooded rice fields. This would force Doolin to come in closer than he wanted; he had to ensure that his own people waited before they determined him to be the enemy. Doolin made it within five hundred yards of the first set of perimeter defenses and then did something that he had never dreamed he would do: He stepped out into the open space for a total of about three seconds, lifted his rifle upside down with his left hand holding the barrel, and then quickly stepped behind a tree. He repeated this five times before picking out a new location closer to the Rock Pile, and again he performed his "I am here" dance.

Judah then stopped and knelt behind a natural mound of earth nearly three feet in height, covered slightly with green reeds. Looking through his field glasses, he systematically examined the perimeter fencing. There he saw the cleared-out and heavily mined rim of space surrounding the base of the rising geological structure. The military facility situated at the apex of the mountain appeared quiet; no movement, no flag or light. He then decided to wait for thirty minutes and began watching the areas he had just traversed, his back side. Charlie was a frequent traveler along the many footpaths in the area and used this region to transport men and material South. Doolin didn't want to get caught from behind in incidental contact with the enemy so close to safety.

He waited twenty-five minutes and was considering how he could get into the camp when he heard the signature sound of blades cutting through the air, the repetitive thumping of a UH-1. It flew over his position once with the right-side door open and a uniformed crew harnessed in place, leaning out with binoculars and searching the ground below. One of them must have seen Doolin, as the chopper banked a short distance from his position and made another pass just overhead. The chopper was lower now as the metal beast slowed and began to descend about fifty yards away, aiming for the crossing of two intersecting earthen banks demarcating the boundaries of flooded rice paddies. Doolin looked up and over from behind the small earthen hill he had chosen as his primitive concealment, and the harnessed door gunner was hurriedly waving to him.

Doolin got up and threw his rifle over his shoulder, loosely hanging on his back, and sprinted toward the helicopter. The pilot in the right seat was studying him, carefully watching this troubling visage. A tinted green sun visor covered half the pilot's face, but there was no doubt he was warily viewing a lean animal-like predator racing toward his ship. The morning ground fog swirled, creating a trailing mist-filled eddy as Doolin ran toward the camouflaged metal structure. The pilot nodded once as Judah was now almost to the radius of the rotating blades. He crouched and reached the side door just as the gunner, still secure in his harness, reached down, grabbed him by the arm, and pulled Doolin up, who rotated his body inside the helicopter. They were already lifting off the ground and immediately began banking toward the Rock Pile.

The side door gunner looked at him and motioned for him to put the headphones on. Doolin did as he was asked, and the gunner spoke slowly into the plastic microphone at the end of the slender metal arm attached to his helmet.

"You must be special cargo, Corporal. Got highest priority orders not more than twenty minutes ago to get you. We were near the old base at Khe Sanh dumping ammunition and were ordered to get over here immediately. You OK?" Doolin nodded yes, and the gunner shook his head. "Well, you look like shit!"

And he grinned, and so did Doolin.

"I guess you can't say much, but where the hell have you been?" the gunner queried.

Judah said nothing, but pointed toward the North.

The man's smile disappeared, and his face went flat. A trace of alarm surfaced as he processed this information.

Doolin remained silent and hooked his arms into one of the nylon straps that served as temporary harness straps to secure passengers sitting on the metal floor.

Within forty-five seconds, they were descending onto the LZ at the Rock Pile. As Doolin exited the chopper, the blades were still rotating as the pilot was intently talking to someone and readying the beast for continued movement.

Doolin glanced back at the door gunner, and he gave Doolin a thumbs-up and a brief nod. The Marine returned the gesture, dipping his chin, but his eyes were searching the gunner's face as he stared at Doolin for a long time before turning his body and speaking something into his microphone. The bird was lifting off the ground again, and Doolin shielded his eyes and face from the air drafts and resultant flying small debris.

The sound intensified and then abruptly began to fade as the UH-1 climbed and banked away from the LZ and off the Rock Pile, moving rapidly over the valley. The beast was gone in twenty-five seconds.

Doolin stood and looked around to see a senior Marine lieutenant approaching. He saluted immediately; the officer returned the gesture and motioned for Doolin to follow him.

As he approached, the lieutenant stated, "Doolin, right?"

"Sir."

"We began to get priority flash traffic concerning you …" He paused, giving Doolin time to respond, but Doolin said nothing; he wasn't sure why the officer was bringing any of this up.

"Yes, four days ago we began to receive quite highly encrypted messages, 'flash com' traffic concerning the fact that you might be coming in or arriving in the vicinity and we were to watch out for your arrival. What is a little unclear is, where are you coming from, Doolin?"

Mallroy had previously discussed this, strongly emphasizing to Doolin that the less anyone knew about the nature of his actual mission, the better. Doolin was simply to say "advanced reconnaissance" and leave it at that. If anyone pressed him, Doolin was to offer minimal information about looking at enemy routes into the South to confirm suspicions already entrenched in the dialogue between different commands. Still, the fact that someone had actually been ordered into the North was highly unusual and thus raised interest in any and all parties. But Doolin was not to bury his mission; Mallroy had specifically requested that he answer questions truthfully while at the same time not offering unsolicited information.

Perhaps, Mallroy had offered, Doolin should reinforce the current belief held by strategists and commanders: a collective understanding that the DMZ was still a very porous barrier, unable to impede enemy troop movement and equipment headed for the South, and Doolin was simply confirming such. While such a response was certainly plausible, and superficially acceptable, anyone with any sense would immediately become suspicious. Doolin's activity coupled with the high-priority extraction and flash communications would not comport with this mundane narrative. They would rightly suspect there was considerably more to the story, and they, of course, would be correct!

Thus, Doolin looked at the lieutenant without emotion, his expression impenetrable. "Detailed recon on enemy violations of the DMZ, sir."

He looked at Doolin and half nodded. Puzzled, but cautious, he stated, "Well, good to have you back. I must say that I have had five encrypted 'twixts' on you from a Colonel Mallroy, highest priority." His eyes were locked on Doolin, his concern surfacing through the façade of calm.

Doolin almost shrugged but remained silent.

The effect was as anticipated. The lieutenant stared at him for several moments, waiting. Knowing that he could not ask Doolin any additional information, knowing that the occurrence of sending a lone Marine sniper into the North was incredibly unusual, if not unheard of, at least by him, and understanding that querying further risked violating the "need to know."

He finally looked away and stated, "We have another bird scheduled at fourteen hundred that will get you back to the world. Just hang out for a bit—no one will really bother you …"

And with that, Judah stood and saluted as the lieutenant stated, "Dismissed, Corporal."

CHAPTER 11

MALLROY IS GONE!

October 19, 1971

Exercitus sine duce corpus est sin spiritu.
"An army without a leader is a body without a spirit."

D oolin could not have known at the time, but his intervention in the North had already spawned serious repercussions. It was not until several years later that all of the information would be available to the young American, and this, through a strange series of fortuitous and highly improbable events. But these future occurrences would involve material that provided a more complete context to what now was a succession of rapidly unfolding measures that Doolin would both hear about and personally encounter as he landed at Da Nang.

Colonel Mallroy was nowhere to be found, having apparently gone completely off-the-grid before Doolin returned from the Rock Pile. It appeared to him that Colonel Mallroy had solidified plans for Doolin's safe re-entry at the Elliott Combat Base, and then he vaporized. As Doolin waited for extraction and return to Da Nang, the same lieutenant commented that the colonel had contacted the Rock Pile's commander every day for five straight days almost two weeks ago. Then all contact abruptly ceased. Was Mallroy now stateside at some meeting? Or what? There was no other information regarding the "spook in chief" Mallroy. Who could know, with Mallroy's skills at deception, what he was up to? He might have been in France on the Riviera, sitting on a beautiful beach basking in the sun.

This same lieutenant who initially had been frustrated by Doolin's unwillingness to elaborate on the visit to North Vietnam was incorrect about getting Judah off the Rock Pile. It took an additional thirty hours for the UH-1 to extract Doolin, and he then began a series of shorter helicopter flights until Doolin was delivered to Da Nang.

Getting off the bird and moving quickly away from the rotating blades, Doolin was looking forward to some real food, not the dried fruit and fish that had sustained him for nearly four weeks. He had again lost almost eleven pounds, and although he was not weakened, Doolin could tell that he was dangerously close to the line between thin and being almost malnourished. But as soon as he was off the flight line and back into the secure compound that normally housed Mallroy, he knew something was up—something not right. A different keeper, a new light colonel, one Lieutenant Colonel Stevens was waiting for Doolin even before he passed through the first security check.

"Doolin," he stated forcefully and, not waiting for confirmation, added, "follow me."

Doolin was whisked through security and turned down the same hallway to the second security checkpoint. Again, they walked through—no search, no hesitation—and then continued further down the hallway past Mallroy's office to a back room subdivided into discrete smaller work areas, each with a Plexiglas series of half walls sitting atop wooden baseboard dividers. This guy walked fast, but Doolin observed that Stevens was watching him with periodic sidelong glances, his pace slowing as if he was contemplating seemingly incongruent data. He ultimately chose one of these tiny partitioned work spaces, evidently at random. There were no personal effects in the space, no individual memorabilia, and he motioned to the stool sitting alongside the desk and the chair.

As he sat, he looked at Doolin and began to open a manila folder he held with his left hand. He slid the contents onto the table and carefully arranged the papers into a perfect stack. All the while he looked at the documents, yet Doolin knew from looking at his eyes that he was focused somewhere else, somewhere distant, debating what he should say. The lieutenant colonel's initial attitude was that of a superior, a boss talking to a common laborer. But as they had walked and Stevens had carefully and silently stolen some glances at Doolin, his attitude reflected in his pace had gradually changed. The more he looked at Doolin, the more Doolin felt the man became confused with the disparity of rank and of whatever data he had been provided regarding Doolin, or this young American's mission.

Finally, he must have arrived at some internal final set of decisions. "Corporal, I have some orders here from Colonel Mallroy. These orders are a bit unique, to say the least; I have never shared classified information with anyone below officer's grade previously unless they were a clerk with security clearance. I have never operationally discussed data or information with someone of your rank."

Doolin's smirk must have shown through despite his best efforts to conceal it. He couldn't help but enjoy this prima donna's uncomfortableness.

Stevens immediately glared and Doolin's smirk turned into a thoughtful frown, instantly erasing the half smile. But then Stevens's eyes softened; he reminded himself to take in the context of an underweight eighteen-year-old Marine, having successfully returned, according to this summary, from North Vietnam on a highly classified but still undetailed mission. There were not many of these sorts of characters wandering the halls, despite the insanity of this war, the changing sides, and the convoluted alliances that existed one day only to evaporate the next. But this kid sitting in front of him was a trained killer—of that, Stevens was sure. Doolin's eyes missed nothing. He was silent in his movement, efficient in his motion, almost fluid as he sat or reached for the door or turned in the room; there was no wasted motion. He had intelligent eyes, wary but not afraid, cautious but not timid. Doolin was, the lieutenant colonel realized, a predator. A lethal predator of other humans.

This "kid" was not a desk jockey, but a real live combatant who lived and roamed free in the harsh reality of an unforgiving jungle with men and women who pursued a strategy to capture, torture, and kill him. And he had not only survived, but the word was, passed directly from Mallroy, that the organization owed this kid, and owed him big time. But what the hell had happened to Mallroy? Stevens was aware the actual circumstances, and they were nothing short of ugly. The whole issue was gravely uncomfortable for Stevens: this kid, the preparation of an almost precedent testimonial by this "bird" colonel, and the notes specifically addressed to Doolin—a handwritten dialogue between colonel and corporal—invoking the highest security status possible. Beyond weird, and then Mallroy's so-called "departure" … how could this have happened? Stevens was one of the few who knew the facts surrounding Mallroy's departure, and the facts were catastrophic.

Stevens was new, having actually met Mallroy in person only about six weeks ago, but he had sensed in Mallroy a need to pull Stevens into his confidence, in part or perhaps specifically because he was new and untainted by office alliances or outside influences. Stevens was not certain, but he had had a creeping intuition that something may have been on Mallroy's horizon and the colonel needed someone to be available to clean up the mess if he was tied up or unavailable. Had Mallroy also had a premonition? Or was he simply navigating in shark-infested waters and making use of every resource to bolster his own odds … of staying alive? This premonition had proved prescient.

The narrative regarding this exhausted eighteen-year-old, however, was nothing short of Hollywood in the eyes of Stevens. He had simply had to reread twice the accounts of Doolin's actions on Black Virgin Mountain, and he would have thought the story certainly exaggerated were it not for the multiple inputs from all ranks and the simple statement from one Major Stein, whose final comments regarding Doolin were succinct: "He is an American HERO! This is not bullshit." Even under combat or any stressful conditions, officers were to complete a dispassionate account of events summarizing any action in a manner consistent with an objective unemotional tenor, but Stein's comments were anything but.

That's nuts, the lieutenant colonel had thought.

But here it was, in black and white and in Mallroy's own hand. And prior to Mallroy's troubling departure, Mallroy had been involved in leaving no resource untouched to ensure that this kid was safe and coming back to Da Nang to be debriefed. He even had a sealed envelope for the kid's eyes only. *Complete bullshit*, Stevens had thought.

He continued, "But here it is … Mallroy—Colonel Mallroy wanted me to extend his most sincere appreciation for your efforts on behalf of the forces of the United States and Republic of South Vietnam. And he wants you to read this first."

Stevens handed Doolin a white business envelope and asked him to open it and read the contents.

"Corporal Doolin: Judah" was handwritten beside Doolin's formal rank.

I want first to express my appreciation to you. You risked your life and future to address a traitor within our ranks. I want you to know how much your efforts have assisted me in pinpointing the source. I am dealing with it. I need you to be debriefed by Stevens if I am not available. You may speak to Stevens as though you were speaking to me. Do not embellish, but more importantly in your case, don't downplay the events, Judah, just explain in detail what you did and what you observed. I will recontact you in the future. If anything happens, remain who you are, Judah, but a parable in "Matthew" is relevant to you: "Gifts are not to be squandered."

Mallroy

Doolin finished the note and thought briefly about the parable before Stevens reached for the piece of paper. He hesitated, but then handed it to him.

Stevens stated, "No loose ends. Mallroy's orders."

Doolin smiled and readied himself for a five-second query before a disinterested dismissal, yet what transpired was anything but a cursory exit interview. Almost ninety minutes later Doolin had finished a no-nonsense, honest summary of events, leaving out the fact that he had shot and killed an unarmed civilian female. Doolin also provided a directed assessment of enemy activity in the DMZ.

As Doolin finished, he simply stated, "I think that's about it," and sat back, looking directly into Stevens's eyes.

He was staring back at Doolin. His face betrayed a look of unease coupled with near doubting amazement. He was motionless; nothing in the room moved. If he had been Doolin's rank, Doolin would have jokingly broken the ice and said, "It's OK to breathe now." But he was not, and the corporal sat quietly, wondering if Stevens thought that he had made this shit up.

Fuck him, Doolin thought.

But Stevens surprised him. "That is a rather remarkable story, Corporal."

He could see that Doolin's face hardened in response to his comment, his face reading as though some prick had just accused the youngster of making up a fairy tale. So Stevens rapidly added, "Mallroy stated … quote, 'This kid's the real deal.' I think I agree with him, Corporal … Mallroy wanted you to know that he is putting you in for a Silver Star." And at this, Stevens smiled as he saw the look of discomfort involuntarily register in Doolin's face.

"That is not necessary—with all due respect, sir."

"He told me that would be your response. Shit, Corporal, you might want to reconsider letting anyone get to know you so well, except maybe your wife—eventual wife or whatever. But you need to reconsider allowing a colonel to have an inside track on your thoughts, Doolin."

This was said with humor, almost genuine affection, but his tone also contained a trace of sadness, as he was processing the events in North Vietnam along with what he still had to tell Judah.

"OK, Doolin. This last piece of business is really unpleasant for both of us, but you, my young Marine, are likely in real danger. I know this sounds sophomoric as both of us are sitting in the middle of an unconventional guerrilla war, but you are in danger of getting killed by someone who is supposed to be a friendly."

Stevens sighed. His shoulders even dropped, sagging momentarily. "I have to share with you that Mallroy was assassinated four days ago. Shot five times as he was waiting to enter the MACV2 compound by three, four, or even more guys posing as foot taxis. They literally walked to his car and, at point-blank range, shot the colonel and his driver, some younger guy from the embassy. He was dead as he hit the pavement.

"This was not a combat kill; it was premeditated murder. Trying to find the guys who ran off and likely disappeared into the back-alley maze area … well, our likelihood of finding them is zero, in my estimation. Colonel Mallroy was very concerned that anyone working in the clandestine area might need to take precautions, especially one Corporal Doolin. I was ordered by him to ensure you were protected. I swore not only a professional oath to him, but a personal one as well … I'm just letting you know."

Stevens had seen Doolin flinch at the shock of the news and paused. "You OK?"

Doolin tried to recover immediately and said carefully, "No, I am not OK," but it came out a bit more forcefully than intended.

Stevens looked carefully at the younger man, who was beginning to stand. "I just know that there is a network of assassins targeting important players in both American and Vietnamese forces. My worry is that you may be on that list. Actually, Mallroy was *very* worried that you are on that list."

"I'm sure he is or was correct, and that suits me just fine," Doolin snapped at Stevens. He was up without permission and clearly having difficulty keeping his emotions under control. Apparently, the young man had deeper feelings of loyalty for this Army colonel than he had realized.

Doolin squeezed his hands tightly to the point where his knuckles blanched white and clamped his jaw, and then he heard Stevens say softly, "Judah, please sit down."

Doolin registered surprise at his Christian name. He partially regained composure and began to sit.

"I needed to hit you with that to judge your reaction. I apologize, but not professionally. What I did was deliberate and purposeful; I do, however, apologize for the personal insult to you. I just had to know you were not involved."

Doolin had started to glare at Stevens but was rapidly processing the disclosure, the full extent of his comments, and anger was transforming into thoughtfulness. He began to logically connect the lieutenant colonel's need to screen Doolin to assess his response. This guy was doing his job, and doing it properly. Stevens's carefully and softly spoken comments did not fully alleviate his anger—in fact, one could call it rage—but it did mitigate, at least to some extent, the full force of the shock in learning Mallroy was dead. He now understood why Mallroy was not here to debrief him, to greet him.

Deep within Doolin's being, he intuitively knew that Mallroy had been eliminated by the CIA Station Chief Haney. He also knew that the fallout from this assassination would not be clean nor limited to a single event. Some of the most clandestine and forceful instruments in the American empire were being used for a corrupt purpose, compartmentalized and concealed from any and all persons other than the ultimate perpetrator. Only this abominable individual would be able to see how the complex assortment of pieces fit together to facilitate success regarding their final goal.

And this goal, of course, was to continue to supply the South with drugs. What Doolin didn't know was that Haney had decidedly changed tactics. The long-held edict of prohibition of requisite reprisals and limiting the eradication of any threats that could harm the lucrative drug trade for fear of inviting imprimatur interest in activities had become optional. The money was just too powerful an incentive.

Doolin was minimally comforted that Mallroy had kept his name out of the typical rigid listing of orders that flowed up and down the structured chain of commands existing between various military bureaucratic centers. But he also knew the system well enough to understand that a single slip of the tongue, an unmasked name of an operative, or a comment by some idiot in the command structure was all that it might take to enable talented sleuths to trace his involvement and thus arrange his premature departure.

Stevens was still observing Doolin, carefully watching. Doolin slowed himself down, got control, and then said, "With respect, sir, what do you want from me? Or perhaps more importantly, what are your plans?"

Stevens smiled a tight smile, for he was pensive, and obviously troubled. "I again have to ask for your patience, Corporal, and if you don't mind, I am going to start by calling you by your Christian name. I am not used to sharing information and strategy sessions with a non-officer of lower rank …"

Doolin had begun to cease his listening, but Stevens immediately picked up on this and held up his hand, palm facing him.

"That, however, is *my* limitation, not yours; I will learn quickly. Judah, I will trust you if I think it appropriate in a manner outlined and requested by Mallroy, OK?"

Now, the Marine was engaged; his eyes were locked on Stevens.

"So …" He paused. "Here we are, and I am not sure what to do, frankly, so let's talk this through. Acceptable?"

Judah barely nodded his consent.

Stevens began slowly and provided context to his narrative. "Mallroy corresponded with me twice in private letters. He knew, as did we all, that those of us in military intel have all of our mail read or screened before being released to the mail service. Importantly, this was a service that was assigned to the military but staffed by low-level CIA employees, as it was deemed a time-consuming nuisance. So, Mallroy knew that he needed to create enough fog in his correspondence to make his intentions opaque. We, in war time, were under a blanket of scrutiny and our letters were watched, and this is appropriate for intelligence services.

"Thus, knowing this, he wrote a short letter inquiring about my father and family followed by a long letter. My father had died four years ago, so this tipped me off that this was a message within a message. In the second much longer letter, he included the following statements embedded in the communication. He stated that he spent time reading the Bible to ease his conscience about losing men in war, and it was in his spare time that he was sort of struck by the intensity in certain ancient stories. Among these he noted the ancient chronicle of Rahab, in the second chapter of Joshua. Immediately, upon seeing this, I realized it was a thinly veiled advisement by Mallroy that he was investigating in real time some concerns within the espionage community.

"Judah, let me help you, if needed, in a little Biblical history to place Mallroy's concerns in their proper perspective. In the letter, he got around to asking me if I thought Rahab in the Bible was accurately portrayed as a spy or as a double agent since he, Mallroy, thought she was just a loyal subject. How could she have committed betrayal of Jericho's king? He said that he didn't put much stock in this traditional interpretation, et cetera.

"So, Mallroy was worried that we had a mole or an agent working against the interests of our government in Vietnam who was thought to be a loyal subject. Further, Mallroy then postulated that Rahab's house was by the city wall, which to me meant that she was inside of the king's fortress city. The

Biblical story was that she alone breached its defenses by offering a way for the men to escape to the mountains. In fact, he wrote the very passage 'Get to the mountain, lest the pursuers meet you. Hide there three days, until the pursuers have returned. Afterward you may go your way.'

"This was a statement that someone inside our government structure itself, not the Vietnamese government, who was thought to be loyal was actually involved in perfidious activity. He tellingly left the paragraph hanging and did not go on with any more comments regarding Rahab. This was like a sign saying 'Here is the problem I am interested in!' But to a casual reader of hundreds of letters, it sounded like a committed Christian discussing a story during Bible study!

"He then asked about my parents and then my son, Judah. He implored me to enjoy the time I had with my 'son' and to cherish our time together. The problem? I have no son, Judah, and as noted, my father died four years ago. Corporal, that 'Judah' he was referring to apparently is—well, obviously it's you! Mallroy went on in the letter with idle gossip about command, who was 'in' and who was 'out,' but eventually got around to asking about my uncle Philbee in Lebanon, Ohio.

"I have no uncle by that name, and Philby is the name of the infamous traitor in the British equivalent of our CIA who was stationed in Lebanon, Beirut. Philby was head of MI6 in Beirut when first suspected by US and British intelligence of being a Soviet mole. So, once again, he gave me direct information in a manner that did not trigger any repercussions, given that our mail is screened. As it should be.

"But the whole letter and clandestine approach ... well, I have to be honest here, I considered this unnecessary and fairly lame, if not outright overly dramatic. Yet now he is dead, and this letter was his last testament. Remember also that I only met him in person within the last six weeks, but Mallroy never discussed any of this with me again. He had a lot on his mind.

"Taken in the context of recent events, it appears as though the likely cause of his death was the investigation of someone in the CIA. He was worried that his correspondence might tip his hand and, more ominously for him, implicate or expose me. I have done some work—in fact carefully checked—and there has been and is currently no one that I am aware of snooping around to examine my activities. Of course, I can't be entirely conclusive here, but it appears nothing unusual has been transpiring. So, his approach was effective, to a point."

"To a point," Judah finally said. "He's dead."

Judah was now locked in, watching him, and Stevens half smiled. "Yes," he responded, "and it does look as though his meticulous caution was as necessary as it was unsuccessful."

"We will have to judge that, as the future is unknown, Colonel, sir."

His gaze, having drifted slightly, shot back to Judah. "Yes, we will … yes, we will, Judah."

CHAPTER 12

LUNDGREN'S DECEIT YIELDS JUSTICE

One Month Earlier: September 3, 1971

Per Angusta ad Augusta
"Through Difficulties to Greatness"

The limited American female nursing staff at US Army 3rd Field Hospital in Saigon found it both necessary and interesting to share idle gossip regarding Christopher John Lundgren, MD. He was, for many, the "catch" they had contemplated for years. A combination of polite Minnesota manners coupled with Scandinavian heritage provided a classic Nordic appearance in his chiseled face and piercing blue-gray eyes. He was physically muscled, lean but strong with an appearance of just stepping out of a shower, clean, fresh, and "pressed" despite the intrinsic humidity and heat of Saigon. He responded immediately and carefully to any question and was seldom abrupt, even when casualties flooded into and exceeded the small hospital's capacity. He wore no jewelry save his grandfather's 14 carat gold Hamilton watch; there was no wedding ring, for he was not attached.

The hospital itself was busy. While not up to American standards of the mainland, this pre-war urban hospital was advanced for Asia and in truth was remarkably well staffed and equipped. Most technology of the day was present, being upgraded by American effort and money. The volume of trauma far exceeded any comparable stateside institutions. A lesser-known fact to the American public was that the few existing Western-style hospitals in Vietnam were modernized and served along with the somewhat romanticized image of updated MASH units, or mobile army surgical hospitals. These military trauma centers had been popularized by the Hollywood movie about serving veterans from a previous war, the Korean conflict, and the TV series with the same moniker was immensely popular. Thus, this hospital, along with dedicated Army and Navy "military only" facilities, broadened the scope of America's medical response to the ever-growing casualty metrics found in Vietnam.

Chris had completed his residency in general surgery with an active-duty military deferral, but upon finishing his mandatory five years and one at the NIH, he sought entry into the Army. Ultimately sent to Saigon to assist in the eroding military conditions after Tet, he saw firsthand the cost of Vietnam's evolving legacy. He had spent eighteen months in Saigon and had six months left before the "big bird" took him home. As his government grappled with an exit strategy he, like many, sensed the end was going to be tragically unforgiving.

Several of the older surgeons had told him to keep a low profile and just operate. But they had also broodingly cautioned him that while his technical surgical skills and judgment would dramatically improve, he had to resist the emotional "darkness" that would grow in seeing so many young lives destroyed. Lundgren had not dismissed this last element, for he knew that this was his greatest challenge—that, and staying alive. He had listened carefully to vets that he encountered in his training. Those from Korea and WWII both recognized and communicated to Chris the hidden scars that many kept from public view. He had wondered if he was to also suffer his own assortment of mental wounds.

Chris had seen the cost of war reflected in their tearful, rheumy eyes, the modest, eternally humble but hardened survivors of WWII. The veterans from this era were becoming less common, but they still existed as senior surgeons or medical personnel. A perceptive, even prescient individual, Lundgren felt their vulnerability even when they joked and dismissed their experiences with patented humorous understatements of their time in war. But when the mask of patriotism and bravado was removed, and when the spectators had gone home, many of these same true heroes suffered memories that scalded the soul.

The vast majority of Vietnam's American vets were much younger, but often they, too, simply wished that they had been the one to perish rather than their best buddies. These men had witnessed a sudden tangled broken shell, a lifeless form who moments before had complained about his feet hurting or the quality of food they all were forced to eat. For these survivors, they had bonded with "a someone from somewhere with some background" different from theirs. Even such casual connections, perhaps not important in the eyes of an outside observer, were the requisite nourishments to those facing possible death. These young kids, most not yet twenty-one years old, had shared the laughs, the frustrations, and the fears, the *pervasive* fears, the collective experiences that ended with that someone lying face down, legs shattered, a riven skull and face, the ground slowly absorbing the coppery remnants of life.

Chris had prepared himself the only way he knew how: careful analysis of the environment he was to inhabit, and a simple request to his Creator. The analysis was ongoing and updated daily, reviewing his surgeries, his management, his choices; the request to God was for him, Chris Lundgren, MD, to bring healing and peace to his patients. The rest, he simply accepted, and thus he worked to save the young men and occasionally civilians who were caught up in this struggle.

He worked without complaint, without drinking, and absent the sarcasm and bravado that insulated most from the pure terror of war. And as he worked, those around him grew to respect, then admire and finally revere him. The female RNs loved him beyond his striking handsomeness, for they saw both the humility and humanity in his care and work every day. His standards slowly transformed the hospital surgical staff. The compliments to different staff members became more common among the collective group, and a clean-shaven and kinder language began to replace the haggard-looking contemptuous "cutters." Their frequent vile outbursts, for any and all who crossed their paths, receded as a tide from a beach, the sand washed of unclean habits. As the atmosphere of professionalism reemerged, the hospital's staff understood within a spectrum of awareness why this had transpired; they looked to a young surgeon from Minnesota who kept to himself but gave freely to his young wounded patients.

As his reputation grew, his actions were sufficient; he remained quietly and intensely focused upon his craft, studying his outcomes and results constantly. He went from major to colonel in one and a half years. Part of this was the attrition in staff; as older surgeons rotated out, the residual staff would fill their shoes and then Army promotion boards would ensure that position equaled rank, as was required. Combat officers despised this ultra-rapid promotion, but this was simply a reflection of the rapid turnover within the medical corps. Chris was outwardly giving no indication of rank, for he was respectful to all and deferred to anyone with input, meaningful input. For the others who liked to hear their audible utterances fill the air, void of meaning or insight, he simply ignored them. But it was not a cruel gesture; even with these people he would give a tight smile underwritten with his genuine humility, stripping the recipient of reprisal.

On a Friday just after eleven thirty a.m., the hospital got a call on the radio regarding four individuals shot near MACV2 in what looked like an assassination, but details were scarce. Two were now en route to Lundgren's facility, the other two taken to another. By chance, there was a lull in the often-frenetic surgical schedule and Chris had just finished a cup of coffee. He was walking near the back of the hospital near the ambulance ramps when Lundgren thus met the "crackerbox" at the ambulance entrance, quickly surveying the two victims.

Both were dead. The younger man had been shot in the chest and the skull. The skull wound alone was enough to kill him; half his left temple was gone. The velocity of the projectile had caused the deformation in his skull as it travelled through soft tissue, vaporizing the surrounding brain and bone. His head was thus asymmetric, a deep divot in the front and side of his face behind his left eye where the bullet had carved out its mark.

Lundgren then looked at the older man. He also had been hit several times, but the terminal event was a grouping of two shots to the top of the head. Lundgren worked out that he must have been bending forward as the gunman shot twice at close range to implode the top of his skull, now a swollen, deformed soft mass of blood, hair, and fragmented bone.

Both of these men had been killed instantly at the site of the shooting, and this fact was evident as soon as Lundgren climbed into the back of the overused ambulance. One of the MPs standing off to the side, a tall man of twenty-six who looked thirty-five with deep lines already forming in his face, his eyes guarded, had been analyzing his notes and was now looking at Lundgren.

He nodded at Lundgren, and the surgeon approached him from three yards. "What is your read of this?"

"Assassination," the MP responded.

"Tell me the circumstances?"

"No, no can do … I can't do that, sir. Investigation is opening now. And even if I was allowed to discuss it, which I am not, I'm really not sure of all of the details. Sorry about that."

"I understand. Can you tell me anything about them? Names, or anything?" Lundgren asked.

The MP looked skyward briefly, considering, and then half smiled, shrugged his shoulders, and said, "The young guy there is a state or likely CIA employee. The older guy here is a full bird colonel—Army Intelligence is what I'm told. I guess that's all I can say."

Lundgren said nothing but nodded. This was an assassination; someone had wanted one or both of these guys dead.

Before he knew it, Lundgren asked, "Is this common?" and immediately regretted sounding like a four-year-old. This was Vietnam; a war was raging and people were getting killed daily, as Lundgren intimately knew via his busy operative schedule.

But the MP did not scoff or even smile and remarkably, in Lundgren's view, considered the question.

"Sir, not sure how much I can tell you with a pending investigation, but NO, this is not normal."

Lundgren looked at the MP. "OK, well, if you need anything …"

Surprisingly, the MP stated, "I do need you or someone to give me a cause of death in detail, slugs if you can dig them out, and the whole nine yards … OK?"

"Sure, but that wouldn't be me. An autopsy will need to be done if you think this is a criminal case, which I guess it obviously is."

"Yes, as you say, it obviously is, but if someone could just examine the bodies to see the wounds, I'd appreciate it. And if you can see a slug, you know to give it to me … the sooner the better. You know what they say—if too much time goes by … not helpful for any investigation. If I have to wait for four weeks for the final report, it is not going to expedite this investigation, if you can understand my need for some speed."

"OK, sure … I get it, yeah. OK."

And with that, Lundgren, the MP, and an Army corporal loaded both bodies onto two separate gurneys. With Lundgren at the head of one, the corporal at the other, and the MP trailing, they wheeled them from the entrance down a central green-tiled hall, turning into a side hallway where they had to form a single file, as the passage narrowed slightly. At the end of the hallway, a room with two doors opposing each other—each with a dark-brown wooden lower half, the upper half holding a frosted glass panel—was labeled in black block letters "Morgue."

The body-laden gurneys were pushed through these doors and as they opened, both wheeled stretchers and their attendants entered a large room with two steel tables, each supported by a central pillar allowing them to tilt bidirectionally.

"Whoa, boys, what ya got there? This is not Christmas time, you know," the older man, still in his thirties, in a white apron similar to a butcher's garb and equally as bloodstained hectored the newcomers. The pathologist and his forensic assistant were busy with an alleged manslaughter attributed to a drunk GI running over an elderly Vietnamese man with a military jeep. Recognizing Lundgren, however, the older man immediately smiled, and his tone softened as he attempted an amended greeting.

"Hey, Chris, what's this? KIA goes to holding and the icebox and I'll get to them as soon as schedule allows, OK?"

Lundgren answered pleasantly but with a tone that brokered little objection, "Doc, these two are likely murder victims and the MP just needs an initial wound check and, if possible, a slug. OK for me to help him out, just for a minute?"

The pathologist examined Lundgren's face, his greeting, and the tone simultaneously. He then said in a soft, almost inaudible response, "Yeah, sure, Chris. Just leave any notes so I can attach them to my report." He motioned Lundgren to take the other table.

Lundgren, realizing that he had in effect ordered the pathologist to comply, attempted to soften his declaration. "You sure it's OK, Fred? Not too much of a bother?"

The pathologist, Fred Kowolski, shook his head, already returning to his existing evaluation.

"Thanks, Fred. Just going to look quickly and then leave them." But the pathologist was immersed in his examination of the elderly man's neck, comparing it to an X-ray displayed on the eye-level light box.

Lundgren asked the Army corporal to stay, as he had worked with Lundgren previously. Lundgren and the corporal undressed the younger man first and reported that two entry wounds were present in his chest, along with superficial but numerous lacerations. The light from a silver metal ceiling lamp extended on its long arm and hovered three feet from the surface of the body. It provided a brightly illuminated cone of light but gave off minimal heat as it highlighted sparkling nuggets embedded in the skin across the upper torso of the corpse labeled "Body #1: Driver."

The light was reflecting off of windshield glass shattered during the attack, distributed unevenly but superficially within the dermis surrounding two separate bullet entry sites. A corpsman cut away the victim's clothes and no other wounds existed, save the deforming single entry into the left temple just above and behind the left eye. Years later, extensive forensic photographs would be taken throughout this process, but this was Vietnam. Resources were limited, and a physician's description accompanying a pre-printed form showing a standard figure representing the body annotated in accordance with the specific wounds would have to suffice. Chris was look-ing at folded paper taken from the body's wallet, now being held up to him by the corporal.

"Says here this guy is Thiem, William Thiem."

He spelled the last name for the young MP as he made notes in a spiral pad, roughly sketching a reproduction of the image before him and bending close to Thiem's skull before slowly shaking his head and muttering, "No chance at surviving that."

He looked up to find Lundgren examining the other body still in a gur-ney, but without the aid of the powerful illumination. Lundgren, wearing rubber latex gloves, was feeling the upper right and left shoulders of "Body #2: Passenger."

"Doc, do you want to bring the light over him but leave him in the gur-ney?" the MP asked. He was hoping to enable a quick and ultimately less cumbersome examination of the second body, but Lundgren shook his head. Lundgren's assistant, the corporal, was on the opposite side of the examina-tion table as the MP stood near Lundgren.

"No, let's do this by the book. Help me move him onto the table."

The noise four feet away at the other examining table momentarily ramped up, almost a detonation as the pathologist and his assistant started laughing uproariously. Then, noticing the collective silence surrounding them, they became instantly self-conscious, looking up briefly before each shrugged nearly in unison and went back to their work. But a few chuckles were heard as they continued.

Lundgren, the corporal, and the MP moved Mallroy onto the table and the corpsman started to remove the blood-soaked shirt. Paradoxically, his khaki trousers were almost unblemished while the simple short-sleeved white dress shirt was nearly completely saturated in a sticky ferrous jelly, its tang mixed with seemingly random congealed clumps the color of darkening copper or sienna.

As Lundgren pointed out the wounds to the MP, he also took time to detail the other injuries to the chest and arms. He watched the corporal re-move the man's clothes and place them on a waist-high steel stand with detached professional interest. The corporal pulled off the trousers and, slid-ing them gently off the legs, he extracted the wallet from a back pocket and again found identification.

He held an ID up to Lundgren, who read the name to the MP. "This man is—or was, pardon me—Mallroy. And yes, he was a full Army colonel." Lundgren frowned as he looked down at the remnants of Mallroy's body, then spelled the last name for the MP.

During this time, the corporal had successfully removed the pants from the body and was placing them on the metal bedside tray, but Mallroy's brown calf-skin belt slipped and fell to the floor.

As Lundgren reached to pick the belt up, the strong brightness of the ceiling lamp illuminated an irregular patched section of sewing along the edge of the belt. The two strips of calfskin had been carefully resewn back together over a length of not quite two inches.

That was odd, Lundgren thought; it looked for a moment like a decent repair job or, conversely, a botched initial attempt, sort of a defective product or "seconds" that might be sold at a discount.

The black thread along the surface of the longitudinal border joining the two pieces running lengthwise was slightly fuller; it was newer and ap-peared to be a replacement thread. It was simply not as worn as the original. But what caught Lundgren's eye was the fullness of the belt's two opposing leather strips, a palpable thickness demonstrating a minimal but discernible step-up in the smooth surface of the leather adjoining the resewn segment.

Something was inside the two opposing leather calf-skin hides making up this belt. Lundgren felt a cold shiver down his spine realizing that he was looking at something that had been deliberately hidden. In light of the al-leged assassination of this man, the contents might have been important, but he just as quickly dismissed this as he thought that the man, Mallroy, likely hid money. Some quantity of cash, some sort of emergency money in case he was in trouble. This was the outlined form of a homemade money belt.

But Lundgren immediately knew this last explanation was inaccurate. This appeared to be an expert job, almost completely unnoticeable, and did not assume the shape of paper money; it was too small and just too thin. Unless it was a folded thousand-dollar bill greater, and then for someone to go to this much trouble for a single currency note was illogical to Lundgren.

Further, who would want to waste time attempting to cash such a large denomination? Where and how could one even convert such a denomination? And finally, while US dollars were almost the gold standard in Vietnam, gold, in fact, was the standard. So, if money was the treasure, then why store paper money?

Lundgren's mind raced as he considered these issues and felt that the hidden material was not money; he was almost certain of it. But then … what was it? He laid the belt on the stand but immediately started to think through his next moves to "procure" the belt. He suddenly realized he was contemplating committing a felony. Interfering with an investigation, tampering with evidence—this was obstruction of justice.

But he knew—somehow, he knew—that his need to understand the contents and its story were almost righteous. He could not explain it; he just knew.

He needed to be out of public view to open the stitching and remove its contents, but taking the belt might be better done in plain sight. He got his chance as he asked the corpsman to get paper bags that could be sealed to transport each of the victim's belongings. Lundgren considered that the easiest way to take the belt was to do it in front of everyone present in the room. Thus, as the corpsman returned, Lundgren motioned for the corpsman to roll the body over and stated to the MP, "Be sure to look at his back side to ensure that we don't miss any other entry wound." Both men obliged and momentarily examined the back of Mallroy's corpse.

As the MP and the corpsman were engaged, Chris slowly picked up Thiem's belongings and placed them into "Bag #1." He then moved toward his intended target, Mallroy's shirt, and, still wearing gloves, folded the blood-soaked shirt and placed it in "Bag #2." Both bags were constructed identically with a folding paper lip coated with glue along the outer upper boundary, allowing the bag to be sealed. Next he picked up Mallroy's pants, folded them, and then reached for the belt, again noting the almost undetectable bulge within its opposing leather surfaces. He began to curl the belt into a tight circle before placing it on the trousers. He positioned the first paper bag on the stand, not three feet from the shoulder of the MP who was bent with the corpsman examining the mid-torso of Mallroy. Then Lundgren positioned the second bag on the same stand and placed the pants within the bag.

He grabbed the belt with his right hand, while still holding the bag with his left, and slid the belt into the long side pocket on the right side of his white physician's coat.

This was the cotton overcoat that hung to Lundgren's knees and allowed physicians to carry the requisite stethoscope, reflex hammer, and other assorted equipment. He then casually sealed the bag while his mind screamed, *THIEF!*

He reached for a single blank 8x11 sheet of paper on the pathologist's desk, picked it up, and folded the paper and wrote Mallroy's and Thiem's names on each side. He focused intently as he fought the adrenaline pouring into his veins and neatly tore the paper along its horizontal crease, then placed each labeled half of paper with the respective victim's name on their respective bag. This, he did slowly and with obvious deliberateness.

Afterwards, he turned and returned to the desk. He picked up a second sheet of paper and also folded it, but this he covertly placed in his pocket, the fold acting as a small paper tent covering the portion of the belt nearest the top or opening of the pocket.

As a last gesture, he moved just behind the bent-over MP and spoke in a voice registering thoughtful confirmation of the lack of trauma to the back of one Colonel Mallroy, "Yes, I don't see any entry or exit wounds in this area. OK, you can lay him back down … gently, guys …" Lundgren stood and turned away from the MP, allowing only his left side to be plainly visible.

Christian Lundgren, MD, had just committed the felony he had previously briefly contemplated, and he knew it. Ironically, he could not understand or really explain why he needed to see the contents of the belt before, or absent, anyone else. He was not objectively certain that anything of intrinsic value was hidden within the two opposing leather straps of the belt, but he knew it was critical to retrieve the contents before deciding what had to be done next. He had never done anything like this before; he had not even ever been cited for a traffic violation, let alone a major violation in the chain of evidence or obstructing a government investigation.

Why? he asked himself again. He later reflected that his actions in the morgue were patently insane. He was incredulous with himself for his rash and inarguably risky actions as he later mulled over his decisions. But he didn't try to explain, for somehow he knew he was correct, that his actions were justified. What he could not know was that the act of taking the belt would prove to contain its own inherent inertia, beginning and pushing forward a quest that would last a lifetime, whose consequences would literally form a palpable ripple in world events.

As the MP and the corpsman gently laid Mallroy's body down, Lundgren removed his gloves and moved to tap the MP on the shoulder. The younger man turned immediately to face him, a perfunctory gesture with eyes questioning the contact.

"OK, stuff's in the bags. Take care." Lundgren pointed to the two sealed paper containers. "Folded and placed. Hopefully they will not pierce, soak, or tear."

Lundgren's right side was still positioned away from the two men, toward the wall, and he casually walked to the doors of the mortuary. He paused and called to the pathologist. "You need any help, Fred?"

"No, Chris, but thanks. I'll get to your cases in a while."

"Actually, they're not mine, just helping him out." Lundgren pointed to the MP and motioned with his eyes for the MP to address the pathologist, which the MP did.

"Whenever you get time, if you could let me know, I'll be happy to come by and observe."

"You sure about that?" The pathologist half grinned.

"Yeah, I think so." The MP grinned back.

"Call me if you need anything else, OK?" Lundgren spoke, looking at the MP, who returned his glance and touched his now ungloved fingers to his brow, a thankful salute.

To Lundgren, he added further, "Thanks, Doc. Appreciate the timely service."

"No problem." And thus Lundgren exited the room, carefully closing the door behind him, and made his way down the tiled hall, turning into a seldom-used passageway off the corridor to his call room where he would have some assurance of privacy.

Lundgren sat on the side of the narrow twin mattress on an iron-frame bed in the call room looking at the belt, examining it carefully. His small duffel bag with his toiletries and a change of underwear sat on the foot of the bed. He pulled the bag close to ensure that he could stuff the belt in the bag if he were interrupted or called for an emergency, which was almost a certainty.

He then re-examined the belt, looking along the newly sewn section about four inches from the buckle end. The bulge was small, but when looking for it, it was obvious. But like the unrecognized abnormality missed on an X-ray, the finding became obvious only when you knew what you were looking for. The thread was the same color, but with close inspection one could discern that it was replaced. The texture, the thickness, and indeed the fullness of the unworn cord betrayed a distinction from its more pronounced threadbare counterpart. The material found on either end of this new segment, while not tattered, was indeed showing its age. In effect, the borders of the 1.5-to-2-inch "revision" revealed no disturbance to a cursory assessment. But the telltale signs were present, and seemingly great care had been taken to conceal the disruptive reconstruction. This in itself fascinated Lundgren.

He got up from the bed and moved across the short distance to the closed door of the call room. Lundgren opened it casually and looked out and then back at the bed as though he was forgetting something. No one was present in the side hallway. This was his real purpose, though seeing no one only relaxed him slightly. But he continued his deception by snapping his fingers as if he had just remembered an item forgotten and re-entered the room slowly and deliberately, closing the door behind him. He then hurriedly but methodically took his straight razor, a gift from his father, out from his shaving kit and using his surgeon's skill, he opened the edge of the belt between the two joined leather straps.

Oh shit! Yep. Someone—Mallroy, most likely, the man just shot twice in the head and once in the chest—had placed a small, very small folded collection of onionskin or rice papers inside the belt. Very carefully, Lundgren pulled them out and looked into the created space between the leather. A small 6x2-millimeter rectangular piece of plastic—actually, it became apparent that it was a sharp piece of thin film; a negative, a single microfilm, or what they called a "microdot" —remained. His eyes dilated in excitement as his thoughts raced. What the hell was going on here?

He began to unravel the thin papers and immediately recognized that there was a series of numbers, some, if not most, nearly sixteen digits long. He reached into his small canvas book bag that he carried between work and his barracks in the officers' quarters and pulled out a pad of paper. Over the ensuing seven minutes, he copied the numerical data found on the onion papers and coming to the last two of eight pages, he recognized tiny writing. He searched for a magnifying glass but realized that he had his intraoperative ZEISS magnifying glasses and pulled these out from their case. While primitive in comparison to the next two generations of eyewear, their precision optics were simply made to last, and Lundgren never gave these up over his ensuring forty-one years of his practice. He switched on the bedside light and positioned the thin rice paper to achieve the optimal focal length, and then he began to read.

> *1–3: Cayman Island: Accounts referenced via Fred Reese and joint audit of 7 accounts for CIA activity Jan 1969 to Sept 1972. Outliers are starred, amount in question $3,546,000 and change. Build-up has been over last 8 months but variable prior to the 8-month interval. Deposits up to $400,000 per month.*

> *4–8: Taiwan: Accounts Joe Sampras, DIA IG Accounting. Audit demonstrates balances for 7 accounts nearly $4,897,000 in unverifiable and unreported "black" installments. Sources unknown, paperwork nonexistent. These controlled by Eric W. Haney, no other source activity identified. IG states would be complete violation of departmental policy, no regulatory oversight.*

And as these rice paper scribblings continued, the tight, meticulous, incredibly delicate handwritten notes continued listing numerical and factual evidence of an immensely detailed investigation and audit. *Mallroy had taken the time to do this?* And it must have been done using the same magnifying instruments that Lundgren was using to read them.

He finished reading and then copied the name Eric W. Haney and the contacts noted, including Fred Reese and Joe Sampras, along with others. Intuitively, Lundgren felt that he was now in possession of evidence from some investigation, and what bothered him was the fact that if these data were the reason that this guy—*What was his name ... Mallroy, yeah, that was his name*—had been killed, perhaps it was also behind the murder of the younger man, Thiem. Obviously, something important was involved.

The "something" was undoubtedly money, but how was it gained, and what was it being given for? Intelligence, drugs, weapons? Lundgren had no way to confirm or investigate. But he could guess, surmise, that this was war, and Lundgren was no fool; he knew the pressures being brought to bear by a cunning and unremitting enemy. Their total and consuming effort was to undermine the validity and effectiveness of the American war effort in Southeast Asia.

All options were on the table, and the North Vietnamese were fully aware of the growing dissatisfaction of the American public with what was now becoming perceived as an illegitimate war. Soon, even the most reasonable of the "silent majority" felt the effort appeared to be emblematic of the faulty bureaucratic hauteur linked to disastrous outcomes of an increasingly untrustworthy government. The war was lost, Lundgren thought. *It is now a matter of how to minimize the injury to our people, our objectives, our allies, and our nation.* A sad departure from the near-unified lockstep of victory witnessed after WWII.

Lundgren sat on the bed, unsettled, pensive, and concerned. Through his incredible, arguably stupid spontaneous act, he had become, in point of fact, the sole proprietor of this material. What was he going to do with it? Hand it back to the MP? He might get a slap on his wrist, but he could explain that he just wanted the belt and then found this stuff. There might be a letter of reprimand, perhaps, but probably not. The war was just too overwhelming, and in truth, no one would really care.

"Chris, if you wanted a belt, just tell us and we will buy you one for 2 US dollars, leather, from Hong Kong at the Saigon market. Best quality, latest fashion … Pierre Cardin …"

But more importantly to Lundgren, what would happen to this material? A man, two men perhaps, had potentially lost their lives over this material and he, Lundgren, suddenly became aware that he needed to understand why. He laughed at his sudden realization, and at his naïveté; he was a child in the forest of any criminal investigation. And what gave him the right to supersede the chain of command, anyway?

But several elements still gnawed at him. The US war machine was huge, a reflection of the superpower status of his nation, left largely intact after a world conflict that saw a magnificent European culture built over centuries largely obliterated in a zero-sum game conflagration. The US was left unscathed, a young lion cub, half adult, half child, eager to take its place on the world stage. And thus, nearly by default, America had emerged as the self-anointed policeman in accordance with FDR's prescient but arguably flawed view of the post-WWII future. Yet within this powerful and capacious national bureaucracy, one had to ask if there would even be an effort to address the deaths of these two people in a conflict that would claim nearly sixty thousand active duty personnel.

Lundgren realized this was not going to occur, and this very fact—the loss or waste of a human life, if not two—troubled him. Actually, it simply pissed him off. He had dedicated his life to the service and care of human beings, to their collective healing done one at a time. The thought that a person could somehow be obliterated, their memory, purpose, and value as human beings totally erased, infuriated him as much as it frightened him. As if they actually had never existed. To Lundgren, it was equivalent to a soul being discarded like the skeletal remnants of a boned fish being prepared for consumption. It simply was not proper.

On a personal level, Lundgren had labored too many hours to save the legions of young warriors brought to him, torn to pieces, maimed, damaged, and permanently disabled. He knew his personal efforts were but a drop in the endless sea of a paradoxically collective effort to protect and repair both the innocents and combatants. On the one hand, the US strove to efficiently kill those deemed to be the enemy, and then turned around and expended great effort and significant resources to save those injured deemed to be friendly.

You could not make this stuff up. Lundgren slowly shook his head; war was truly an insane environment.

But to witness two such examples … the slowly simmering chaos of this war was beginning to accelerate and would almost certainly relegate this double homicide to the "Cold Case" file. It would eventually be ice-cold, effectively tossed in the trash and forgotten.

Nope, bullshit … absolutely not going to happen, he thought, even if his world was but a tiny microcosm of the overall theater of conflict. He could not allow this!

He could not be certain, but to all appearances, this man and his colleague had been assassinated not one hundred yards from the entrance to MACV2, the location housing the war's intelligence services. And for all Lundgren knew, he was the only surviving entity with any real interest in understanding what this evidence represented. Arguably, the young MP and his superiors would pick up the case, but for how long? How long before they were transferred to another duty station and the circumstances, context, and specifics of this case were left slowly ossifying into a fossilized relic?

NO! Chris Lundgren could not allow that to happen. For the remaining years of his life, he could never fully grasp why the death of these two people had upset him so deeply. In life, he had never known them; in death, he had spent no more than twenty minutes with their physical remains.

But soon he stopped thinking about the why and accepted his duty. He felt, if not knew, that he owed these two unknown casualties the decency of an investigative effort. They had been killed, and for what? The "for what" he now held in his hand.

CHAPTER 13

HOMEWARD BOUND

March 1972

Ab Inconvenienti
"From an Inconvenient Thing"

Six months later, thirty-six hours before Lundgren's PCS—or permanent change of station, his rotation back to the States—Chris had by chance entered the hospital cafeteria. It was long after the change of shift, nearly eight p.m. or 20:00 hours, and there he encountered the pathologist, Fred Kowolski, MD. Kowolski was the archetypical pathologist and had been the apron-clad man working in the room when Lundgren, the MP, and the corpsman transported Mallroy and Thiem to the morgue. Lundgren had met him, befriended him, and secretly wondered, if not with some degree of risible speculation, how he might likely behave on a first date.

Fred was from a tight-knit family in Milwaukee, devout Catholics. He himself had been an altar boy who furtively suffered exposure to the execrable sexual depravity of a homosexual priest. At the age of eight, the priest began to intrude upon Fred's personal space, putting his hands on his shoulders, then around his waist. These episodes were brief, but enough to hint to Fred of their impending malevolence. But this passed, and it wasn't until three weeks after his tenth birthday that Father Paul slipped his hand inside the front of Fred's pants and grabbed the boy's genitals. Fred tried to move away, frightened, shocked, and stunned by the betrayal. The priest placed his strong arm around Fred's shoulder and in a continuous movement pulled the boy to him, kissing him while fingering his penis. Fred was able to extricate himself but only after another kiss, his mind reeling in response to this personal assault.

Fred never told his parents; he was too ashamed and confused by the actions of this man, Father Paul. The priest was so revered by his mother and silently respected by his father; how could he have possibly engaged in such behavior? But Fred took pains over the next three years to maintain a safe distance from this man, and this time as an altar boy coincided with his explosive physical growth—nearly seven inches over three years—and at nearly five feet, eleven inches, Fred was an imposing figure by the time he was thirteen years old.

Fred was, by nature, an ebullient soul with twinkling blue eyes and a bit of a ski-jump ramp for a nose, but it added premature character, making him appear a bit older. Coupled with a solid jaw, he had an attractive masculine face, if not actually handsome. A gentle and meticulous individual, he had nevertheless dismissed the actions of this reprobate priest as this man's shameful issue and not any of his own participation. He knew now that he had not encouraged or facilitated this deviant behavior in any way. And so, remarkably it was through prayer—the use of the communication with God that the priest had long encouraged in his parishioners—that Fred asked and reached a decision, approved by the Creator.

Thus, on a Friday evening in November after mass, Fred, now almost fourteen years old, asked the priest to accompany him into the small wood-paneled sacristy with a heavy oak door hung on silent brass hinges. As the door silently closed, just as quietly Fred whirled with the full force of his man-child frame, uncoiling like a sidewinder striking at its prey, and buried his fist in the elder man's face. The force of the impact caused a blowout orbital fracture and permanent loss of normal sight in the priest's right eye. Fred's action unequivocally announced the termination of their relationship, their association.

Nothing was said by the priest—he knew better—but as Fred stood over him, he quietly related to said priest that his time of trying to deflower young boys had come to an end. The old man, crumpled in the corner of the room, was wedged between the wall and an elegant mahogany chair. He tasted blood in his mouth, and it was also dripping from his nose. His head felt as though it had been struck with a wooden baseball bat. Fred further assured him that if any word ever reached Fred, by any manner, gossip, rumor, or truth, that such behavior had resurfaced, Fred personally would extirpate said priest's genitals and stuff them in his mouth. Although Fred could not see his own face, it reflected a pent-up rage that would give even the most hardened warrior pause, a rage seen only in those who have experienced violation of their souls.

The elder man was shaking violently, his nose oozing blood, his right eye swelling shut, face asymmetric as the skin grew purple red, the physical trauma causing bleeding just below the dermal layer, but it was the stench of urine that terminated the unilateral conversation. Fred left the small sacristy and shut the door gently behind him, head held high, and never again let the experiences with this reprobate enter his mind.

Now, as a professional, Dr. Kowolski's attention to detail and his memory were nearly equal to Lundgren's; in fact, at times it might be argued better. He intuitively felt comfortable with organization and patterns that made sense, and his extraordinary mastery of human anatomy and its components, its various tissues and cellular patterns, represented this inherent need to place a degree of order into his observational processes. Coupled to this remarkable memory that could recall these patterns and extrapolate their myriad natural plasticity of shape and geometry, Lundgren was certain that Kowolski would eventually author manuscripts or even a full textbook on his insights into the variations of histological pathology.

Lundgren often consulted Fred, and within their separate overlapping tours they had become comfortable and respectful of each other's skills. Kowolski was prematurely balding, his thinning wispy light-brown hair no longer covering a shining pate. His manner was methodical, his jawline strong, and his somewhat chunky features belied the fluid movement that embodied his professional activity and the acuity of his mind. He wore black framed glasses, and while few people can be said to have their appearances enhanced with these clunky Army-issued frames, Fred Kowolski, MD, actually looked as studious and learned as he truly was.

The hospital canteen and cafeteria were combined; several soft-drink-dispensing machines were arrayed along the far wall opposite the glass-fronted commercial steam tables where hot meals were provided to the staff. The midsized room with fifteen tables, each with three plastic-backed chairs, was open twenty-four hours a day. Coffee was always available, and sandwiches were placed in the cold food bar near the cash register at the far end of these four stainless steel hot food bins. On this day the pathologist sat at one of the tables nearest the middle dispenser, the Coca-Cola machine, and had an open file he was reading, nearly oblivious to his surroundings.

Lundgren walked into the commodious room. Only one other couple was in the room: two female RNs, white miniature caps pinned to their heads, white uniform dresses covering their white-stocking-clad legs, both smoking and exchanging the day's gossip. Lundgren immediately noted Kowolski and thought briefly about simply leaving him to his solitude, moving by him out of the room, as Lundgren was not that hungry or thirsty and the man looked to be intently studying a file or some chart. But then the pathologist looked up and smiled briefly at Chris, then frowned, and the suddenness of his reaction piqued Lundgren's curiosity. It was as if Kowolski was remembering something after looking at him. An odd combination, even for Kowolski.

Then the pathologist stood and almost eagerly waved Lundgren to his table. As the surgeon approached, the pathologist was sitting again and surprised Lundgren as he took part of the file or manila chart he was reading and turned it toward Lundgren so the surgeon could clearly see the heading "TOP SECRET."

Lundgren stopped dead in his stride and looked up, focusing intently at Kowolski, who was already scrutinizing him, their eyes locked into each other. Kowolski, with a slight motion of his right hand while glancing toward the nurses, ever so slightly beckoned Lundgren to sit, and the surgeon carefully slid into one of the plastic-backed chairs.

"Chris, you were the one who brought these two people into my morgue nearly six months ago or so," Kowolski softly stated.

"Actually, it was exactly six months ago and three days. I am due to leave in thirty-six hours—PCS move to Madigan Army Medical Center, Tacoma, Washington. Two months or so there, and then I am done. Are you sure you should be showing this to me?"

"You brought the bodies into my morgue; you are the surgeon of record and a cosigner on the death certificates. Yeah, I think it's OK. Why, you worried you'll be arrested or something for looking at a medical record, doctor?"

"Well, one that begins with a 'Top Secret' security identifier makes me take pause, Fred."

"Since when did a sawbones ever express humility or fear? I am shocked."

"Last time ... what do you want me to look at?"

"Well, there is a reason I'm asking you to take a look. They are asking me ..."

Carefully, Chris ventured, "Who is asking ... and what are they asking?"

The pathologist smiled, realizing that he had sprinted ahead without context or clarification regarding the data conveyed in the folder. "The 'who' is some upper-echelon Army intel group. The 'what' is anything that I left out that might possibly be helpful. I guess they mean like trajectory of the shots, how close—anything that could identify or shed light on any aspect of this assassination."

"So, it was a hit?"

"Yes, according to the Army … here, take a look. Your insights and comments may be helpful. You have seen a ton of these kinds of wounds."

"Unfortunately, you are more than correct, Fred."

"Yeah, I know, but you are leaving this hellhole. I still have six months left."

Lundgren glanced up as he was starting to read and saw the starkly naked candor of pain in his colleague. He realized that Fred Kowolski, MD, had also begun to pay a price for his participation in this war. It was one thing as a pathologist to diagnose ugly cancers in seventy- and eighty-year-old people, entering the later stages of their allotted time on this planet; it was quite another to be hip deep in nineteen-year-old Iowa and Missouri farm boys with their heads shredded from the modern weapons of war. This form of forensic pathology was disquieting to the soul.

"You OK?" Lundgren asked.

"No … I am tired of seeing boys who should be in the back seats of Ford convertibles screwing their high school sweethearts lying cold on the slab in my morgue without legs and arms. It gets old really fast, Chris."

Chris simply asked, "What and where are you going after you get Stateside?"

Kowolski, confused, looked at him. "I have no earthly idea. I still have two years after—that is, if I get out of here."

"Well, you are getting out of here, and I would appreciate it if you would call me. I will keep in touch when you are ready to PCS, unless you are going be a lifer."

"No, I can't do this for another year, Chris. I can't do it …"

"Yeah, I understand. So, you look me up. We need a hotshot pathologist to make the program top-notch."

Fred looked genuinely surprised, unable to hide the impact of this genuine compliment. "You serious? Where are you headed?"

"I am very serious, totally, and I have no idea, but it would be an honor to have you with me and our surgical program wherever I land. It may not be of interest for you, but you will be invited to join me, and you will have the right of refusal, OK?"

Fred smiled and his face softened for an instant; his eyes lost focus and perhaps almost misted, but it was gone as he looked at Lundgren and said, "I would be more than happy to join you wherever the hell you end up … I think." Both men smiled.

Lundgren lowered his eyes to the folder and saw that it was a narrative composed of three rather long paragraphs over two and a half pages of typed single-spaced lines on quality bonded paper. The first paragraph began with the events that preceded the assassination and were completely unknown to Lundgren, but three sentences into the report, he felt a chill tickle his spine.

> *Col. Mallroy appears to have been carefully reconstructing the fiscal linkages and political contacts supporting the successful VC drug trade throughout the South and specifically within Saigon and Da Nang. These activities are felt to be directly sanctioned by Democratic Republic VN leadership. Mallroy's interviews at embassy (see Appendix A-1) and State (Dept.) (Appendix A-2) note his careful (and of significant interest to leadership of Army Department 112-B Section C) potential exposure of US Govt. employees cooperating with VC in effort to further illicit successful drug profit. Several off-shore Bank Accounts, used for US Govt. covert action, potentially corrupted through laundering significant fiscal resources for personal use of those involved.*

The news that US government employees were cooperating with Charlie to make money while their fellow citizens fought and died in this unbelievably bizarre excuse for a war was mind-numbing. His heart had picked up and was panging in his chest; he had difficulty finishing the document. Skimming to almost the end of paragraph two, Lundgren read the following, sensing his heart actually pause and then skip.

> *Consideration of Mallroy's activity resulting in targeted elimination raises several very troubling concerns, including primarily: 1. Murder of USA officer, either result of cooperation or direct premeditation of above-noted alleged off-shore account users. 2. Cooperative planning requisite to enable pinpointing Mallroy's activities and vulnerability leading to MACV2 ambush …*

Lundgren stopped reading as he felt his stomach lurching upside down followed by a sense of nausea. He looked at Kowolski and found him still staring directly into his eyes; neither man uttered a word, but Kowolski motioned with his eyes to continue reading. The end of the last paragraph on page two was no less unsettling.

> *Col. Mallroy appears to have violated several specific USA regulation(s) in successful, or at least partially successful, exposure of US Govt. personnel potentially involved (Appendix A-3). Mallroy also seems to have employed (freelance) civilians and US Army assets to assist his efforts. At least one individual (HDT-US State Dept. empl., US Embassy-Saigon: Appendix B-1) admits to being paid by Mallroy for clandestine monitoring of US Govt. employee of interest. (Source of funds for activity unknown.) Two additional Saigon US embassy personnel currently being questioned. Of interest, US Marine E-3, (MOS-8541?) kept off-record, performed communication outside authorized C-O-C in field. Unverifiable individual, but strong circumstantial evidence (personal interviews of MIBARS support staff) supports Mallroy's continual utilization of individual. Lt. Col. Stevens, Marine reconnaissance, Mallroy's vice, 1st MIBARS TDY, on loan 1st Recon., denies use of MOS-8541 sniper. Individual known only as "Mallroy's kid."*

Lundgren read the final words and thought the entire war effort reflected this cloak-and-dagger byzantine opacity. The only problem was, the same obtuseness intended for the enemy often clouded the US efforts even more, as one hand often literally didn't know what the other was doing.

Lundgren finally lifted his eyes from the paper and sighed audibly, at which time Kowolski said sympathetically, "Yes, it is incredible, Chris. We have the college boys in the embassy or State or CIA enjoying the sights while making money, and all the while the grunts and we lower-class types get fed into the meat grinder. It gives cynicism a new meaning."

"It certainly does."

Lundgren did his best to hide the rapid focusing of his mind as he recalled the contents of the belt that now made sense, given that the numbers were very likely bank accounts that Mallroy had been investigating. Kowolski must have sensed something.

"You OK? Is there a problem, Chris?"

"You mean beyond the fact that some of our guys are supporting the enemy to make money, the very definition of blood money? No, Fred, there is no problem. I want to fucking vomit."

Lundgren stood up from the table and extended his hand. "Fred, I meant what I said about looking me up. If there is any pull that I possess, you have a job."

Fred stood and firmly grasped Lundgren's hand. "Thank you, Dr. Lundgren."

And with that, Lundgren turned to go and as he walked out of the room, the swinging double doors bouncing shut behind him, he was totally focused on what he needed to do. Should he return the material to the MP and allow the investigation to go forward?

How far would it get? Who would actually follow up? The war was not going well, and those in the know understood that a "drawdown" was beginning, a fancy name associated with leaving a lost cause. A fancy way to hide the fact that a superpower was going to lose this war to an agriculturally based society embracing seventeenth-century values. The crimes of this war would be buried with the thousands of dead from each side. No one would care what happened to these two people, murdered or KIA, friendly fire or intentional murder; no one would want to look into it.

He was certain, however, that they were casualties of this war. But no one cared.

In this last thought, however, he was wrong. At that moment, eighteen-year-old Marine sniper MOS-8541 was completing his final mission after a self-imposed six-month extension. He was carefully picking his way through the highland mountain formations of South Vietnam near the Laotian border, and he would pick up the trail of this investigation. But he would not begin for years, and not on this continent. Lundgren himself was not finished with this, either, although he did not know it at the time. For this same eighteen-year-old Marine cared deeply about one of these men, and Lundgren's "procured" data would eventually reignite the quest.

But those outcomes were still years in the future.

CHAPTER 14

FIVE YEARS AFTER LEAVING VIETNAM

September 1978

Et Reversus est Tenebrae et Lux
"Returning to Darkness but Then to Light"

t was the earliest portion of a lazy morning, the nocturnal sounds of the desert giving way to the day. Doolin sniffed the air and it was already warm, dry. A gentle breeze buffeted his face as he looked out over the shades of brown and gold with the trident-silhouetted still shadowed saguaro cacti slowly becoming clearer as the first rays of the sun began to touch and illuminate the eastern sky. It was a beautiful environment—unforgiving and demanding, to be sure, but still with a unique beauty that made it readily understandable how the Native Americans had cherished their land and wanted it preserved without malls, fast food restaurants, or highways. The red-brown dust already coated his boots and would be carried and deposited throughout this land by forces older than time. Little rotating swirls of wind—transient mini tornadoes, only gentler—these "dust devils" were the product of the baking heat of the day and would happily dance as teens did at some fifties sock hop.

Doolin automatically checked his surroundings. Almost all of the group was still under the influence of a mind-numbing mixture of alcohol, marijuana, and heroin. There were other substances preferred by some, namely LSD, quaaludes, or magic mushrooms, but alcohol, marijuana, and heroin were the common mixtures, and they were also deadly. Every two weeks or so, someone in their group became extremely sick or simply passed out, never to reawaken, and was left to be discovered by passing motorists, cheap hotel clerks, or police. Their identification was often removed and thus missing, an order from Bagshaw; he didn't want to make it easier for the police and was completely without feeling for the eventual grieving parents.

As Doolin studied the surrounding beauty, he felt Bagshaw's eyes. He was their nominal leader, and yes, there he was off to Doolin's left, over his shoulder staring right at him. Like Doolin, he did not partake in the chemical festivities each night, but unlike Doolin, who never partook, Bagshaw did occasionally. His actions were deliberate and intimidating, communicating his force and potential for violence to all, even the women who rode with the bikers. He preferred a different girl each night, and relationships between a woman and another biker did not factor into his insatiable appetite. In fact, Doolin intuitively suspected it probably further aroused him. He wanted simply to dominate and harm anyone who came within his orbit of activity.

And thus he ruled their twenty-five-to-thirty-person mobile group with a combination of animal instincts and selective use of the aforementioned mixture of alcohol and illicit drugs. Favoring a woman might mean that he paid attention to her and deliberately plied her with a combination of illicit heroin and marijuana, sapping her of all resistance, inhibition, and dignity. She would awaken still foggy from a night of vague debauchery, only to actually find aching in her shoulders that had been pinned back as someone had immobilized her during sexual violence; pain in her hips, where she may have had her legs spread for hours; and of course, exquisite tenderness in her genitals, both orifices violated at will and repetitively. Bagshaw sometimes took delight in his buddies sharing his fun, with or without the woman's ability to understand or realize her circumstances.

It was not uncommon for a woman to disappear within the week after he had taken her, either running or returning to her home, broken, raped, and now understanding that the high school ideas of romance associated with bikers were similar to that of war: the reality was far from the ideal. But disappearance was not the norm; most of the women simply retreated to their female friends within the group and waited to endure another night when Bagshaw decided it was her turn again.

Two months ago, one of the guys, Guider, had objected to Bagshaw taking his woman. This resulted in a Bagshaw-initiated altercation that escalated from a verbal trading of insults to ultimately one that left Guider beaten, his jaw broken and skull crushed. He had lain unconscious, dying in the dirt, behind some cheap adobe structure. The next morning, after his woman had been "released," she went to find Guider, but he was gone and never seen again. Surprisingly, she did not leave but became one of

Bagshaw's "regulars," the bond between the two perhaps forged within the twisted principle of the dominant male.

Trouble was that Guider had never had a chance; he was hit from behind by Bagshaw several hours after the two had their initial verbal exchange. Bagshaw had used a ballpeen hammer to disfigure his skull, render him unconscious, and then just beat the unconscious human being, apparently enjoying the damage he could inflict on a defenseless individual. In truth, Doolin was not even sure that Guider had survived the initial hammer strike, as it likely led to intracranial hemorrhaging and probably immediate death. It might seem that such predictable violence would ultimately render the perpetrator vulnerable to some form of retaliation from other members of the group, but this would be an incorrect conclusion.

All groups have their own interpersonal dynamics, and Bagshaw used two other guys to reinforce and maintain his position. Overtly deferring to them and highly solicitous of their opinions, he gave each individual the belief that their opinions were important and often determinative. However, it was all just for show; if they had demanded something Bagshaw didn't approve of, then their fate would have matched that of Guider's. But this was Bagshaw's instinctive predatory use of other human beings: empowering and then manipulating two of the weaker and less intelligent individuals, who would then support what they perceived as their collective will on the group. In reality, it was Bagshaw's rule, and their actions were only to assist him in enforcing his stipulations on the collective. Everyone just went along, and the flow of illicit chemicals no doubt was an essential aid in keeping the status quo among these psychologically compromised and physically threatened people.

This was undoubtedly also why Bagshaw never let Doolin out of his sight; he instinctively knew Doolin was different. The man had probed Doolin several times in an effort to predicate his past. He thought Bagshaw was most worried that he was a plant, law enforcement or some DEA guy. But Bagshaw also was apprehensive that when the inevitable came and he had to take Doolin down, Doolin was somewhat more "versed" in a skillset that might make the outcome of Bagshaw's actions less certain.

Doolin, in turn, felt that leaving his person exposed or vulnerable in any way to Bagshaw or his buddies was tempting an early departure from this life. So, the two men lived in the in-between world of mutual distrust and growing concern about the other's intentions. Doolin admitted to himself that Bagshaw seemed to at least partially accept his history when one of the other guys, Stroey, actually validated Doolin's past in Vietnam.

Stroey himself had been an Army ranger. Doolin was more than a bit surprised that Stroey, and in fact the Rangers within his company in Vietnam, had heard of a particular US Marine sniper who had fought and saved some folks at Black Virgin Mountain. This in itself created two potentially troubling concerns for Bagshaw: First, this information set Bagshaw on edge, as he didn't want to acknowledge to anyone—himself, most importantly—that there was a male who may just be more dangerous than him. Someone who had killed and done it often and was good at it. Second, a trickle of doubt ran down into his consciousness that he could not, in reality, intimidate Doolin, no matter how quiet or seemingly accepting he was when Bagshaw acted out his Faustian behavior. Doolin had already decided that he would stay out of Bagshaw's way. The fact that Doolin was even part of this lawless biker group, roaming throughout Southern California and Arizona, was testament to how distorted his moral compass had become.

After completing his mandatory twelve-month tour in Vietnam, it had been extended into eighteen by his own hand, as Doolin found the independence of being up-country in keeping with his needs. While it is true that Doolin took orders from a mammoth corporation called the US Joint Military Command Vietnam, he found their influence on his day-to-day activities negligible, as he stalked the enemy alone and far from the safety of sheltered bases or camps. Mallroy had intervened and made Doolin disappear administratively so that in reality Doolin took orders from him, and Mallroy had kept him on a very loose leash.

Doolin had realized then that those six months alone would be his last; his silent movement, uncharted and largely unaccounted for, would never again occur once he returned to the reality of living in the US. And so, for his last six months in Southeast Asia, Doolin had moved as a ghost. He became rather adept, if not truly skilled, surviving and almost flourishing within Vietnam's unforgiving ecosystem of diverse topography. Their highlands and plateaus in addition to their rice paddies and riverbanks became comfortably familiar. He embraced the land, and the land in turn made him invisible.

The enemy knew of his reputation, an American who moved with stealth and expertise, a man who killed seemingly at random, and they were afraid. Even their battle-hardened commanders were consistently uneasy within the established paths of guerilla infiltration into the South. Doolin had moved as a shadow, silently choosing his timing for killing enemy troops, as he felt such actions fit the very loose mission parameters given him by Mallroy.

Once Mallroy was gone, assassinated, the colonel's replacement, Lieutenant Colonel Stevens, did not alter his mission parameters. The result, however, was that Doolin gradually lost the distinction of what constituted a "legal" target from one that he felt needed to be eliminated for his own safety. At that point, the legality of the kill was the last thing Doolin considered.

And while it would become increasingly difficult to self-justify some of his past actions the more time accumulated after leaving Vietnam, while in-country Doolin hadn't flinched over his decisions. Yet the souls taken increased in number and ignominy, despite his somewhat foggy conviction at the time that their sacrifice enhanced his chances of survival. Some were simple farmers who caught sight of him; they looked up at the wrong instant as he moved between trees or rocks, providing them a glimpse of an American soldier, and then they were gone. Some may not have actually seen him at all, but Doolin didn't want to take a chance, nor did he want to roll the dice regarding their potential of going back to their village and reappearing with fifteen of Charlie ready to systematically search the area. But Doolin hadn't considered the long-term impact on his own eventual self-acceptance. His actions at the time were justified by survival of the only person who counted: Judah C. Doolin.

Anyone in these rural areas was VC until proven otherwise, and understandably so; if they wanted to live, they cooperated with Charlie. If they wanted their daughters to escape gang rape or their sons to live to see the next day, these rural villagers cooperated. And regarding their identification of an American in their presence—or more importantly, their timely alert being given to Charlie, who was always in the area—meant increasing the likelihood of Doolin's death, or worse, his capture. And so, the Marine had acted with repetitive brutal finality.

Of course, Doolin realized that killing of any kind would alert both the enemy and the population that someone was out there enacting what amounted to a campaign of terror, but no one could be sure who it was or what "side" was represented. Was it a traitor within the rural Viet Cong, an informant being paid by the Americans? Or perhaps an unrelated vendetta for a past insult, a wrong or breach of marital fidelity? His actions were often difficult to view as any coordinated effort by a single American, and the practical impact was that these disparate possibilities protected Doolin. This "pragmatic" protection, however, did not ease the escalating self-doubt that his actions were in truth nothing more than murder—cold-blooded murder. But Doolin felt as long as Charlie didn't find him, then the end always justified the means, especially in war. Judah, however, would eventually learn this supposition was incorrect.

It was only now, five years and many sleepless nights later, that the enormity of his transgressions were becoming evident. It was only now that Judah began to accept both the consequent actions he had taken against the murky justification for their need. A very slow path began to emerge in his subconsciousness toward reconciling these activities and the realities of war with some form of viable future for himself. While he had managed to return physically unharmed from Vietnam, Judah had suffered inherent mental, if not spiritual injury too. Remarkably, he had managed to stay out of the hard drug culture, but he had self-medicated with alcohol for nine months. Consequently, he had been drunk most of the day and night; his appearance would have shocked even his commanders used to seeing him return from weeks out in the jungle.

Doolin had become an animal, partaking in a diet of a 2-carbon fragment: ethanol that numbed the pain and minimized the frequency of the intimate images of those that he had killed. It was not consistently effective, but it was all Doolin would allow himself to partake. Still, the image of his mother and her disappointment, if not shock, would not leave him as he lived in that netherworld of drunken stupor and mindless anesthetized comfort. Yet other times, the smell of his past activities—the rotten egg vapor immediately following a discharge of his rifle, his altered breathing—and the pure, almost supernatural focus he had experienced moments before the trigger reached its limit and the gun kicked its heady approval, the round screaming toward the target ... all of these were images never further than a silken shimmering dream away.

Doolin awoke one night with his .357 Cobra near his face and knew instantly that it had been in his mouth. He could taste the metal residue. He sat up and looked at the beautiful symmetry inherent in the weapon's design, the cold blue-metal surface unforgiving and disciplined. Judah knew it was time to begin climbing out of his self-made hell and rejoin the other members of the human race, those that still had lives left to live. But this was not a quick journey, nor, as it turned out, was it to be a straightforward ordeal. And in truth, several times he thought he just might not succeed.

Somehow, this aspect of his past hung on Judah Doolin like a vaporous shroud, emanating a subtle but unequivocal telling energy to anyone adept at sensing it, to those who were perceptive. The current possessor of such talents, however, was a copredator with the moral grounding of a rabid animal. For this is what Bagshaw was: a killer, or more accurately, a serial murderer. Bagshaw didn't want balanced odds; he wanted total assurance that his action would end inevitably in the death and humiliation of his chosen prey.

Doolin thought for many sleepless nights about the differences between men like Bagshaw and himself, especially after the final six months in Vietnam when at least seven innocents had perished as the result of his unauthorized and never reported kills. He tried to comfort himself that at least he was an enemy combatant and he was often, if not continually, within the enemy-occupied environment, a single man up against overwhelming odds—but it didn't help much.

Thus, Judah had seriously considered a portion of his past actions nearly equivocal to Bagshaw's, and perhaps in the net impact they were. Lives had been taken by both men. The faces seen in Doolin's scope surfaced even now, almost clearer than when he had pulled the trigger and the round penetrated the human flesh, extinguishing their life's spark. Lives taken … how were his actions any different? But Doolin's government, the United States of America, had demanded these actions. He had been ordered by his government to kill armed enemy soldiers, collaborators, and allied civilians. Most reasonable people would find the actions between these two men so different as to invite ridicule in any genuine comparison, yet now Judah could not find it in himself to entirely excuse his actions. Farmers and others who might have been entirely innocent but nevertheless became his victims, such as a woman in a cave, suggested to him that the hard outcomes were perhaps more closely related than many might consider. Ultimately, however, Doolin had been in war, and Bagshaw was a sociopath; the similarities were technical, the comparison inherently flawed.

The two men were presently behind a run-down roadside store selling beer and gasoline, but in reality were offering illicit drugs to those who knew the owner; Bagshaw and his biker group were the mobile suppliers. Up from Mexico, the lower-quality brown heroin was being imported into the States via multiple conduits, and a favorite low-cost but low-quantity method of transport was the biker gangs of the 1960s and '70s. Bagshaw worked for one such group, later to be called cartels, originating out of Culiacan that would later become one of the dominant suppliers for the US.

Begun by Pedro Aviles Perez, he was the first of many to realize the business opportunities from consolidating and running his operations as a corporation. Their activities began as a business but were never far from the blood and violence that accompanied this most dangerous of professions. By the year 2005, the legacy of these drug lords, as they became known, were among the most remarkable examples of survival of the most vicious and had turned large swaths of Mexico into a lawless, corrupt "narco-state" stacked with the bodies of both competitors and innocents. But it bears remembering that selling a product that is unpopular usually means the industry dies, and in the case of the tons of illicit material being transported into the US, the material was more precious than gold and sold even more readily.

The gas station was, in fact, a beat-up, dilapidated version of a small dusty, enclosed two-room store adjacent to a two-pump open-air fueling island. Behind the station there were five dirty, run-down tan-colored adobe units that served as rooms for guests. No one would use these for weeks, and then the bikers would show up and occupy them for three to four days before moving on. Doolin's group of bikers had been there for three days and were getting ready to leave later in the day.

The store, with its weathered linoleum floors and dirt-encrusted windows, was attached to a one-vehicle garage that was essentially a single building thirty yards in front of the adobe structures. There were two electric glass-doored coolers filled with Budweiser and Pepsi, condensation covering much of the glass, and in the single room flies buzzed while an occasional tiny scorpion scurried across the floor. Standing shelves stocked with candy bars and potato chips, along with breath mints and maps, completed the offerings. Cigarettes and chewing tobacco lined the wall behind a counter with a paint-chipped cash register that never had more than forty dollars in it.

The unkempt, balding, and greasy semitoothless owner smelled even worse than he appeared in his armless T-shirt and stained blue jeans, wearing scuffed-up cowboy boots and exposing a long leather scabbard enclosing a combat knife attached to his worn belt. The small but deadly nickel-plated Ruger Blackhawk, a six-shot pistol, was hidden in the small of his back. This was not a kid-friendly stop, and the single public restroom was beyond salvage—a malodorous stench permeated its enclosure, where a stained sink accompanied a toilet that had not been serviced in four months. In the space behind the public area of the store was the rather well-organized second room with tobacco products and a walk-in refrigerator used for the surplus beer and wine.

The dead bolt on the door leading to this back room was heavy. The doorframe was made of reinforced steel and set in cinder blocks with steel rods running the entire height of the wall. This was, in fact, a safe room to be used when any form of enemy appeared, with a narrow eye-level sliding peephole or vedette in the steel-gray paint-chipped door. It was easily and quickly accessible from the storefront, an escape during any threatening activity. The windows were slits with heavy steel bars spaced at six inches preventing entry. The back door was also reinforced metal, gray and dented, with two dead bolts on top and bottom and thick hinges welded to the heavy frame. The door handle encased an expensive lock composed of remarkably heavy reinforced steel and aluminum with its own internal deadbolt.

In the corner of the room, the most fastidiously maintained area, were the illicit products for sale. Here, the owner kept meticulous records; he never wanted his supplier, one of the Mexican cartels, to consider that he might be cheating or skimming. Such activity was never a good idea. But the business in this line of items was brisk, and he kept a low profile and lived off the profits that by all accounts were better than any other product he dealt in. He kept his eyes open and his mouth shut. Twice in the last thirty months, a person had been killed in or near his shop and he just never said anything, knowing quite well who had committed the act and what the repercussions would be if he talked to law enforcement. Thus, when the events of this day were revealed, he had seen it all before. But then again, he himself would have admitted that there were surprises yet to unfold.

INTO THE LIGHT

It was now after six thirty a.m. and Judah turned slowly to face Bagshaw, who had not allowed him out of his sight. The ex-sniper nodded briefly and slowly walked back toward his room in the last crumbling adobe. Doolin concentrated on whether this was the moment that he would have to act to defend himself from some cowardly attempt by Bagshaw to eliminate him from the group, from life. He listened intently for any shift in the gravel, any movement, but there was none, and as he passed behind a corner of the middle adobe, he slowed and turned back to look at Bagshaw. The biker had moved off toward the main structures of the gas station and had his back to him. Doolin could have ended it right there, shot him mid-back and not had to worry about the prick, but he just didn't have it in him. Judah was beginning his slow recovery from the depths that only those trained to kill for their country experience, and he did not want to step back into the darkness again.

As he turned back toward his room, out of the corner of his eye he saw a county sheriff's police car roll slowly to the front of the station. Quietly, silently they stopped. The car doors opened and two men exited the vehicle, again carefully minimizing any sound. A big man nearest Judah carefully guided one of the doors back against the side of the car but did not engage the locks; the other man left his door open, all done in near silence.

This immediately set off rather significant alarms in Doolin's head; this was not a routine visit or stop. The driver was a big muscular black guy, at least Doolin's size, his hand on the grip of his pistol. The other was a blond somewhat shorter stocky man who communicated something with a nod of his head to his partner. And then they separated slowly, the big black guy coming toward Doolin's location and crossing in front of the car, but he did not see Doolin. He walked silently, each step weighed carefully as he passed alongside the garage's side wall, moving to the back of the structure. Then his gun was out, and Judah knew this was going to be a problem.

Doolin had reached his adobe and because the front walls of these structures formed a gentle arc with a small central parking area, located behind the station, Doolin had a clear view of the big man's backside. He stopped at the furthest wall of this last adobe structure, crouching to ensure he was minimizing his profile against the front corner of the plaster-sided sleeping quarters. Those inside were still unconscious, in reality still anesthetized from the night's festivities. The telltale odor of liquor and marijuana still permeated the air inside of the nearest room and seeped out from the windows and door.

Judah waited to understand what was happening and what he needed to do. He briefly considered walking away into the desert and sitting down, enjoying an extension on the early morning stroll among the cacti with the rising sun. But he couldn't leave; he was too worried as to what was going to—*bang*!

Doolin knew that sound. A large-caliber handgun and then a return of several shots, four or five, from a different handgun, and a scream. And around the opposite corner, from the one this big sheriff occupied, Bagshaw came running with blood pouring out of his shoulder. Immediately, both men recognized the other and Bagshaw fired first, hitting the officer in the right leg just below the groin. The guy screamed out, twisting uncontrollably around, losing his gun in the process as it discharged harmlessly into the dirt.

Bagshaw came running to the guy from fifteen yards away and then stood over him, his gun pointed at him from three feet away.

"Fucking pig!" he shouted. "Your fucking buddy is dead, motherfucker!"

Doolin was now the one now running toward Bagshaw, and instinctively knew what he had to do. "Hey, great shot!" he yelled. "Really fucking great shot, man. You got him."

Bagshaw looked up and scowled at Doolin. He momentarily looked uncertain but then waved his gun up and down.

"Fucking right I got him. His partner also … fucker's a dead man but got off one shot and hit me. Cocksucker."

Doolin reached behind to the small of his back as Bagshaw looked back down to the officer, preparing to put a final bullet into him.

What Doolin failed to understand was that once Bagshaw discharged his final shot into the deputy, this sociopath had already decided that the next shot would be in Doolin's chest. But then he never got that opportunity.

The young African American was holding his leg and staring at Bagshaw, his eyes wide with fear, his jaw locked, grimacing in pain.

Doolin pulled out his four-inch Colt Python, laughing as he silently pulled back the hammer.

As Bagshaw lowered his hand, a merciless smile appeared on his face. He was enjoying the sense of near unlimited power as he readied for his kill.

It was to be his final attempt … ever.

Doolin said, "Put it between his eyes, man."

And just for an instant he looked at Doolin with the vicious smile curling the corners of his mouth even more, but it lasted for only a split second.

Suddenly, instantly, his smile faded. And before his arm could reposition, Doolin fired once at point-blank range.

His forehead cratered with an initial explosive, almost concussive sound, then there was a whipping, swooshing sound of wind howling through denuded branches followed immediately by the back of Bagshaw's head exploding.

Blood and tissue hit the back wall of the garage. He collapsed, gun still in his hand. His legs twitched involuntarily for several seconds, but Judah did not see them; he was already assessing the sheriff's leg. It would be lethal unless he got to a hospital and received help. Judah read his name badge from his uniform.

Doolin reached down and cupped the officer's head. His hands were remarkably still, steady. "OK, McGill, stay with me, guy. We got to get you to a hospital, or you are going to be in trouble."

Looking up, he searched the opposite back corner of the structure for any new people. So far, none.

Doolin immediately ripped off the white neck bandana that he wore. Unfortunately, he was so pumped with adrenaline he also ripped off the gold necklace and cross his mother had given him. It had remained where it always was, tightly wrapped within the bandana, and as Doolin wrapped McGill's leg, he didn't realize that part or all of the chain was gone from his neck; he had no recognition of its loss.

But he did strangely sense that his mother's blessing was with this young guy who had taken Bagshaw's bullet. Judah would never know how, but in that moment he knew she was smiling as he tended to the man. He winced as Judah tightened the tourniquet.

"Stay with me now."

Judah knew that he had to get him back to the car and that he needed to call this in. He pulled the officer up and carried him fireman style, with his body over his shoulders, and held on to his good leg and one arm. McGill was a big man, but Doolin's adrenaline-fueled state moved him with ease. The officer was now almost unconscious and in shock.

Doolin reached the car and as he laid the big man on the back seat, he moved around the rear end toward the driver's side. He caught a glimpse of the man's partner, covered in blood. He had managed to crawl out of the store but was lying in the doorframe only two-thirds of the way out, his legs still keeping the door ajar; the man was motionless.

Doolin grabbed the radio and spoke carefully and succinctly, "Citizen calling for emergency assistance for two officers down. One believed dead and one seriously wounded. Need immediate medical assistance to transport an Officer McGill with large-caliber gunshot to right upper medial thigh."

Almost instantly a voice crackled, "Who is this? Identify yourself."

"Listen, you need to get medical help immediately to Scenic Gas on Indian Route 15, just north of the cutoff road. Move now! If you can use or call in a medivac or whatever you guys call it, that would be advisable—he has limited time."

The voice was now alarmed and angry. "Who is this, and what—?"

Judah cut him off, "Get your ass in the air, mister, or you are going to lose this man, NOW!"

He dropped the mic as he saw Bagshaw's two buddies, guns drawn and moving cautiously from the far side of the store, the opposite side of where Bagshaw and McGill had gone after each other. They were clearly stoned and yet still dangerous. Judah pulled the rear driver's side door open and cupped his hand to McGill's ear.

"Listen, McGill, we are about to have trouble here. Got to go, otherwise I would stay with you. You got a rifle in this car?"

In and out of consciousness, the young law officer motioned with his eyes to the trunk and Doolin immediately felt for his keys. "Unlocked, switch released," McGill managed to sputter.

Doolin moved rapidly to the trunk and popped the hood. Bagshaw's nearest man, Lester, screamed, "Fucking cop!" and started running toward Doolin.

Inside of the trunk was a modified M-16, single shot, clip fed. Doolin instantly grabbed it, pulled back the slide chambering the round, and whipped into a crouched position at the bumper of the car. With thirty-two yards left, Doolin put two shots into Lester before he had even raised his gun. His back exploded, a thin red spray erupting from the vicinity of his left shoulder blade. Lester stumbled, both knees collapsing, and hit the baked dirt- and stone-covered surface as he fell face down into the rust-colored gravel.

The second man, Sigler, now knew that someone was armed and firing; he had just witnessed his cohort die.

Sigler turned to flee, and at forty-five yards Doolin hit him three times in the back, the last shot hitting the top of his neck at the base of the skull. He was without thought, pain, or life when he crumpled to the ground.

Doolin had a ridiculous half smile on his face. *There is going to be new leadership in the group*, he sarcastically thought. But his smile was for McGill—that this man still had a chance, and that Judah had assisted him.

For Doolin, the targeting skill required for each of these two idiots was negligible. Shit, hitting a guy at thirty-two yards was like pissing into a commode. The forty-five-yard moving target was technically a bit tougher, but not really.

Then there was quiet. In fact, there was almost a serenity to the morning now, and Doolin went back to McGill. "How are you? You OK?"

He rolled his eyes in Doolin's direction, and Doolin said, "It's OK. Zone cleared. I mean"—he smiled—"you're safe now."

McGill, weakly but still conscious, asked, "Who are you?"

He smiled again and said, for no other reason than it simply crossed his mind, "Semper Fi." Judah patted his hand.

He checked on the tourniquet, tossed the M-16 into the open trunk, and moved quickly to retrieve his bike, then he left.

Remarkably, none of the other people in their biker gang were up; it wasn't seven o'clock yet, and the wonders of chemical addiction were on full display as Doolin maneuvered his bike out of the station and into the desert. There, he picked up a seldom-used road, or more aptly a path with a single lane—two tire ruts that quickly became a single footpath. Doolin was moving fast and only slowed and looked back after about seven minutes.

He was headed south on this dirt path, going a bit fast for safety, but he put another ten minutes behind him and then pulled off the dirt road and into the shade of a saguaro and a small stone overhang fifty yards off the road. There, he rested and thought through the events. Doolin did not know if McGill would live, and if the cops came and saw all the dead bodies, they might think that an epic gun battle had taken place.

What Doolin could not have known was that the cops did arrive nine minutes after he called, six minutes after he had kicked his bike to life. If the trauma helicopter had arrived from the south, they would have passed directly over Doolin, but they came from the northeast and immediately saw four sets of blinking lights emanating from four recently arrived police cruisers. What they found profoundly and collectively shook the gathered assembly, but they did manage to save McGill, although he would walk with a limp for the rest of his life.

The senior officer surveyed the carnage and shook his head. He went over to offer his respect and gratitude to McGill, thinking that this kid had killed three guys all while crawling to the car. Some asshole had called it in, and for that Kressler was grateful, but he was impressed with this young black guy—he was the real deal. But then, it was not entirely surprising; the kid was a Marine and had briefly served in Vietnam. Still, it was a striking demonstration in courage and fortitude.

Kressler went over to McGill just before the paramedics lifted him into the air ambulance.

"Some work, kid. Tough but necessary. I stand in awe of you, young man."

But McGill had shaken his head, grimacing in pain although the morphine had begun to work. He still managed to say, "I didn't do anything. Some guy, the one who called you ... and ..." before he became a bit somnolent, the morphine really kicking in.

Kressler recoiled a step upon hearing this. *What the fuck ... what? Someone saved this kid's life while taking out three bad guys? Bullshit! That's crazy! But ... ?*

Kressler watched as the helicopter carrying McGill lifted off, creating a huge dust cloud, and then banked, picking up speed as it headed to the nearest medical facility that could work on the wounded man.

Doolin waited until eight thirty p.m. to begin his slow, much more careful journey south into Mexico, crossing the border at a desolate unmonitored area. Doolin's goal was to get to Yecora, Sonora, a small isolated town that could afford him some rest and might just provide him time to let the events associated with Bagshaw and the young officer fade somewhat. It was strange, but Doolin felt that he had done something worthwhile for the first time in months. In fact, it might have been years since he had done something that his mother would have endorsed. It became evident to Judah then that as his enthusiasm for the righteousness of his nation's war effort had faded, so did the belief that what he was doing at its behest was OK in the eyes of his Creator, his God.

Systematically slaying other human beings for no other reason than some abstract difference in political orientation was not compatible with an enlightened outlook per his Creator's judgment. At least this was Doolin's opinion, and he didn't think he was alone, judging from the reception that most of the American Armed Forces were getting from their own civilian population, with many of the guys being spit on by people at airports and bus stations across the country.

Judah had reflected on what he might do if someone unleashed a portion of their oral secretions on him, and whether he would or could ignore them or potentially beat them to death. To that effect, he had pretty much decided that looking into their eyes was likely to be the most effective response. If indeed they had a soul, a conscience, or any humanity within them, then the brief but instant transposition of his pain to them and their sanctimonious behavior might effectively communicate the contextual depravity of their actions.

It might just linger within them, seeping into their dreams, perhaps for years, that they felt that such activity was necessary to foist upon the real potential victims: those who had been asked to fight this war by the absurd rules made up by Ivy League dilatants. But it had not happened to Judah thus far. Getting off the chartered jet from Honolulu at San Francisco and processing through the perfunctory readmission to his country was a vivid reminder of what groupthink was all about. The band, flags, and the moms and dads and families cheering—no outsiders were allowed to disrupt the celebratory and, albeit brief, festive mood.

It wasn't completely successful, however. Doolin noted several family members examining him and quietly sharing comments as he deplaned and walked through customs. Apparently, his size and haunted appearance concerned these happy, overfed people who were used to seeing returning Americans looking victorious, not gaunt or self-reflective as to the horrors they had visited on others of the human species.

Doolin wasn't in a good place, he ventured, but then how could he have been? And if someone had argued that he should "roll with the changes," then they had not experienced what visited Doolin every night as he closed his eyes, the images of those he had killed reappearing to demand explanations of *"Why me?"*

Helicopter Ride and Recovery

Once in the helicopter, a paramedic called Liston attended to the leg of Officer McGill. What he saw surprised him as he slowly undid the expertly applied tourniquet, letting blood flow briefly to the lower portion of the leg. He then retightened it and packed the wound with sterile bandages before cutting away the trouser leg and tightening up the new contraption being used called MAST wraps, or military anti-shock trousers, developed in 1903 by a surgeon. Like so many prescient developments, it was not appreciated and thus not commonly used before the Vietnam War, where it was "redeveloped" and deployed to save troops. Later, the entire conceptual basis for MAST would come under heightened academic scrutiny, but this was state-of-the-art in the 1970s.

What had initially surprised Liston was the gold metal peeking out from the folds in the now blood-soaked bandana. Once the helicopter landed and the surgeons took the young sheriff to the OR, the bandana was removed from the leg, and out fell a necklace attached to a cross. This was gathered as evidence by this same older sheriff named Kressler, who had driven to the hospital to check on McGill. Kressler seemed fascinated, yet actually frowned when he realized the contents that the bandana had hidden.

It was also interesting to Liston that Kressler did not leave the waiting room of the ICU or the hospital room that McGill was moved to for three days. The nurses confirmed and were equally impressed by this crusty older man's attention to McGill, bringing this weathered police officer coffee and even sharing their snacks with the man. He was constantly on the phone in the room, talking quietly, or out in the hall speaking to various other police who came by in an uninterrupted chain of visitors to ensure that this young kid was going to recover. And recover, he did.

Kressler had been a member of the force for eighteen years and had a craggy face, deeply lined by sun and wind, despite his straw cowboy hat with its broad sloping brim. He was always clean-shaven, except for a bushy mustache that had a hint of gray and rolled up at the two opposing ends. His light-blue eyes were the color of wildflowers growing alongside of cattle paths. Kressler was the embodiment of a law officer: direct, cautious, but unafraid. His mind was like the cutting edge of a straight razor, eliminating extraneous data and able to find the essential evidence in seconds.

He tolerated no bending of the rules. Himself a prior enlisted soldier with the Army in Korea, he demanded conformity to the integrity he saw as inherently just within the culture of law enforcement. He had come to an age where he viewed most crimes as done by people in need, either of something that society forbade or something that their soul demanded. Larceny was done to supply the habit of drug addiction, and as long as it was without injury to innocents, he was almost gentle with the perpetrators. Murders were likely to be between those who knew each other and often were crimes of passion, a lack of discipline and instant loss of control in the setting of an alcohol- or drug-induced haze.

When confronting the surviving party, shaken and becoming gradually aware of the enormity of their act, the fog of their chemical imbalance waning, Kressler intuitively understood their building sorrow and often was rather careful in his handling of this surviving perpetrator. Some commented that he demonstrated a degree of professional restraint that actually bordered on tenderness. But for those occasional unrepentant and still hostile, his methodical, by-the-book process of incarceration was direct, immediate, and emotionless.

The only two mortal sins Kressler would not forgive were being a "dirty cop" and harming a child. Those who knew him well were quiet about the rumors of his beating a father, or rather a pathetic excuse for one, nearly to death after he had discovered him violating his eight-year-old stepdaughter routinely and violently. The child was placed in protective state custody; the man went to the ICU and never had vision restored to his left eye and needed a cane to ambulate. There were rules, and Kressler knew them and lived by them. Rules were seldom to be broken, according to him, but if so, then deliberate and mature acceptance of the consequences were mandatory.

And thus Kressler, over the ensuing three days, sat in the room without fail, listening to McGill sleep and breathe without effort. McGill's African American mother now sat in the other chair, watching her son, while Kressler contemplated the necklace and cross that he held in his hand. He had met McGill's mother upon her arrival at the hospital. She had traveled from Texas. He had taken her in his arms and whispered in her ear that God would protect her son and that he would thus recover; Kressler had promised her. In 1974, the embracement of a black woman by a large white man wearing a cowboy hat, a gun, and a badge was unusual, and to see his tear-filled eyes was almost unknown. The rest of the all-white group of officers had stood in a semicircle behind Kressler, hats in hands, respectfully murmuring their support for the woman's son.

Kressler was still staring at the cross found within the bandana that had squeezed shut the hemorrhaging artery, holding its life's force in place until the surgeons could reconstruct the artery and the leg. Kressler rolled it over in his hand. There were three letters, MCM, and a very tiny 18 carat stamp along the back of the cross, verifying that it was solid gold. He wondered not for the first time whether this was intentional or something else—a taunt for law enforcement or simply an act of kindness, possibly from one soldier to another?

The radio operator had specified to Kressler that the communication from this "somebody" was direct, unexcited, and professionally specific. Kressler found the lack of excitement extraordinary, considering that a gun battle between three men ensued within seconds, with two people being killed. This somebody had protected his officer, kept him alive, and demanded without emotion, yet directly and precisely, that they get help to McGill immediately.

McGill had surfaced from his profound sleep earlier during his recovery to tell Kressler that the guy was definitely military, and almost certainly an experienced combat veteran. He, Mr. Somebody, had handled the entire situation like someone in the middle of a firefight in Vietnam, according to McGill. This meant to both McGill and Kressler that this "somebody" had immediately acted within recognized boundaries of training to assess and kill what he perceived as a threat to either himself or McGill, or both.

It meant also that this guy might be a bit harder to either identify or apprehend. Importantly, McGill had confessed to losing his gun after or at the time he was shot and had prepared to meet his Maker, or at least take a round in the head from Bagshaw, who had been wanted in three states with outstanding felonies. McGill had also admitted to not hearing or even knowing someone was behind him when suddenly a guy was yelling encouragement to Bagshaw, and then the unthinkable: this guy, Mr. Someone, shot Bagshaw in the face and pulled McGill to safety.

The forensic team had collaborated the happenings that McGill related; in fact, there was almost an identical summary in the chain of events. The body of the man at the corner of the station was identified as Bagshaw and he had been shot at point-blank range, with plaster foot impressions and photographs confirming that Mr. Someone had stood in back of McGill and then carried him to safety. There were partial fingerprints on the trunk of the police cruiser and the M-16. Kressler knew he would submit these to the military, starting with the Marines, in an attempt to identify their owner's name. Part of Kressler wanted to arrest this guy, as he was, judged by his actions, just a little dangerous. But part of him also wanted to thank him for saving McGill.

Mr. Someone had acted with speed and deliberate force to take down three individuals, one a dangerous and violent felon, the other two wanted on drug and assault charges in both California and Arizona. Now, all three were in the morgue, and the mystery man was gone.

Interviewing the remaining members of this biker group had procured eight arrests for outstanding warrants for various crimes, mostly drug related. But unsurprisingly, there was little they could offer about this Mr. Somebody; he apparently had provided very little or perhaps no additional information to his fellow bikers. He was described by the members of this loosely affiliated gang as quiet, withdrawn, a loner, and so on, and no one even knew his real name. Even a consensus label for him was absent; some called him "the tall guy," and some simply called him "that guy." But the overall image that Kressler pieced together was that Mr. Someone was deliberately careful and silent.

Of growing curiosity—indeed, a degree of side interest for Kressler—was the fact that he was never seen to use the illicit product that the gang sold or transported and apparently never drank alcohol. This made Kressler not only grudgingly respectful, but slightly uncomfortable. Who was this guy, and was he potentially hiding in plain view? Was he undercover? The interview with the sleazebag owner had not gone well, as Bagshaw had killed him moments before Kressler's two boys first pulled up. Apparently, the entire sequence of events was an unfortunate case of mistiming in the face of Bagshaw's depravity. So many of life's true outcomes are indeed a matter of timing.

Kressler considered his options and felt in his gut that this was the group involved in the transportation of sizable amounts of heroin into the country, or at least several members were. What he could not have known at the time was that Bagshaw was also responsible for seven murders, including the owner of Scenic Gas. Kressler deeply wanted to speak to this unidentified "helper," as there were undoubtedly little golden nuggets of inculpatory evidence to be gleaned.

He reached over and patted the slightly trembling hand of McGill's mother, Roberta, and asked if he could get her some coffee or a glass of water.

"No, thank you, Sherriff, but I am grateful for your attention to my son."

Her eyes filled with tears, and Kressler squeezed her hand. "He's going to be just fine, Roberta."

She looked directly into his eyes. "They say someone protected him after he was shot. Is that right?"

She was a small woman but had significant girth, wearing a loose brown skirt to just below her knees and a worn rose-colored blouse. Roberta's hair was gray, short in its natural tightly curled appearance, and her smooth dark chocolate skin appeared remarkably youthful except near her eyes, where wrinkles and lines were deeply etched. Her hands reflected a lifetime of arduous domestic work, endless hours of sweeping; her knuckles were enlarged with age-related arthritis, her fingers no longer delicate, showing small scars from past injuries.

Roberta's eyes were intelligent, knowing and yet sad, perhaps even disappointed. They reflected a life of hard work, but one of systematic prohibition from equal prospects common to the times and her social position. Yet there was also fortitude, a strength that slowly surfaced in her eyes for those willing to look, and Kressler made a habit of looking. Kressler never before had discussed a case outside of his professional sphere, and yet something compelling arose in him as this gentle mother of six searched his eyes for a response.

"Well, I'm not sure of the exact events, but here is what I know, and I ask only that this exchange remain between the two of us. Is that OK?"

Roberta nodded slightly, affirming his request.

"It appears that at a critical moment, your son told me directly that someone stepped in and prevented the bad guy from doing any more harm. This same protector then carried your son to the police car and got on the radio and called in assistance—actually *demanded* that we get our asses in gear and get him to a hospital."

Again, Kressler made it one of his rules to seldom use improper language in the presence of a lady, but he felt at peace with Roberta. After raising six kids, he knew she had heard worse, and he wanted her to know that everyone had responded with a sense of urgency to save her son.

Even though nothing else needed to be said, Kressler continued, "The final act by our protector was to take down two additional bad guys who decided to come in later and try to finish what the first creep started, and I can only say that both of these losers never got close to your son. Our man made sure of that."

"Do you know who he was?" Roberta asked.

"That's the million-dollar question. Apparently not even those people hanging together in the group of bikers even knew the name of this guy. It amazes me, but it sounds like he was in the group for almost nine months and no one had or has a clue as to his name. I naturally suspect that at least a few are deliberately hiding his name, or what they called him. But for most of them, well, to be honest, I really don't think they know any more about this guy than we do."

Although Kressler had by this time put out feelers to the DEA and the undercover narcotics branches of both state and federal authorities, he was pretty sure this man would not be among their plants. But this, he did not share with McGill's mother.

Dallas McGill—probably named after the city where he was born, perhaps when the family was moving on to West Texas—was breathing easier and sleeping a bit less as his body healed and he recovered. A couple of times he woke with a start, and it was obvious to Kressler, who had seen too much in his career to deny or ignore the signs, that McGill was reliving the moments of terror when Bagshaw was about ready to kill him. But these dreams were coming less frequently now, and it appeared young Dallas was on the mend.

McGill's mother turned toward Kressler and said, "It's remarkable that this man stepped in and saved my son, yes?"

"I would say yes, definitely."

She nodded but to herself, as if she had reached a decision. "Well, God has provided this man to save my son, whoever he is, and I am blessed to receive this man's actions."

Kressler was now looking intently at the woman.

"Yes, God made him come to my boy's moment of need, and this means this man is a blessed person, Sherriff." This was said without question, a fact as logical to her as the elemental geometric proofs were to a budding mathematician. "Now you must decide on how you will deal with this man."

And with that, she reached over and patted Kressler's hand, rose from the chair, and left the room.

Kressler—alone now except for Roberta's healing son, sleeping and safe—looked up at the ceiling and smiled, knowing at that instant that Dallas McGill's mother's insights were both prescient and correct.

He murmured, "Shit!" and again smiled, thumbing the cross he held in his hand. He too rose from his chair and walked quietly to the door, leaving the room.

CHAPTER 15

MEXICO

September 1978

Servus Servorum Dei
"Servant of the Servants of God"

I t took Doolin three days to get deep into Mexico. Traveling mostly at night, he initially used dusty dirt back roads to slowly climb the plains toward the small town of Yecora residing in the rising plains of Sonora. He ended up taking Federal Highway 16 or Yecora-Cuauhtémoc, which was pretty much deserted, watching the dust and desert become slowly green with trees and rolling hills as the elevation increased. He knew that when he entered Yecora, looking for the Catholic church Neustra Senora de Guadalupe, he needed to find Lopez. Judah turned off on Calle Nogales and headed north for several blocks until he eventually found Benito Juarez Garcia and turned off this onto Martinez and arrived at his destination.

The church was a prototypical sun-baked Mexican sanctuary of worship so characteristic of small towns in El Pais. Off-white adobe with twin towers in the front, each capped by a rounded top, the whitewashed cylinders giving way to faded red-tiled caps, appearing as equal halves of a large globe. Set in between them on a pale rectangular façade was a single large cross situated on the plastered wall above the doors, along with part of the outer wall that was the front boundary of the narthex. The nave ran for almost thirty feet before the chancel and sanctuary. The sacristy was off to the left side as one faced the long central aisle, its floor smooth flagstone from the nearby riverbed that held water in the early spring. The rectangular roof over the nave was composed of baked clay tiles supported by old pine beams and sturdy walls of brick and clay, a peeling whitewashed stucco covering the walls interrupted by handmade elongated Gothic stained-glass windows that were the pride of the parishioners.

The two large varnished antediluvian wooden doors were pockmarked and partially stained from rusting iron latches, the red-brown color blending into the wood and fading. The doors were surprisingly silent in their movement, almost noiseless, blocking the intense sunlight and noise from the spiritual atmosphere within the sacred domain. Multicolored light from each of the arched biblical-themed windows provided a spectrum of rainbow-colored radiant beams illuminating the dusty swirls kept in perpetual Brownian motion. The ethereal nature of the unnaturally quiet but pleasant emptiness of the deserted church was a refuge to the very few who sought to enter.

Doolin had spent several weeks during his visit to Black Virgin Mountain with an Army ranger by the name of Sebastian Lopez, who went by the moniker Lopez. It is impossible to explain how quickly close relationships form within the pressure cooker of combat. Judah had met Lopez minutes before he was engaged in protecting his defensive firing position and his right flank from advancing VC Special Forces trying to breach the defenses of the lower zone at Black Mountain.

Lopez's best friend Tucker, a happy, outgoing kid, had extended a welcome to Doolin mere minutes after his arrival, but he was killed in this same attack Doolin's first night in camp. Lopez had been shocked by the permanence and suddenness of the loss of his young friend. For days he had sat quietly in his hut, staring out into the emptiness of the valley and paddies below. At times his eyes could be seen to fill with tears, and his interactions with fellow troops trickled away until they were nonexistent. His gaunt face was partially hidden under his helmet, his rifle propped against his knees. In short, he withdrew.

As in all of history, it was infrequent for Doolin's young generation to experience such a sudden or irreversible outcome as the violent death of a friend of the same age. Grandfathers "passed away," and older uncles might suddenly die, but this was the extent of the shock brought to Doolin's peers as less than fully developed men. Their innate ability to handle such stress might have even been less than previous generations, but Doolin was not sure about this last point.

The popular trend as Doolin grew up—and one that was only to propagate in both scope and absurdity, taken by parents, psychologists, and school boards—was to shield young people from disappointment. To provide prizes, awards, and celebratory recognition for participation and actually for just showing up. Judah guessed he understood his parents' generation's need to attenuate disappointment or the pain of not winning; they were, after all, survivors of WWII. The idea was that such an emotional bromide would minimize difficult moments, allowing equanimity.

Doolin still remembered Lopez smiling when he had articulated this concern, thinking that such experiences actually might have delayed their generation's contextual understanding of reality. Doolin had communicated this to Lopez deliberately, even aggressively in an attempt to intrude into his sorrow and solitude. He eventually responded to Doolin's concerns, knowing both what Doolin was attempting and yet gently expressing his appreciation by answering his probing. But Lopez answered that he was not so sure that any approach protected people from the harsher realities of conflict.

Instead, Lopez made it clear to Doolin that every generation had had their lives irreversibly changed the moment they experienced the horror and cruelty of war. But he agreed that Vietnam had indeed eliminated any soft landing, as there was nothing starker than seeing your friend's lifeless eyes staring off into space when a moment before he was driving you crazy with stories of his high school sexual exploits. Conversations like these resulted in Doolin's growing respect and affection for Lopez in the time they shared at Black Virgin Mountain.

When so much of everyone's personal energy was consumed by the need to remain human, to hold on to characteristics learned in their formative years from parents, priests, and teachers, such conversations as those shared with Lopez were necessary to remind each of them that Vietnam was the aberration, not the norm. War—arguably intentionally—engaged in a systematic and painful stripping away of these very elements of humanness. The smell of freshly cut grass or wheat, the crispness of spring rains washing away the remnants of a cold, sterile winter—these were the elements of living, the bedrock of routine. It was not the twisted, crushed muscle and bone accompanied by the odor of a coppery liquid running freely from an abdominal cavity. It was not the red pulp of macerated tissue that only moments before was your buddy talking about his first time with a girl in the back of his parents' Chevy. Thus, they clung desperately to each other's willingness to challenge these horrors with a belief that tomorrow would bring the restoration of goodness back into their lives.

Doolin thought back to the intervals of humid days and nights spent with Lopez. In between sniper activity, mortar harassment, and full-fledged attacks, Doolin had grown to enjoy the comments from Lopez, his perceptive but youthful wisdom, his honesty. The haze of grief had slowly lifted in the remaining weeks spent with him on Black Virgin Mountain, but he was never the same. Lopez's youthful exuberance and almost careless, boundless enthusiasm had died along with Tucker. His ebullience was dented, deformed, and then cynically he hardened—a requisite adaptation to the brutality of war, to the pernicious impact of loss.

Yet he never completely abandoned his desire to assist others, and as he recovered, he began to attend to the needs of some in their military group. He would check each man for skin rashes, bug bites, foot blisters, and so on. He would dress them after checking with the "doc," their actual medic, and gradually Lopez became remarkably adept at such skills. So much so, in fact, that their medic asked Lopez to assist him after any major engagement when bandaging and inspection of injuries was necessary.

Doolin's last day there had followed a fierce exchange wherein Charlie had nearly overrun the camp, and Doolin had become an adrenaline-filled, terror-driven killing machine. In the end it was surmised that Doolin had saved several of his colleagues, including their CO, but the exhilaration of his accomplishment was lessened by the self-realization of his effectiveness as an instrument of death. Doolin had missed Lopez before he left. In fact, Doolin did not even look for him; he couldn't bring himself to query if he had survived. In truth, he was terrified that he might not be able to handle the news if Lopez had perished. And then Doolin had caught the mechanical bird back to Da Nang, never confirming Lopez's status.

Now, on the other side of the world, Judah was surprised by the cool gust of air that embraced him as he pulled open one of the large doors and entered the narthex. His eyes gradually became accustomed to the ambient illumination provided by the sun pushing light through the hand-crafted stained-glass panels. They were beautiful panes of multicolored glass, each piece carefully placed within soft leaden boundaries, each beginning at shoulder height and spaced at regular intervals along each wall until they reached the sanctuary. A large wooden cross carved from pine hung at the center of the furthest wall, and candlesticks on a waist-high wooden communion table with a closed Bible occupied the center position.

Judah walked down the shiny but uneven floor of the center aisle. The surface of the river rock and flagstone, worn smooth, was cool to the touch. He made as little sound as possible. Doolin had not been raised Catholic but had spent summers in a small town in the upper peninsula of Michigan, routinely attending mass with his grandmother. He had always understood, or at least he thought he discerned, the purpose in the centuries-old traditions intricately woven into daily and Sunday services. People need predictability, if not some purposeful habit in their lives, and it often was most relevant to maintaining their spiritual health. Not unlike military traditions and ceremonies, there was reason and meaning in both their origins and continuance.

As Judah neared the altar, he saw off to the left a small woman bent and kneeling. She was almost at floor level, her legs folded and tucked under her as she leaned forward in the pew, motionless and silent. A rosary was clasped in her right hand; a length of its chain hung freely.

Situated above her shoulder, to her left, Judah's eyes were drawn to a simple wooden plaque attached to the transept wall between colorful stained-glass windows. It appeared that names were etched into the plaque's surface. Above the names were the words *Nuestros Angeles Caidos*. The first name was Sgt. Ernesto Sanchez, Khe Sanh 1968, and Doolin immediately realized that even here, in this small isolated Mexican village thousands of miles from the killing fields that had been Vietnam, relatives mourned the loss of fallen Mexican American veterans.

A hooded figure watched this young man enter the church and walk silently down the narrow nave toward the center crossing. The woman remained silent, praying.

Suddenly, the hooded man realized he had seen this walk previously. He slowly began to recognize its owner, and with this recognition came surprise, joy, and then a gentle wash of pain. But the shrouded figure watched in silence as the man reached the crossing separating the nave from the small quire and apse, the rough wooden altar in front of him. Slowly, the man sank to his knees in the center of the crossing and bowed his forehead, touching the smooth flagstone of the floor.

In the presence of God, the man began to silently weep. His shoulders dipping and rising, his head remained still against the cool stone of the floor.

The man wearing the hood bowed his head even lower and clasped his hands in prayer as tears also filled his eyes.

Doolin had tried but failed to control himself. As he entered the church, gradually moving deeper into its structure, he sensed he had floated along the main isle, gliding past the simple rough wooden pews. Judah had felt he was being pulled toward the altar as if the cross, prominently situated in its center, was communicating with him.

Past images, gentle faces of those seen through the perpendicular markings of his scope, rose to face him. The scope's crosshairs had formed its own Christian symbol, and it also had spoken to him. Not in anger, but in disappointment and regret. The images long ago seen through the scope's markings met Judah's gaze, but they now were looking at him before they also bowed their heads in supplication, awaiting the force of his bullet. The rounds that had crushed and deformed their bodies were not present, but their simple gesture of forgiveness, bestowed upon Judah, provided by them, washed over him.

He was unable to stand, and his cheek lay against the cool smooth flagstone as his tears rolled freely onto the floor, forming rivulets pulled unevenly across the topography of nature's stones. Doolin asked God to end his life. He now realized he had done too much to be forgiven; he had served no purpose other than to kill others of his own kind. He simply couldn't pretend to fathom the price extracted by war on his soul anymore and just wanted closure—permanent closure.

Part of Judah C. Doolin had died in Vietnam, perhaps his naiveté that human beings were incapable of nearly unlimited cruelty. Was he so deformed as to represent only this aspect of his species? The potential for unimaginable brutality? This was a truth, and often truth comes in fits and starts and is hurtful. It was in this moment that he finally was able to tally the extent of war's viciousness and his role within its singular theater of the absurd.

This discordant reality exists in each of us: the ability to attend church and the joy derived from a daughter's wedding melding into the savagery, the brutality, of killing unarmed villagers and burning them, their belongings, and their remains. Each aspect of our behavior is valid, and each is predicated on the environment's impact on a sane person, the insanity of violence and cruelty rationally understood within a contextual reality. Judah was not the first and certainly would not be the last to marvel, to be fundamentally and irrevocably shaken, and to ask for understanding as these truths unfolded before him.

As he lay there, Judah suddenly felt a cool hand gently caress the back of his head. He bolted up and found he was looking into the dark but serene eyes of the tiny lady. She smelled slightly of lavender and lemons. Her slight figure bent down, almost touching him, her goodness come to rescue him. He bowed his head again, his forehead touching her outstretched arm.

Her eyes communicated a lifetime of struggle but composure in its presence, an existence spent at the margins of society in her tiny adobe-walled, steel-corrugated-roofed structure just outside of town with no running water. She half smiled, a toothless but tender gesture, her coarse gray hair chaotically peeking out from beneath a white scarf tied under her chin. She slowly wrapped the rosary around Judah's left wrist, deliberately holding his arm with her hands, and then she too bowed her head.

She began to pray, and Doolin lowered his head even farther and found himself holding both her hands within his left hand. After almost a minute, she looked up at Judah and he returned her gaze. There was no judgment, and her eyes spoke of tenderness. A timeless understanding of the trials experienced in this lifetime.

It was at this time that Doolin saw a hooded figure in a brown robe belted at the waist. A large crucifix was draped around the neck and as his eyes cleared, Judah could see the beard and the familiar eyes of Lopez.

Doolin's body must have reflexively flinched at recognition of Lopez, but the hooded figure's smile quieted Doolin's unease and Judah smiled in return. Lopez softly said something in Spanish to the lady and she slowly stood. Doolin did not let go of her hands, and she in turn held his. Reaching up and touching Judah's face, she said, "Vaya con Dios." And Doolin smiled weakly, her genuine affection a temporary healing salve.

"Gracias," he murmured.

And with that, she slowly shuffled back to the pew, picked up a tattered straw bag, and then turned to walk down the outer aisle to the back of the church, where she exited through the large doors. The sunlight was momentarily blinding as its wedge of illumination created ethereal red, blue, and yellow shafts of light, the contrast allowing the outside reality to penetrate their quieted domain.

Doolin turned back toward Lopez; he was looking at Judah, his eyes at peace and his very countenance solemn but welcoming.

"Hey, Marine," he said quietly, almost whispering.

And as Judah attempted to respond, he hesitated, not knowing how to correctly address him. "Hello … Father?" he offered.

Lopez smiled. "No, Judah, I am a brother to the old priest here in town. I am his legs, his arms, and his eyes, but I have not been ordained. I wear the robes as I have committed myself to God."

Judah smiled and spoke softly, matching Lopez's tone, but not his tranquility. "You look well."

He smiled, his teeth bright in the colored spectral light from the Gothic windows.

"Come with me. Let's sit and talk for a bit."

And Doolin rose, his knees a bit tender from their embrace of the river-smoothed stone. He followed Lopez back around to the sanctuary and then to a small door that led into an office. Two of the walls were lined with permanent shelves with scores of books, some expensive-looking with leather bindings, others paperback, but all looked to have been used. Their surfaces were worn, their spines uneven and lined; they had been read, perhaps even studied.

In the center of the room, positioned in front of two elongated clear windows, was a plain but solid wooden desk, remarkably organized and clean. A Bible, leather bound and large, sat off to the right and a single lamp was positioned on the center of the desk near the outer edge. An empty ecru-colored oak chair, also sturdy but with arms worn smooth and slightly darker or stained, had a small light-blue cushion in the center of the seat and was pulled slightly back from the desk. The desk lamp was on; it gave a small oblong cone of light, enough for reading. The single whitewashed wall was empty save the wooden crucifix that hung on the wall opposite the windows. A smooth, thick red-clay-tiled floor, uneven but swept clear of any debris, betrayed only the subtle scuff of Lopez's worn leather sandals.

He motioned to one of two simple wooden chairs in front of the desk and Doolin slowly sat, enjoying the sunlight as it caressed his upper legs. Lopez sat quietly behind the desk and looked at Judah for a long time, slowly shaking his head as if in disbelief.

"How did you find me, Judah?"

"I remembered our conversations. You told me you were coming here after the war. You did not, however, tell me you were going to become a priest." Judah smiled.

"Again, I am a brother, a committed believer, but not ordained." He smiled back as if reminding a child of important distinctions.

"Oh yeah, sorry. Well, you are close, right?"

Lopez laughed slightly in spite of himself. "Yes, I guess you are more correct, at least in some ways, than you realize."

The door moved slightly and the sweet aroma of a lightly scented woman drifted into the room. And as she entered she was suddenly startled, almost gasping when she saw Judah's presence. He immediately stood up and acknowledged her presence, extending his hand.

Lopez, sensing her discomfort, stated, "Maria, this is Judah, a close friend—no, a dear friend of mine from the war. He saved my life, Maria."

Judah immediately objected, "No I—!"

"And he is a bit argumentative!" he interrupted and laughed, and so did Maria as she looked into Doolin's face for the telltale remnants of the past conflict she had seen so permanently etched in Lopez.

She was striking, a beauty, which is just as much an understatement as to call the Sistine Chapel a building. Deep brown eyes formed almond-shaped pools of inquisitiveness; her jet-black hair was pulled behind her head with a simple sterling silver barrette with a center turquoise stone, a straight, almost pencil-thick polished silver pin holding it in place. She had high cheekbones, almost angular, and full lips with a slightly cleft chin. Her skin was the color of light sand but smooth, with a slightly reddened bloom in the cheeks.

Maria wore no makeup and a simple string cord around her neck holding a wooden cross the size of a half-dollar was her only jewelry, if one could call it such. No earrings, no painted fingernails, and only the very faint smell of lavender. She was about five feet, five inches tall, and although she wore a white peasant's blouse, her full breasts refused to be hidden. Her red skirt ended below the knees, revealing slender but muscular legs. Doolin immediately understood that she was in love with Lopez.

She looked from him to Judah, searching Doolin's eyes to determine goodness or evil, the consequence of a war that the world believed unjust. She must have seen elements that satisfied her, as she offered her hand and simply said, "Welcome."

Doolin wanted to inhale her scent and not move.

Lopez was grinning as Doolin turned from her to him and sought to understand their relationship. But it was not a boyish smile or an expression in any manner disrespectful of Maria; it was simply *Yes, she is beautiful, Judah*, an affirmation of their visual sensory feedback.

Lopez began to sit and motioned for Maria to take a seat next to Judah, for which he was eternally grateful.

"Judah has come to …" He paused, leaving space for Doolin to explain.

Doolin respected Lopez. He did not know Maria, but he felt that her presence in his life implied a deferential mutual acceptance between the two, and so Doolin simply told the truth.

"I had to leave the States."

Lopez's eyebrows raised ever so slightly. Judah did not look at Maria but felt her penetrating visual examination.

"I pulled a deputy sheriff out of a gun battle, shot in the leg by the alleged head of our biker gang … the latter not a man you would approve of, Sebastian. He was going to finish his work and kill the deputy. I had to kill him and his two buddies; the deputy, I think, is OK. So, I had to leave."

There was absolute silence. Lopez looked at his friend and slowly nodded his head.

Doolin still had not yet looked at Maria. Almost without emotion, he said, "If this creates a problem for you, I will leave immediately. I am OK by myself and can live on the road."

Lopez's tone was serious but gentle. "Judah, you may stay here as long as you like. Forever, if you want."

Immediately, Judah felt a wave of relief wash over him—gratitude, perhaps, but also deep respect accompanying his affection for Lopez.

Lopez must have sensed this and simply smiled, nodding at Doolin.

"Maria," he said, "Judah will need to be put to work, so let's get him a list of things that you want done, OK?"

It was at this point that Judah turned to face her, and as she looked at him, the intensity of her gaze betrayed the gentleness of her statement. "Could you do a little fix-up around the church?"

Doolin smiled. "That would be therapeutic."

She shook her head slightly. "God has provided you here to do His work."

Judah's smile disappeared as he immediately understood her sincerity. "Maria, I will have to work for centuries to get right with God. And I am not sure anything I do will square my relationship with the Almighty."

"Judah, you may now begin to understand my chosen path, yes?" Lopez's question was simple but direct.

Doolin intuitively grasped that Lopez, like himself, was looking to cleanse his soiled sense of self; his soul needed to be washed of the horrors and the depravity of actions taken during the war. He had been a good soldier, but he had done what was necessary to live and survive, and that invariably meant killing other human beings.

He saw Lopez's eyes mist and felt rather than saw Maria tense. "Yes, Sebastian, I do understand. And I hope this provides you peace, and I guess a meaningful …"

Lopez again addressed Maria, "Would you show Judah to his room? Then let's get him to work while he is still of a mind ..." He finished with a chuckle.

Doolin rose and Maria was already up and beckoning him to follow.

As the church extended behind the office, there was a narrow hallway that essentially served as a modified storage space. It had been previously cleared sufficiently to place a bed and a chest of drawers made of rough wood, but it was solid, and Judah glanced at what he assumed was to be his temporary abode.

Doolin looked at Maria and asked, "This is not intrusive as to your collective activities?"

She looked at him. "No, you are welcome here. In some ways I sense that you being here is part of a greater plan. Sebast—Brother Sebastian has ..." She paused. "Needed your presence. I can feel this now."

Doolin studied her face carefully. The considered thoughtfulness of her demeanor had transitioned into one of contemplation and analysis.

"I am not an evil person, Maria, but I have dwelt where evil exists and have not come through unscathed ... unscarred ..."

"I know ... but that is what God has intended for you."

Doolin wondered, not for the first time this day, how he could rationalize these statements with what he knew existed in the world.

"Let us hope—" He stopped, and then it just came out, "No, let us *pray* that you are correct."

She looked at him and stated, without emotion but clearly with conviction, "I know the difference between evil and goodness. I know you are a man of decency."

"How could you possibly—?"

"I am not certain that I can explain it, but I know this to be true."

She reached out to pat his arm and turned to leave.

"Maria, how old are you?"

"I am twenty-four years old. My parents are both gone, my brother was murdered by those who sell drugs, and I was taken and raped by these same men while my brother, Fernando, lay bleeding, dying, but they will not define me or who I am or who I become. One day, they will have to explain this to God."

The words were carefully chosen, flattened pieces of communication. Her face seemed to float in the small room. And as Judah stood there, numb, processing her naked honesty, a truth within the harshness of her past, she quietly left the room and closed the door without a sound.

Not for the first time there was anger in his soul, and there was knowledge—unquestioned, definitive intuition. Identical to that which Judah had previously experienced, a rushing premonition like that encountered the first night at Black Virgin Mountain.

A reckoning was speeding toward him, one he could not slow, could not run from, and could not change. An accounting that was God's judgment on him, on his past, on Judah's value as His instrument. It was calling for Judah; it was awakening. As if from a deep slumber, it was beginning to stir ... to make its presence known.

Doolin knew that he would live through whatever God requested of him, for it was not a divine servitude; it was a choice that Judah had already agreed upon. In fact, it was precisely what he had asked for.

For the next six weeks Doolin worked on and around the church, fixing areas of the roof, the windows, and floors. He reconstructed the wooden door to Sebastian's office and tinkered with the hinges until the closing was silent and exact. Even Lopez was impressed. Sebastian noted the fact that while he was the "committed one," perhaps Doolin should reconsider, as there was a good legacy for carpenters in Christianity. They had both laughed but only briefly, as Doolin saw the vestiges of pain in Sebastian's eyes. His friend's gaze fixed on the uneven tiled floor. He was remembering Tucker.

It was as if the war was an unwanted companion for each man, at times enveloping them, a watery bog slowly, gently pulling. Struggling delayed but did not prevent slipping eternally under the surface. The end was eternally approaching, acceptance of the inevitable. Both men could not escape or truly leave Southeast Asia; there were too many memories.

Lopez had taken it upon himself to begin after-hours school programs to boost the basic learning opportunities for the children of the town. He related to Judah that it had started slowly, with only two or three children participating, but within three months he had a class of twenty-four regulars, and both he and Maria taught more advanced grammar and basic mathematics such as long division and multiplication. Judah saw that Lopez was actually very good with the kids, and as a teacher, well, he was superb.

He took concepts long forgotten and made subjects both interesting and at times very fun, with each of the kids competing to get to the head of the class for spelling or multiplication. Maria followed him with paper and pencils and erasers so that the kids could do their exercises and participate. Judah watched several of his classes and found himself nearly yelling out the answers to the speed multiplication drills Sebastian conducted. Sebastian would then finish at about six thirty p.m., and the parents would be waiting in the nave of the church to take their kids home. These were mostly women but occasionally men would come, some in from the fields, or a couple of guys would occasionally stop by when they were in town during a rest interval from their long-distance trucking jobs.

Lopez also routinely toured his parish, walking up to forty-five minutes to the far outskirts of the town to visit those in need. He might bring food, or a bit of over-the-counter medicine that in Mexico could be anything from penicillin to morphine; the need for a physician's orders was often optional. He chatted with and advised his "flock," and this guidance was at times counter to the established order within the town. He encouraged some of his parishioners, for instance, to push but not demand better wages from the growers in the region.

These were the same people who controlled the town's finances and were supported by the local police. But his comments, he believed, were carefully crafted concerns that would not be immediately threatening to the established order of the town's power elite. He knew, as does anyone, that no matter the surroundings, there is always an established order. Thus, Lopez was disciplined in his verbal challenge to the status quo. It therefore made this town among the most pleasant environments Doolin had ever experienced, save for the existence of the drug traffickers who freely roamed.

While a relatively new social element in town, they rapidly made their presence and their potential for deadly violence known. Unfortunately, the town was well situated as a hub for transportation through northern routes of distribution to the United States. Thus, as product came up from Central America, various routes were in play to ensure that the maximum tonnage of product reached the US since there were still haphazardly effective American-sponsored anti-narcotics law enforcement efforts operational throughout Mexico and in Central America. Thus, Yecora was one of several distribution ports that enabled the budding cartels to efficiently shift product transportation to ensure avoidance of capture or destruction.

Efficient drug trafficking had begun in earnest about five years prior, long before Doolin arrived. Initially there was rapid turnover, as the cartel organization was very loose and discipline was lax, but in the last two years the templates that would become the hallmark of future success for these multimillion- and eventually multibillion-dollar enterprises took root. To this effect was the enforcement of whatever "contractual" terms were demanded by the employer, and any infraction usually was met with the unpleasant demise of the offender.

In addition, any and all who impeded the organized systematic product transportation were eliminated—usually violently and often gruesomely in order to deliver a message to potential coalescing public objections. Finally, the police or those in authority were paid off, and initially this was more difficult than perceived by many later observers. A culture of complicity was absent in the early days, and police and army units were independent and hostile to the idea that they would succumb to money or threats. But the methodical elimination of those who stood in the way of the cartels, in addition to the violent public murder of their families and relatives, eventually silenced their objections, and the money was too potent a weapon to be ignored for long.

Thus, if your choice was to see your family tortured and then murdered—not to mention experience your own painful death as well—or to receive significant monetary compensation to look the other way as the cartels sold product to the hated gringos from America, well, this was not a difficult choice for a growing number of officials in Mexico. The culture thus gradually changed until Mexico had no real or sustainable independent law enforcement. The money grew exponentially, and the operational expertise of the cartels grew as well. These cartels were on a path to become as large as or larger than any of the Fortune 500 companies in any of the nations of the world, and their operational proficiency rivaled these corporate entities in their collective intellectual competitiveness.

It was not long before Doolin came in contact with their workforce. A group of six or seven men who walked past the church daily before entering a cantina about a half block from the church's front door made it clear that their activities were not to be disrupted. They also made it clear that they believed they could do whatever they wanted.

One late dusty afternoon at about 3:55 p.m., the group left their warehouse two blocks from the church and as they passed its front doors, a stray dog wagging its tail in search of food approached them. One of the men bent to rub its ears and said something, as all humans do to an animal in search of contact or food. But then one of the man's companions suddenly produced a Glock and shot the dog three times, killing it and causing his dog-loving companion to dive for cover, shocked by the sudden gunfire.

The other men in the group roared with laughter and shouted obscenities in rather harsh, sarcastic tones to their coworker now lying in the street. The guy got up from the ground and was initially furious, but recognizing that his companion still had the gun in his hand, ready to use it again if needed, he shrugged instead. They all shared a continuation of the laughter, not missing another step on their way to the cantina. An hour after they had gone, Lopez retrieved the dead animal and buried it behind the church.

Maria had warned Doolin that this cantina was a front for illicit drug purchases in the setting of a run-down but rather busy bar. The men were from a larger gang that supported the infrastructure of the drug trade, loading and shifting produce in the trucks, big semitrailers, or eighteen-wheelers that routinely came in and out of Yecora.

Their leader was a handsome savage. His raven hair was slicked back and scented with cream, his fingernails manicured and lacquered, always clean-shaven with a perpetual tan. Expensive clothes, Ray-Ban sunglasses, and a gaudy yellow-gold Rolex watch with a diamond-studded bezel announced the self-importance of this man who drove a Corvette and visited the small town two to three times weekly. Doolin never confirmed if some or all of these men were involved in the death of Maria's brother or in her subsequent sexual assault, but he strongly suspected that these crimes were typical of their breed, and some of them were likely at least peripherally involved.

For her part, whenever Maria saw them, either outside the church or from its grounds, she immediately retreated into the building and hurriedly went to Sebastian's office. She made it a point never to be on the street between 3:30 and 4:30 p.m., as that was when these men often were leaving their warehouse. Doolin had carefully observed this one afternoon as she walked to the church from her tiny house not more than three blocks away. Upon seeing four of these men, who must have left the warehouse early, she almost ran to the church's side entrance.

Doolin had the door open for her and as she hurriedly approached, he beckoned her inside and then slowly closed it. One of the four stared after her and then at Doolin. He could feel the man's predatory assessment, sniffing the air as to Doolin's vulnerability being "ledgered" against this man's future actions. Doolin took note of him and, like in Vietnam, almost unconsciously began to plan his response. This automatic rejoinder was troubling for Judah. He knew this was something he was trained to do, and he was good at it, but Judah also knew it was not in his best interest to pursue this plan of action if he were to ever shed the horror of his past.

Predictably and unfortunately, Doolin did not have long to wait before such concerns were realized. Thursday evening, nine weeks after his arrival, Lopez was returning to the church after he had walked two of the children home. He had prearranged this task with their mother, as she was waitressing late and could not wait for them. About three blocks from the church, he saw too late after rounding a corner that there were five men waiting for him.

As Lopez approached, a bearded man with a single scar running down from his left eye, the apparent leader, "politely" asked for him to "accompany" them to the cantina. At first Lopez refused, saying he had services to perform in the church. The bearded man swiftly slapped Lopez in the face while another rested the barrel of a Colt .357 Magnum in the small of Lopez's back.

Lopez asked, "What do you want?"

The bearded man smiled viciously. "I think you should not ask questions, my friend. If we wanted you dead, you would be dead already."

The group moved slowly and deliberately to the cantina. An old man watched the scene, hidden within a doorway beyond the church in a building across from the back entry to the cantina. He had been sweeping inside the structure and had mopped its floors when he heard the commotion. Should he tell the brother's friend, the new tall man who drove into town on a motorcycle two months ago? Both Lopez and his friend would now be at increased risk.

As Lopez entered the cantina, the smoke from several of the patrons created a blue haze that formed halos around the naked bulbs descending from the unfinished ceiling. The music was softer than he had anticipated; the bar was rough wood with a cheap tiled counter surface and an old iron footrest nine inches from the floor. There were two glistening curved metal necks forming the draft beer spigots that divided the countertop in two, each half running nearly seven feet. Behind the bar countertop was a dirty wall with a single 3x7-foot mirror bordered in wood. Two ceiling fans lazily turned, one making a repetitive grinding sound with each revolution of its five-blade structure. At the far end of the bar, the well-groomed amoral Corvette-driving animal sat lazily on a stool, one elbow propped on the bar countertop.

He smiled as Lopez was led over to him. A young woman of fifteen sat on the barstool next to him, her blouse open with no bra, her young breasts exposed. She began to hide her face from Lopez as he looked in her direction but a sharp retort from Escobedo, the suave barbarian leader, stopped her from shielding her face. She turned slowly, reddening slightly as she did, to look at Escobedo and then Lopez.

Lopez saw the dilated pupils, the signs of fear, as did Escobedo. Sitting next to her, he smiled mercilessly, reached into her blouse, and caressed her right breast. He slowly rubbed his thumb repeatedly over her pink nipple until it became erect, taut. The young girl tried to smile but was too ashamed to pull it off convincingly in the presence of the robed Catholic symbol standing next to her. As Escobedo got up from the stool, with Lopez standing three feet from him, he slapped the girl in the face, nearly knocking her off the chair.

Lopez moved instinctively and grabbed Escobedo's arm to prevent a second slap, and in doing so the two men collided with the force of this encounter, displacing Lopez's lunging arm. His hand caught in Escobedo's expensive hand-tailored shirt, tearing off two front buttons.

Escobedo reacted immediately and screamed, "Fucking prick!"

His scented oiled hair became displaced as he instantly stepped back and viciously kicked Lopez through his brown robe, connecting expensive Gucci slip-ons with Lopez's groin.

Lopez doubled over, collapsing to his knees, his head jerking forward and down. Escobedo kicked again and his right foot landed in Lopez's face.

There was an odd attenuated, hollow sound as if a pumpkin had been dropped on stone. Lopez's head snapped back, and blood shot out of his mouth as his eyes fluttered near the limits of consciousness.

Escobedo then screamed, "You fucking ruined my shirt, you asshole!"

He again viciously kicked at Lopez's face but caught him in the neck, just below the right ear.

Lopez's head popped sideways, and for an instant he saw stars. He struggled to get to his feet when the blows from four other men began to rain down on him. He collapsed, lying on the cantina floor, and for almost sixty seconds they beat him, continuously striking his head, back, and groin with their fists and booted feet.

Escobedo pulled up his hood to examine his face and yelled, "Get this fucking robe off of him!"

With that order, two of the men pulled the robe off of Lopez to reveal an already bruised and contused torso and head. Swelling had begun, colored with a faint purple over both eyes, and his lips were three times their normal size.

Escobedo leaned down and half yelled, "You fucking prick! I brought you here to tell you to stop providing shit ideas to your followers, you asshole. My people don't want you stirring up the locals. You get that, you fuck?!"

And Escobedo slapped Lopez hard across the face, sending blood flying out of the beaten man's nose and mouth.

The young girl was sobbing. As Escobedo registered her response, he grabbed her by the hair and pulled her off the stool. He brought her face close to his and whispered, "I will have every one of these men fuck you until your ass and cunt are shredded, and then leave you in the alley for the rats. Shut the fuck up."

The sounds stopped, but her shoulders continued to shudder. Her eyes were clamped shut.

He then spoke in a mechanical, emotionless voice, the voice of a scientist recording the geological novelties of a new rock. It was a voice without pity, without human connection. "Take your blouse off, and do not make me say it twice."

She struggled but pulled her arms out of her blouse and sat half naked on the stool, her chest still heaving, splotches of pink and light red irregularly spaced over her fine blemish-free skin. Her nipples were no longer erect, her ample breasts moving up and down as she struggled to control her emotions.

Escobedo stared at her youthful feminine beauty and then returned his attentions to Lopez. He grabbed him by the ear and pulled his face up.

"Father, or whoever you pretend to be, stop talking to the natives. Stop stirring up trouble or you are a dead man. Perhaps it's time for you to leave town."

He jerked his head toward the door and four of his men grabbed Lopez and dragged him across the now nearly empty bar. They took him out the rear door and dumped him, like trash to be discarded, outside the back of the bar.

Inside, Escobedo was washing his hands and eyeing his fifteen-year-old captive. He smiled to his men, the only patrons remaining; everyone else had scattered and left the bar with the first slap applied to the woman. Now a total of five of his men plus the barkeeper remained—seven men and the young girl. He stood and faced the girl, pointing for her to stand by the stool. She obediently followed his command. She stood five feet, four inches tall and facing her, Escobedo pointed at her and then down to the floor. With his thumb and index finger, he unzipped his pants.

In the alley, Lopez struggled to right himself, half leaning, half falling onto the adobe brick wall that formed a back boundary to the cantina, separating it from the alley. He staggered into the alley and immediately felt the presence of an arm attempting to hold him from falling. It was one of the uninvolved bar patrons guiding him back to his church.

At the outside gate to the priory, the patron said, "You must be careful, Father. This man is vicious."

The old man who had been sweeping and mopping had waited and then moved from the doorway where he had remained hidden, waiting until the group took Lopez from the alley through the brick wall opening and into the back of the cantina. He had remained for five minutes, worried about a lookout or that they might possibly decide to reenter the alley. The man had then moved to the church two blocks down from the alley and crouched by the back of the building, deciding if he wanted to get involved. He thought that Lopez had even odds of not surviving this encounter. The old man did not want to get his family involved; his son had been one to object to this new brand of bandito and had paid with his life. He did not want more of his family's blood spilled.

In the end, he decided that he must tell this tall man, the newly arrived friend of Lopez. Instinctively, the old man knew this friend was a military man, a trained combat man—someone who would likely be unafraid of anyone or anything. The old man wished he had the power and training to take on these animals, but sadly he did not, and he dared not put the remainder of his family at risk. But this new American, he was quiet, unobtrusive, but his eyes saw and captured everything. His movements were those of a wildcat in the jungle: deliberate, efficient, and conclusive.

Lopez was leaning against the gate and the patron still had his arm around his waist. Lopez's head throbbed, and he felt close to needing to vomit. He tried to thank the man who supported him, but he sensed someone else was close.

Lopez thought to belatedly correct this man—to draw a distinction between his status as a brother and not an ordained priest—but he stumbled slightly and then heard a click, but the gate had no latch.

"Move and I will blow your fucking head off." Doolin had placed the barrel of his .357 Colt Python at the back of the patron's head; the hammer of the weapon had already been pulled back.

Both Lopez and the patron froze.

Lopez spoke first. "Judah, this man came to my assistance."

"Yeah, sure, Sebastian, after he witnessed you getting the shit kicked out of you."

"Judah, he came just before you did." And with that the barrel moved and the hammer slid back down, silently returning to its rest position.

"Fair enough. One of your parishioners just notified me three minutes ago that you went into the cantina. I was on my way over there, but I had to get my gun 'cause you wouldn't let me carry it in church."

This last was said with impatient understanding: a younger brother upset that his older sibling had been correct, even proper, but had been harmed by an indifferent reality.

"I saw them dump someone, you, out the back door. It was dark, so I couldn't be certain, but I thought it was you."

Doolin moved to assist the man and get Lopez through the priory door and into bed. As he shifted his friend into the room and down onto his simple narrow wooden bed, he reached for the light on the nightstand and switched it on.

The patron silently backed away from the bed, his eyes wide in terror as he took in the injuries Lopez had sustained. He silently moved to exit the room and closed the door. He melted into the night, and he was gone. He could not let the predators see him with Lopez or his American friend. He still had a family to protect.

What Doolin saw sealed his decision for future action regardless of what his friend was about to say. Lopez saw it in Doolin's face and quickly said, "Judah, let it go ... there has been enough violence already."

"I will do what God directs of me, Sebastian."

The words had tumbled out. Doolin nearly smiled in amazement as he heard his own voice utter these unyielding pronouncements; it was by His authority, and it had become absolute. Doolin had suddenly and with finality begun to grasp that he was but a simple crude instrument for the Lord's work. It was that elementary, and he was at peace with the outcome, whatever it was to be. But he knew he must answer the Lord's commandment.

Doolin had also begun to understand the unspoken truth, perhaps the most poignant tacit legacy of war, that for many of the survivors exposed to combat and the instantaneous decisions to fight for their very existence, a beast was let out of a cage buried deep within every person. For many of those exposed to this personal, physical form of warfare, that beast, once let out, roamed freely, rewarded for its plunder and predatory excesses. For many of these same individuals, this creature refused to be recaged and found ways to remind its keepers of its terrible potential. It was, for many, a realization that they simply could not live with, could not accept. And thus, they drank or drugged themselves into oblivion—not out of weakness or shame, but to impede this monster and its quest for freedom to hunt again. Doolin had never been completely successful in neutralizing this force, and yet perhaps now he would allow it to serve God and let the Creator judge the outcome.

Lopez looked into Doolin's eyes and saw the transition into acceptance and faith. He had witnessed this before. Not often, but he knew the signs of an individual's acceptance of inevitability—inevitability seen as God's message. He tried to smile, but it hurt. He wanted to warn Doolin, but he knew this was wasted effort; Doolin already knew and seemed to welcome whatever fate awaited him.

So, Lopez allowed Doolin to lay his head back on a pillow and as Doolin grabbed a wet washcloth, Lopez prayed for him to understand the message God was delivering, to harness the force that he knew Doolin possessed and to use this for good, not pure violence.

"By the way, Sebastian, where is your robe?"

"Probably in the cantina. They stripped it off of me."

"Well, I guess that is as good a reason as any to go back to that place, right?"

"I guess." He managed a painful weak smile. But Lopez also knew his friend and understood that whatever Doolin would accomplish within the spirit of God's work, it would contain a singular characteristic typical of Doolin.

And with this acknowledgement, Lopez then prayed for Escobedo, for he knew the man had only a short time left in this life.

Suddenly, there was the unmistakable aroma of Maria in the room. The old man had apparently run from Doolin to Maria's house to tell her of Lopez's fate. Maria looked at Lopez and the back of her hand reflexively moved to her mouth as she sucked in air, horrified at the image of the man she admired, respected, and had befriended—the man she also loved. She fought back tears and rushed to sit on the bedside, holding his face in her hands.

"Oh, Sebastian, my God—what have they done to you?"

"I got into a little disagreement" was all he murmured.

As Maria took the wet cloth from Judah and dabbed Sebastian's cheeks, removing dried blood, Lopez looked up at Doolin. "Judah, you remember who you work for, yes?"

"I will remember, Sebastian. I could not forget."

Maria suddenly rose. "Señor Doolin—Judah, may I speak to you?"

Doolin was already moving out of the priory when Maria caught him at the door.

"What are you going to do?"

Doolin only half smiled. "I need to get his clothes, Maria … and I need to finish my mission." This last part was said softly, almost a whisper, as Doolin was somewhere far from Mexico, *hunting in the tropical jungle, feeling the light rain of the Vietnamese evening.*

She could not entirely make out his eyes in the faint light, but she felt their intensity. Maria also sensed, enclosed within the finality of Doolin's almost inaudible statement, a tome of haunted memories.

"I must go with you," she stated.

Doolin suddenly refocused.

"Absolutely not. I think that would be unwise and would put both of us in danger."

Then, without warning, she wrapped her arms around Doolin and looked up into his face. "Judah, you must be careful! I cannot stand to lose another person, and one who I love as a brother."

Doolin tensed ever so slightly and then wrapped his arms around Maria, lowering his face to touch her forehead with his lips.

This was Lopez's woman, and he would do what was necessary to protect them both.

His characteristic boyish bravado surfaced momentarily, and he stated, "Wow, you smell better than I remember."

She looked up at him and slowly shook her head, his playful attitude masking his carbon-steel commitment made to God.

She looked back up into his eyes and said, "You must be careful. They are animals."

Doolin now wanted to live, to tell her that all was going to be fine. But he knew intuitively that his time with both Lopez and Maria would be limited, no matter the outcome. He nodded once and turned into the night, mentally performing an inventory of his weapons.

His .357 Colt python; his fourteen-inch K bar knife, used to kill silently; and his Berretta 9mm with sixteen rounds, counting one already in the chamber, and his silencer. He hoped they would be enough if he needed them—if he was given the chance to use them. But he felt already that his purpose was clear, and its outcome nearly assured. How he knew this, he could not understand; if someone had asked him to articulate its logic, he would have been at a loss to provide any rationale. But just the same, he knew it to be true.

He moved quietly out into the night. The sounds of the small town encircled him as he padded almost silently out of the priory across the dirt grounds to the back of the church. He slipped behind the dirt-encrusted wall separating the alley from the back boundaries of stores, houses, and shops. Its clay adobe brick was nearly shoulder height, protecting him from view as he crouched and approached the back of the cantina. Doolin felt but did not see Maria behind him, following at a safe distance, equally quiet in her approach. He would have preferred she not be near him, but that was an argument he had already lost.

He stole across the alley to the back of the cantina and waited nearby; he sensed a backdoor lookout but could not see one. The muffled din of rock and roll music provided a steady thumping rhythm that could be heard through the closed door. Doolin realized this might be difficult if the doorman had a gun, as the guy might fire first at any sound, potentially ending Doolin's night prematurely.

And then the aroma of Maria passed him, and as she walked up to the back door she said to the shadows, "May I come in? I am here to collect Brother Lopez's robe."

The man stepped out from the shadows and Doolin could hear him chuckle. "Sure, Señorita, you are welcome, but you should stay awhile."

As he turned to face her, Maria had maneuvered her position so that now the lookout had his back to the alley. Suddenly the blade of the K bar plunged into the man's right lateral thorax, and his neck and head both violently jerked and then stretched vertically. Doolin's viselike grip held the man, now entrapped. With a single rapid continual movement, the knife blade was forced upward and pulled viciously along the natural curvature of the ribs posteriorly. The wound widened and instantly blood poured from his chest, soaking the man's shirt, down his abdominal side, covering his hip and right leg to the knee.

Doolin's actions were deliberate, as he had been trained; he had created an insurmountable impediment for the lookout to create pressure to yell, since the chest cavity was no longer sealed and air flow directed toward the vocal cords was absent. The man's air now had a new larger gaping, ragged opening to the outside, and the sickening sucking and sputtering sound told Doolin he had created the type of wound desired.

A split second later the knife was out of his chest and plunged deep into the anterior lateral base of the man's neck just behind the right clavicular head, or the juncture of the collar bone and sternum. Again, a single rapid, brutally quick pullback and the triangular junction of three major blood-filled conduits was severed and then ripped beyond repair, and the man's life force indiscriminately poured into his ruined chest cavity.

Doolin held him tightly, immobilizing the body as the man briefly struggled, but his strength and indeed his life ebbed quickly and Doolin slowly allowed him to slide to the ground. The ambient light seeping from the doorframe to the outside rear of the cantina was enough for Maria to see firsthand what Doolin was capable of; she had just witnessed classic United States Marine tradecraft for the elimination of a sentry or lookout. Doolin wiped his arm and hand on the cleanest part of the man's shirt and retrieved his Berretta from the top of his jeans, attached the sound suppressor, and checked the chamber. He looked at Maria's face but could not see her eyes. He jerked his head, indicating that he wanted her behind him, and she complied.

Doolin walked up to the rear door and opened it. Music and light flooded to the outside alley, and he paused ever so briefly to adjust his eyes to the indoor ambient light. He stepped in and saw that there were four men closest to him, one in front of them, and one behind the bar. A lone very young woman was perched on a stool next to the man in front of the bar counter.

Doolin walked in at normal stride, almost nonchalantly, and as the first man recognized that he did not belong, Doolin raised the Beretta and shot him in the face, the back of his head exploding like bursting multicolored party favors accompanied by a distinctive popping sound. He walked further into the near-empty cantina and rapidly repeated the deadly choreography a total of three more times. Two of the men never even looked up but were dead before they slid from their chairs.

As the man sitting at the bar turned, he belatedly processed that this moving form was not one of his men, was not supposed to be present. The handsome man with the gold Rolex reached for the Glock in the waistband of his pants, but Doolin shot him in the shoulder attached to the moving arm. Escobedo screamed—the weapon, partially grasped, flew out of his hand and skidded across the cantina floor. Doolin then shot him in the other shoulder. The barkeep ducked behind the bar, and Doolin shot three times into the thin wood just below the countertop. The wood splintered as the three shots clustered at the immediate location of his disappearance. Undeterred, he then fired eighteen inches to the right and left of the man's original position; the sound of a heavy thump followed. Then silence. Doolin popped out the Berretta's clip and slammed a second into place.

The young girl, now sitting slack-jawed at the bar, stared at Doolin, her eyes dilated with terror. She had urinated while sitting on the stool. Doolin looked at her and motioned with his chin for her to leave by the back door and the girl jumped off the seat and ran smack into Maria, who was now ten steps behind Doolin.

Maria said something to her in Spanish, and the young woman started to cry. Maria held her, her face buried in Maria's shoulder and chest, as the girl sobbed almost uncontrollably. Looking at Doolin, Maria slowly surveyed the carnage of his last forty-eight seconds of work. She was shocked, stunned by the speed of this man's lethality; he had eliminated the lookout and the bar's six inhabitants in less than three minutes.

Doolin had glanced at Maria and frowned, but understanding her role in caring for the young girl, his temper dissipated. As he turned back toward the man in the tailored shirt, he saw that he had crawled toward his Glock. Doolin quickly kicked it away and it slid across the uneven floor to the base of a table leg. The man crawled to the end of the bar, and Doolin readied himself; if he showed a weapon, he would die instantly. If not, then there was time for a few questions.

The man reached the end of the bar, turned, and lunged back at Doolin, but too slowly, showing a machete that had been strapped to the far end of the bar. Doolin easily sidestepped the man and tripped him, sending him to the floor, where a quick heel to the man's wrist loosened his grip on the thirty-inch cutting blade.

He put the gun to the man's head and said, "Let me help you sit up on the stool."

Doolin assisted him, pulling him up and pushing him down onto the stool.

He then pulled back about three feet away from Escobedo and while bending back over, out of leg reach, Doolin picked up the machete.

Escobedo sputtered, "F-fuck you, asshole, you're a dead man. Do you know who I am?"

"Yes, in point of fact, I do. You are the alleged human being who has others kill for him, rapes young underage women, and thinks he is to be afforded the respect and honor reserved for the president of Mexico, yes? You are also going to die tonight, no matter what you do, say, or think."

This quieted Escobedo immediately. His eyes widened slightly, enough to tell Doolin that the outward armor or bravado, the demonstrative elegance of power, had been penetrated and was beginning to rapidly evaporate. Escobedo began to understand that this man was not going to be intimidated. So, he tried another tack.

"You want money? I can give you two million in cash in twenty minutes."

Doolin only smiled.

"OK, five million! Give me twenty, maybe thirty minutes."

The man grimaced in pain, as both of his shoulders were shattered from the Berretta's lethality. His left shoulder was bleeding, but it appeared to be slowing already.

Doolin gave the man a sympathetic, somewhat disquieted look, sharing in the embarrassment allotted Escobedo's naïve attempt at negotiation.

With this, Escobedo began to panic and screamed, "Fuck you! I will have them cut your balls off and stuff them in your mouth, you fucking asshole! And I will have them rape this cunt"—with a wavering and weakened left arm, he tried pointing at Maria—"until she bleeds to death! Your friend, that stupid priest, is already dead!"

Doolin slapped him with the barrel of the Berretta, chipping his front upper teeth and splitting his lower lip. The man began to whimper.

"Please, don't kill me, please! Money—I have money and … and some stuff. Anything you want."

Looking at him again, Doolin registered discomfiture for a coward. And then Escobedo began to cry.

Doolin looked at Maria and motioned with his chin for her to leave with the girl. She slowly shook her head no but whispered to the girl.

Maria then kissed the girl on the forehead, and although the young woman initially stumbled, she righted herself and walked out wearing Maria's shawl, pausing to look back at Escobedo. In perhaps her first act of healing, she spit on the floor in his direction, lifted her chin, and exited via the back of the cantina quietly.

Maria, Doolin, and Escobedo were alone.

Doolin asked, "Who is your boss?"

Escobedo, not yet approaching the parameters for blood-loss-related shock, shook his head and smiled. "Señor, you and your people are dead. The woman is pretty and will be used and enjoyed before she dies. I will personally fuck her in the ass until she bleeds." Steadying himself with his right hand on the bar countertop, he grimaced but managed a faint chuckle.

Doolin had heard enough; the futility of obtaining information without overtly torturing this man was now apparent. But he would not limit his actions despite Maria being present.

"I think not."

The ex-Marine raised his arm and with one swift, powerful arcing stroke, he brought the blade down on Escobedo's right arm three inches behind the right wrist, severing his right hand from his arm.

Escobedo was stunned and he screamed, his back arching upward and his legs shooting forward off the stool. He then began to wail, his pupils widening with horror as he realized his hand lay on the bar counter and his shortened arm was rhythmically pumping blood freely into the air.

Maria shuddered, then turned to the bar and vomited.

Doolin brought his face next to Escobedo's ear and stated clearly and slowly, "Now, my friend, goodbye. Your time is over, and you will not be missed. You will unfortunately not be able to keep any of your promises made here tonight."

He stepped back as Escobedo slumped over, his shoulders slack but bobbing slightly as he sobbed. The man's head was bowed over his lap, neck exposed, his left hand attempting to stop the hemorrhaging from his cleanly severed right wrist.

Doolin brought the blade down with as much force as he possessed, aiming and successfully striking the back of Escobedo's neck. It cut through the skin and muscle and dove between the cervical vertebrae, the bones of the spine, almost through to the anterior neck muscles. Blood exploded upwards. A sickening gurgle and then a sucking sound and a red geyser sprayed upward, cresting and arcing over the bar countertop. Then rhythmically, beat by beat, the flow lost force before bubbling freely down the back and sides of Escobedo's residual cervical stump, the floor, and the bar front, now painted red.

There was a gathering silence, a second strike of equal force, and then the head rolled onto the bar counter. The detached body fell off the stool and hit the floor with a thud; the spastic jerking of his legs lasted twenty-two seconds.

As Doolin turned he saw Maria, her eyes wide, her hand over her mouth, pressed hard, fighting for control. She was beginning to shake; she turned and retched again onto the floor as she struggled to maintain her upright position. Doolin was somewhere else, scanning for unfriendlies, immune to the horror he had committed or the needs of Maria.

Doolin walked past her, but not before he turned and grabbed Escobedo's head, lifting it by his long slicked-back black hair. A surprisingly pleasant aroma emanated from his expensive hair cream, now mixed with the metal coppery tang of hemoglobin from his blood. Doolin headed to the back door but paused when he realized that Maria was not moving.

He walked back to her and extended his free arm for support, which she took, still shaking, and she let him lead her out the back door. One arm holding Maria, the other holding the head of the once powerful drug enforcer of Yecora.

Once outside, he turned and gently leaned Maria up against the same adobe wall that, not more than forty-five minutes previously, Lopez had struggled in pain to stand against. Doolin walked the perimeter, scanning his surroundings, deliberate, methodical, and emotionless in each sector he viewed, the Berretta in his free hand. At the front of the cantina in the soft light from the single outside naked bulb above the front door, he found Escobedo's Corvette and placed his detached head on the hood near the windshield. He then turned and headed back to Maria, accompanying her back to the priory to check on Lopez. Doolin never spoke a word.

She had seen him at his worst. He had again become one of nature's most efficient predators. The beast of war and combat had been let loose, free once again to roam and destroy. But was he like those who used violence and intimidation to humiliate and break human beings, to strip them of all dignity? What Maria did not, *could* not know was that Doolin was at that very moment asking God's forgiveness, asking Him to guide him back into the light and remand this beast that dwelt deep within him to a sealed secure prison, never to be let out again. Judah waited for God's answer. He waited for His judgment.

The mangled bodies of seven men who in life were accustomed to intimidating, abusing, and harming innocents now lay within the dingy, eerily quiet cantina. The music had stopped. Doolin had met their viciousness and raised the level of retribution to a near incomprehensible level. The men who had so often laughed and found humor in the fetid scent of fear from the innocent had at last shared in the same dreaded pong themselves. They had encountered a killer, a man trained to cull the herd with maximum efficiency, bereft of emotion or hesitation. Their collective insolence and moral obloquy had angered the Furies, and they had answered with a heart-stopping avenger named Judah Connor Doolin.

Doolin reached Lopez with Maria in tow. His friend was now sleeping with the easy cyclic movement of his chest, belying the events of earlier in the evening save the puffy distortion of his eyes and face. Judah turned toward Maria and took her face in his hands, gently holding it up to his, and looked carefully into her eyes. A soft touch of his lips to her forehead, tender, affectionate, and warm. He spoke softly to her.

"I am sorry, Maria. You have seen ... well, you have seen the darker side of my being. I am soiled beyond any redemption, beyond hope, beyond any salvation. I cannot be forgiven for what I have done, and tonight is only a small portion of the evil that lurks within me. I have to leave, and I hope that I have not complicated Lopez's life too much. But what is done cannot be undone."

Maria moved her face onto his and held him with her arms, not kissing and without passion, but with growing tenderness coupled with an awareness of the power held within this man.

"My dearest Judah, you may be many things, but I cannot accept that you are purely evil. No, I cannot accept that this alone describes you. You are indeed capable of extreme violence, I ... I cannot understand ... you are very dangerous. Before God, I ask if you are ... maybe you are one of the avenging angels that God has directed to clean up parts of His imperfect world. I do not know ... I do not understand what I have seen. But you have responded in the only way ... the only way that protects the innocents.

"Perhaps I will ... perhaps *we* will see you in the future, Judah. Sebastian and I may join you some day, but not now, as there is much to do. We may call for you, and if you send for us, we will come. But now ... now you must go. I don't want to know where. No one will ever know that I care deeply for you, Judah Doolin. I am in love with this man." She turned her eyes toward Lopez, who was now awake. "I am his, but you will also reside in my heart, Judah Doolin."

Doolin had wanted her but understood this was impossible, and he was truly happy for his friend.

Yet still he asked, "How can you stand to be near me when you know what I just did … .what I am capable of?"

She smiled slightly, her eyes meeting his. "I am a religious woman, Judah. I believe in God's works. Perhaps you have a greater purpose; you are His instrument. This, you already know."

One last gesture, a soft brush of her lips against his, and then he turned to gather his things and leave.

At 10:45 p.m., one hour and forty minutes after the devastation visited on Escobedo and his men, Doolin was on Federal Highway 16 heading north back to the United States.

CHAPTER 16

FROM MEXICO TO MALLROY

Mid-November 1978

Fiat Justitia ruat caelum.
"Let justice be done though the heavens fall."

T he aftermath of Doolin's vengeance threw Yecora into a virtual panic. The police had tried to locate both Lopez and Maria within hours of the unfolding events, but the couple was gone. The authorities also searched for the man on the motorcycle who was a friend of the Catholic brother, but he was also missing. Three days later, senior leadership in the cartel brought the local police before them and demanded an explanation as to what had happened. The authorities were clueless. The warehouse manager for the cartel had visited the cantina early in the morning after finishing his shift and found evidence of a massacre. He nearly lost the contents of his bladder when he saw the unique hood ornament sitting on the shiny Corvette. After, he had quickly entered the cantina and called his bosses, as bodies were everywhere, and one was missing its head. Both the cartel leadership and local law enforcement personnel conveyed their shock at the suddenness as well as the level of violence displayed. The police chief sat nervously with a senior lieutenant of the cartel and could offer no assistance.

There were initially rumors that Lopez had participated, but little by little the beating of Lopez and the reaction of his military friend became known. That one man had caused all of this destruction was initially dismissed as absurd by cartel bosses, but no one in town had been a witness to the events. The fifteen-year-old girl had driven with her mother to San Diego to begin a new life. Whispered utterances from the old man mopping eventually made their way to the bosses, and it appeared as though Lopez had been too severely beaten to do anything, leaving this guy on a motorcycle as the principal architect in the elimination of an entire segment of the cartel's workforce.

Lopez and Maria had relocated to Canada to seek and live with his relatives in Toronto. They applied for residency as refugees from the drug wars, and both changed their names. They would not return to Yecora, and Doolin played by strict rules; he told no one and never attempted to contact Lopez or Maria. Doolin was only a bitter and frightening memory, almost a phantom within nightmares for many peddling narcotics south of the border.

The townspeople, for their part, were stunned. That someone had stepped up to render harm to those of the cartel and *survived* was unprecedented. The drug corporation itself was unsure about how to ultimately address this unusual set of circumstances. They looked for someone to punish, someone to use as an example, but in truth they knew, as did everyone else, that the single man of consequence had vanished. Things slowly quieted, and the illicit business of narcotics continued. But the leaders of Mexico's most rapid growth industry would not stop looking for this "special" gringo.

As Doolin traversed Northern Mexico, he slowly doubled back to the northwest. He had directed his route north and then east when leaving Yecora, ensuring that anyone watching or following would initially, at least, begin a trek to the Gulf. But once north of Chihuahua, he began to pick his way in a generally northwest direction. He used his navigational skills honed and long ago perfected in Vietnam to continue to his destination: a reentry into the States, but not via a legal port of entry. And since he remained off of the main thoroughfares, he found that he quite enjoyed the solitude of the natural beauty of the desert.

Many of the roads had no names, and indeed the only issue for him was to ensure that he could get gasoline and not leave himself stranded somewhere. But what surprised him was the sense of tranquility and serenity that he began to enjoy the more he traveled into the emptiness of Mexico's sparsely populated northern regions. Staying away from the cities, the towns, and even the villages, he only ventured into their confines when he absolutely needed food, water, or gasoline. This meant, in reality, that he could go for five days—much less than in Vietnam, since rain was uncommon here, if not rare.

He worried about Maria and Sebastian, but they both had been adamant that they would be OK. They had demanded that he leave promptly to ensure their collective welfare. Thus, he was now on his own and actually felt a sense of freedom and safety, as he knew this was territory where he held a distinct advantage if challenged by anyone. He was the endemic predator in the semi-wild country of Mexico. Anyone else, especially heavy-handed enforcers from some drug syndicate, were likely to be fish out of their geographic waters in this area. The city was different, but out here, he was unrivaled in his training and ability to identify and eliminate any potential adversaries.

The environment also gave him time to think, to reflect carefully over events, some of them five years old now. The drone of his Harley's engine, the open blue skies, and the empty surroundings, at least void of human beings, allowed Doolin's mind to wander. He had entered that stretch of land where the saguaro cacti began to appear. Their habitat was surprisingly defined, geographically present in Northern Mexico, Southern Arizona and California, and almost nowhere else. Along with the cacti, he also saw the wildcats, deer, and coyotes, which were mostly nocturnal. Sidewinders and tarantulas were also common, as well as the ever-present scorpions.

But Doolin loved the eventual nightfall, the appearance of the stars that seemed to paint the night sky like a work of Seurat pointillism, luminous and beautiful. He marveled that the light he saw was perhaps millions of years old, traveling nearly an infinite amount of time to reach a small blue-green planet and the retinal cones of a young man contemplating the experiences of war.

As he rethought the sequence of events that had led to the death of Mallroy, he intuitively felt that Haney was to blame. Almost assuredly Haney had not pulled the trigger—in fact, he might not have even been in the country—but Doolin was certain that he was behind the murder of the man who had become his instructor and friend. An individual who had opened a pragmatic, if not trenchant window into the historical destiny of the US military-civilian government complex.

Doolin had respected Mallroy immensely. The reasons for this were many, but perhaps more salient were the specific actions this "full colonel" had taken regarding Doolin himself. Mallroy had engaged in an interest to educate Doolin as to the reality of modern warfare and explored the genesis of the Vietnam conflict, and he had done this because he saw several qualities that were remarkable in this young man.

Doolin would have been surprised, and indeed humbled, at the energy and mental effort that Mallroy had expended on his behalf. First, and in Mallroy's eyes the most impressive feature regarding Doolin, was that the young man was a pure warrior: unafraid, committed, and comfortable with aggression but restrained in his desire to deliver violence. This latter willingness to unleash combat energy depended upon the "totality of circumstances"—a phrase that had nearly caused Mallroy to go speechless when Doolin had uttered it, for it unmasked that this kid actually was grounded in decency but also wanted to learn, to advance his understanding of his surroundings.

His parents had been a heavy influence on Doolin, no doubt, but in Mallroy's eyes Doolin was a warrior, an authentic soldier who carried within his conscience the essential elements of understanding linked to compassion. Doolin himself had expressed as much to Mallroy. This was the struggle for Doolin, as these elements ebbed and flowed over the months of combat exposure. For this young man, a balance was essential. The alternative was to become a rage-filled animal, unable to distinguish between combat and murder.

Further, Mallroy felt that in this, Doolin was like those that pushed their country's history along. Mallroy had spoken often with Doolin as to the former's belief that history's legacy is one that stumbles, lurches along, and operates with no inherent value system. It is up to the individual, acting alone or together with others pursuing a worthy cause, or prescient leadership to guide any movement to rectitude, to justice.

Mallroy understood that Doolin had read enough to know of the political and personal inconsistencies among our so-called "Founding Fathers." These were men, and they exemplified the norm rather than the exception in their personal weaknesses or flaws. But these individuals were similar to history's other people of stature or, as some would say, of historical importance. They were human beings, and thus they were inconsistent and imperfect. The emotionally inspiring language of the American Bill of Rights was authored by men who owned other people, who owned slaves, but these same flawed individuals were those who in turn drove their collective expression forward with justice and hope as a species, race, and culture, and as a nation.

Doolin had voiced to Mallroy that only those who continued to seek goodness, fairness, and honor could permanently bend or shape the future. Wickedness would ultimately be corrected and, at some point in the future, abolished. It might take time—often too much time—but evil would fail. It might and often did rear its awful ugliness again, but time, like the water and wind in the karst caves of Vietnam, would wear down its impact as nature's variables did to limestone and gypsum.

Those seeking a righteous future needed their intent to be one facilitating greater justice than that found in history's past. If lives were sacrificed in this noble pursuit, well … Mallroy understood that Doolin thought this was acceptable up to a point, but both men did not endorse the idea that "the ends justified the means," for Doolin, like Mallroy, was not an adherent of Machiavelli, nor of the "winner take all" at any cost philosophy. Otherwise, as a people, they were in effect enabling a culture of Darwinian survival dictated by the strong over the weak. And Doolin could not embrace or support, mentally or by force of arms, either an American or Vietnamese outcome based on an implicit Darwinian paradigm. For both men, the weak, the defenseless, and the innocent needed protection, a commitment by the strong to protect these most vulnerable people. To protect their future, one that perhaps might not mirror what Americans or US leadership thought best.

Perhaps a reflection of Doolin's growing maturity was his fundamental commitment, even at the cost of his life, to principles allowing liberty and freedom of choice for his fellow citizens who cared precious little for him. People who now chose to burn the American flag or scream at and spit upon him as they manifested their anger toward him and their government.

And this was perhaps the most remarkable aspect of Doolin's character, in the eyes of Mallroy. Aware of these contradictions within his capacious young mind, he understood and even accepted the duality within our species: love and hate, night and day, each accompanied by the ever-present and shifting gradients. The young man, while dealing with the intrinsic pain caused by his personal actions during the war, was processing them within the context of history. These actions were committed by an individual raised in a Christian home and taught by loving parents to respect all life. This was naturally a burden for Doolin, heightened by his especially close relationship with his mother. She had taught him to give aid and comfort to other individuals, but instead he had become a trained killer. It was just that simple; it was just that complex.

At one such time in the future, the kid would eventually render a judgment upon himself as to the righteousness of his actions or the perversion he symbolized. The kid was, after all, a sniper, and one very good at his assigned task. His tally book revealed an unofficial record for the number of kills of enemy combatants, and whether this would be held internally as appropriate or not would decide Doolin's ability to move forward with his life. For someone so young, Mallroy held Doolin in near awe.

Mallroy had seen this in Doolin, through discussions and through questions that were direct and even at times aggressive, but the young man seemed to enjoy the probing by the senior officer. Mallroy had understood that Doolin would live, die, or be killed in pursuit of his duty. Whatever obligation was assigned to him—even with his integral reservations about his personal conduct within a conflict that might be nonsensical, unjustified, and historically immoral—Doolin would choose duty over any other option. Thus, Mallroy had decided to protect him; Mallroy wanted Doolin to live to see the war's end and be the force for good that he envisioned for him.

But Mallroy also witnessed in this young man a need to fit the pieces together in an attempt to understand the request for violence from superiors. Doolin struggled with the taking of life when certainly other strategies might yield satisfactory or equivalent results. This almost dismissive concern by the nameless bureaucracy as to the impact upon those conducting the requested acts enraged this young man. Mallroy recognized that Doolin would not hesitate to kill in defense of both comrades and justice. Even the abstract manifestation of something so elusive as "honor" would, in Doolin's mind, ensure that moral integrity was maintained; this was enough for this young man-child to unleash his deadly force. But senseless killing trickling down through the sterile layers of government policy was often unacceptable to him. And yet, he fulfilled his duty. This self-imposed, if not rigid boundary between black and white, right and wrong, in a world that paradoxically screamed for shades of opacity and grayness fascinated Mallroy regarding Doolin.

Keeping the kid out of harm's way had proved a bit more difficult than Mallroy actually anticipated. He just kept doing things that were described by other officers and commanders such as Stein as "heroic" or "life-saving." His tenure on Black Virgin had proved almost catastrophic, ending with Doolin saving Mallroy's friend while being nominated for the Navy Cross. Mallroy had smiled in spite of himself as he shook his head in wonder. *You can't make this stuff up,* he thought. Some people were just marked for significance, even greatness, and he had begun to wonder, to seriously consider, that perhaps young Doolin was such a person.

For Mallroy, unfortunately his destiny was not to survive the war. Someone had assassinated the colonel while Doolin was on his way back from North Vietnam. This series of events still was emotionally raw for Doolin, even years after the event.

As he felt the Harley's steady power and its rhythmic drone, he took in the desert beauty and let his mind refocus on the events of five years ago. Lieutenant Colonel Stevens had related to Doolin that Mallroy had been shot multiple times near the US Embassy compound in Saigon en route to the second HQ used until the Army's operations grew so large that a new facility was needed. The building's purpose at the time of this event was little known, but it was used for Army Intelligence and housed those undertaking espionage activities in Vietnam. Mallroy had been visiting the embassy and on his way to the clandestine center for reasons that took both Stevens and Doolin nearly six weeks to unearth.

Doolin could not be certain, and he never quite confirmed that it was in response to Mallroy's plan to ensnare EWH that somehow something had gone awry, but he had suspected as much. In fact, Doolin felt that Mallroy, when he had advertised falsely that "an Army colonel was for sale" to a high enough bidder, had marked himself for death. Doolin had even considered telling Mallroy to forgo this part of his plan, thinking it was too simple and transparent. Haney would see through the thinly disguised veil, he thought. Mallroy had set this up to gain access and to understand hidden connections, but perhaps someone, or Haney himself, had rapidly identified Mallroy's real purpose and decided to eliminate the troublesome Army colonel.

Stevens and Doolin had pieced together several details in the weeks after Mallroy's death. First was that Haney had been given notice that Mallroy was indeed for sale to his network of illicit drug commerce for South Vietnam. Overtly, Haney had bitten hard, but the concern that Doolin had at the time and felt more so in the years since was whether Haney had done this for show. Had Haney wanted Mallroy accessible to enable Haney to pull the lever for the colonel's elimination? But Mallroy was in a position to assist the illegal heroin distribution, and thus Haney was provided an ideal set of circumstances to further his business. It would also let Mallroy get close to Haney.

Haney, through intermediaries, had arranged for Mallroy to be brought into the process, but incrementally, as the criminal hierarchy was always worried about plants or double agents. All was going well; Mallroy was working through the Vietnamese general's contacts, and they were allegedly blinded to Mallroy's deception. Unfortunately, Haney was not, and slowly he began to piece together that Mallroy was in the process of making a series of very subtle and careful inquiries regarding Haney. This very fact alarmed

Haney, as it should have, since Mallroy was working through CIA contacts that he himself had personally vetted to examine the movement of Haney and his connection to laundered money.

Someone somewhere had slipped and provided Haney a clearer view of Mallroy's real interests, and the door slammed shut. Haney moved quickly to transfer funds and to put dummy financial records in place for several of the smaller accounts so that both the CIA and Mallroy would reach dead ends in looking for such deposits and people to connect back to Haney. Haney could also reasonably argue that at least two of these smaller accounts were part of operational plans to entrap dishonest police or military personnel and this was the beauty, the game within a game. But he also knew that the enormity of his dark assets, if discovered, would cast doubt on any credible story of their legitimacy—or Haney's. It was therefore important that only a couple of these lesser deposits be discovered, and only if absolutely unavoidable. But even these smaller accounts should optimally be kept secret, lest they lead to the big ones. The big ones, known only to Haney, had to stay completely dark or he risked everything.

But Haney went even further. Doolin and Stevens never knew the details, but Haney finally crossed the red line he had repeatedly warned others never to traverse. He knew Mallroy's reputation and that this Army guy was committed, intelligent, and aggressive, but even Haney hadn't counted on the rapid progress that Mallroy made in unmasking both Haney's illicit activities and the enormity of the money reserves under only a single CIA officer's control.

Thus, one rainy steamy afternoon, with humidity soaking the armpits of anyone standing or even sitting outside for three minutes, Haney shared his intentions with General Nguyen Trong Ang. In a tense one-on-one meeting at the end of a routinely scheduled mutual defense gathering of involved personnel between CIA and military from both South Vietnam and the United States, Haney had motioned quietly for Ang to stay behind.

In the rather plush conference room, with a large oblong rosewood table that comfortably sat nine, the sound of the fans rotating over the table provided a repetitive soft brushing of metal on metal. The table had a tasteful centerpiece of carved green jade, a nine-inch shallow curved bowl partially filled with water. Three delicate white flowers floated on the surface. Only two of the carved rosewood chairs imported from Hong Kong, each with a white cushioned seat cover, were occupied. Everyone else had left but still Haney waited, silently looking at Ang. Haney and Ang were diagonally facing each other at the rounded end of the elongated table, its charred-red surface silky smooth.

Approximately seven minutes after everyone had exited, Haney knew that they were totally alone; their portion of the building was now empty. He was also aware that no active surveillance of the room, either audio or visual, was being maintained when he extracted a folded 4x6-inch sheet of paper from his inner shirt pocket of his hand-tailored linen suit. He simply passed Trong Ang the paper with a name written in black ink and said, "Eliminate him now."

Mallroy's life was effectively over.

Not more than five days later, Haney let General Nguyen Trong Ang know that Mallroy was going to Saigon to speak to someone at the US embassy. After this, Mallroy was to go to the old MACV headquarters, where apparently he had a scheduled meeting with superiors. The building was located across town from the embassy, separate and distinct from the main facility for covert operations located at the new $28 million structure near the Ton Suh Nut Airport. This Mallroy, in Haney's concerned view, wanted to meet with someone in military intelligence after seeing a contact at the embassy. The CIA derisively called Army efforts to address and utilize covert assets an "oxymoron" given the lofty, if not sanctimonious, self-image of the CIA. But Haney was worried Mallroy was cross-checking information, linked to a growing appreciation that Mallroy was particularly effective. And Haney did not make a habit of underestimating his opposition. That could prove fatal.

Unknown to most was the fact that MACV's remnant presence in the building housed a remarkably effective intelligence effort, with deep penetration into several Viet Cong groupings. But it was different than the CIA in that "wet"—or active—measures were routine for the Army's covert activity, as opposed to mostly paper shuffling and observational efforts of the local CIA's assets.

The building itself was a beautiful relic of the French occupation, a modified French colonial structure surrounded by barbed wire forming a second perimeter within a wrought iron fence. Its front was a pale mustard yellow with white-trimmed French arching windows, originally with darker ochre shutters. The entrance had twin white grooved pillars and there were no eves, but it was topped by a mansard tiled roof. The structure's true occupants and their activities might have been guessed by the multiple radio and high-frequency antennas and emitters located along the tiled roof, thick as trees found in the Vietnamese highlands further inland from the coast.

Haney had a CIA contact inspect travel logs for the colonel, since higher-ranking officers had to provide data on their movements. He thus knew that Mallroy was making two stops in Saigon, and this increased Haney's options for an effective solution regarding the troublesome colonel.

Personnel working from within the building were forbidden to wear uniforms, and activity within the building was deliberately but fraudulently cast as a mind-numbing administrative section of the military run by civilians. In reality, the senior leadership of Army intelligence met and worked in this building, their actions hidden from much of the surrounding military and indigenous population. They were a small but tight-knit group, as they were obsessed with security.

These "gorillas," as the CIA disparagingly called them, understood that whether in war or peace, but especially in war, poor or loose security gets assets killed. They took their job seriously; there was an absence of hubris, and a cold reality of potential harm penetrated their clandestine culture of frequent wet operations. Here, Mallroy needed to obtain additional approval for his ever-escalating security clearance requirements, as he was now encountering impediments as he meticulously worked his way through the byzantine world of hidden money. Haney watched his progress through a network of informers and direct monitoring of bank maintenance records, the activity within his dark accounts. Haney was also observing Mallroy's increasingly successful approaches to several accounts, two of which Haney was using for the bulk of the dark money.

This was undoubtedly part of Mallroy's escalating efforts to identify Haney's true nefarious activities. Haney was growing restless—no, actually, he was beginning to get extremely nervous. Haney was certain he was identifying the forensic footprints of someone coming behind him and checking on accounts, his activities, and their connections to other accounts. He knew this had to be Mallroy, but he worried Mallroy might have others who were now aware of these accounts and might be independently conducting their activities and reporting back to Mallroy. They were closing the loops around the true dark money mega-accounts, the ones Haney was never going to be able to explain, and Haney was watching this with ever-growing alarm.

Mallroy, on the other hand, had assumed that if Haney's activities were legitimate, Haney would have already called a meeting with Mallroy's superiors from Saigon and put an end to his efforts. This would have been possible, if not probable under an established administrative umbrella wherein each government entity, CIA and Army, were allowed to review the other's planned and ongoing operations, but only in the most general or broadest terms. Still, this was occasionally done, and while underutilized, the review process was in place to prevent incidental screw-ups. The unfortunate reality, though, was that each government entity operated individually with barely concealed disdain for the other, as if each operated in a vacuum.

This administrative arrogance could and historically did lead to a potential crossing of wires where failing to inform each other of vital information occasionally impacted ongoing operations of one or the other. The result of such "siloed" organizational activity was in its most mild form juvenile, but in a war zone it had certainly resulted in unnecessary casualties, including deaths of friendlies. One group's operations might harm the other's if there was a shared ignorance of mission goals; it was that simple.

It was maddening for the Army to uncover poorly conceived CIA plots that undermined existing Army needs and vice versa for Army plots that directly exposed CIA assets to the enemy. The typical response was a shrug of the shoulders by either one of the organizations. They simply didn't communicate very well, because they despised each other. Haney's lack of effort to administratively "slap" the hands of Mallroy, if Haney knew that Mallroy was investigating the CIA officer's activities in itself, was suggestive of a potentially disreputable motive. It smelled like Haney was nervous about confronting Mallroy, and this was not the norm. When CIA operations could even be remotely troubled by Army activities, the CIA literally went batshit crazy in publicly admonishing the guilty responsible military culprit.

Not having screamed about Mallroy's investigative activities looked to Mallroy like Haney might not be able to—because the accounts and the suggestive enormity of their balances confirmed unspeakable treachery. Or perhaps Haney didn't know about Mallroy's probative efforts; Mallroy didn't believe that Haney was that naïve or stupid not to watch his backside. And of course, this was true. Haney could not take the chance of having an open meeting where Mallroy might already know enough to expose Haney's accounts or his activities. This exposure, in an open forum with senior leadership present, was inexplicable. To produce documents regarding Haney's fiscal largesse would be catastrophic—he couldn't risk that. Mallroy had to go.

But this need by Mallroy to meet with his superiors and gain approval for further security clearance along with additional authorization for his unmasking of dark accounts created a potential opportunity for Haney. Mallroy's need translated into needing approvals from senior officials at both the embassy and the mini-MACV. Traveling between the locations, Mallroy might not request a driver to take him. Thus, this would likely expose him to an ambush either leaving or entering a taxi or a government automobile en route between the two sites.

Haney wanted to ensure that Mallroy was dead, but he wanted no traceable connection to him. This was the ultimate reason he wanted no meeting between the two organizations pitting Mallroy's investigation into Haney's activities. Any event that occurred after such a meeting, even if Haney had successfully traversed the meeting's potential threats, would then seep back to him, and others might become interested in connecting the dots between a dead Army colonel and his interest in Haney's activity. The implied connection would have been accomplished, and this could not be allowed.

Haney and Trong Ang worked in concert to distort the itinerary of Mallroy's limited travel between the two heavily guarded compounds. What remained unknown to Stevens and Doolin was that the meeting in the embassy had gone well, and Mallroy had indeed discovered, confirmed, and exposed the movement of money between two previously dark accounts that Haney had control over and repeatedly used. Yet, Mallroy had not yet shared this with anyone—a hesitancy based on Mallroy's need to ensure that "due process" was followed. One simply didn't go around accusing their own government officials of treason without ironclad, indisputable, undeniable proof. Mallroy, with his background in the "shadow world," knew that he had to be certain beyond appearances, since hidden agendas might legitimately underwrite and explain Haney's activities.

Mallroy now needed to go to MACV and lay out the preliminary information to his seniors. The next step was to ask for the necessary official and sanctioned legal authority to penetrate the banks and examine all identities associated with the accounts in question. Since these accounts were "dark" they, by definition, had imaginary dummy cutouts acting as their holders. This made the actual identities opaque unless formal assistance of the banking officials was obtained, and confronting banking officials with imprimatur authority was thus necessary.

Mallroy's argument was to be that cross-checking in a time of war was vital. If such activity unmasked irregularities, requisite discreet or direct open enquiries should commence. Any ruffled CIA feathers would ultimately undergo the forcible correction to the incommodious reality that Army Intel had actually employed clever investigative assets and not the Neanderthal prototypes popularly portrayed by CIA Ivy League dilettantes. There was always an advantage found in shocking your competitor into the disquieting awareness of your competence. In fact, Mallroy might enjoy this more than whatever truth he uncovered.

If Haney was innocent or if there was a valued strategic rationale for the existence of these dark money accounts, so be it. Even though the appearance of liquid assets involved in numerous highly questionable transactions might actually be just that, if sanctioned by leadership at the CIA and used for America's protection or benefit, their existence and use would be appropriate, even potentially of value. Further, Mallroy's senior leaders could demand from CIA equals their confirmation of a semiobscure station chief's requisite need for operating huge dark money accounts. Under what pretense would such vast amounts of money in the hands of a single man be judicious?

But still, Mallroy played by a set of rules that allowed "due process" for the accused. It was possible that Haney had constructed a remarkable penetration into Charlie's activities that would render these accounts reasonable and valid. But even this possibility might be better discussed, because it might be that Haney's activities, if sanctioned, could still be at cross-purposes with Army mission objectives. Thus, knowing a bit, just a *bit* of each other's goals might avoid embarrassment or even endangerment of field personnel.

But if Haney's accounts were unknown to or unsanctioned by higher-ups in the agency, then the ax would fall. They would personally bring Haney to account; the CIA likely would handle a renegade operative quietly but effectively. All of this was contingent upon a careful, traceable, but quietly accurate forensic analysis of assets moving through these shadowy accounts. The analysis had to be correct.

The day in question found Mallroy leaving the embassy as he slowly walked toward the front exit to access the taxi stand and public transportation. In the main hallway leading to the heavily fortified entry, a routine but thorough search of all persons and materials leaving the embassy complex occurred. To the left were two hallways lined with offices and to the right, a glassed enclosure providing light to the massive entry hall, benches, and public telephones along the far back wall. A dark-haired man sweating through his tailored cotton shirt, in spite of him wearing only a loose-fitting necktie and cream-colored linen pants, intersected Mallroy's path. Unknown to Mallroy, the embassy liaison officer was in reality a mid-level CIA officer.

He quietly but deliberately fell in step alongside the Army colonel. As they walked not more than twelve steps toward the forming line at the front security checkpoint, they both slowed. Mallroy caught the odor of expensive cologne as the man came nearer Mallroy's personal space but stopped before intruding beyond the tacit comfort zone observed in Western cultures. The young embassy officer audibly moaned; the growing queue was slowing the exit from the building and delaying important meetings for the powerful and influential. The sweet-smelling linen-clad man assumed he belonged to this class.

As he turned to Mallroy, he said, "First this unbearable humidity, and then yet another problem here. Look at the length of the lines. The drivers are even worse … some are actually dangerous. I'm taking my car, if you need a lift. I'll drop you off if it's on my way."

Mallroy stopped and viewed the growing line in the front of the building. He immediately turned to the young man and said, "You with the embassy?"

"Yep, going over to MACV. Got a meeting at thirteen hundred."

Mallroy habitually calculated the odds of this being an incidental versus deliberate contact.

By design, the younger man in the linen suit had already begun to turn away and depart down the hall that led to the back of the facility and procurement of automobiles. This route traversed the multiple corridors and offices housing support staff. He was not waiting for Mallroy, and as the younger man walked away, he considered that his attempt had failed. He had planted the hook and, in accordance with Haney's request, waited to see if the colonel in civilian clothes would bite. But he had been told not to make the effort to transport the colonel obvious.

Mallroy was buoyed by this offer of transport because he did, in fact, want to get to MACV reasonably quickly. He was indeed anxious to lay out the damning evidence that implicated Haney. After a moment, he chose to break out of the long line, turning to follow the linen-clad figure. It was Mallroy's only mistake. Unfortunately, it would be his last.

The liaison officer was an ambitious junior underling of Haney, William Thiem, who was receiving nearly $3,000 a month, sometimes more, for what he thought was participation in a black ops program to catch VC embedded in the RVN police force. He was completely unaware as to the source of the money, but when he started getting envelopes marked "Top Secret— Internal" from Haney in a sealed diplomatic pouch filled with $100 bills, he was so shocked and then excited that he went to extreme lengths *not* to ask or report the gains. Haney had mentioned that the money would accumulate and be used to "purchase information," thus explaining the practical need to keep it off the books.

Haney had joked with Thiem, "Can't file expense reports for bribe money for corrupt Saigon police, now can we?"

Haney had provided the opportunity to enlist Thiem for his plans by inviting him to the Rex in Saigon on Nguyen Hue Boulevard at the corner of Le Thanh Ton. Over an extended lunch, Thiem had been asked by Haney to encourage Mallroy to ride with the young man in his car from the embassy to MACV, knowing such a trip was on the colonel's itinerary. Haney had shown a picture of Mallroy to Thiem and told him that the Army officer would likely not be in uniform, but in civilian attire.

He had also assured Thiem that such a ruse was justified to probe Mallroy and to query him, if possible, as to operations that might ultimately interfere with CIA plans. William Thiem had initially thought this odd, in part because such a request involved activity that was "beyond his pay grade," but also because Thiem could not understand what he could possibly ascertain from a veteran covert asset on a fifteen-to-twenty-minute ride. But Thiem readily agreed, flattered that such a high-ranking CIA officer—a station chief, no less—had picked him to assist in ensuring that no conflicting plans were afoot.

What Thiem could not know, however, was that Mallroy was always going to be a target of assassination, in addition to the individual giving him a ride, and this now happened to be Thiem. Whether the logic of Haney's request held substance was debatable, and perhaps given more time and scrutiny Thiem would have thought twice, but the youngster's ego was flooded with pride at being tapped to assist a station chief. It was a simple message Haney had imparted, and Thiem had accepted it at face value. The unspoken message to Thiem was that this "idiot" Army colonel might spill some valuable information, and as Haney finished, he rolled his eyes as confirmation. This sealed Thiem's willingness to partake in the ruse and assist his "better." This occurred not more than five days before Mallroy's scheduled appearance.

Thus, on that day, Thiem had observed that Mallroy was indeed not in uniform as the Army colonel approached the large central receiving hall leading to the front entrance of the facility. William exited an office assigned to junior liaison staff and joined Mallroy as the two approached the front exits of the building and the growing line. The young CIA officer briefly took up position walking alongside Mallroy, initiating this single sentence of small talk as to the "unbearable humidity" as both men approached the crowded embassy exit. He then uttered his prearranged statement regarding the delay caused by the security at the front facility exits.

Continuing his rehearsed lines, the comments regarding his desire to drive himself, followed by his seemingly offhand offer of dropping off the older American gentleman if convenient, were accomplished. Thiem was already beginning to effortlessly glide away from the central area to the labyrinth of interconnecting hallways that housed the working offices of the embassy staffers and led to the building's rear area carpool.

Nothing more was said, but this information was immediately processed by Mallroy. *Deliberate or incidental?* He momentarily considered if he should get outside and take a random taxi. After all, he was in no immediate hurry, and the less anyone knew of his travel, even in the city, the better. While the embassy's assigned drivers were able to pass through the checkpoint into the MACV headquarters, avoiding an unnecessary delay, they could also be working for two employers, with Charlie being one of them. This was probable in some instances, and the shocking lack of security vetting was to chronically plague the American war effort.

Further, balanced against the time Mallroy might wait for the driver, he might actually get to his destination earlier if he just hopped into a taxi and exited in front of one of several MACV entrances. But he would also be defenseless, both in the taxi and in the front of MACV prior to entering. Thus, this young guy's offer seemed remarkably fortuitous.

However remarkable it may have been, it was not fortuitous.

Mallroy turned and caught up to him in three quick steps before asking, "Hey, you sure you wouldn't you mind giving me a ride? I actually am going to MACV myself."

"Oh, that makes it easy. No, I've got to get over there, and many of us bounce between the two areas. It's no problem."

Mallroy thus made his only mistake. He smiled and said, "Great, thanks."

A Vietnamese janitor mopping the hallway, pushing a cart with a mop and a galvanized gray-metal pail, observed the entire exchange as the two men headed toward the back of the embassy. He worked for General Nguyen Trong Ang's men, but his real employer was the People's Liberation Armed Forces of South Vietnam: Charlie. He slowly stood from picking up paper scraps in the hallway and walked over to the bank of public phones along the right side of the entrance. These were public phones and were monitored by the embassy, but a call to a number at a tailor shop in Saigon raised no red flags.

As he approached the phones, he deposited two coins and dialed a number provided to him by General Nguyen Trong Ang's men. A two-ring effort followed by his sudden replacement of the phone in its cradle provided the signal that General Nguyen Trong Ang had requested. Thiem was driving Mallroy.

The route through Saigon was irrelevant. The key to operational success to kill Mallroy pivoted upon a single fact: Traffic entering the MACV compound was limited to a single entrance for vehicles. It was a deliberate gauntlet ending at the heavily fortified MACV security entryway. As such traffic was funneled into a single lane approaching from a tree-lined four-lane city boulevard, the extreme right-hand lane allowed a ninety-degree turn into the checkpoint; this was the only allowed approach, designed to reduce potential guerrilla assaults that might employ several simultaneous pathways to overtake the garrisoned entry. The city street leading up to the fenced-in structure was lined by small shops and upper-end cafes, some with sidewalk tables under canvas umbrellas to keep the frequent warm afternoon rains off customers. Several of these shops possessed narrow passageways to back alleys that then opened up to a maze of small conduits known in detail only to the inhabitants that frequented them.

The opposite side of the street possessed larger restaurants and more exclusive shops that catered to Americans and foreign tourists, these days mostly composed of journalists and diplomatic personnel. In the center of the street was a single continuous linear copse of groomed trees planted in a four-foot earthen lane separating the opposing lanes of traffic. This was composed of taxis and buses in addition to trucks, scooters, and bicycle-taxis or cycled rickshaws. These latter human-powered taxis were everywhere; often their T-shirted, rubber-sandaled owners could be found lounging in the various safe zones, protected from the larger self-propelled buses and trucks. They were likely smoking American cigarettes and drinking

American-imported Coca-Cola. Like people everywhere, they were communicating the latest gossip of their culture.

Among the outdoor tables at the New Paris Café, 150 yards from the American checkpoint for MACV-2 were four bicycle transporters sequestered near the safety of the curb. If viewed for the last hour, the curious might have questioned the collective wisdom of denying rides to at least seven people who had approached them for transport to nearby destinations. Instead, they stood next to or sat in their single-seated pedestrian transports, talking genially but actively directing riders to other cycle taxis. These other human couriers were continuously arriving from other destinations, depositing customers next to the café's outdoor seating and taking on new traffic. Tucked under the four cushioned seats of each transport was a Russian Makarov 9mm, each loaded with a maximum number of rounds, and as they talked and sipped their bottled beverages, each incrementally moved slightly closer along the curb while staying safely distant from the security checkpoint. All four were now curbside within the safe zone reserved for rickshaws and bicycles. Further into the street, six or seven feet from the curb, the backed-up column of automobile traffic stretched from in front of the café to the entrance of MACV2.

The expensive custom tailor almost directly across the boulevard had double French doors that remained open at this time of day. The overhead fan swirled air in a mirrored fitting room just inside of the doors, and the back rooms allowed customers to change in and out of linen suits and light wool-linen blends. A beautiful twenty-nine-year-old Vietnamese woman with almond-shaped brown eyes and raven hair wearing a subtle orange áo dài moved in and out of the shop, at times catching the eye of one of the four men working the cycle taxis. As she exited the store's open double doors, she placed a vase of flowers alongside the entry. It added a degree of beauty and sophistication, clearly inviting to the well-heeled clientele, but it was also a clandestine message that the car carrying Mallroy and Thiem was en route. At that very moment, it was six blocks from MACV2's entrance.

The four men, each highly trained and assigned a specific role, began to move into their respective positions. Two were the primary assassins, one was backup, and one was to clear the street of any heroic-minded pedestrians allowing rapid escape through the back of the café into the tangled maze of alleys and narrow passages.

As Thiem drove, he made small talk with Mallroy, careful as to not appear too interested. He simply asked him where he originated from and how long he had left on his tour. Thiem was well trained and commented mostly on the chaotic Saigon traffic; he apologized once, telling Mallroy that he might have saved time taking a taxi. This was, of course, not true, and Mallroy smiled briefly and expressed his appreciation to Thiem, realizing that he had likely saved forty minutes between waiting for transportation and the ride over. Mallroy was ahead of schedule, and the "fortuitous" ride would allow him to get back to his office late in the day instead of the next morning.

As the café came up on the passenger side of the car, the scooter and bicycle traffic, including the cycled rickshaws, clumped into a desultory mass at the corner. People, scooters, and automobiles were all fighting for limited space as traffic slowed to a crawl, and then a policeman in a white uniform and white chin-strapped pith helmet directed the river of metal and people to briefly stop.

The temperature was 88 degrees, the humidity at 100 percent. Mallroy sat with perspiration beading up on his forehead and freely dripping from his chest and armpits. The traffic cop, an impatient middle-aged man, then waved the intersecting snaking flow along, and for forty-five seconds there was a continuous cacophony of horns and engine noise. Brightly colored blue, yellow, and light pink moving transports weighed down by produce of nearly infinite varieties competed for space with people, all streaming together in front of Mallroy and Thiem. The two Americans sat a couple of cars behind the front with Mallroy, per habit, scanning the surroundings.

He caught view of a single bicycle rickshaw driver standing fifteen yards from the corner, thirty-five yards from him in a direct line that formed the hypotenuse in the triangle of the two crossing streets. The man was looking at him directly, and then rather abruptly put on sunglasses and turned to speak to another man on his right shoulder. The other man did not turn toward Mallroy, but at a somewhat unnatural, almost hurried purposeful pace moved toward an unoccupied rickshaw.

Mallroy was struck by this second man's appearance. A warning light in Mallroy's subconsciousness began to slowly glow, although he couldn't articulate precisely why. This man appeared deceptively relaxed as he strode away from his colleague to his own parked bicycle rickshaw, but then he disappeared from full view. The colonel might have dismissed this if it were not for the first man turning back and, although wearing dark sunglasses, appearing to look directly again at Mallroy. A confirmation?

And then under the cushioned pillow of his rickshaw passenger seat, sunglasses never leaving Mallroy's direction, the man sought something, lifting and tilting the padded cover partially as his hands explored the area beneath. Mallroy could not see what he wanted or if there was even an object in the space being searched.

The traffic began to move again, and Thiem turned slowly right and rounded the corner. Thiem expertly avoided two people who slowed in front of him before joining the MACV2 line parallel to and seven feet from the curb. As the car eased into the MACV2 security line, Thiem forcefully tapped the brakes a bit harder, as a man in his thirties was suddenly crossing directly in front of them. This man, also with black-framed sunglasses, put out his right hand, touching the hood of the car just on the driver's side of the Ford Galaxy emblem. Mallroy suddenly was aware that a second man was walking briskly from grouped bicycle taxis toward the stopped car.

He was the same man who had previously been looking in Mallroy's direction, and he was carrying something close to his right hip. Mallroy was in the act of rapidly attempting to open the door when thunderous explosions began both in front of and beside the car.

The man touching the hood had leveled his firearm at Thiem, using his left hand, and fired six times at near point-blank range into the semirounded windshield of the Galaxy, all six shots clustered above the steering wheel. Thiem's chest was torn open and two rounds hit his head as he slumped, the last round entering his left temple and exploding the side of his head.

The car lurched forward, causing the man at the front bumper to jump up, landing partially on the hood of the car. His torso slammed onto the metal hood as he simultaneously rolled, expertly regaining his footing as he now crouched at the left front tire. The car stopped its forward momentum as it smacked into the rear bumper of the preceding car in the MACV2 line four feet from its original position, shattering the left headlamp.

Mallroy attempted to use the door as a shield, but there were now two of them on his side of the car. One man, the one he saw first, fired through the window of the passenger door, catching Mallroy in the shoulder and neck. Mallroy attempted to shield himself, but the other man from slightly behind the door, equal in position to the car's right back tire, fired into the now half-open door, literally hitting Mallroy in the top of his head twice as he was ducking below the window of the door, killing him instantly.

The fourth man focused on onlookers, and the traffic cop. The officer directing traffic finally realized what was happening and, while stunned, started toward the unfolding carnage. At a distance of twenty-five yards, the fourth man shot him, emptying his automatic into the traffic cop and wounding two innocent pedestrians, one critically, as the hail of bullets traversed the intimate space around the cop. Hit four times in the chest and abdomen, the pith-helmeted officer lived another two minutes.

The four men then moved into the café, accelerating but not running. An off-duty American Army supply officer rose from a back table inside of the café to confront the lead man and was killed instantly with two shots to his chest. The group was then out the back door and, as ground fog exposed to the early morning sun, evaporated into nothingness.

SUBSEQUENT EVENTS

Stevens and Doolin had pieced together much of the timeline and the series of events that ended Mallroy's life, but there were significant gaps in their knowledge. These gaps were not answerable, and for both men the inability to verify who was directly behind Mallroy's murder left them with wounds that likely would never heal. But this was yet another legacy of their experience in Southeast Asia.

For Doolin, it was both a professional and intensely personal loss, and as he left Vietnam, he had to accept that he would likely never be able to address the perpetrators nor fully understand the circumstances in specific detail that led to Mallroy's death. He was convinced that Haney was involved, but then among the violent reprisals and chaotic environment of Saigon in the early 1970s, could Doolin really be certain? He intuitively understood that he must relinquish his frustration, as he was never to completely appreciate the details. Nor was Doolin ever able to settle the emotionally raw open account due his mentor, friend, and protector, Colonel Alfred K. Mallroy.

But Doolin was wrong. All unpaid bills come due.

CHAPTER 17

FIVE YEARS AFTER LEAVING VIETNAM

November 1978

Ambulans in Lucem
"Walking into Light"

Doolin slowly and carefully traversed the arid topography of Northern Mexico, sticking to back roads that were sometimes gravel, sometimes deeply rutted. The engine of his Harley murmured smoothly, his ride a reflection of his meticulous upkeep. He had purchased a 1969 FLH Electra Glide 1200 cc bike, fitted with the Shovelhead engine, from a kid in California. He thought he remembered the kid's name, Frazier, who unfortunately had just been convicted of selling marijuana. Doolin had known he could get the bike through the kid's lawyer for pennies. The kid was fatigued emotionally, worn down immediately after his conviction and sentencing, and he was also destitute, apparently owing his attorney money. Thus, the Harley was advertised in a local paper outside of Sacramento, and Doolin had first thought the price was a mistake. He insisted that Frazier receive a fair price and said he was not going to cheat the man based on his emotional lability. Some might have argued the final price was even a bit generous, being more than the asking price.

But the thirty-three-year-old, now convicted and sentenced for selling small amounts of marijuana, was from Missouri and had been in the Army in '68, perchance at the time of the Tet offensive, trapped within the ancient city of Hue. The experience had stripped him of his confidence in life's serenity, basic goodness, and meaning. He had witnessed what all combatants experience in war: needless death, cruelty shaped by necessity, and split-second decisions with horrifying results.

Upon returning home, Frazier had retreated into a drug-induced haze to

311

erase or at least try to attenuate the monstrous horrors that he had seen, and perhaps even committed. Doolin sensed an intimate connection to this lost soul when visiting him in jail to finalize the sale. He had seen firsthand the vacant, haunted look in this young man's eyes. Like so many veterans who had been pulled from the ennui of high school—girl-chasing, sports, and mother-enforced church on Sunday—his life had been irrevocably altered. Within six months of leaving his idyllic Jefferson City suburb, the absolute brutality associated with trying to stay alive within the stark habitat of unannounced firefights with an elusive committed enemy had forever taken its toll on this young man, as it did for many traversing the centuries of human conflict.

He had wandered the streets in Sacramento, his disembarkation point after twelve months in Vietnam, following an unceremonious discharge. They had snatched his youth, taught him how to kill, and then forced him to engage in the depravity of armed combat without rules. In seconds, the Military Code of Justice had become an abstract, irrelevant legal primer historically composed by those trying to limit the human race from backsliding into oblivion.

Finding it impossible to achieve steady work, his nights were a dream-filled kaleidoscope of mangled bodies and screams that awoke him drenched in a cold sweat. He often smelled the unique pungent odor of burning human flesh and hair, his nausea welling up in him to the point of actual retching on certain early mornings. Doolin did not know any of these specifics, but he sensed their presence immediately upon meeting Frazier. The expressionless eyes, the limpness inherent in his every movement.

Had Frazier told him about Hue, Doolin would have nodded silently, immediately understanding the isolated loneliness that encircled this former high school football standout. Had Frazier told him about Hue, both men would have remained quietly somber but a bond between them would have slid into place, a blood-earned rite of kinship. Such is the shared empathy of those who have dwelled within the valley of the shadow of death.

Doolin had unnecessarily thanked Frazier for selling him the bike and had even promised to keep it in proper working order. The attorney had thought this humorous, but he would never have understood the brotherhood of injured souls who were now wandering within the borders of the American nation. The bike was black and silver, and while it drew some attention to him in the small towns and stops, especially in Mexico, he deliberately kept the bike dirty, covered with a thin coat of road dust. Dirt did not mean neglect, however, as Doolin kept the machine in top condition. He actually enjoyed his seemingly endless tinkering performed on the bike to ensure optimum performance.

What Doolin could not know as he slowly navigated the narrow dirt roads in Mexico's northern desert was that at this very same moment, his former executive officer on Virgin Mountain, Major Nathan Stein—a man he had saved from certain death—was sipping terrible coffee while looking over the reports and detailed accounts of a particular quintuple homicide at a rural gasoline station occurring six months previously. He sat at his desk in the cramped district attorney's office that he had recently joined and pondered the events. One law officer was killed and one apparent semi-innocent drug trafficker, along with three of society's less desirable characters. Stein was intrigued by several elements of the reported events but also had significant confusion as to who had actually saved the wounded law officer.

Stein had also left the Army and was now a talented but emotionally wounded junior employee with Arizona's expanded Yuma County law enforcement. For Stein, the war, in similar fashion, had taken part of his life; his innocent and naïve belief in glory and valor was gone. He had lost his wife while risking his life for what amounted to a flawed political hypothesis of strategic containment: Vietnam. They had been high school sweethearts, but she grew tired of his constant dialogue of honor and duty and thus, in his absence, she sought an excitement that in truth sheltered a desperate narcissism within a rather shallow identity. She saw herself as a happy and fulfilled social butterfly; others viewed her through the optics of self-indulgent sanctimony. Often after cocktails at a local watering hole in Southern Georgia, she let it be known that her inner thighs could be spread for the asking. Her parents had nearly disowned her. In fact, her father had slapped her across the face one evening, the moment he unequivocally understood the repeated pleasure she took in the intimacy of men other than her husband.

Her husband wrote to her daily, but it was during his mid-tour homecoming that he tasted the bilious agony of her recurrent voluntary indiscretions. An alcohol-fueled irate statement one night regarding the large red-purplish scar over his cheek, a confirmation of her rather copious enjoyment of other men without "deformities, either intellectual or physical," had eviscerated Stein. He had gone back to Vietnam to die. His life's meaning was gone, and his belief in anything wholesome or good had vanished. And then Doolin had interfered.

This young, quiet, serious Marine, a remarkable kid from Chicago, had not only saved his life in the cauldron of vicious combat, but had subsequently told him that the single most important thing for Stein to hang on to, the "thing" that Stein would be most proud of in his entire life, would be his damn facial scar!

Coming from an eighteen-year-old, Stein was stunned at Doolin's complete unconcerned confidence in the veracity of this statement. To Doolin, his observation was so obvious that it brokered no dissent. His commander wore the permanent sign of a warrior, and this honor would always, from the inception of our species until its final potential demise, carry significance. The species was, in effect, hardwired to respect, if not venerate courage.

And this mark was one of valor, of action, of honor in Doolin's world. It would gradually reassume these qualities in the mind of Nathan Stein as he underwent his rebirth after the war. While Stein was an officer and clearly older than Doolin, neither the difference in rank nor age prevented Doolin from sharing his nearly perfunctory observation with Stein. Nathan Stein never forgot that statement, the man who made it, or Doolin's surprise in the necessity to have such an observation validated. As the years passed, Doolin's comment had indeed been proven accurate. Stein, each morning while shaving, took note of the pale white line on his face and felt a calm acceptance, even serenity as to its presence, and always thought of Doolin. But such feelings were hard-won.

After Stein had returned from Vietnam and left the Army, he began to rebuild his life. It was a difficult and a surprisingly long journey. The pain and betrayal by his wife, Jennifer, was still palpable and made its presence known at least twice a day: in the early morning, as he faded from somnolence to encounter a new dawn, and in the transition into a troubled sleep when his own dreams, a panoramic replay of Vietnam, began. But he sensed that he had crossed a boundary with Doolin on that mountain in Vietnam and entered an unknown territory of sorts. This mystic terrain was a land wherein his actions and future personal conduct reflected not only on him, his life individually, but on the survivors of this desolate crusade in Southeast Asia. These were his brothers, his soul mates, having survived a common horror-filled experience only to then endure the reckoning of that survival. His future actions and life's direction would bring either honor or shame to the collegium.

He gradually began to feel a necessity to demonstrate, to both himself and others, that he was not stained with shame or dishonor—that his life was not a wasted, misguided series of mistakes. He was not a "baby killer," as the long-haired "flower children" dressed in colorful garments espoused. The men with beards and long hair often had a strange, hesitant reflexive expression when seeing their short-cropped uniformed opposites. The young women, most braless and some quite attractive, had nevertheless insisted as such as they hurled insults and their own body fluids at the soldiers leaving the airport at a federal disembarkation site. They screamed that the veterans returning from an ignoble war deserved to die, but Stein had resolved he was going to live.

But it was not easy. For nearly six weeks, he sat listlessly in his parents' home in Georgia. Not watching TV, not reading—only eating and sleeping when he could, and staring out of his bedroom windows onto the partially manicured green lawn of the backyard. Finally, his father, who had seen the effects of war on friends and colleagues after WWII, accepted that his son, his beautiful boy, was suffering and that as a father, he must do his utmost for his child. His mother, too, understood that while their son had returned, he was not the same and perhaps was never again to be the stalwart, disciplined, honor-obsessed young man that they had watched enter the military.

Initially, they had let him drift, hoping the loving confines of his childhood surroundings would replenish him. But then his father had decided "enough." He confronted Nathan after four days of him not leaving his bedroom except to meet his body's needs, and his father told him it was time to restart his life, to move on. His father revealed that his child was not the first, nor would he be the last to try and survive the depravity of human cruelty unmasked in the theater of armed conflict. His father had spoken gently and yet conveyed with the last vestiges of parental authority that his demands of "renaissance" were not open to challenge.

Nathan, sitting on his bed, had watched his father struggle to find the right words, the right tone, to push him to begin his recovery. His father, for his part, had prayed to the Creator to help him save his son, who miraculously had returned without physical injury, save his facial scar, but was obviously deeply troubled by the war's impact. Both men had looked at each other and, through shared tears, decided "triumph over despair." And thus, Nathan Isaac Stein began his recovery by touching his father's cheek with a soft kiss and then mowing the grass in both the front and back yards.

He then commenced a detailed and systematic restoration of the landscape surrounding the house, trimming bushes, planting shrubs, and cultivating different flowers in the open areas near the back fence and boundaries of his parents' large double lot. Nathan inserted pavers and smooth river rock to border the dirt-filled shrub and flower beds, separating it from the grass that he watered and fertilized. His mother watched, fascinated, as her son transformed her entire yard into a beautiful sanctuary of vibrant green vegetative life. His father sat with his wife at the kitchen table, both looking out into the backyard, and smiled with her as their son labored, at times for twelve straight hours per day. He meticulously changed the surroundings of the house to that of a carefully kept park.

Stein never asked for assistance, never asked for money, as he would get in his car, drive off, and then return with plants, shrubs, and beautiful flowers. His mother would come out in the middle of both the morning and the afternoon with lemonade, iced tea, or water and just set it on a small portable bamboo stand, available for her son to quench his thirst when needed. Voicing her only concern softly to her husband, she wondered if either of them could maintain the beauty that their son had bestowed upon their oversized suburban lot. Ever more frequently, neighbors came by to comment to both parents how incredibly beautiful their yard and surrounding land appeared. Some wanted a tour; some wanted the name of the company "responsible" for the transformation of their property.

Late in July, Stein's sister Lisa returned from a summer session of college at Vanderbilt and viewed the activity of her only sibling. She could not quite believe the verdant beauty and sculpted pathways that now crisscrossed her parents' nine-tenths of an acre. It was like entering an enchanted forest with vibrant flowered boundaries and molded gardened expanses. Lisa had always been a bit intimidated by Nathan, by his intellect and force of personality, but his love for her melted any fear she ever possessed. The net effect was that she was nearly in continual awe of him, and she thus had followed his life's path carefully. She greatly admired his dedication, his belief, his commitment to what he saw as correct.

Lisa was just under five feet, five inches tall, a rich, thick red-brown mane of hair framing an oval face with full lips, unstained straight teeth—as she drank no coffee—and extremely pale, nearly iridescent white sclera surrounding remarkable deep green eyes that missed nothing. Her nose was straight and, she lamented, too big, but others saw just enough balance to prevent her from being "cute," and thus "beautiful" was the term often substituted. Lisa's figure had transformed a bit later than her peers' but she was shapely, her breasts full, if not a bit pendulous given her small-boned frame. She turned heads even though she dressed modestly; she could not dissuade onlookers of their visual interest. The younger Stein, however, did not suffer fools well. Her friends were often older, and she listened with interest to the uncommon, perhaps even rare professional women she encountered.

She had been just as injured as her brother when her friend, now Nathan's ex-wife, had wandered. Jennifer's betrayal was to both Nathan and Lisa, and to the families involved. But to Lisa, the actions had confirmed her long-held suspicion that Jennifer reflected the moral vacuum so typical of segments of modern American life.

The bounty that her generation enjoyed had been a fortuitous inherited combination of valor and economics. The blood spilled in Europe and Asia by her parents' generation during the Second World War, coupled with the hasty, nearly explosive growth of the country's undamaged manufacturing potential, had created an infrastructure and consumer market never before witnessed in recorded history. The children of her generation thus were the recipients of parents who had suffered, fought, and won a conflict, creating this decisive historical inflection point. But Lisa Stein had long wondered whether she herself had been born one hundred years too late. She found the preoccupation with money and material wealth irritating, if not outright unsettling, and often thought of her generation's obsession with material "things" an unsustainable distraction, for she viewed existence through a lens of purpose and meaning.

Lisa herself was similar to her brother, fascinated by history and the actions of men and women over eons that had shaped the collective understanding of the world and approach to life itself. She debated in college and wrote for the university student newspaper, but Lisa found that she was frequently at odds with her classmates over the interpretation and significance of modern events. She often confided in her father and mother, and later to Nathan, that so many of these contemporary events, when viewed through the optics and lessons of history, provided a markedly different set of conclusions than if grasped only through the contemporary frenzy.

Conclusions, unforeseen shortcomings, and dreaded implications were often so easily missed, misinterpreted, or misconstrued without the emolument of time, the prioritizing vantage point that history provides. The shrieking hysteria of today's ill-informed mob, Lisa felt, reinforced the actual tragic conclusions of Isaiah Berlin's prescient essay from the 1950s. This expository tongue-in-cheek essay noted a modern interpretation of a single line from an ancient Greek poet, Archilochus of Paros. And whether entirely accurate or not, "The fox knows many things, but the hedgehog knows one big thing" was felt to underscore the disparity between those who used the lessons of history—the foxes—and those who "just knew they were right" —the hedgehogs. History had a way of demonstrating that the more certain you were of your exalted knowledge and insight, the greater the risk that such certainty actually represented a state of reduced wisdom to be exposed by history's inherent sorting routine.

Lisa had talked to both her parents during her brother's tour, and tangentially they had collectively shared their concerns about Nathan. Her parents had witnessed the withdrawn, haunted transformation of their son as he returned home and communicated this to Lisa, but only partially. When Lisa arrived in late July, Nathan had been home for three months. She now was observing a wholly different person than the one who had passed wordlessly through the front door to her breathless shocked parents only months earlier.

Her brother was tanned, fit, and in fact surprisingly muscular. He was methodically purposeful as he worked a distant corner of the backyard, digging in the dirt and arranging flowers and bushes. As Lisa passed around a gentle curve in the stone pathway leading to a sequestered area of the backyard, she stood silently, watching him. For over a minute she observed his forceful disruption of the soil and then tender positioning of flowers and shrubs. Finally, she decided to break the silence and intrude on him.

"Hey, Nate."

His head whipped around as he recognized the voice from his childhood. That voice, sometimes laughing, occasionally in tears—that voice was a sacred entryway into his past. As he turned, his face, flushed and wet with perspiration, lit up and the grin was spontaneous, the first to grace his face in months.

"Hey, kid. Welcome home."

She began to say something but before she realized it, she was running to her brother and literally flew to wrap her arms around him, sobbing almost uncontrollably into his shoulder.

"God has protected you, Nathan," she heaved.

He held onto her tightly, taking in the fresh-scented aroma of her hair, the surprisingly strong embrace of her arms enveloping him.

He cooed, "Yeah, Lisa, I was lucky in many regards." He slowly released her but she held firm, then pushed back to arm's length.

She looked up at him. "Do you really feel that way?"

"Gradually, yes," he admitted. "Not before, but now, yes, slowly it is becoming clearer to me. Let's say it is not a good experience for anyone and leave it at that."

"Yes, I can imagine," she stated. Then correcting herself, she said, "No, I *can't* imagine, I think. That is the point, isn't it?" She looked up at him, questioning.

He nodded slightly, but definitively. The silence began to gather.

"I am here for you, Nathan, for anything and everything you need. I mean it, I am desperate to please you, to assist …"

"I know," he stated, his eyes far away, his face tight and now searching. Then he refocused, forcing that set of memories into a locked room, and smiled at her, a second smile after years of emotional prohibition. "Would you get me a lemonade and one for you as well? Let's sit out here."

And almost before he finished speaking, she was almost running to the kitchen, returning immediately with two glasses of ice and lemonade.

As they sat, they began to talk. There were no barriers, no embarrassments, no private shame.

She started with something that she knew would surprise him and yet would be irritatingly humorous.

"So, I've decided to spread my legs for the entire Vanderbilt football team."

"Which years? Please say it's only the varsity."

She laughed in spite of herself, as he was ahead of her, as was the norm. Nathan had moved quickly to grasp her well-intentioned ploy to humor him and cut through the distance of time and past ugliness.

"I've decided to do the same," he said.

She threw her head back and in the most unladylike fashion gave a deep, genuine belly laugh that was remarkably satisfying to both. Lisa spilled a small portion of her lemonade as she continued to convulse with laughter. He knew it was genuine, and he laughed in turn.

Their mother, with the kitchen windows open, heard fragments of their shared dialogue, their laughter, and suddenly, in front of the kitchen sink, she felt her legs weaken. She knelt, her knees gently touching the hardwood floor as her eyes filled with tears, and these, too, lightly caressed the floor's surface. Their mother looked up toward the ceiling, clasping her hands tightly as she gratefully whispered her infinite thanks to God.

She remained in this position, rocking ever so slightly back and forth, for almost three minutes. Then, slowly, she rose from her supplication and continued washing the dishes from the morning meal. She was humming a tune from the 1950s when both of her children later walked through the door for lunch, and she felt as though she were nearly walking on air as she laughingly scolded them for their dirty hands and soil-stained clothes.

They each smiled at her false admonishment, for they saw the intense sparkle in her eyes. She had not experienced such happiness in years.

As Lisa sat with her brother, she felt alive, felt whole for the first time in months.

"Don't forget you have a sister with lots of young, beautiful friends with big boobs like mine."

Nathan had begun to sink again, the memories pushing back, but with this he smiled again and said, "Well, give it some time, but I'll definitely take a rain check," just shaking his head in mock disapproval.

Lisa mockingly cupped her breasts with each hand, lifting them slightly within her blouse, and he shook his head but laughed. "Stop it, I am beginning to worry about you!"

But both knew he did not mean it.

"Lisa, there is one thing I need some help with."

"Anything, absolutely anything."

Lisa knew this was about Jennifer, but she was emotionally prepared. If Nathan asked, she would find Jennifer and, short of killing her, honor whatever Nathan requested.

But instead, what she heard shocked her, for what he spoke of was a man. A man he owed his life to.

"There is this guy that actually was flown into our camp and was a Marine sniper. Odd for this guy to come to us and not be Army, but then the war had so many weird elements that I stopped trying to understand or find anything rational for most of these events."

"Do you know his name?"

"Yes … he is, or was, Lance Corporal Judah Doolin. I don't know his middle name, or even if he has one."

"Would you describe what a Marine sniper does? What is his role or responsibility, Nathan?"

He sucked in a breath involuntarily and paused, then looked at her.

"Well, kid, he positions himself in a good spot and, using his skills as a marksman, kills individual enemy soldiers from a variable distance. It's a lonely job, and in my mind, a particularly terrible duty. It's pretty personal for a lot of these guys. They keep a book and record their kills."

She shuddered. "You mean like a scorebook?"

"Well, yes, I guess that is one way to look at it."

"What other way can you look at it, Nathan?" she nearly screeched and then quieted quickly. "I'm sorry ... it just seems like this is kind of a sport or something."

"Well, there is other information about the execution of the shot, the surroundings, the distance, the settings for the scope—you know, technical issues. But you are correct, it's not for the faint of heart. I couldn't have done it. And yes, Lisa, some of the guys get really twisted in their roles; they actually treat it like a sport. Being the best and most accurate, it becomes a competition of sorts."

His sister only looked at him, visibly shaken, slowly shaking her head side to side.

"It sounds unreal, but then so does doing what you had to do." She grabbed his hand and squeezed it. "My gracious Lord, Nathan, what you had to do in the name of our country. To fulfill policy by a bunch of old men in cigar-smoke-filled rooms looking at the world map like a chess board. You guys had to do the work."

She slowly looked into his eyes as hers began to fill with tears. "How did you ever survive, my lovely brother?"

"You know, there were people who wanted us there to help and assist them, Lisa. It was not a consistent or uniform consensus either way, but it was not the mindless stereotypic newsfeed of anti-Yankee bullshit that so many of the people have come to believe."

He paused, his voice barely above a whisper as he continued, "There were committed Vietnamese who wanted America to back them as they resisted the tyranny from the North." Sounding a bit more analytical, he added, "Unfortunately, we were in a civil war, and the struggle has to be ultimately decided by them, without interference from any outsiders, or there is the retribution associated with the label of being puppets of a foreign government.

"The most amazing thing is that Roosevelt strongly resisted the efforts from the French in reasserting their colonial oppression of Indochina after

WWII, after the Japanese were defeated."

Lisa was intently looking at him, proud of her brother's intellect and capacious mind, of his inherent flexibility grappling with arguments that likely had filled the halls of government not twenty years before.

"And here we came, not even twelve years after WWII, beginning to supplant the French in fighting what is a vestigial remnant of their failed attempt at reasserting colonial rule. We might as well be in India trying to reassert British control of the subcontinent. And Lisa, that is why we lost this war, mark my words."

He slowly was shaking his head again, disappointed in his analytics of global strife, but more disillusioned with his own country's naïve understanding of the competing paradigms.

She, however, smiled at his succinct review of history's near-predictable course, as scholars would later argue these were the foreseeable consequences of a young superpower's hubris: Vietnam.

"We were on the wrong side of history in this one." Nathan again looked at her but smiled warmly, his peroration over, drawing her into him. His dues were paid, his family safe.

Not wanting to break the mood, but she cautiously asked, "So what is the deal with this guy ... Dolin? Doolin?"

Carefully, softly, he began, "Well, he is responsible for me being here. For me being able to tell my baby sister that I love her and that she is absolutely NOT allowed to do the whole Vanderbilt football team, only the varsity."

While she smiled, she immediately understood the gravity of his statement. Her brother did not give freely of the commodity "loyalty," and he also was somewhat reserved with "respect." She even had thought at times he was a bit judgmental or even stingy, as he held himself, and all people, to a rather high standard, but here he was. She could tell from the inflection of his voice and his demeanor, his soft sigh, that he held this individual in a special place.

She ventured, "So, I would have thought that all of you guys watched out for each other. Am I wrong?"

"Yes and no. As a group, of course, we did try to protect each other, but there were acts among our collective or general behavior that were so remarkable, so selfless, so absent the intrinsic desire to protect oneself that these rare actions were celebrated among us. And we lived with the knowledge that few among us possessed this level of courage. This kid—I call him a kid … he is four inches or so taller than me, and he is anything but a kid in his world view, I would guess—but this guy was incredible, simply, utterly unbelievable in what he did, and part of his actions saved my life."

She detected a nearly imperceptible aura almost a cloud pass over him, the reliving of some memory as he involuntarily flinched. "He ran at the enemy who had me pinned down and was about to kill me. He ran at him, screaming like a wild animal and shooting, while the VC tried to shoot back at him after I was literally trapped. Doolin shot him and killed him before he even had a chance to fire on me. I watched from behind a rock, balled up like a newborn infant, afraid, terrified. I saw this young, crazy individual run into a hail of bullets that for the grace of God, and only He knows why, didn't touch Doolin. I don't know how he missed getting hit, but he came at the VC like a man possessed.

"I saw him as he came closer and closer. His eyes were wild, like on fire, and he was firing his weapon at the enemy and killed him. He then turned and took on several other VC. He was a one-man killing machine … he saved me."

Lisa was looking at her brother, watching him intently, feeling the very fiber of his being. As he finished, his fingers were blanched white, his hands clasped together. His face had gone slack, but his eyes were alive with fragments of memories reemerging and floating within him. What she saw astonished her, for she was witnessing Nathan, a man she had known from birth to be fearless and strong, speak of this other man in terms that she herself would have previously used to describe her brother. In fact, she still would use them to describe him. But Nathan's own comments about this guy Doolin were stronger, more emotional, and apparently equipped with supportive evidence.

She spoke softly carefully, "What is it that you want, Nathan?"

"I need to find him and to thank him."

She involuntarily sucked in air. "Is that a good idea? I mean, is it good to stir that hornet's nest of memories for either of you?"

"I have no idea … it's a good point, but my soul will not rest until I see him or thank him, or even say a prayer over his grave if that is the outcome."

Tears were now flowing freely down Lisa's cheeks as she grappled to understand and accept the incredible standards of honor and sacrifice that these men still attempted to hold, in spite of the realities they had faced.

She knew this was going to be difficult, if not nearly impossible, but she also instantly grasped that it was beyond essential that they find this man, Doolin. The particulars would be a challenge, to say the least. For one thing, neither of them knew whether this man was still alive; he obviously could have perished in the war. For another, there were no national databases available to them that would divulge any information to lead them to this man, and even if they had had access, how relevant was the data? It had been years since the event. Nathan said it was six or seven years at least.

But Lisa was trying to tread cautiously, thinking and wondering before she said spontaneously, almost without thinking, "Sounds like a good summer detective project for me."

His head popped up, and he looked at her. "Perhaps it is more appropriate for me to handle this. I know I asked for your help, but I suddenly am not sure, Lisa. Perhaps there is no need for you to spend your time on this matter. Maybe it is for me to get done."

"That is where you are completely wrong, my brother. The love I have is for you and you alone, and I would not pass up the opportunity to assist you, even if you put me in prison!"

"Well, with your proposed activities with the Vanderbilt football team, I may have to."

She raised her left eyebrow and a smile began to creep over her face. But she quickly transitioned into an analysis of where and how she would begin her search, and as she became more thoughtful, her smile disappeared. She knew her brother needed her help and that he likely could not accomplish finding Doolin on his own.

"I need his full name, middle included, or as much as you can give me. I need to know date of birth, city of birth, et cetera. If I am going to track this guy, I need to get started with some hard data."

"And how would you go about that?"

"The same way we research anything, Nathan. You know that." She grinned and so did he, realizing that she was not going to relinquish her enthusiasm in assisting him to find Doolin.

"OK, but only until school starts, and then you have to give it up."

Her lower lip jutting out in a mock pout, her eyes twinkled, happy to see her brother reassert his interest in life. "OK, if you say so."

"I do."

CHAPTER 18

TWELVE YEARS AFTER LEAVING VIETNAM

1985

Tempus Fugit
"Time Flies"

O ver a decade later, the demons associated with Vietnam had been wrestled into a controlled sealed room in Doolin's mind, absent from his daily routine and surfacing only occasionally. His life had basically been salvaged, and he had made his feeble amends with his inglorious sordid past. Judah was a paramedic, serving the greater South Side of Chicago. He was often the only Caucasian willing to go into the public housing located in that part of the Windy City.

Doolin was frequently asked by the company that employed him to man the mobile units that attended trauma victims, which in this area of the city meant gang-related shooting victims. He became adept at plugging holes and getting IVs started. Doolin had even put in a chest tube, receiving severe criticism from the ER resident physician but praise from the senior staff surgeon and the police officer who had witnessed the sixteen-year-old dying before Doolin popped the tube into his thoracic cavity. When these victims were alive, with any chance of recovery, Judah could get them safely to the emergency room at Cook County or one of the other trauma units serving the Near South Side.

Judah no longer drank alcohol; he did not smoke, and he had still never used any recreational drugs. But he worked continuously and really, truth be told, had little other life outside of his "family," comprised of fellow EMT/EMS colleagues, the various staffs of the ERs, and of course the police who routinely responded to the same calls Doolin received.

His only other regular activity was attending classes in a new college that

Mayor Richard Daley, the first Richard Daley, had built by unceremoniously clearing the ghetto on the Near South Side by the Eisenhower Expressway. The resulting structure was a concrete academic institution that looked more like a multilevel parking garage in its first years than a hallowed ground of learning, but for the children of immigrants populating Chicago's surrounding neighborhoods, the price was right. The quarter-established schedule of three-month blocks for the academic year meant that hopping in and out of classes could parallel work-related scheduling opportunities for many of these same working students.

There was no on-site living at the school when it first began; it was a commuter university in the 1970s and was still held in low esteem during this period of the 1980s by the communal national academic world elite. However, its validation was soon to emerge in the form of a top-rated business curriculum, a no-nonsense law school, and an outstanding engineering program. The collective perception by those sanctimonious existing universities, who claimed that the University of Illinois at Chicago Circle Campus was in effect a junior college requiring four years to matriculate, reluctantly gave way to a new member with inherent geographic and political advantages. So close to the city, it was able to optimize joint work-study programs founded on reality-based corporate need instead of pompous academic "political correctness."

Doolin had always been comfortable with any form of education; in truth, he had missed formal scholarship. His last real involvement before his EMT training was in sniper school over a decade previously.

And so he had enrolled in classes, as the quarterly tuition was only $212 in the early '70s and combined with advanced placement scores, he was able to work long hours and yet dash to certain classes. In two and a half years, Judah graduated with a degree in biological sciences. During this time, he sort of made a name for himself among the EMT/EMS community, as he was willing to go into darkened hallways in the public housing high-rises. He would announce his presence and say that he was there to help the individual or family who had called. Occasionally, the elderly woman to be picked up was the mother of a drug dealer, and so he became familiar with a group of wealthy but rather violent felons who fought continuously for territorial and fiscal advantage within the culture of illicit narcotics trade within the South Side of Chicago.

He was not immune from violence, however; he had been stabbed twice—once seriously in the abdomen (again!)—and shot at twice, with a ricochet round tearing into his left shoulder but not penetrating very deeply. He recovered rapidly from each wound. Flashes of Vietnam had pervaded his daily routine for each of the subsequent intervals but ended in full recovery. His ambulance company held their breath as they waited for him to sue, and when he did not, they attempted to reward him by asking what routes he wanted in hopes of getting him as far away from the epicenter of violence as possible. Of course, he would not consider this and continued servicing his familiar neighborhoods, much to their initial amazement, subsequent suspicion, and eventual respect.

They could not truly fathom his intent, or more truthfully his need; their aperçu simply could not grasp the salutary effect of his braving danger to assist those in need. He simply was performing a task that God Himself had requested of Doolin. These people required assistance, and when others wouldn't or couldn't within these neighborhoods, he could deliver it.

Their collective but blinkered viewpoint rendered that self-survival and safety were paramount; he knew in his soul that his Creator had provided him with a second chance. God had commanded him to risk his well-being to serve others as a way of paying off his debt, or at least that was the mindset that kept Doolin moving. He had a second chance for a new life, a chance of redemption. The choice was really not at all difficult. The years of elegiacal self-doubt had been surrendered to doing *something,* and he could not abstain or truncate his obligation.

Judah had become familiar and in fact was on good terms with a trauma surgeon at Cook County named Chris Lundgren, who worked a fair number of Friday and Saturday night shifts. Doolin saw him usually once in the early evening and then at dawn. The rest of the time, Doolin was out on calls and Lundgren was in the operating room piecing back together individuals who, by any rational metric, should have been allowed to expire; more than a few of these individuals were not society's upstanding citizens. But Lundgren's attitude was similar to Doolin's: a life is important, and he was not assigned to judge. He was only required to mend, and that he did.

It was only years later that Doolin found out he had been a Yellow Beret, one of the drafted physicians initially deferred to the National Institutes of Health. Lundgren's history was rather odd in that despite being done with training and free from any immediate required military obligation, he spent only one year at the NIH before volunteering for active duty—not just military service, but in-country service. As a result, and directly proportional to the trauma he cared for in Saigon, Lundgren become extremely proficient at his "job," or more correctly, his profession. He was calm under stressful conditions, didn't scream or yell at people, and treated most everyone respectfully, a novel set of traits in the 1970s for a trauma surgeon.

Lundgren also was a remarkable surgeon, working at light speed with few mistakes. Comments by colleagues noted his deft, stable movement, saving precious minutes during operations. His operative mortality was low, his infection rate remarkably small, and his patients generally grateful, although some went right back to finish the botched "hit" and ended up killing their target or getting killed trying. The upshot, however, was a man of considerable skill with every female nurse, married or not, trying to bed him. Some might have been successful, for all Doolin could surmise, but for the ridiculous hours that this guy spent in the operating room. As it was, his "extracurricular" activity was minimal, only adding to the effort of some of the more focused female RNs. But he was forever in the operating room and then disappeared when not on duty.

Clean-shaven with blond hair that had begun to gray at the temples, about five foot eleven, his blue-gray eyes would rapidly take in the initial presentation. Lundgren's teeth were ultra-straight, perhaps one of the early recipients of orthodontic correction, because they were near perfect. His high cheekbones and flat, lightly wrinkled forehead ran into an aquiline nose that was prominent but not oversized. His skin was clear, and his beard, if ever allowed to grow, was reddish, but he would shave even at the hospital after spending all night in the OR.

The surgeon was surprisingly muscular, but if one looked closely, he walked with a very slight limp that he strove to conceal. But when he was tired, the limp emerged, and this was when those who knew him aimed to reduce his physical effort in the time between operations. Although he might come out of the OR having soaked his green cotton top with perspiration, he would immediately head to the locker room to shower and change. Thus, he was ready for the next interaction with a patient and family, well-groomed and bearing the essence of a professional. This was his way of showing respect to families, even though many were of the city's "downtrodden." He didn't care; they were his patients.

As Doolin later got to know him professionally, Lundgren emphasized that these families needed to know that Lundgren respected them. Thus, his clean and groomed appearance reflected this simple statement of deference. When Judah first heard him say this, the younger man was stunned; Lundgren's extraordinary reputation was already made, and many doctors after all night in the OR looked like they themselves had awoken on a park bench. But this surgeon would not allow his appearance to suffer, as it meant something to the family and patient to have a clean, well-groomed physician at their bedside. He demanded this of himself. His comments and his actions would live with Judah forever.

With nurses, colleagues, and people like Judah telling him all sorts of data simultaneously, Lundgren would become that television persona of the competent superman ordering tests on the fly and optimally prioritizing who was first, second, and so on as to who was urgent in heading to the OR. When he was working, the place ran efficiently; he did not get flustered, and he would occasionally talk to the nurses about cases. And in this, Doolin was willing to verify that on at least on two occasions, Lundgren discussed what he thought were his intraoperative mistakes, saying that he had missed such and such and that he had to pay a bit closer attention to the possibilities of hidden injuries. The first time Doolin heard him during such an exchange, the young man's mouth fell open, and Judah thought the nurse speaking with him felt the same; the staff was unaccustomed to someone of his stature just being honest about mistakes, or at least his perceived mistakes.

Judah respected him immensely for this quality. For the female nurses, Doolin could only imagine it added to his attractiveness. The other physicians were very loyal to him as well, perhaps in no small manner related to his honest, straightforward characteristic of occasionally reviewing his self-perceived shortcomings. Everyone else, of course, thought he was infallible.

Doolin's relationship with him forever changed one early morning as he attempted to bring in a seventeen-year-old female who had been shot in the upper abdominal area, the bullet or fragment entering her right side while standing in the front entryway of her apartment in the 1800 block of South Kildaire Avenue. She apparently had not been involved in any illicit activity in any way but had been in the wrong place when a gun battle broke out between two rival gangs over a territorial dispute regarding heroin distribution. The bullet flew into her after striking a metal banister on the concrete landing, and as it turns out, only a reduced or partial segment of the lead projectile entered, tumbling as it pushed through her soft tissue and entered her body. While the banister likely saved her life, slowing the lead bullet, its residual velocity was enough to create a problem.

She was screaming hysterically, doubled over and lying on the ground in a fetal position, when Judah arrived and initially looked her over. Blood had stained her simple white sleeveless blouse near the center. The covering was held in place with four plastic rounded buttons. Doolin told her to be still while he undid the bottom two. He could only see a small, less than a centimeter wide tear in her right upper quadrant of her abdomen, about four inches below the ribs, but the entrance wound was nearer to the midline of the body than her side. Doolin looked at her and she was sweating. He noted that her neck veins appeared engorged, *really* big, like a large rope pushing up under her skin traveling to the base of her ear and jaw. Her pulse was also fast and weak, but what confused Doolin was that the amount of blood on the blouse and the pavement was not consistent with massive blood loss. But then, of course, she could have been bleeding internally, and that made sense because of her fast pulse, almost 120 bpm. Still, the large distended neck veins did not fit this simple picture of excessive internal bleeding.

Doolin yelled to his partner Ronny Jamison, a 305-pound former Illinois State defensive tackle, to bring him the BP cuff and positioned her so that her head rested on a folded blanket. He began to talk to her in reassuring but a no-nonsense manner.

"What's your name?"

"Monica Shaw."

"How old are you?"

"Seventeen, and mister, my belly hurts bad. Help … don't let me die, OK?" She moaned, closing her eyes.

"Monica, you are not, hear me, not going to die, but I need you to do exactly what I say. I need you to be quiet while I get your blood pressure, OK?"

"Yeah, but help me please … please, man, it hurts."

"OK, OK, just let me get this quick."

Jamison was at Doolin's side and grimaced when he saw the blood but handed Doolin the cuff. Immediately, Doolin took the reading.

The red lights and alarm bells were activating in Judah's brain, as the pulse was about 125 bpm and her blood pressure was about 110 over 97.

This girl was beginning to show signs of a condition Doolin believed was tamponade, or when fluid accumulates in the sac around the heart within the pericardial sac. The fluid, in this case principally blood, accumulates and stretches the sac to its maximum, sort of like an overfilled water balloon, and then the internal pressure in the sac begins to rise rapidly correlating to the amount of fluid leaking into it. Since the sac can't expand, the pressure builds up. But here was the real problem: Since the heart is within the pericardial sac and the fluid causes increased pressure in this sac, it acts like a glove, surrounding and compressing the heart. The more the pressure goes up, the more the glove squeezes the heart. And well, a heart that is compressed can't expand and fill normally, and a heart that isn't filling, therefore, can't pump blood. No pumped blood means you die.

All the signs were accumulating, and Judah began to understand that they had no time to get her to the emergency room; she simply was not going to make it. He had heard one of the surgeons tell an intern that with trauma and a virgin pericardial sac, sometimes just 50 or even 30 cc of blood—a small amount relative to the volume in each person—was all that it took to entirely crush the heart with pressure and complete the tamponade effect.

Doolin looked at Jamison and his reflected expression must have communicated Doolin's dread. His eyes momentarily dilated, and he clenched his jaw.

"Judah, what should I do now?"

"Get on the radio and get Lundgren."

"You want his nurse?"

"No, I want him and only him. Now, OK, Ronny?"

"Judah, he ain't coming to the radio for us, you or me."

"Just tell them I need him now, OK?"

"Yeah, sure." He frowned and shook his head, communicating, *It's your funeral, friend.*

Doolin placed the largest IV he could and readied his patient for the gurney.

"Ronny, I need you now!" Doolin shouted. "Get that box behind the driver's side seat, OK?"

"Son of a bitch, Judah, make up your mind, man! Hey, they say, 'Who the hell do you think you are? Doc's in surgery.'"

"Tell those assholes to connect you to the OR."

And with that, Judah turned to the girl and told her, "Do not move. I will come back for you in one minute."

Judah ran the twelve yards to the bus, as they called the

ambulance—crackerbox when he was in the Marines—and grabbed the mic from Ronny.

"Who is this?" Doolin just about screamed into the mic.

"This is Robert Pek. Watch your tone, Doolin, you are on an open frequency."

"Have you gotten Doc Lundgren?"

"You think you have him at your beck and call, Doolin? No, I don't have him, and what do you want? Who do you think you are anyway?"

Judah's tone suddenly flattened, all emotion gone, but it communicated a menace like the reemergence of the biblical Moloch, the vaporous shadow of imminent death waiting for possession of someone's soul.

Pek was one of the self-anointed elites with a two-year degree from a junior college who carried himself above the rest of his colleagues. Forty-five pounds overweight, thick-necked with atrocious dental hygiene and thinning perpetually greasy hair, his breath could stop a grizzly bear thirty seconds after its awakening from six months of hibernation.

All of the EMTs knew that he couldn't handle being out in the field, couldn't make decisions under stressful conditions, for he was a paper warrior. One who could give outstanding, carefully orchestrated briefings for the hospital staff but had never seen field emergencies, never tasted his own fear, and would do anything and everything to ensure that this situation never changed. His fellow EMTs collectively despised him but ignored him as long as he didn't interfere with their operations. And of course, he did everything he could to insert himself into their itineraries and activities.

Doolin spoke clearly and almost quietly.

"Pek, if you don't get Doc on the mic in thirty seconds, I will rip out your throat from your weak-assed neck and stuff it up your overused asshole and watch you bleed to death in front of me. I have killed better men than you. Now do it."

Ronny was standing three feet from Doolin. He was motionless, eyes wide in shock and holding his breath. Doolin smiled a wicked, savage, no-quarter-to-be-given, no-mercy smile and stared at Ronny.

Ronny was, for the first time in two years that Judah had witnessed, afraid, and he actually backed slightly away from Doolin.

"Ronny, for God's sake, come here." Judah motioned to him.

"Judah, they ain't going to be OK with that," he said anxiously, pointing at the mic.

"You don't say." Doolin smiled, a bit warmer, as he kept staring at Jamison.

"Man, I ain't never seen … ain't never seen that in you …"

"I'm sorry, Ronny. Don't take it personally."

"I know, but Judah, you're … you sort of became …" His partner searched for the words.

The mic came to life; it had been nine seconds. "Judah Doolin, this is Dr. Lundgren. May I assist you … ?"

Ronny's eyes were now glued on the mic. He thought for sure Doolin was getting canned on the spot. While his eyes did not convey fear, dreadful anticipation might have been an understatement. Ronnie just looked at Doolin, his head shaking ever so slightly, waiting for the hammer to fall.

But Judah held his ground and rapidly explained to Doc Lundgren.

"Sir, I have a seventeen-year-old with a penetrating wound to her abdomen, five inches from the costal margin, nearer the midline. Heart rate one-twenty, BP one ten-over ninety-seven, neck veins prominent and not collapsing, and she is tachypneic. I think she is in tamponade, and I don't think I have time. It's fifteen minutes or more to get to you."

"OK, listen to me, Judah. Get her into the back of the ambulance and get her sitting up at about forty-five to sixty degrees. Do it now, OK? I'll wait."

"OK, out." Judah and Ronny flew back to her side and loaded her, the IV, and the bandages onto the gurney and then into the ambulance in twenty-seven seconds.

Judah got back on the rear mic. "OK, Doc, she is here with me sitting up, head at about forty-five degrees."

"Judah, repeat the vitals," and Judah did.

The pressure was now 90 and the bottom was muffled but almost 88 he thought, and the pulse in this young woman was 165 bpm. She was sweating profusely, her skin was blue-tinged; she was dying.

Doolin's eyes were locked on his young patient. A form of tunnel vision had replaced Doolin's normal observational skills, and he almost missed Lundgren's request.

"Judah!" Lundgren was now yelling over the radio.

"Yes, sir," startled, Doolin responded, and the tunnel vision disappeared.

"You have to make a decision. If you bring her in here, she is going to die en route. If you do what I ask of you, you have a good chance of killing her … but you could also save her life, if you do this correctly. And if you don't, you and I could get in big trouble, *big* legal trouble. Now, it's your choi—"

"Let's go, sir, please," Doolin interrupted. "We don't have time, she looks rough."

Judah spoke with urgency but calmly. He now had a plan and the fear, the paralysis of losing his patient had transformed into requisite action—into serene composure.

Doolin heard the satisfaction register in Lundgren's voice; even on the radio, it was clear. "OK, pour the betadine over her chest and listen carefully … we have no time."

The surgeon rapidly walked Doolin through, in the next twenty-five seconds, a procedure commonly known as pericardiocentesis: sticking the needle into the pericardial sac to relieve the pressure, allow blood to come back into the cardiac chambers, and allow good pumping to ensue. The only issue for both of them was that this was something that advanced cardiology trainees or cardiac surgeons got to learn within their formalized training.

It was not a procedure that you started doing in the middle of the night, in the back of an ambulance, by radio communication with no senior physician monitoring your every nano-move and without any formal medical degree or training—EMTs should not apply! Oh, and usually there was an absolute requirement for sterility, but Judah knew this was not possible at the 1800 block of South Kildaire Avenue.

A total of thirty-three seconds elapsed from Lundgren's initial comments before Doolin pushed the needle into the final two centimeters, already four centimeters into her chest. Doolin felt the "pop" Lundgren had predicted would occur and immediately pulled back the syringe's plunger, but held the syringe in place. Fixed in space, the plunger came back into the large syringe Judah was using, blood flowing freely into its cylindrical 50 cc capacity.

As Doolin pulled, passing 25 cc, he could sense the young woman's response. Ronny had been holding her hand and told Doolin that her pulse had disappeared completely just as Doolin pushed the needle into her chest beneath the xiphoid process and pulled back the plunger; after, he couldn't be sure, but he thought he felt the pulse again. Yes, the pulse was indeed there—it was rapid, but it was also stronger.

She came back from the pasty cyanotic lethargic silence that marked her attempted passage into celestial eternity and firmly stated, "Fuck, man, that hurts," and started to grab for the needle.

"Hey, stop! Monica, stop!" Doolin yelled, and she froze. "This is keeping you alive. Do not touch it, and bear with me … Ronny, drive."

"Judah, I ain't never driven the bus."

Ronny was no fool. He knew how to drive; he was just careful, if not overly cautious.

"Ronny, please, for God's sake, drive and go with the lights and noisy shit you love, OK? Just don't kill us!"

Ronny now chuckled and jumped out the back of the "bus," slamming the doors. He sped toward the emergency department, lights and sirens announcing their passage through the Near West Side of Chicago's southern first precinct. Judah kept the needle in place, and every thirty seconds he pulled it back and got about another 12 to 18 cc of blood.

Jamison drove like a man possessed and reached the emergency room entrance five minutes faster than anyone else could have. In fact, both Doolin and Ronny later agreed that only Jamison would drive from this point forward. He was good, he was careful, and he was fast.

Doc Lundgren was at the door and immediately jumped into the back with Doolin and the patient. He examined Doolin's work and smiled. "Perfect."

As Doolin was now ready for Lundgren to take over, he started to get up and the surgeon stated authoritatively, "Oh no you don't. Stay there and keep doing what you were doing. I'll tell you when you are done, OK?"

A bit startled, Doolin recovered quickly. "Yeah sure."

And as he turned his head, Doolin could see the man smiling; Lundgren was actually happy.

The surgeon proceeded to give Monica more fluid, but nothing to dull the pain from her gunshot or Judah's needle in her chest. All the while, he was giving orders to four nurses and two junior surgical trainees to ready the OR and get a bunch of other tests and lab work done, now drawing blood from her left arm himself.

Doc Lundgren was like that; he always moved to personally do what needed to be done.

They then transferred the young lady to a hospital gurney and as Doolin sat on the side of the moving bed, still focused on not moving the needle and cyclically withdrawing a bit of blood every thirty to forty-five seconds, they traversed the tiled floors of the giant hospital and were suddenly in the OR. Doolin didn't get to see much of the preparation of Monica by the anesthesiologist or really anyone since his focus was on Monica and the damn needle in her chest. Then suddenly, Lundgren told Judah, "OK, I'll take it from here."

As Doolin began to exit the area housing the OR suites—he had never been up to see them before—the chief nurse, Mary O'Neal, stopped him.

Mary was a woman with a reputation. She was also a woman who had a secret—one that involved Doolin, although he had no idea. She was in her late sixties—sixty-nine, to be exact—and by all accounts should have been long retired, but the hospital would not consider this, and she had not yet thought it necessary. Her beauty had faded slightly, but her sharp blue eyes, once accentuating a face that had stopped men in hospital hallways, now demanded respect; her intellect underscored her natural integrity. The woman's figure had changed—settled, she admitted, and her slightly fallen neckline, not quite doughy, was emblematic of this. Her waistline, too, had given way to gravity's law. Not obese, by any means, just not flat and hard as it once was.

The formerly trim lines delineating her legs also had changed but were still surprisingly muscled. Mary's chin had a slightly prominent cleft, and her skin over her pale but rose-tinted prominent cheek bones remained taut enough to hint at the beauty of her youth. Her teeth were small, still attractively white, not the darkening yellow of others whose aged incisors demonstrated decades of coffee and tobacco pigmentation. A minimum feminine overbite resulted in a permanent expression that suggested caution and thoughtfulness, yet her manner was commanding.

She had been a young RN during the last two years of WWII and witnessed the horror of combat in the mangled young men who clutched her gentleness as drowning victims to a float. She had seen their crushed bodies, their ebbing lifeless eyes replacing the vibrant hubris so recently filled with patriotism and purpose. And during these formative years, watching the impact of horrific combat, in her youth she struggled to retain the optimism of her childhood. Mary's nights were populated with dreams that often ended in her failure to save the youthful faces of men so recently aged beyond their time. Kneeling on a small shoreline, she would frantically reach for their faces and they would sink, slowly disappearing within black water, her hands unable to pull them to the surface. Some nights this dream came twice, but most often only once. She accepted it with equanimity, as the small price she was asked to pay in comparison to the honored lives that had passed into oblivion.

She slowly came to understand the requisite essentials of trenchant re-alpolitik. It caused Mary to broker minimal tolerance for any ingratitude or dismissal of these heroes, these boys who were so often ephemeral in her life, but significant. She also disdained the "proper" societal view regarding her gender's need for protection or shelter. Her generation's coming of age in the cauldron of a world conflict had forever stripped away the careless ennui of cocktails and the typical obsession over proper social interactions on Friday evenings. Mary had repeatedly felt death's impending verdict in the form of countless twenty-something year-old men grasping her hand, feebly calling out for a mother's lost presence, their grip gradually weakening as they slipped into heaven's embrace.

Such were the days that had made her life, and where she had formed an enduring friendship with a recent graduate of Vanderbilt University, a brilliant young RN born in Tennessee who had graduated over two years earlier than her classmates. Mary O'Neal loved this younger woman as a sibling and cared for her as she would her sister. At the end of the war, both moved back to the Midwest, and both took up positions at the same prominent Chicago hospital.

Life was good; collective joy had erupted after the war, and the country was breathing its full measure again. Mary's loyalty, however, was put to the test nine years after the war ended when her friend's young life fell apart. This brilliant, pretty "Vandy" graduate was accused by her husband of being impregnated with another man's child. Was this a lie? Mary never knew but suspected that the babe, now the man Judah Doolin, might not have been of this woman's husband. The life of Margaret Catherine Mahoney, the brilliant young RN and wife of Frank O'Brian, was about to collapse. The era of reasonable legal and social treatment of both marital parties was yet to arrive; a woman without a husband, one verbally shamed by calumniated accusations of adultery, entered into a dark spiral of societal disdain and personal isolation that left them unprotected and vulnerable.

Her husband threw her out, taking all of her belongings save the gold cross she wore around her neck. Their two daughters, he left with her to feed, clothe, and raise on her own. Now pregnant with young Doolin with nowhere to go and no family to turn to, Mary took her in. Mary kept Margaret and her two girls safe from any further predations of those who read the wind of her friend's misfortune as Serengeti jackals sense injured strays. Margaret's humiliation was finalized and locked in place by the exaggerated efforts of those other RNs who secretly were jealous of this young woman's intellect and position and took the opportunity to communicate their horror and shock to all who would listen. Of course, more than half of these same young women were themselves engaged in extramarital relationships, enjoying the post-war reprieve with a particularly sanctimonious form of *bon viveur*.

Several of the RNs, however, who witnessed the catastrophic turn of events impacting Margaret chose to stand behind their embattled brilliant younger colleague and protect her and her newborn when the birth finally came. Mary had, in fact, been one of the rotating transient "mothers" to Doolin after his birth. He lived within the hospital for weeks, a form of temporary residency within the pediatric ward in the early 1950s since Margaret Mahoney O'Brian had apparently suffered a psychiatric event that now would be classified as classic post-partum depression—a severe case. The other RNs quietly determined they would care for her child, feeding him and nurturing him as if this child was their own.

In fact, two of the younger RNs became so close to this infant that when the Doolins came to take him home to adopt him, these RNs required gentle prodding from Mary and others to release the child to his new family. Margaret's two daughters were taken in by relatives until their mother was released from court-ordered psychiatric care, deemed safe to resume her mothering.

Mary, too, had nurtured the babe, he without a family, and had given testimony to God Himself that if the authorities were going to place this child in one of those awful state agencies, she was going to take him and disappear. She would keep Margaret's child safe and raise him as her own if needed. On her knees in the early evening hours of December 1953, within a large cold, empty stone-walled Church of Rome on Chicago's West Side, Mary had asked God if her planned illegal act was permissible. Was such an act sinful or righteous?

She felt God smile at her plan. She left the church grinning, and the priest of first-generation Polish immigrants who happened to be at the front door smiled in return. Then, somewhat perplexed, he stared after her, unable to deduce the source of the radiant face that had floated past him as Mary exited into the frosty night.

Thus, she formulated the remaining details. She had a brother who was a police officer and a cousin who was a lawyer. She had no clue how to accomplish the specifics of her startling epiphany, but she would sacrifice her life to ensure that Margaret's child was provided a decent home, a chance. She might not have fully grasped the enormity of what she contemplated, but she knew enough to understand that documentation related to the origins of a child could be purchased through illicit, dimly lit back channels.

But the plan ultimately was unnecessary.

What Judah Doolin could not have known was that this no-nonsense nurse with the reputation of a Marine drill sergeant thus knew more about his origins than he did himself. She had often contemplated his fate while holding him as an infant, smiling over the softness of the soles of his newborn feet, the texture of his lanugo scalp hair, and the intense curiosity found in his young questioning eyes. Mary had herself rested peacefully in a rocking chair at the nursing station, holding him with his face pushing against the fullness of her white uniformed breast, his breathing steady in the rhythmic tranquility of a newborn's sleep.

She also wondered about his biological father. Mary despised the man who had harmed Margaret, but she did wonder if the man who had fathered this infant was actually her husband or another. But because of the shame and harm her friend's soon-to-be ex-husband had visited upon his wife, Mary swore to her Creator that this man would not ever be allowed to see or have access to the son he abandoned. But was this child even his?

Mary knew that her young friend was nearly destroyed, as she had spent almost twelve months forcefully institutionalized for what amounted to severe depression after Judah's birth. Stripped of her family, her daughters, and her civil and medical rights, she experienced a legal form of enforced incarceration without trial. Mary ultimately lost track of her Vanderbilt prodigy, but in what was a final desperate expression by her young friend, Margaret C. Mahoney O'Brian had given Mary the cross necklace that hung from her neck and asked that this be given to her infant son. A son whom she would never see again, never hear his infant or maturing voice, never witness his development into a man of substance and honor.

Margaret had given the cross to Mary as she lay nearly catatonic in the post-partum section of Illinois Masonic Hospital, her eyes uncharacteristically dull, but not lifeless. Mary had taken the necklace, kissed Margaret's hand, and swore before God that the living being who was to be named Judah C. Doolin would receive this item. Somehow, some way, young Doolin would come to understand that his mother was limited to providing only two items for her infant son: one was this cross, and the other was life itself.

Ultimately, Mary had met the Doolins and approved of them and their intentions of adopting him immediately. She saw their goodness, their humility, their desire to provide this infant with a good home. She would wait, but she would also act in whatever manner necessary to ensure they were able to "procure" him.

She had pulled Virginia Doolin aside in the hospital corridor, away from the nursing station and separate from her husband, on the afternoon they had come to first see young Doolin. She held both of Virginia's hands and with tears forming in her eyes, the same eyes and hands that had embraced scores of young men dying from combat as they clutched this gentle nurse's firm grasp, she passed the cross to Virginia and told her of its origins. Virginia did not say anything, but her eyes became glossy, and she simply pulled Mary into an embrace that signified language was inadequate and unnecessary. A covenant, sacred and steadfast, had been made.

Mary had resolved that if the Doolins were denied access to the infant, she would enact the plan squared with her Creator. She would simply disappear with young Doolin. She would smile at this later, looking back over the years at the audaciousness of her idea—never acted upon, but only she knew how very close she had come. Judgment upon her was irrelevant; the rest of the world could eat dirt! Most importantly, and completely unknown to Judah Doolin, was that Ms. Mary O'Neal had been a lifesaving friend and endlessly supportive "older sister" to his biological mother, Margaret Catherine Mahoney O'Brian, precocious Vanderbilt RN graduate and WWII officer.

Doolin, a hardened Marine combat veteran, would gasp if he knew that this same Mary O'Neal now faced him again over three decades later.

It had been a long time since Mary had held young Doolin as an infant. He was now six feet, three inches tall, muscular and handsome, showing a rather striking resemblance to her friend. Yet it was the intensity of wonder and curiosity registering in this man's eyes that instantly reconnected with her, transporting her back almost three decades. She remembered looking down into his eyes as he rested his face on her breast, bonding with him in a manner that only a woman and infant can experience or understand.

It was almost as if time stood still. She could almost smell his comforting newborn musk, and she had to turn away from him as her eyes became moist. Mary also sensed immediately his compassion and that he had taken his intellect from his mother's prodigious brilliance. But she also saw darker vestiges of past events in a man much older than his stated age, and she could not see his cross.

"You are Doolin? Judah Doolin?"

"Yes, ma'am."

"Please follow me."

Judah must have hesitated a bit, because she smiled and said, "Dr. Lundgren wants you to scrub into the case."

It was stated as a matter of fact, in a tone similar to one used with Lundgren's trusted colleagues who routinely managed difficult cases with him.

Doolin was speechless for a moment. "You are certain he wants me in there with him?"

She turned and faced him and said simply, "Yes." Mary walked down the tiled corridor and extended her right arm toward the door labeled "Surgeon's Locker Room."

"Change in there. Don't leave your wallet or valuables. If you need, I'll wait here … give them to me."

Space and time bent a bit. Doolin thought he must have been dreaming. Here was this lady who had a reputation that would rival some of his sergeants in Vietnam, and yet she was not only being kind to him—she was sort of being … well, sort of being motherly.

"OK, give me a minute" was all that Doolin could manage.

Entering the hallowed ground of interconnecting hallways for the twenty operating rooms in Cook County Hospital, Doolin again felt like he was getting off the bus in Parris Island boot camp in 1969. He sensed similar anticipation, heightened alertness, and even wonder concerning events transpiring beyond the doors opening into each suite. And again, these were mixed with a degree of uncertainty and apprehension. Mary O'Neal carefully instructed him in scrubbing, showing him both the technique and timing of his cleansing activity before Judah was allowed to enter the surgical suite. He noted her approval in his careful and thorough preparation.

There was an element of familiarity in this preparation. Doolin had once also repeatedly bore a similar analysis of his rifle, a careful inspection of his rounds and equipment including his scope and water before he took to the harsh confines in Vietnam. Doolin could not share this with Ms. O'Neal, but somehow he felt that she must be feeling this also, as she was respectful but matter-of-fact in her instructions.

Cap and mask on, Doolin backed into the door as she called to the circulating nurse that he was ready and needed a gown and gloves. The door closed behind him and Doolin stood there, dripping water and residual soap suds from his elbows, as he was shown how to gown. He was intently focused on each aspect of this ritual, and only at its completion did he look to the table and see Doc Lundgren there, methodically working. His hands were out of view, but the rubber gloves reached midway up his forearms, as did Judah's. He kept them out in front of his body, upright, palms facing his chest.

"Judah, come over here and stand by Grace. She is the scrub nurse ... a real tough girl ... but the best, and she gives me my equipment."

Grace laughed a natural, light chuckle and shook her head slightly side to side.

Lundgren announced, "Ladies and gentlemen, this is Judah Doolin. I am going to make a surgeon out of him."

With this, the circulating nurse stopped moving. The anesthesiologist exchanged sustained eye contact with the scrub nurse and the operating technician, positioning the retractor slowly, looked up and locked eyes with Doolin. Apparently, the sentence uttered by Doc Lundgren had been unprecedented.

Doolin's importance, stature, and character had just been validated.

"Judah, let the lessons begin." Lundgren immediately started naming different muscles, fascial layers, and instruments. Judah wished he could have told someone that he was overwhelmed, but this wasn't the case; he began to immediately memorize, classify, and actually enjoy this first exposure.

At the end of the case, Judah helped Lundgren "close" the wound and Judah began, under his supervision, to sew and layer the abdominal tissues. Later in Doolin's life, he would laugh at this introduction to medicine. No one in the current age would believe that without credentials, verification by state and federal licensure bodies, and statements, Doolin had been both sane and of good character enough to be allowed into an operating room and assist a surgeon. Of course, they would be wrong.

The environs of medicine remained rooted in a sophisticated, if not mostly traditional apprenticeship; only slowly did government and society call for tighter input on training and validation of character from those who were inclined to join the profession. Arguably, this was long overdue, but the reality in the latter half of the twentieth century found the gravity of this profession still closer to the tricolored barber pole than the hallowed halls of technological wonder. Judah was entering this profession in a somewhat unique manner, but entering it, he was.

Thus began Doolin's relationship with Lundgren and Ms. O'Neal. Judah was indeed the "chosen one," and while some EMS and EMTs might have been jealous, most everyone was accepting of the new role that he was to play. He made sure that he earned their respect through diligent work and attention to detail, and Judah was also focused on not disappointing his new mentor, Dr. Chris Lundgren.

But Lundgren also had a secret buried in his past that Judah could not have foreseen, and remarkably, it involved him.

ABOUT THE AUTHOR

He is no one special or of much interest. Frankly, he is a nobody. His literary talent is marginal at best, but he has struggled to communicate a tribute to those who have surrendered their lives at the behest of this nation's interests, even if said interests were misguided or flawed. For in honor and faith, they fulfilled their duty. He also reveres those who have lived through the nightmare of war; the specific conflict is irrelevant, as the staining of the soul is perhaps the most troubling legacy of human conflict. May the survivors find a livable peace and a lovable remembrance of their fellow human beings who gave the ultimate gift: their existence.

www.ingramcontent.com/pod-product-compliance
Lightning Source LLC
Chambersburg PA
CBHW051135030726
47504CB00004B/879